A Murder in Zion

Nicole Maggi

Advanced Reader's Edition:
This is an advanced reader's edition from uncorrected proofs.

OCEANVIEW PUBLISHING
SARASOTA, FLORIDA

ISBN 978-1-60809-638-1

Published in the United States of America by Oceanview Publishing
Sarasota, Florida

www.oceanviewpub.com

10 9 8 7 6 5 4 3 2 1

PROLOGUE

Whoever said "a journey of a thousand miles begins with one step" had obviously never hiked The Narrows. Thigh-deep in icy river water, Darby cursed her life, cursed her ex-husband, cursed the person (probably a man) who had designed the waterproof hiking boots that were rubbing her heels raw. But mostly, she cursed herself for thinking that this trip would be the cure-all, the *aha* moment, the thing that brought her back to herself after seven long years wasted on a man incapable of emotional maturity. Seven long, *fertile* years, waiting for a man who wasn't "quite ready" to have a baby, thinking every January that maybe this would be the year he'd change his mind, that if she just showed him pictures of her best friend's adorable twins or babysat her niece one more time, he'd see the light . . . *stupid*. Stupid, stupid, stupid Darby.

"Slot canyon ahead," the guide called back, and a titter went through the little group she'd been buddied up with at the outfitters when she'd booked the hike. This was something her ex had always wanted to do, but she was the one with the better job and the savings account, so while he was shacking up with some other successful woman he wouldn't impregnate, she was taking the trip of his dreams.

"Hope it's wider than the last one," muttered Jo, a forty-something woman with purple hair twisted up in a ponytail. She was with a friend; "mom friends," they'd called each other when they'd introduced themselves, and Darby had tried not to wince at the phrase.

Her mother had warned her. Two weeks before the wedding, as they were packing up the gifts from her bridal shower and making a list of who gave what for the thank-you notes, her mother had turned to her and said, "You know, if he doesn't want a baby now, he's probably never going to want one."

Darby had paused in the middle of writing *KitchenAid* and stared at her mom. "You don't know that."

And her mother had just given her a soft, worrying look, the same look she had on her face on the wedding day, the same look she had when, seven years later, Darby had told her, over dinner, that she and Jack were splitting up.

"You'll do fine," Jo's friend reassured her. "You're braver than you know."

Darby wished she was brave. She stuck to the middle of the group, not wanting to get caught in anyone's conversation. She didn't want to explain she was here out of revenge and spite and a desperate need to find herself again after feeling lost for so long. The last few years of her marriage, her head had felt fuzzy, like she'd had a hive of bees between her ears that were constantly interrupting her thoughts with their buzzing. It was never quiet in her head, not until Jack moved out, and then it was too quiet.

They crested over a small rise and the water level dropped down to her ankles. After a few steps, one of her poles got caught between two river stones. She tugged at it, the cold, clear water sloshing against her legs. One of the men in the group stopped beside her. "Here, let me help."

"That's okay—"

He yanked her pole out of its jam without waiting for her permission and smiled kindly at her before rejoining his girlfriend. Darby exhaled hard. She could've done it herself if she'd had the chance. The rest of the group passed her while she took a pull of water from her CamelBak, hiding her face so they couldn't see the red in her cheeks.

The guide, Hal, looked back and stopped too. "Great idea, Darby. Let's all take a short rest and drink some water."

"How 'bout some vodka?" Jo said.

"Hey, I have no jurisdiction over what's in your Hydro Flask," Hal laughed. "But I sure wouldn't want to sidle through a slot canyon with anything but a clear head."

"Don't worry, I'm waiting for the hotel bar tonight," Jo said. The Narrows was a sixteen-mile trek, but their group was only going eight miles—four out and four back. By the time they got back to the hotel, just outside the park entrance, Darby didn't think she'd want to do anything but collapse into her bed and sleep well into the next day.

Overhead, a hawk circled and let out a single cry of longing that echoed across the canyon. Darby tilted her head back and bathed her face in the bright blue sky, the streaming sunlight. The red canyon walls rose up all around them, smooth and jagged all at once and impossibly wild. It was another world, ruled by nature, dwarfing the little group of seven tiny, unimportant human beings who dared come into its realm. Darby breathed in deep, a tickle behind her eyes. It had been a long time since she'd been awestruck by something. Awe wasn't something she felt in her everyday life.

Maybe this trip wasn't such a waste after all.

"Alright, let's move on. We'll have to go single file after this bend," Hal said. When they started moving again, Darby found herself at the head of the pack, just behind Hal. "Doing okay?" he asked her over his shoulder.

"I'm great," she said. Physically, it wasn't a lie, but she didn't think that Hal was asking about her mental state, and he probably didn't want to hear all about her divorce. She had a therapist for that.

"Kinda gives you a new perspective, doesn't it?"

"What does?"

"This." Hal waved his arm to encompass everything that surrounded them: the river, the cliffs, the hawk, and the sky. "It's hard to be stressed about anything when you're out here."

"Except whether you're going to drown in a flash flood."

Hal snorted. "Fair enough."

Darby grinned at him. She actually wasn't too worried about drowning in a flash flood; she'd checked the detailed weather forecast obsessively, and the outfitters had a meteorologist on staff who had the final say in whether a group went out or not. The day was clear and dry, not a threatening cloud in the sky. But flash floods were known for their fickleness; they rose without warning, tearing through a perfect day with absolute savagery.

The group finished their water break and rounded the bend. The river narrowed, growing thinner and thinner until the canyon walls stood barely a breath from each other, their vermillion surface worn smooth by millions of years of water rushing through them, eerie in how much the color looked like dried blood.

A set of boulders complicated the entrance to the slot, and Hal stopped the group. "I'm going to give everyone a hand up," he said, "so I'll be at the back as we navigate this one. Don't worry, it's a short one, maybe only a quarter mile." He held his hand up to Darby. "You first."

"Me? But—"

"Yep, you." Hal's voice was soft but firm, a current running beneath his words that steeled Darby's spine. She took a deep breath and gripped his rough, calloused hand. He hoisted her onto the boulders, keeping his grasp as she climbed down the other side and entered the slot.

There was no room to turn around and watch her fellow hikers file in behind her—no choice but to keep moving forward, and the metaphor of that wasn't lost on her. The walls undulated around her, so close that her shoulders brushed against them. At one point she had to duck beneath a crag that jutted out at the height of her head, her poles dragging in the ankle-high creek that wound its way through the canyon. It was dead quiet, the sound of the other hikers' voices muffled with the closeness of the walls, and for a moment Darby stopped. If a flash flood came roaring through here, right now, at this very moment, what would she regret the most?

It wouldn't be her marriage. She'd loved him, and she'd tried, so hard. She couldn't regret that effort. It wouldn't be her job, and it wouldn't be that she hadn't had a child. She had plenty of years left to have a baby, even if she had to do it on her own. No, her deepest regret was not loving herself enough. That she'd spent so much time worrying about whether everyone else loved her while ignoring the person who really, truly mattered.

That ends now, Darby decided in that moment, standing in the quiet, her feet submerged in the cold creek encased within the ruby walls of Zion. *The moment I emerge from this canyon*, she thought, *I'm going love myself fully and put myself first.*

Behind her, a peal of laughter from Jo broke the spell. Darby nearly laughed out loud herself and moved through the slot canyon as though she'd been there a thousand times before and her feet knew the way on their own. The dappled sunlight grew brighter and warmer until she stepped out into its full strength and breathed in anew.

The river widened and deepened here, rushing over rocks with a loud burbling. Darby drank her water and walked a little way out into the river, waiting for the rest of the group. The cliffs rose above her, cragged with tough-looking trees clinging to the rocks. It was so quiet, aside from the river, and for the first time in a long while, Darby listened to her own thoughts without someone else's crowding in. She smiled to herself, walking further along the river, leaving the group behind as they began to emerge from the slot canyon behind her.

Up the river, something bright blue glided in the water, its manmade color a contradiction to the natural reds and greens and browns of the canyon. Darby squinted. It looked like a parka. *That's too bad*, she thought, *someone is going to miss that.* The parka snagged on a rock, bobbing up and down a little, the motion slower and heavier than she would expect from a simple jacket. She took a few steps closer. Something about the parka looked wrong; its shape was too defined, too full . . . her feet kept moving towards it, her gaze fixed on the oddity of it, her mind trying to wrap around what she was seeing. Parkas weren't supposed to have white, blue-veined hands attached to them, or hoods full of human hair

. . .

"What is that?" she asked, and she felt the presence of the other hikers turn to her, shifting to see what she was looking at. Out of the corner of her eye, she saw Hal come up next to her, but she didn't turn. She was still trying to comprehend the impossibility of the parka, trying to make her mind accept it, but she couldn't—not even when Jo screamed, not even after Hal unclipped the satellite phone from his belt and radioed the ranger station, his words sounding distant though he was right beside her, saying, "I need search and rescue out here. There's a body in the river."

CHAPTER ONE

Emmeline Helliwell stood on tiptoe, balanced on a rickety plastic crate, her hands reaching for a box on a shelf while she tried not to drop the phone cradled between her head and shoulder. "I can't do it, Stace," she said into the phone. Her fingertips brushed the box, still frustratingly beyond her grasp. "I can't go flying off to Acadia."

Her soon-to-be former boss sighed his trademark sigh in her ear. "You're my only agent not assigned to a case right now—"

"Then someone is going to have to double up." Emme stretched her arms so much that her shoulders screamed, until she was finally able to hook her fingers around the side of the box. "There is no way I can go to Maine. Not with—*everything*." She grunted on that last word as she tugged the box toward her. The weight of it propelled her backward, right off the crate, as the phone flew out from its precarious perch. With a cry, she landed flat on her back, the box crashing down next to her. Luckily, the piles of various crap that covered the floor broke her fall. "Goddammit." She sat up and pinched the bridge of her nose. A headache was forming.

"Emme? Emme? You okay?"

Emme lifted herself onto her elbows, slid off a stack of folders, and scrambled around the floor on her hands and knees until she found her phone. "You see? This is why I can't fly across the country, Stace. The house is a mess." *And so am I.*

"I thought you were making progress." There was a creak on his end of the line, and Emme could picture him in his big swivel chair, the leather crackled and worn, looking out over Yosemite Valley from his office at the ranger station. "And have you heard from Addie?"

"No. Both to making progress and hearing from Addie." Emme scooted herself to a patch of bare floor against the wall and leaned back, breathing deep to dispel the swoop of fear in her gut whenever she thought about her sister. "My mom had a lot more stuff than I realized," she said, her gaze involuntarily going across the room to rest on the jar that held her mother's ashes.

"Maybe taking a break from it will be good for you. Clear your head," Stace said. She could hear the strain in his voice and knew the pressure he was under; there were only thirty-three agents in the Investigative Services Branch of the National Park Service, and he was on the verge of losing one in her. But though she was still two weeks out from her last day at the ISB, her feet were already out the door.

"I love how your version of 'clearing your head' involves a crime scene."

"That used to be your version too," Stace reminded her. "Once upon a time you were only too happy to let a good case erase all your problems."

"That was before." Before her mother had died. Before her sister had gone AWOL. Before Hannah DeLeo.

"Emme, everyone makes mistakes."

She wanted to reach through the phone line and strangle him for all the times he'd said those words. Yes, everyone made mistakes, but not ones that got someone killed. That error hung in the air between them, across the miles from Utah to Yosemite. "I need to stay in Springdale," she said. "If—when—Addie comes home."

"Look, we're pretty sure it's the Backwoods Bandit," Stace said, and Emme could hear papers rustling on his end of the line. "The M.O. is the same: cars parked at trailheads, left rear window smashed in, those stupid little thank-you notes tucked into the backseat—"

"The Backwoods Bandit operates in the Southeast." Emme nudged the box she'd pulled from the top shelf with her toe. "He's never been that far north. Also—" She sat up straight. "Did you say left rear window? Because he always breaks the right rear window. We could have a copycat on our hands." With a swooping feeling, her gut twisted and she slumped back against the wall. "Nope. Not getting sucked in. Send someone else, Stace."

"You know, you still work for me for two more weeks."

"What are you going to do if I don't go? Fire me?" She didn't mean for the bite in her voice to come out, but there it was, the edge that she always seemed to be walking these days.

There was a pause. Finally, Stace said, "Okay," the same soft okay he'd uttered when she'd slid her resignation letter onto his desk. "I'll let you off the hook on this one. But you do still have two weeks left on your contract."

"As if you could let me forget."

"Ha. I'll check in with you in a few days." The line beeped as he hung up.

Emme held the phone up in front of her and pressed Addie's number from the recent calls list, a motion so fluid and instinctual that she didn't even realize she had done it until the phone went directly to voicemail. Addie's cheerful voice bit into her. *I can't answer the phone right now. Please leave a message and I'll call you back as soon as I can.*

"Addie, it's me. Again." Emme swallowed. "Just—please call me back. Please. I need to know you've gotten my messages, that you know what's going on." She waited a moment, as if listening for an answer. "Okay. Bye." She hung up, shoved her phone into her pocket, and pressed the heels of her hands into her eye sockets. Pops of color and light exploded behind her eyelids. Silence stretched across the house, the only sound the ticking of the copper clock her mother, Sunny, had bought at one of the local artisan shops in town. When she counted to a hundred and twenty ticks, she blew a hard breath out and pulled her hands away from her face.

The mess in the living room mocked her. The piles she'd deemed for trash or donation seemed infinitely smaller than the ones she still had to go through. She picked up the stack of papers she'd fallen on, folders of Addie's report cards going back to elementary school, and hesitated. She couldn't throw them out without Addie's permission. With a groan, she dumped them onto the *To Be Determined* pile she'd created which had grown bigger by the day. At least she didn't have to worry about her own elementary school work. There were no mementos of hers prior to middle school, nothing from before she was eleven, when they'd had to run from their home in the middle of the night, taking only what they could carry.

She crawled over to the box that she'd pulled off the shelf and caught the writing scrawled on the side in black marker. The sight of her moth-

er's handwriting still jolted her heart, a tangible piece of her, so close that
if she just reached her hand back her mother would squeeze her fingers.
It took a moment to register the words written on the box. *Emme: Cases.*

With a shaky breath, Emme pushed the lid off the box and peered inside. Newspaper clippings were stacked haphazardly, some inside folders
with names on the tabs, others loosely tossed in. Everything had shifted
when the box tumbled from the shelf. Emme thumbed through the
folders, walking through the graveyard of her past cases, each name like a
fresh wound. In every article, Emme's name was carefully highlighted in
yellow, like some sort of macabre Playbill for murder instead of theatre.
Her throat tight, Emme moved the folders to the side. A loose clipping
that had probably been on top before the box fell fluttered onto her
lap. Emme froze. The headline blared out at her: Body Found in Grand
Canyon Identified.

Emme jammed the lid back on the box. Her mother may have kept the
articles because she was proud of her daughter's work, but Emme had
lived through each of those clippings and didn't need the reminders. She
began to drag the box to the trash pile, but instead of depositing it, she
whisked the box up into her arms and marched out the back door.

The morning sun had crested over the mountains that ringed Springdale, bathing the red rock cliffs of Zion Canyon in ruby light. The sky
was clear blue without a cloud in sight. It was a hiker's dream, and no
doubt the trails in the park were crowded. Emme dumped the box next
to the old stone fireplace that sat at the edge of the property, surrounded
by overgrown grass and splintered Adirondack chairs. There was a small
stack of wood next to the fireplace and a weather-beaten box of long
matches on the ledge above it. Emme made a little pile of kindling out
of twigs and dried leaves that had fallen from the branches of the oak

tree arching over the backyard, stacked three logs into a triangle the way she'd first learned in wilderness training so many years ago, and lit the kindling. The flames ate through the leaves quickly, nibbling at the logs for a few minutes before bursting into a crackling ring of fire. Emme sat cross-legged for a long moment, her vision blurred by the dancing of the flames. The heat flushed her face, burning away any remnants of lingering tears.

She pulled the box to her side and lifted off the lid. One by one, she drew out the folders and tossed the clippings into the blaze, watching each one blacken and curl, turn white, and wisp away into ash. As each article went into the flames, she remembered how there was something in every case that broke a little piece of her, how the six years she'd been on the job had chipped away at her. It wasn't just the Hannah DeLeo case. It was years of seeing the ugliest side of humanity in some of the world's most beautiful places, a juxtaposition that should be impossible but was all too real. She emptied the box, turning each of her cases into smoke, until the only piece left was the article about Hannah. She held the thin paper up, the ink from the newsprint darkening her fingers.

The body found in Grand Canyon National Park has been identified as Hannah DeLeo, plural wife of Elijah Murdock, son of religious leader Abraham Murdock. DeLeo, who was not legally married to Murdock, was found strangled to death just off the South Kaibab Trail near Skeleton Point, about 8 miles from Bright Angel Campground where, three days before her body was found, authorities had been called to the couple's campsite for a domestic disturbance. Though Elijah Murdock has not been charged with DeLeo's murder, he remains a person of interest and his whereabouts are currently unknown.

"Anyone who sees him should consider him armed and dangerous and contact law enforcement immediately," said Emmeline Helliwell from the National Park Service. Abraham Murdock, the head of the Warriors for Armageddon, a secretive fundamentalist community located in Redwater, UT, could not be reached for comment.

It was the only article in the box about Hannah's murder. By the time Abraham Murdock had called the authorities to report that Eli was dead—presumably by his own hand—Sunny was in the hospital, never to return home. There was a picture accompanying the article, not of Hannah—the Murdocks had never released a photo of her, or even acknowledged her death—but of the trail where she'd been found. The photo was in black-and-white, but Emme could see the orange dirt in her mind's eye, the canyon ravine at the edge of nothingness. The wild beauty of the place felt disturbed by Hannah's body, clad in bright green hiking pants and white t-shirt, her limbs splayed out, her eyes wide open to the sky. The couple who had found her hadn't moved her, not one inch, before Emme got there. "We thought she was a mannequin at first," the man had said, and the woman burst into tears and buried her face in her boyfriend's shoulder. Emme saw how he held her close, how gentle his hand was on the back of her head, and how easily he could crush her skull on the rocks at their feet, if he wanted to.

She blinked to clear the memory. Her mother knew how Emme had screwed up this case, how she'd failed Hannah . . . how she'd failed *her*, and yet she'd still kept the article. With a hard exhale, she crumpled the paper in her fist and threw it into the flames. Her gaze fixated on it as it transformed from black to white and then to nothingness. She might have two weeks left on her contract with the National Park Service, but in her mind she was already done. She twisted around to look at the

Craftsman house and the A-frame building that sat in front of it: The Sunny Spot, her mother's bakery. It had been closed since Sunny had gone into the hospital weeks earlier, but the moment she was officially out of the Park Service, Emme was going to reopen it. Leave all this tragedy behind her and build a life where the biggest complication was bread dough. Except—her mother had named Addie a co-executor of her will, and she needed Addie to sign off on the bakery's transfer to her name. Emme turned back to the fire, which bloomed taller as another log caught, and bounced her knees. She wanted to move into that future and put her broken days as an investigator behind her. But she couldn't until her sister came home.

Her pocket vibrated, jolting her. She reached in to grab her phone, willing it to be her sister reading her mind all the way from Tanzania. But when she looked at the screen, it was Stace's name that lit up, not Addie's. She clicked *Accept*. "I told you, I'm not going to Acadia."

"This isn't about that," Stace said, his voice low and serious.

Emme's insides twisted. He was going to ask her for another favor. "I can't go flying off to wherever, Stace, you know that."

"I don't need you to go flying off to wherever," Stace said. The knot inside Emme tightened. "I need you to drive ten minutes into Zion National Park. There's a body in The Narrows."

Chapter Two

There are three ways into Zion National Park. From the south, Zion Park Boulevard runs right through Springdale, funneling visitors past the iconic sign and into the main visitors' entrance. Drive north along the scenic road through the park and pull off to hike up to Angel's Landing, or around the Emerald Pools, all beneath the perpetual gaze of those red cliffs towering high to the sky. The Virgin River snakes its way through the entire park, wild and wide, rushing and roaring in places, and calm and quiet in others.

Emme held onto the bar overhead in the open-air Jeep as it rumbled along the park road towards the Temple of Sinawava. From there, they'd have to take the easy Riverside Walk to access The Narrows. One of the most famous hikes in Zion, The Narrows takes you into the actual river, beneath cliff faces worn smooth by millions of years of erosion from water and wind. Most people came from the south, or "bottom up," along the paved Riverside Walk to its end point where you have to climb over the low stone wall. Descend into the river, and you're in The Narrows.

Emme gripped the bar tighter as the Jeep jolted over a pothole. So much for sliding under the radar in her last two weeks on the job. Damn Stace; he knew her too well. Zion was her backyard, and he knew she wouldn't refuse an investigation on her own turf.

"Should be there in a few minutes." Theo, the ranger who was driving, shouted to her over the roar of the engine and the wind. "Then we'll have to hike in."

Emme nodded in response. She would do a preliminary investigation—one last favor for Stace—and get someone else assigned to the case. If there even was a case. Most deaths in the parks turned out to be accidents.

Theo pulled the Jeep into the small lot at the Zion Shuttle Stop #9 and they hopped out. Emme walked to the back of the Jeep. She slung her pack over her shoulders, tucked her water bottle into its side pocket, and grabbed her hiking poles. There was a steady stream of people on the Riverside Walk; it was one of the easiest hikes in the park, more of a walk than a hike. They threaded their way around the other walkers, who moved aside when they spotted Emme's wide-rimmed ranger hat and flak jacket with the words FEDERAL AGENT emblazoned in yellow on the back. The trail was only a mile long, and she and Theo reached its end quickly.

They scrambled over the wall, down onto the rocky banks of the Virgin River. Emme tilted her head back and breathed in the bright blue sky. It never failed her, this view, this canyon. She'd first stepped into The Narrows when she was eleven, worn out and weary from weeks on the road with Sunny and Addie, still shellshocked from the punch her father had landed on her jaw and her mother's immediate decision to finally get the hell out of that house. They'd driven for miles and miles, past cornfields and dairy farms, over the Rocky Mountains and into the red rock canyons of the west, landing at the place where other pioneers from the east had settled a hundred and fifty years before: Zion. They'd only gone a mile or two that first time—Addie was in a carrier on Sunny's back. Walking along the banks of the river with the canyon rising above them, Emme finally felt safe. Secure. *Home.*

She swallowed the tightness in her throat and brushed past Theo so that she was in the lead, weaving around the day hikers. "Are you here about the body?" one of the hikers called to her as she passed, but she ignored him. *No comment* was always the ISB's official party line until they were ready to make a definitive statement.

The banks of the river grew thinner and thinner until at last they had to step into the water. Emme dug her poles in, cold water splashing up to her shins, soaking her waterproof pants. She hadn't put her neoprene wetsuit on; it was still warm for this time of year and the wetsuit restricted her movement, something she didn't want today when time was of the essence. Had the hikers pulled the body out of the water yet? How many fingerprints and footprints had interfered with the scene?

A mile and a half in, a skinny ribbon of water tumbled from high above into the river below. A group of hikers stood in the water, gazing up at the canyoneers rappelling down the side of the cliff. Theo's walkie crackled. "What's your ETA?"

"We just hit Mystery Canyon," Theo responded. "Fifteen minutes or so."

A quarter of a mile further, Orderville Canyon Junction brimmed with hikers taking pictures and selfies of the towering crimson cliffs, rising so high above their heads that only a thin sheen of sunlight spilled onto the river below. Emme stopped to take a drink of water. The year after they'd moved to Springdale, her mother had woken her and Addie early one morning and loaded them onto the shuttle that stopped along the road to the park, not saying much until they had reached this spot. Here in this natural cathedral, with the quiet of the canyon surrounding them, so early in the morning before the tourists took over, Sunny had hoisted Addie to her hip and put her arm around Emme's waist. She looked up to the sky, and said, "Your father's dead."

It was a curious thing, to learn of someone's death and feel nothing but a sweet relief flooding her veins. Addie had burst into tears; she'd been too little to know what their father really was, but old enough to understand that she would never see him again. Emme remembered listening to her sister sob and watching two hawks circle high above the canyon, calling to each other with a plaintive cry, and thinking that the hawks mourned her father more than she did.

A row of three rangers stood at the mouth that led out of Orderville Canyon, blocking anyone's progress deeper into The Narrows. The one in the middle jerked her chin at Emme and Theo. "They're up past Wall Street, before Big Spring."

"Did they pull the body out of the water?" Emme asked.

"I think so. They just radioed a few minutes ago asking how far away you are. They sound wigged."

Of course they were wigged. They'd gone out for a gorgeous hike in one of the most beautiful places in America under a perfect, cloudless sky and found *a fucking body* in the river. Emme just nodded and, with a glance back at the tourists congregating beneath the cliffs, rounded the bend onto Wall Street.

The canyon narrowed significantly here, the walls undulating in rhythm with the river. That morning with her mother, they had hiked in silence until Emme said, "We could go back to New York. Now that he's gone." It had been a struggle that first year in Springdale, with Sunny working two jobs to make ends meet, often leaving Emme in charge of Addie. Returning to New York would be familiar, at least.

But Sunny had arched her neck back so that the sun fell full on her cheeks. "And leave this place?" A month later, the check had come from her dad's lawyer, insurance money that Sunny hadn't even realized she was still entitled to, and within a month she'd bought the house and the bakery.

They hiked over a collection of boulders and into a slot canyon. Emme turned sideways and sidled through, ducked beneath jagged outcroppings. She could hear voices ahead. Theo's walkie crackled again, but before he answered, the walls of the slot opened up and Emme emerged into the open.

The group of hikers were clustered on the other side of the river, several paces away from a human-shaped form on the ground. They'd draped a jacket over the body. "Dammit," Emme muttered, shaking her head as she picked her way across the river. She couldn't blame them; no one wanted to sit for hours waiting for the authorities to arrive with the open eyes of a slowly decaying dead person staring at them. But it didn't help the preservation of the scene if it was a crime.

A tall, gangly man with an orange bandanna tied around his long, sandy-brown hair stepped forward as Emme reached the group. "Hey," he said. "I'm Hal, from Zion Outfitters."

"Hey, Hal." She shook his hand. "I'm Agent Helliwell. Were you the one who found the body?"

"No, that was Darby. She spotted it first." Hal motioned to a woman about Emme's age who was sitting on the ground, huddled between two other women. They were rubbing her back, but dropped their hands and moved slightly away as Emme approached. She crouched down so that her gaze was level with Darby's and pulled her notebook out of her pack. "Hi, Darby. I'm Agent Helliwell, but you can call me Emme. You okay?"

Darby nodded in a way that said she really wasn't okay, but she wasn't going to admit it. "I guess—as okay as I can be?"

"Can you tell me exactly what you saw?" She kept Darby talking, until the paleness in her face slowly faded away as she became more solid in her answers. "Show me where the body was when you first saw it." She let Darby guide her out into the middle of the river and stood there for a moment, let her gaze glide from the riverbank up, up, up the canyon walls.

"Do you think—he fell?" Darby asked.

"That's what we're going to find out," Emme said, throwing her a small smile. She jotted everything down in her notebook and made a little sketch of the scene. The cliffs were so high here they blocked out the sky. The thing was, there wasn't a trail at the top of them, not like Mystery Canyon which spilled from a ten-mile scramble through the canyon into The Narrows. In order for someone to fall from this point, they'd have to be seriously off-trail. Not impossible, but already Emme's mind was spinning, trying to make things fit, and she had to rein herself in. *Just take good notes,* she told herself, *so you can pass them on to another agent with a clear conscience.*

Theo was on the shore gathering statements from the other hikers, and Emme knew she couldn't put off looking at the body any longer. It wasn't a shock to her anymore, but there was still a moment of breathlessness, of realization that she was kneeling beside a life that had been snuffed out. She sent Darby back to the group and walked over to the jacket-draped figure. She pulled the jacket off. Too bad for whoever had sacrificed it; now, it was evidence.

Dark-haired male, she wrote in her notebook. The decomposition wasn't that pronounced yet, so he either hadn't been in the river very long or the cold water had acted as a natural preservative. The thing about water was that it was either an investigator's friend or enemy: it either protected its spoils, or it destroyed them. She squatted down at the victim's side. There were impact injuries all around his face, black and blue and purple, red streaks like cracks running down his neck. So he *could* have fallen . . . as she reached out to go through his pockets, she caught a better look at his battered face, the way his nose sloped at its end, the beaded necklace tangled around his neck. Emme fell back on her haunches, landing hard on the rocky riverbank. "Holy shit," she muttered softly, but it was loud enough that Theo glanced at her and disentangled himself from the group to walk over.

"What's wrong?"

Emme pulled her hat off her head and held it to her chest to keep her hands from shaking. "I know him."

CHAPTER THREE

The only time Emme had hiked the entire sixteen miles of The Narrows from the "top-down" was the summer after she'd graduated from high school. She and her friends Max, Brianna, Tim, and Amy had piled into Max's dad's Range Rover and driven through the East Entrance, windows down, singing loudly and off-key to Linkin Park along the way. They'd camped along the river, and Max cooked such a good meal over their campfire that they'd nicknamed him Mountain Max. Snuggled into a sleeping bag, with the top of her tent open to the night sky above, it seemed that all the possibilities in the world were spread before her, ready for the taking.

But whatever possibilities had spread out before Max that night, they were all dashed now.

Emme gazed into Max's wide-open eyes, staring forever at the cliffs that rose above them. The last time she'd seen him was a few years ago, when she'd come home for Christmas and met up with a group of high school friends at Cap's Landing, the local bar at the edge of town. They'd fallen into an easy conversation about life and how it hadn't quite lived up to their expectations yet. She searched his guileless face, now filled with an emptiness that would never be replenished, and tried to reconcile those memories with the sight before her. They seemed like two trains passing each other in the night, never fated to connect. Emme looked north, where the Virgin River wound in a loose coil through the canyon. It was entirely possible that Max had hiked top-down and been camping overnight; the designated campsites were only a couple of miles upriver. He could have had an accident at his campsite—fallen and hit his head on a rock, perhaps, then drifted downriver.

She peered closer at the wounds around the base of his neck. *Blunt force trauma*, she scribbled into her notebook, *possibly from a fall*. One spot bloomed darker than the rest, right where his spine met his skull—the point of fatal impact, she suspected. God, how fucking unlucky. Emme pinched her forehead. "Mountain Max" had been no joke; she remembered him as an expert outdoorsman who knew this park like the back of his hand. When she'd seen him last, he'd been working for one of the outfitters in town. But Mother Nature had a way of laughing in the face of expertise. A simple misstep could be your downfall out here in the wild.

"How do you know him?" Theo crouched beside Max. Emme fought the urge to shove him away. Death was such a private, sacred thing, and she wanted to leave Max to it, allow his soul to cross over, or whatever it was that souls did when they left their body.

"I went to high school with him. He's local."

"Shit." Theo, too, removed his hat and scrubbed his hand through his short blonde hair. "I guess even locals can misstep and fall."

"I don't think he fell," Emme said slowly. "Not from up there, anyway," she added, jerking her chin to the cliffs that towered over them.

"The only trail that leads to the cliffs is south from here, at Mystery Canyon. He couldn't have fallen from there and floated *up*river."

"Maybe he was off-trail."

"Maybe," Emme echoed. That didn't jibe with the memory of the Max she knew, but people changed . . . and often the ones who considered themselves experts were the first to flaunt the rules. "I think it's more likely that he hit his head on something up near the campsites, fell in the river, and drifted down to here."

Theo raised his eyebrows. "The question is, did he hit his head on his own, or did someone hit it for him?"

"Well, that's a question for the medical examiner." Emme ignored Theo's sharp gaze on her as she stood back up.

His radio buzzed, and he walked upstream to answer it. "The rescue helicopter's on its way," he called back to her a moment later. "ETA probably a half hour or so."

"Thanks." Emme began a slow walk around Max's body, taking photos at each angle and collecting samples of the pebbles and dirt in the place where the hikers said his body had snagged. There were rangers with more specific forensics training than she had, but the landscape of a wilderness crime scene changed so fast; it was a race against time with the wind, the river, the heat, and the cold, and she had learned to take samples when she could. And it would help out the agent who took over the case.

But as she snapped a close-up photo of Max's injuries, something uncomfortable and insistent gnawed a hole in her gut. Passing the case on to someone else would be harder now that she knew the victim. Someone would have to inform his family, and pushing that task onto a stranger felt cruel and wrong. And once she did that, they'd want to know exactly what happened, and they'd want her to be the one to figure it out. She'd be fully ensnared by then, unable to disentangle herself. The roots would keep pulling her deeper back into the ISB.

Emme straightened, tucked her phone into her pocket, and ran her hand over her hair. This was likely an accident. Once the medical examiner attested to that, she could cut those ties and walk away, straight into the end-date on her contract.

The sound of chopper blades cut through the air, distant at first, getting louder. Emme took one last look at Max before search and rescue put him in a body bag, before the M.E. sliced him open. She wanted to remember him here, surrounded by the canyon that he loved. Tilting her head back, she breathed in the undulating red cliffs and the small patch of sky visible just above them. If there was such a thing as a soul, Max's would stay here, forever at home in The Narrows. *Rest in peace*, she thought.

The chopper appeared above the cliffs, blacking out the sun and throwing the canyon into shadow. The hiking group huddled on the riverbank, and Emme spotted Hal handing out beef jerky. Her stomach growled and then immediately flopped over. She'd had nothing since breakfast, but the thought of eating now, next to an old friend's lifeless body, made her sick. She took a drink of water instead.

Theo joined her on the riverbank, and they both watched as the helicopter descended as far as it could, the force of its blades rustling the hardy brush that grew in the cracks of the cliff walls. A hatch opened in the underside of the helicopter and a long basket emerged, slowly lowering down to the ground on a thick black cord. Emme could see the rescue team inside the belly of the chopper and waved up to them. Theo's radio beeped. "Do you need one of us to come down?"

Emme shook her head. "Tell them we can manage."

When the basket hit the riverbank, Emme dragged it next to Max's body and rolled out the heavy black body bag, moving with conscious precision to keep her mind from spinning out. She'd have to tell Max's parents and his—did he have a sister? Emme thought she remembered a younger sister, a year or two behind them in school. It would be better coming from her than some random ranger from the park . . . she blinked, shaking her head a little, and unzipped the bag with a loud *zzzziiippppp* that tore through the canyon.

Theo positioned himself at Max's shoulders and Emme grasped his ankles. "On my count—one, two, three." They hoisted his body into the bag on the stretcher. Without lingering, Emme pulled the zipper back up, swallowing his once-vital life into a pit of black vinyl. She fastened the straps, made sure they were secure, and signaled to the rescue team. Slowly, with an odd sort of reverence, the stretcher lifted from the ground, up, up, up . . . Emme arched her neck back to watch Max's final flight, her throat tight, heat gathering at the back of her eyes. She'd been on too many of these scenes, but never someone she had known.

When the chopper had him, she looked over at the hiking group, their heads bowed in respect as Max's body was removed. The helicopter lifted itself out of the canyon, up and away, restoring sunlight as it disappeared. Emme picked her way over the rocky bank to the hiking group. "Hey everyone, thanks for sticking around." She pulled out her notebook. "If you didn't give your information to Theo, please give it to me. I need names, phone numbers, email addresses, where you're staying and dates of departure."

As she'd suspected, Theo hadn't been as thorough as she or any other ISB agent would be. Without Max's body there, the air felt lighter, her head felt clearer, and questions were swirling into focus: *Had Max been camping overnight? Was he alone?* For each case Emme worked, she created a board with every detail and clue pinned carefully into the cork. She could already see the board forming in her mind's eye and blinked hard to erase it.

"We need to head back if we want to beat sunset," Hal said. The group gathered their stuff and set out. Theo sidled into step with the woman who'd found the body—Darby—leaving Emme to fall in behind them. She let them all go ahead of her through the slot canyon and paused before she entered it, turned to survey the river and the vermillion walls rising to the sky, empty now of hikers and helicopters and dead bodies. Shadows lengthened along the ridges of the cliffs, the sun beginning its afternoon descent into dusk; they would be hard-pressed to beat sunset now, but Emme had never been scared of darkness in Zion. It was a different park after nightfall, wrapping anyone brave enough to venture out in a diamond sky dusted with stars, the lonely sound of nocturnal creatures calling to each other, and an acute knowledge that this world didn't care much about you. It had too much to do to bother with one tiny, insignificant person, too many other things to worry about than one solitary body in a river. Listening to the water as it flowed end over end past her, Emme wondered once again what had happened here, and if the canyon would ever reveal its secrets.

She stayed a few paces behind the group as they trekked back, listening to Theo awkwardly hit on Darby, who didn't seem to mind, and the woman with the purple hair tell her friend that now she had something to post about in her true crime Facebook group. "Don't do that," Emme muttered, but she couldn't really officially prevent her from posting on social media about it. It wasn't a crime until she proved it was a crime, and she couldn't do that yet. And even if there was a crime here, the case would be pushed onto another agent when Emme's end-date arrived. She would deliver the terrible news to Max's family, but that would be the end of it.

Orderville Canyon was nearly deserted now except for a few straggling day hikers. They glommed onto Hal's group and one of them hung back, trying to look casual, as if Emme couldn't spot his intentions from a mile away. "So, what do you think happened?"

Emme glanced sidelong at the hiker. He was tanned and broad-shouldered and not too long ago, she would have postured right along with him until they ended up in bed together. But now, she felt nothing but annoyance. "I really can't say until the ISB investigates further."

"What's the ISB?"

"Investigative Services Branch." Emme kept her tone clipped and professional. Factual answers only. "We're the branch of the National Park Service that investigates crimes in the National Parks."

"Isn't that, like, state law enforcement's job?"

A small, smug smile pulled up the corners of her mouth in spite of herself. "No, because it's federal land. Every crime that happens in a National Park is automatically a federal crime. The state has no jurisdiction." It was still there, that flash of pride that shot through her when she told someone what she did, the rare and unique place she held as an ISB agent. She tried to squelch it, but it just bubbled right back up.

"Wow, I never knew that." He grinned at her, showing off very white, straight teeth. "Remind me never to commit a crime in a National Park."

"How about just don't commit a crime?"

"Or that." He laughed, then pulled his face into a semblance of somberness. "So, you think this is a crime?"

"Like I said, I really can't say. We'll treat it that way until we learn one way or the other." They emerged into Mystery Canyon, the cliffs bare of rappelling ropes and canyoneers. Dusky shadows stretched their long fingers along the river. "I have to hustle to catch the rangers back at the Visitors Center before they leave. It was nice chatting with you," she added, even though it hadn't been any different than the thousands of conversations she'd had over the years with all the looky-loos who elbowed their way into a case just so they could tell their friends "*I was there.*" She dug her poles into the river and fired away from the hiker, who had that look on his face like he wanted to ask "just one more question" that would turn into about twenty. When she reached Theo, she knocked him in the arm, startling him out of telling Darby the best place to get a drink in town. "Would you radio the Visitor Center and tell them I need all the permits pulled for The Narrows from the last few days?"

"Oh—sure. Darby, maybe I'll see you at Cap's Landing later?"

Darby smiled, sweet and warm and genuine. "I'd love that."

Emme glanced over at Theo as they broke away from the hiking group for the last stretch before Riverside Walk. Maybe she'd underestimated him and his ability to hit on women. "Cap's Landing? That's not exactly tourist central."

"*Bingo,*" he said with a sly grin. Emme rolled her eyes.

By the time they got back to the Jeep, the sky was purple, streaked with deep pink that made the cliffs glow in the falling light. Theo handed her a blanket, which she gratefully wrapped herself in for the chilly ride back. Twilight rose fast in the park, the sunlight fading upwards along the canyon walls. It would be a few hours before the stars lit up the sky, but Emme could feel them hiding just behind the dusty cloak of sunset.

They pulled into the Visitors Center as it was closing, a stream of tourists trickling out with their gift shop purchases, back to their campsites or hotels and their easy lives. Emme muscled her way against the tide of foot traffic and slid in through the door of the Center, Theo on her heels.

Inside, a few stragglers in the gift shop stood in line waiting to check out, and the rangers at the information desk were tidying up. One of them looked up as Emme and Theo approached, a round-faced Mexican woman in her twenties, her nametag reading Ranger Garcia. "I have those permits, Agent Helliwell," she said, pulling out a file from beneath the desk with the same sharp, eager gleam in her eye that Emme recognized as the kind of ambition she used to have.

"Great. Help me go through them? We're looking for Max Kerchek's."

They split the pile in half and started flipping through each sheet of paper. Emme had only gotten halfway through her stack when her finger froze over Max's name, written neatly on the designated line. "He was a walk-in. Yesterday." Emme ran her finger down each line of the permit. Most wilderness permits in Zion were obtained a month before the trip, in a mad-dash online booking. If you missed out on that, you could go for the long-shot lottery a week before. And if that failed, you could show up early the morning of your trip, get in line before the desk opened, and hope there were enough permits available for the day, the best option for procrastinators and non-planners. So either Max had procrastinated, or the trip had been a last-minute idea. Emme's gaze paused on the line Total Amount Paid. It was $15, the price for one to two people. Next to it, in thick black Sharpie, was a neatly printed number 2. "He wasn't alone," she murmured.

"Pardon?"

Emme looked up. "Is there any record of the person he was with?"

Ranger Garcia shook her head. "No. He was probably alone when he obtained the permit."

If Max was with someone else when he died, where was that person? Surely they would have tried to get help if he'd injured himself. But Theo had told her that the only call to the ranger station from The Narrows in the last day had been from Hal, after they'd found Max's body. She scanned the permit again. "He was assigned to campsite four," she said. "Did anyone report anything at the campsites last night? Or turn in anything that was found?"

Garcia checked her log book. "No. We can send someone up there in the morning to see if anything was left at the site."

"Do it." Emme handed the permit back to her. "Can you make me a copy of this? And pull all the walk-in permits from yesterday and give me the list of those names and contact information," she said. Garcia nodded and started to pull the permits out of the box.

Theo raised an eyebrow at her. "What do you need to contact those people for?"

"To snag a day-of permit, you have to get here super early and hang out until the desk opens," Emme explained. "Maybe one of them remembers something about Max's companion."

"Cover all bases, eh?"

Emme cocked her head. "Yes. That's what a good investigator does. Nothing is ruled out until everything but the truth is ruled out." She was tired and hungry and cold and damp from the river and still had to do the worst part of her job before the night was over. She was not in the mood for being second guessed by men. Ranger Garcia handed her a file with the permit and the list of names; it was frustratingly thin, but Emme knew from experience that soon enough it would be stuffed with autopsy reports, witness statements, photographs, and scribbled notes. Her mind was already sprawling outward into all the possibilities, to the lists of questions she had for the rangers who'd been on duty at the East Entrance station yesterday, and for anyone else camping at The Narrows campsites last night, and for all the other top-down hikers . . . and now she had to drive out to Max's house to tell his family he was dead. "Goddammit," she said out loud as she slid into her car. She turned on the engine and leaned her forehead onto the steering wheel. It had only been half a day, but she was already exactly where she told herself she wouldn't go: waist-deep in the quicksand of this case with little hope of pulling herself out.

CHAPTER FOUR

The moon rose above the mountains that encircled Zion Canyon as Emme steered her car along the road to the Kerchek home in Rockville, the next town over from Springdale. The gears in her brain churned as she drove, but the pieces would not connect. Something was stirring in her—something she didn't want to look at, something she wanted to lock into a tiny box and keep away from the light.

Her headlights swept down the long driveway that led to the large, log cabin-style house. The front door opened as Emme came to a stop next to a mud-spattered Jeep Rubicon; Washington County was a small-town place where people didn't pull into your driveway at night without a good reason. Gathering her breath, Emme turned her car off. She took her Smokey hat from the passenger seat and put it on her head. This was official National Park Service business, and the uniform was her shield against the damage she was about to do.

On the porch, the small, wiry woman who had stepped out the front door was joined by a younger woman—Emme recognized her as Max's sister. As Emme approached, she stepped halfway down the porch stairs and peered into the darkness. "What's happened?" she asked without preamble.

Mrs. Kerchek joined her daughter on the step. They reached their arms around each other's waists, and Emme's heart squeezed at the intimacy of that gesture, such a simple mother-daughter thing that she would never feel again. She tried to inhale past the tightness in her chest. For however bad the news she was about to deliver was, at least they had each other to hold onto.

"Mrs. Kerchek, I don't know if you remember me—"

"Oh please, call me Laura. Of course I remember you, Emme. You used to come over and watch movies in the basement."

"Yes, that's right. I'm—"

"I was so sorry to hear about your mother, dear," Laura interrupted, her eyes darting nervously, as though small talk would save her from whatever Emme had come here to say.

"Thank you. That means a lot."

"This is my daughter, Gwen. She was a couple of years behind you and Max at Hurricane High."

"I remember—"

"What's going on?" Gwen cut across their chit-chat. "You work for the Park Service, right? Where's Max?"

Emme slid her Smokey hat off her head. "I'm so sorry. I was brought in to investigate a body in The Narrows. I'm terribly sorry to tell you that it was Max."

"What? That's not—no," Laura stumbled backward and collapsed onto the top step. "No, no no no no no no . . ." Gwen sank beside her and looked up at Emme, disbelief widening her eyes.

"Are you sure?" She held her mother as Laura pressed her fist to her mouth. "What happened?"

Emme latched onto the question, something tangible to anchor her in the sea of grief that was starting to flood the porch. "We're still investigating. It looks like he may have fallen and hit his head—"

Laura moaned, a sound that tore at Emme's insides. Gwen pulled her close. Emme swallowed. "We'll have more answers after—after the medical examiner sees him," she finished softly. She watched her words register across Gwen's face, her acceptance of what Emme was saying, until she crumpled into her mother and they sat shaking, holding onto each other.

Emme looked away, trying not to intrude on something so private, so personal and sacred. No matter how many times she'd have to deliver this news, it never got easier, and grief was unique to each person. But as she listened to their sobbing, she fought the urge to cover her ears. It echoed inside her, twisting her around until she was back in her mother's hospital room, watching the nurses switch off the heart monitor that had flatlined a few moments before . . . she shook her head to clear the memory. *This isn't my grief,* she told herself.

Gwen turned her tear-stained face up to her. "Were you—the one who found him?" she asked, her voice hoarse.

"A hiking group found him, but I was the first ranger on the scene." Emme used the moment to dig a fresh packet of tissues out of her bag and hold them out to Gwen.

"Thanks." Gwen pulled out a tissue and wiped her nose, all while keeping an arm around her mother, whose face was buried in her shoulder.

Emme inhaled a deep breath. "I'm so sorry to do this, but I have some questions I need to ask." She glanced at the open front door. "Can we go inside?"

Gwen smoothed her mother's hair back from her forehead. "Mom. Mama. Emme needs to question us."

"No," Laura whispered. "No—"

Gwen looked back up at Emme. "Does it have to be now?"

Emme's forehead crinkled. "It would be very helpful to the investigation if we did it now as opposed to later."

"Let's get it over with, I guess." Gwen gathered her mother and helped her into the house. Emme followed them, her footsteps heavy.

Inside, the house had a large, open layout with wooden beams running across the cathedral ceiling. Family photos jostled for room on the mantel above the stone fireplace that dominated the living area, and two oversized couches faced each other, topped with pillows that said things like LIVE LOVE LAUGH and FAMILY IS EVERYTHING. Emme spotted a smiling photo of Max on one of the end tables, dangling from a cliff on rappelling ropes and grinning madly at the camera.

"That was taken on El Capitan, in Yosemite," Gwen said, seeing Emme staring at it. "Have you been there?"

"Yes," Emme said. "That's where I started as an ISB agent." She didn't elaborate on her first case there, when a completely shitty excuse for a human being had downloaded a trove of child sexual abuse images onto his phone while staying at the Ahwahnee Lodge.

"You must've been to every one of the National Parks," Gwen said. She was covering the space with chatter, Emme recognized, that would soon be filled with an endless grief.

"Not quite," Emme replied, still looking at the photo. "I haven't been to Alaska or Hawai'i. Or the Virgin Islands. But most of the ones in the continental U.S. I've been to." She pointed to the picture. "Would you say that Max was an experienced climber? His gear looks pretty expensive."

"Oh yes." Laura spoke from one of the high stools at the bar that ran along the kitchen. Tears still flowed from the corners of her eyes down her cheeks, but she seemed to have entered the lull that comes after the initial shock, before the bone-deep grief settles in. "He worked for REI after high school and took all of their trainings."

Emme took her notebook out of her bag and wrote *experienced climber, REI, had training* as Gwen moved around in the kitchen, putting a kettle on for tea. She examined more of the family photos—Max on the back of a pack mule making its way down the Grand Canyon, Max and Gwen and someone who looked like their dad at the top of Angels Landing. Emme glanced around the room. "Where's—Mr. Kerchek?" *Good God, she was going to have to deliver this horrible news a second time . . .*

"My dad died of Covid, early in the pandemic," Gwen answered in a hoarse voice. Laura dropped her head into her hands, her shoulders shaking with renewed sobs.

"I'm so sorry," Emme said, feeling like those three words were too meager to stretch over the enormity of their losses. She remembered Max's dad as the hunting-and-fishing type who told corny jokes that they'd all rolled their eyes at in high school.

"Max and I had come home to quarantine, and then we just—never left." Gwen rubbed her mom's back until the kettle whistled. "I'll get the tea, if you'll grab a few mugs from that cabinet," she said, pointing above the counter.

The tea poured and served, Emme climbed onto one of the stools and watched mother and daughter over the rim of her mug. Even wrapped in their grief, a thread of envy wove its way through her, the way they completed each other, how Gwen knew to fix Laura's tea with a drop of milk and honey without asking, Laura's hand on Gwen's arm as they sat next to each other. She took a swallow of tea, coughing a little as its heat scorched her throat, and set her mug down on the counter. "When was the last time you saw Max?" she asked, poising her pen over her notebook as she waited for their answer.

"He left very early Tuesday morning," Gwen answered, "before either of us was awake. He left a note—it's there, on the fridge, under the Grand Canyon magnet."

Emme slid off her stool and went over to the fridge. The note was written in a messy hand, like someone in a rush who didn't spend too much time writing longhand. *Camping in the park, probably no cell service. Be back on Thursday*, it read. Emme snapped a photo of it. She turned to face the two women. "He left on Tuesday?"

Gwen nodded. "We were expecting him back this afternoon. When your car pulled into the driveway, we thought—we thought you were him." Her voice broke, and Laura covered her face with her hands again.

Emme looked down at her notebook to give them a minute, but her mind raced. Max's permit had been for last night—Wednesday. If Max had left on Tuesday, where had he spent that night? "You're sure it was Tuesday?"

"Yes." Laura raised her head. "I'm sure. I had a doctor's appointment that morning that he was supposed to bring me to," Laura said, her voice

rusty with the tears that still dappled her face. "It wasn't like him to skip
out on stuff like that. I was annoyed," she finished in a whisper, cupping
her cheek in her palm.

Gwen reached out and gripped her mom's shoulder. "It was odd. He
usually planned his trips—even short ones—well in advance. It wasn't
like him to just take off without at least waiting for us to wake up so he
could say goodbye."

Esme scribbled *left home Tuesday/obtained permit on Wednesday.
Where did he spend Tuesday night?* in her notepad and looked up. "Did
Max have a girlfriend?"

"No," Laura answered right away. She glanced at Gwen to back her
up.

"Not that I knew," Gwen said. Her eyes darted to the side, so quick,
but Emme caught it.

"Are you sure?" Emme pressed.

"He would have told me if he was seeing someone," Laura said.
"We—we were very close, especially since his dad . . ." A fresh wave of
sobs tore from her throat, and she tipped sideways into Gwen. Emme
slid off her stool. Her insides were heavy and tight, like the air inside the
house had been sucked dry. Gently, she placed her card on the counter
and nodded to Gwen, hustled to the door, and slipped out.

On the front porch, she bent over double, breathing hard in and out of
her nose. But even the deepest breath couldn't fill her lungs. Everything
felt stuck, like her insides were coated with flypaper. Their grief was
suffocating her; she needed to get away, far away, so she could breathe
again. She hurried down the front steps, but before she reached the
bottom step, she heard the door creak open.

Gwen stepped out, twisting Emme's card in her fingers. "We're not in a real good place to answer questions right now," she said, glancing over her shoulder.

From inside the house, Emme could hear wailing. She stepped backwards, trying to get it out of her earshot. "Of course not," she told Gwen. "I'm so sorry that I had to even question you at all."

"You're just doing your job." She bit her lip, the card still making its rounds through her fingers.

Emme tilted her head. "Was there something else you wanted to tell me?"

"No," Gwen answered quickly—too quickly. She held the card up. "I'll call you if I think of anything."

"Gwen." Emme's mind twitched between pressing Gwen for what she was withholding and letting her off the hook.

"Yes?"

"We didn't find Max's phone on him," Emme said, a split second after deciding to let her off the hook. "It's likely it was lost when he—when he fell in the river. Did he have a laptop?"

"Yeah, he did." Gwen jerked her chin back toward the house. "I'm pretty sure he left it here. Do you think it might help you?"

"It would be very helpful, but I can't guarantee you'd get it back." Emme looked up at the sky, where the stars had finally come out. "If you want to take time and back it up onto an external hard drive, and then give it to me, that would be fine."

Gwen nodded. A gust of wind blew across the porch. She hugged herself. "Okay," she said, and backed up into the house, closing the door with a soft thud.

Emme looked at the closed door for a long moment, imagining the grief that roiled behind it. Another burst of wind scattered dead leaves across the driveway. Hunched against the cold, she made her way back to her car.

CHAPTER FIVE

The moment her Bluetooth connected in her car, before she was even out of the Kerchek's driveway, Emme called Stace. He picked up on the first ring. "I've been waiting for your call. Whatdya got?"

No *hello* or *how's it going*: that was Stace when they were digging into a case. When they weren't, he would talk your ear off late into the night over a bottle of bourbon, and Emme had lost count of how many nights he'd done just that. She never minded. Stace had a few lifetimes worth of stories, even before he joined the National Park Service as one of the first Native American rangers. "I knew the victim," Emme said.

Stace made a little strangled noise that was a combination of sympathy and curiosity. "Who were they? What happened?"

"I went to high school with him. It looks like he probably hit his head, then fell in the river."

"So—an accident."

"Probably," Emme said, but her gut squirmed. "There are a few things I need answers to before I determine that."

"Such as?"

Emme slowed behind a RV going about fifteen miles below the speed limit and tapped her fingers on her steering wheel. "Well, his permit for The Narrows listed two people. But whoever he was with never called for help or contacted the authorities and hasn't turned up at all."

"Humph. Odd."

"Also, the injuries on his head and neck—they don't seem consistent with a fall. Not from a great height, anyway."

"Well, that's for the medical examiner to decide," Stace said. "Did you notify his family?"

"Yeah, I just left there."

"So what are your next steps?" In the background, Emme could hear the creak of Stace's swivel chair, perhaps as he reached for his pen to jot down notes on what Emme was telling him.

"They're sending a ranger in tomorrow morning to check out his campsite." The road widened into a passing lane and Emme zipped around the RV, past the wide wood-and-rock *Springdale: Zion Canyon* sign welcoming her back to town. "And I have a list of people who were getting permits at the same time as him to call. Maybe one of them saw the other person he was with."

"Good. Let's touch base tomorrow afternoon to see where you are with all of that."

"Actually," Emme's hands tightened on the steering wheel. "I was hoping you could get another agent down here to take over."

There was a long pause on the other end of the line, filled with the sound of Stace's even breath. "No, Emme," he said at last. "I'm not going to do that."

Emme slammed on the brakes as a couple of tourists ran across the road. "What? Why?"

"This is your hometown park, you *knew* the victim, and you want someone else on this case?"

"Stace, I have one foot out the door, and I have so much to deal with right now—"

"I know, Emme. I empathize with that. Trust me, I do." Stace's voice softened and lowered. She could almost see the glimmer in his dark eyes; if she was there in the room with him, she knew he'd be putting his arm around her shoulders, giving her a little shake. "But I need you on this case. First of all, I don't have anyone I can spare. Second of all—I think one last case will be good for you."

"You don't know what's good for me," Emme snapped. She bit down on her lip so hard she tasted blood.

"I think, in this situation, I do," Stace said, his tone so gentle that Emme wanted to reach through her Bluetooth and strangle him. "Besides, you probably don't even have a case. It sounds like it was an accident."

Her gut squirmed again with that thing she wanted to keep in a box away from the light. A missing companion wasn't enough to call this anything other than an accident; maybe that companion had even met their own accident somewhere else in the park. She reached the bakery and turned onto the narrow lane that led past it to the house. "I'm home now, so I'm going to hop off."

"Emme—"

"It's fine, Stace," she lied.

"Keep me posted, okay?"

"I will." She hung up and turned off the car. The house in front of her looked claustrophobic, full of tight, maze-like rooms, completely different than the Kerchek's wide-open home. She sat staring at the front door, its bright purple sheen mocking her. When Sunny had bought the house, the door had been weather-beaten, faded by the sun and the wind, a sad shade of the illustrious wood it had once been. *What color should we paint it?* Sunny had asked her two girls. Before Emme could answer, Addie had shouted *Purple!* Almost thirteen by then, and too cool for the pinks and purples that had dominated her childhood, Emme had rolled her eyes and groaned *Please no.* But Sunny had just laughed and brought Addie with her to the paint store the next day and come home with a shade called Violet Sunrise.

There were nicks and dings and dents in the door all these years later, but Emme knew that when she repainted the damn thing, it would be with a bucket of Violet Sunrise.

She got out of the car but couldn't make herself climb the steps to the front door. Instead, she detoured into the bakery. The lights were on, and when she entered she found the manager, her mother's righthand man Jaspar, sanding the legs of one of the old, battered tables. "Hey."

"Hey! Where have you been all day?" He pushed himself out from under the table and dusted his hands off. His soft green eyes searched her face. "You don't look okay."

Emme sighed and glanced back toward the bakery's kitchen. "Do I smell something? I'm *starving.*"

"I made a couple of quiches, trying out new recipes. Onion and rosemary, and bacon and sweet potato."

"I'll take the bacon one."

"You got it."

Emme watched him disappear into the kitchen, a wave of gratitude washing over her. Jaspar was Sunny's "third child," as she liked to call him, ever since he'd wandered into Springdale after a months-long cross-country ramble and fallen in love with the town that served as the base for Zion National Park. After hanging out at the bakery for its free Wi-Fi for five days, he'd finally just asked Sunny for a job, and she'd handed him an apron on the spot. By that time, Emme had long since moved out, but she remembered the first time she'd come back to visit and spotted this soft-spoken, tall tree of a man taking biscuits out of the oven. Her mom was a cautious judge of character, and if she trusted Jaspar, then Emme did, too. In fact, Emme had a bit of a crush on Jaspar when they first met, which quickly tempered into a friendship when she found out he was gay.

The adrenaline of the day was wearing off and the lack of food was making her lightheaded. She pulled a bottle of orange juice from the fridge in the front of the cafe and settled herself at one of the tables. She popped the cap off the juice and took a long drink, letting its sweetness envelop her tongue. A tight heat crept up from her chest and into her throat, but she shoved it down, told it to go away until she could be alone in the house with all the lights off.

Jaspar reappeared, carrying a tray with two plates and the piping-hot quiche, steam rising from its golden surface. It smelled rich and delicious, a world away from the earth-and-water scent of The Narrows and the thin air of grief at the Kerchek house. He cut her a generous slice and set the plate in front of her. She dug in, the buttery crust dissolving in her mouth. "Thanks, Jaspar."

"Anytime." They ate in silence for a few minutes before he met her eyes across the table. "So. What's up?"

"Stace called. They found a body in The Narrows, so I had to go in." She took a swallow of juice. "Do you know Max Kerchek? I went to high school with him."

"Sure. He was in here a lot, used to order chai lattes." Jaspar sucked in his breath. "Oh shit—was it him?"

Emme nodded. "It looks like he hit his head and fell in the river. They found him up past Mystery Canyon, near the turnaround point."

"That's awful. Does his family know yet?"

"I just came from there."

Jaspar's forehead wrinkled and he laid his hand on Emme's arm, stopping her as she lifted another forkful of quiche to her mouth. "That couldn't have been easy for you."

Emme swallowed the lump in her throat down along with the bite of quiche. "It wasn't. And now Stace won't send someone else to take over."

Jasper raised an eyebrow. "Why would you want someone else to take over?"

"Because!" Emme waved her arms in a circular motion over her head, encompassing the bakery, the house, the town, the world that somewhere held her sister. "With everything I'm dealing with?" Jaspar leaned back in his chair, the wood creaking with the movement, and folded his arms. He just stared at her, not saying a word, until Emme set her fork down with a bang on her plate. "Don't look at me like that."

"Like what?"

"You know exactly like what." Emme jabbed a finger at him. "How can I possibly take this on, too?"

"Because it's your job," Jaspar said simply.

Emme dropped her arms down to the table, her shoulders hunching. "Not for much longer."

Jaspar put his elbows on the table, leaned his chin on his hands. "Are you really going to quit to run the bakery? Is that what you really want to do?"

Emme looked out the front window of the bakery. The soft glow from the streetlamp up the road illuminated the tourists on the sidewalk, walking home from dinner. A few peered into The Sunny Spot but hustled quickly away when they saw the CLOSED sign on the door. She turned back to Jaspar. "Yeah. It really is."

"Well, in that case . . ." Jaspar pushed away from the table and stood up. "Can I show you something on the back patio?"

"Sure. Is there coffee?"

"I'll fire up Il Duce."

Emme followed Jaspar into the back. Her mother had been old school when it came to coffee, and the espresso machine she'd installed in the bakery was an ancient Italian monster that she'd bought on eBay. The thing never broke down, and they'd all affectionately called it Il Duce for the way it crushed all of its competition around town. After he made two espressos, Jaspar led Emme to the patio. "So, your mom had mentioned wanting to do this a number of times, but just never got around to it." He waved his arm around the rustic porch, which was outfitted with a jumble of cozy, mismatched outdoor furniture. "We basically lose this space once the weather turns cold. But more and more, the park is still really busy throughout the winter. I think we could redo the porch, install a gas fire pit in the center, maybe station heat lamps around the sides, add some warm blankets for people to curl up in . . . we could really utilize this space and make it a fun hangout for the tourist crowd."

Emme turned in a slow circle. She could see it in her mind, hikers gathering at the end of a long day in the park, swapping stories about how slippery the chains were up on Angel's Landing or how high the water got in The Narrows. Many of the motels up and down the Boulevard didn't have lounges, and The Sunny Spot was close enough to all of them that people could wander over before or after dinner. "Maybe we could finally get a liquor license."

"I think that would be a big draw." Jaspar sat on the arm of an Adirondack chair. "I figured now would be a good time to do it, since the bakery is closed temporarily anyway."

"How long do you think it will take?"

"Probably a few weeks. I need to get a permit for the gas line, but I know some people. I think I could get that expedited. The liquor license will take longer, but we could always open it before we had that in place."

"It's a great idea." She sipped her coffee, let the rich bitterness envelope her tongue. "Thanks, Jaspar."

"You know I'll do anything to help out. I owe Sunny a lot."

We both do, Emme thought, but she didn't say it out loud. She didn't know how much her mom had told Jaspar about their past, about what drove them out of New York and all the way to Springdale, about the solace they'd found at the base of the soaring red cliffs of Zion Canyon. "I think I'm going to turn in. It's been a long day and I have a lot to do tomorrow." She moved across the patio, but on the top step of the back stairs she turned. "Hey, do you know if Max was seeing anyone? Did he ever come in here with a woman, like on a date?"

Jaspar tilted his head. "He used to come in with some of his climbing buddies—I remember, because we had a long conversation about our favorite spots around Utah once during a late-afternoon lull. He was far more experienced than I was, though. Why?"

"His permit was for two people," Emme said.

"Well, that doesn't necessarily mean it was someone he was seeing romantically. It could've been one of his friends."

"True, but where are they?" Emme drummed her fingers on the table. "Why haven't they come forward?"

"Maybe something happened to them, too," Jaspar said, shuddering slightly.

"That's possible, but the river's been calm the last few days." Emme gave a little shake of her head. "If they both fell in, we would've found the other body already."

"You know, The Sunny Spot wasn't the only place that Max was a regular," Jaspar said. "He hung out at Cap's Landing a lot, too."

"Yes, he did," Emme murmured. Their old high school friend Tim, who had also been on that trip into The Narrows after graduation—his dad owned Cap's Landing. She hadn't been back to the bar since Sunny died. All those people, offering their condolences . . . she lifted one shoulder. "I don't know if I'm ready to be out in a crowd."

"I'll go with you," Jaspar offered.

Emme pressed her lips together. It would be helpful, questioning people who maybe knew something about who Max had gone into The Narrows with. "Okay. Let's go tomorrow."

"Why's it so important you find this other person, anyway?"

Emme balanced on the step and drained the last of her espresso. "Whoever they are, they were the last person to see Max alive."

*****

It was almost a relief to ignore the towering piles of crap in the living room and work on Max's case the next morning. Blue sky stretched over the mountains, the puffy white clouds making shadows on the red cliffs. Emme settled herself in the lounge chair on the front porch, a steaming cup of coffee on the little wicker table next to her, and called the medical examiner to confirm that they had received Max's body.

"We will call you when we've completed the examination," the M.E. told her firmly, and didn't even wait for her thanks before hanging up.

Emme rolled her eyes. *Fucking M.E.s.* Too many hours with the dead gave them very bad people skills. Next, she requested Max's cell phone records, hoping it would take less time to get them than the 72 hours they quoted her. Then she pulled out the list of five walk-ins that the ranger at the Visitor Center had given her. The first one went to voicemail. The second one said he remembered Max but was pretty sure he was alone. The third one told Emme, "I don't talk to the fuzz," when she identified herself as a federal agent, and hung up on her.

The fourth person on the list answered after five rings. "Hello?"

"Is this Ruby Cunningham?"

"Who's calling?"

Emme launched into her introductory spiel. "Oh, okay," Ruby said. "I figured you were a telemarketer. I get so many freaking spam calls. How can I help you?"

Ruby sounded young and curious, like someone Emme probably would've hung out with in college. "You purchased a walk-in permit for The Narrows on Wednesday morning, yes?"

"Yeah, I did. Wait, is this about the dead guy they found?"

"It is, actually. He also bought a walk-in permit that morning."

"He did?" Ruby let out a low whistle. "That's eerie. So—what does that have to do with me?"

"I'm wondering if you saw him." Emme described Max: six-foot, dark hair that waved to the left, brown eyes, wearing a bright blue parka, dark pants, and Merrill hiking boots.

"Oh my god, that was him?" Ruby groaned. "That's awful. He was right in front of us in line. My friend and I couldn't stop giggling about it because he was so hot. He's really dead?"

"Listen, Ruby—this is really important so think carefully." Emme poised her pen above her notebook, optimism that she'd actually have something to write this time building in her. "Was he with someone? Was there someone in line with him?"

"No—"

The optimism deflated and her pen tipped forward.

"—not in the line, but there was a woman outside the Visitor Center that he met up with."

Emme sat up straight. "Are you sure?"

"Positive. I remember because my friend said, 'God I hope that's his sister,' and then he kissed her like super sexy, and we were like, 'okay, I really hope that's *not* his sister.'"

"Can you describe her?"

"It was far away, but she was definitely blonde. Probably in her like mid-twenties? Medium height, I think? She had on a purple puffer vest. I really liked the color."

"Is there anything else you can remember?"

"Not really, cuz the people behind us were getting mad that we were holding up the line gawking at them. Oh—they both had camping backpacks. That's about all I saw."

"When you say 'camping backpacks,' do you mean that they were carrying a lot of gear?"

"Yeah, they definitely looked like they were going to spend a night in The Narrows. Maybe more than a night. Those packs looked stuffed to the gills." There was a crackle and a muffled voice beyond Ruby's on her end of the line. "Is there anything else, Agent Helliwell? My mom needs me to drive her somewhere."

"No, that's all. Thank you, Ruby. This has been very helpful."

"Glad I could help," she chirped. "Now I have something to tell my friends at the bar tonight." The phone clicked off.

The last number on the list also went to voicemail. Emme circled the last thing she wrote—*camping backpacks/lots of gear/stuffed to the gills*—and began to mind-map around it with all the possibilities: they were planning on being out in the wilderness for more than just one night, or they had overpacked. Given Max's wilderness experience, that was unlikely. Perhaps his date was not as experienced as him . . . Emme kept drawing a line back to her note, *more than just one night.* Had they been camping elsewhere in the park on that unaccounted-for Tuesday night? If they had, they didn't have a backcountry permit, or a reservation at any of the campgrounds.

Emme circled her note, *blonde/mid-twenties/medium height/purple puffer vest,* again and again, until those words stood out more than anything else in her notes. This woman, whoever she was, whatever her relationship with Max, was the key to everything. Once Emme had her, the whole case would unlock. She could give Max's family the answers they deserved about his death, shut the book, and move on. Emme put her pen down before she scribbled a hole into her notebook. She hitched her hope onto her visit to Cap's Landing that night, that someone there would know who this woman was—not just for Max's sake, but for her own.

CHAPTER SIX

C ap's Landing sat at the edge of town and down a side street so that tourists couldn't easily find it. A collection of mud-splattered SUVs and pick-up trucks filled the gravel parking lot. It was still early; a thin ribbon of pink threaded across the sky, but Emme knew that by the time the stars appeared, the lot would be so full that there'd be some tense moments later in the night as people tried to figure out who had blocked them in. She navigated her Subaru Crosstrek into a spot at the far side of the lot that allowed enough space to get out without having to wrangle keys away from a drunken townie. She and Jaspar hopped out of the car, their boots kicking up dust as they made their way to the door.

A Miranda Lambert song greeted them inside. It was already crowded and loud—not quite shouting level, but it would be there soon. A handful of people clustered around the pool table, watching the game in progress, bottles of local craft beer in their hands. Emme followed Jaspar to the bar, where they slid onto two of the few open stools. Emme swiveled away from the bar and surveyed the room. There were several faces that she recognized: a trio of park rangers, people who ran the

other shops and restaurants in town, and a couple from her high school
that she'd seen around town over the years. It had been months since
she'd been in Cap's, but the place never changed. The constancy was
comforting.

Behind the bar, her high school friend Tim stood pulling a pint of
beer. Though his dad—Cap himself—still puttered around, Tim had
pretty much taken over the bar in the last few years. He looked up as
Emme and Jaspar approached. "Hey, Emme, how're you doing? I was so
sorry to hear about your mom."

"Thanks, Tim."

"Was there a service? I didn't hear anything about it, or we definitely
would've been there."

"Not yet." Emme gave him a lopsided smile. "I'll keep you posted."

"You think you'll reopen the bakery soon?"

Emme glanced at Jaspar, the only hint she needed to give, bless him.
"We're making some improvements," Jaspar answered. "Seemed like a
good time to do that."

"Oh man, I've been at my dad to renovate. Or at least get rid of the cash
register and get a digital POS system. No one pays with cash anymore,"
he said, waving to the end of the bar where an ancient register that was
probably state-of-the-art in the early 80s sat like a squat little gnome.
"But he's stubborn." Tim sighed. "What can I get you two? On the
house."

"You don't have to do that," Emme said.

"Are you kidding? After all the free muffins your mom gave me when
the bar wasn't doing well? It's the least I can do."

"I'll take a pint of the Dead Horse Amber," Jaspar said, nodding to
the row of taps in the center of the bar.

"And I'll take the Happy Valley Hefeweizen," Emme said. "Thanks, Tim."

He placed two coasters in front of them and returned a few moments later with the foaming pints. When he'd set them down, he pressed his elbows on the bar and leaned toward Emme. "Word around town is that you found a body in the park."

Emme picked up her beer. Foam spilled over the rim and splashed her finger. She took a sip while Tim watched her, steadying herself for what she had to say. She rested the glass back down on its coaster, watched a dark rim form around its base. "I did." She reached across the bar and touched Tim's forearm. "It was Max Kerchek."

"What?" Tim jerked back, his hand splayed flat over his heart. "Are you serious?"

"Unfortunately, yes."

"Oh, man." Tim rubbed his face. "Poor Laura—first his dad, now him. Wait—they know, right?"

"Of course. I saw them last night, as soon as I left the park after identifying him."

Tim motioned for someone behind Emme to come over. Emme swiveled to find Amy, another high school friend who worked as a waitress at the bar, making her way over, wiping her hands on her apron as she walked. "What's up?" she asked. "Oh, hey, Emme. How're you doing?"

"Max Kerchek is the body they found in the park," Tim said. Emme resisted the urge to smack him. She would've delivered the news in a much gentler way. After all, Amy had also been on that trip in The Narrows after graduation and knew Max well, too.

"Oh no." Amy sank onto the empty stool next to Emme. "Oh, that's terrible. What happened?"

"I'm still trying to figure that out," Emme said.

"Hang on." Amy jabbed a finger at Emme. "If you're looking into it, that must mean you suspect a crime, right? Don't you only investigate crimes?"

"Well, I have to determine if a crime even happened," Emme said. "So that's what I'm doing."

A shadow darkened the bar as a tall man with coppery hair leaned in between Emme and Amy. "Could I get a refill on the Dead Horse?"

"Sure." Tim grabbed a fresh pint glass and pulled the tap down. The amber-colored liquid swirled into the glass.

"I just can't believe it," Amy said, tilting to the side so she could talk to Emme around the backside of the Dead Horse-refill guy. "Max Kerchek is the last person I would've expected to die in the park."

The copper-haired man glanced at Amy and then Emme. "Excuse me, did you say Max Kerchek?"

"Yes," Amy answered. "Did you know him?"

"No, I—well, I'd spoken to him, but I'd never met him. We were supposed to meet tomorrow." Tim handed the guy his beer and he stood frozen, the foam dripping over the rim of the glass onto his fingers. "Are you for real saying that he was the body they found in the park?"

"Who are you?" Emme asked. "Why were you meeting him?"

A loud buzz reverberated from the guy's back pocket. He yanked his phone out, muttered "excuse me," and walked away from the bar. Emme watched him go. "Have you ever seen that guy before?"

Amy shook her head. "No, never." A burst of boisterous laughter echoed from one of the booths in the corner. As Amy glanced that way, they signaled for her attention. She hopped off the stool. "I'll be back."

Tim leaned his elbows onto the bar in front of Emme and Jaspar. "You guys want some food?"

"I'll have a burger," Jaspar said. "With a split order of fries and onion rings."

"And I'll take a turkey burger," Emme said. "Tim, do you know who that guy is? With the red hair?"

"I saw him at The Ugly Mug this morning getting coffee." Tim made an apologetic face. "Sorry, but I still need to get my coffee."

"That's okay," Jaspar said with a laugh. "We won't hold it against you."

"But he's not a local, is he?" Emme scanned the bar, looking for that coppery head of hair, but the guy had disappeared, perhaps outside to take his call.

"I don't think so."

The door to the bar burst open, but instead of the mysterious redhead, it was Theo, with Darby by his side. He spotted Emme and nodded at her, then led Darby to a booth underneath the set of windows that ran along the wall. Emme drained the last of her beer and hopped off her stool. "I'll be right back."

"Hey, Emme," Theo said when she arrived at their table. "You remember Darby?"

"I do, yes. How are you doing?" Emme asked, putting a hand on Darby's shoulder.

"I'm okay." Darby gave her a little half-smile over the top of her menu. "Did you find out what happened to that poor man?"

"Working on it."

"Did you find out who his companion was?" Theo asked.

"He was with someone?" Darby asked, laying her menu down. "Are they okay?"

Emme pressed her lips together. Theo wasn't a law enforcement ranger, but he should know better than to go shooting his mouth off in front of a girl he was trying to impress. "I have not located his companion."

"Did they find anything at his campsite?"

Emme shook her head. She'd heard from the rangers that had trekked into The Narrows to Campsite Four. Other than the remnants of a fire ring, they'd found nothing. So either his companion had cleared everything out, or Max had fallen into the river before he'd set up camp.

"So there could be another body floating somewhere in The Narrows?" Darby shuddered.

"He didn't die in a flash flood, so I think that's unlikely," Theo said, reaching across the table to pat Darby's hand. Emme narrowed her eyes as Theo's words replayed in her head. *Exactly*. It was unlikely Max's companion—the woman in the purple puffer vest—had also had an accident. So where was she?

"Were you working on Wednesday?" Emme asked Theo.

"Yeah. I was at the South Entrance until about eleven, then got sent up to the East Entrance for the rest of the day," Theo said, running his finger down the list of all the different burgers on the menu.

Emme leaned against the post that separated their booth from the next one. To access The Narrows from the top-down, you had to pass through the East Entrance. But Max and whoever he was with would have been there early in the morning, probably right after he'd gotten his permit. "You don't remember seeing him, do you?"

Theo shook his head. "It was a pretty quiet afternoon. All the top-downers were already on the trail."

"I figured. Did anything else happen that day? Anything out of the ordinary?"

"No. It was a pretty typical day. Oh, wait." Theo lowered the menu and looked up at the ceiling, as though he was pulling a memory from a closed corner of his brain. "This happened before I got there, but the ranger that I relieved told me that some guy had shown up demanding to get into The Narrows. He didn't have a top-down permit, and he threw a fit when Carey wouldn't let him pass."

Emme straightened. "And you didn't think to tell me about this yesterday?"

Theo shrugged. "It didn't seem connected. Is it?"

"Everything is connected until I prove it's not," Emme said. Her fingers were itching to take notes, but her notebook was back at the bar. "What else did Carey tell you?"

"That's pretty much it. The guy caused a scene, so Carey kicked him out of the station and he drove off in a huff." Theo rested back against the cushioned leather booth. "There was an entry in the log about it. I can send that to you."

"That would be great. And have Carey call me. If I don't get him first," Emme said. Theo nodded and caught Darby's eye across the table. They smiled at each other, inside a private bubble that Emme wasn't allowed in. "Have a good dinner," she told them and sidled back to the bar.

"Find anything out?" Jaspar asked when she'd climbed back onto her stool. A moment later, Tim set their food down in front of them.

"Maybe. Did that redheaded guy ever come back?"

"No. Why?"

"Hmmph." Emme picked up her turkey burger and took a big bite. Smoky barbecue sauce dribbled down her chin, and she licked it away before it could escape onto her shirt. "I want to know why he was meeting with Max."

A couple of stools down, Tim set a bottle of 801 Pilsner in front of a woman that Emme didn't recognize and rested his elbows on the bar. "I heard they found him in The Narrows," he said.

The woman took a swig of beer. "Drowned? But the water level isn't very high right now. I was just there last week."

A man sitting on the other side of the woman leaned in. "A friend of a friend of mine was leading the group that found him. They think he fell."

Tim glanced over at Emme, and she busied herself with her burger so that he wouldn't know she was eavesdropping. "Did your friend say where they found him?"

"Between Wall Street and Big Spring," he replied. The woman next to him nodded, and Tim straightened. There wasn't a soul in the bar who didn't know exactly where that was, who hadn't hiked there at least half a dozen times themselves. You would think that living at the base of Zion Canyon it'd be easy to take its beauty for granted, but Emme didn't know anyone who did. The park was as much their home as the town was, and each of them knew its landscape like they knew the layout of their own house.

"He couldn't have fallen from the cliff at that spot," Tim said. "There's no trail up there."

"Maybe he fell further up and floated down," the woman mused.

"Or didn't fall from the cliff at all," the man said. "He could have tripped or something, hit his head and fell into the river."

"Maybe he was murdered," the woman said, so casually as she sipped her beer that Emme's stomach flipped over.

"Jesus Christ and all his Latter-Day Saints." Amy slammed her tray down on the bar between Emme and the woman with a clatter. "He was a real live person. Can we not talk about him like he's an episode of *Dateline*?" Her hands shook as she wiped them on her apron. "For God's sake, he was just in here last week, alive and well and telling his girlfriend he loved her."

Emme froze, her burger halfway to her mouth. As Amy turned away from the bar, she caught her eye. "Can I get another napkin?" Emme asked, holding up her sauce-covered fingers. "I've made a mess."

"Sure." Amy lumbered off to the servers' station in the corner behind the bar.

The woman swiveled back to Tim. "But *what happened?*" she pressed.

"Amy's right," Tim said. "This is giving me the creeps." He spun his back to her and began to wipe down the shelves that displayed the bar's extensive liquor collection. The woman slid off her stool and wandered over the pool table, the guy who was the friend of a friend of Hal's following.

When Amy returned with her napkin, Emme gestured to the stool next to her. "Can you take a break for a minute?" Amy plunked herself onto the stool and arched her back. "How have you been?" Emme asked.

Amy sighed. "My dad's going through chemo, so I'm helping out at their place a bunch. Between that, and the kids—which includes my husband, ha ha—and working here . . . it's been a lot." She reached out and touched Emme's knee. "But you don't need to hear about my woes. You got plenty of your own. I was real sorry to hear about your mom."

"Thanks." She pushed the plate of fries toward Amy, gestured for her to help herself. "It's been tough. And now this thing with Max . . ." She let her voice trail off and took another bite of her burger.

Amy pressed her palm to her cheek. "I can't believe it. He was so out-doorsy—and smart about the outdoors, you know? Do you remember we all called him Mountain Max on that trip we took into The Narrows after we graduated?"

"Of course I remember. I couldn't stop thinking about it yesterday when I was—when I saw him." The snapshot of Max's bruised and broken body flashed in her mind, and for an instant she envied Amy, that she didn't have that image stuck in her brain forever.

"God, how traumatizing." Amy shook her head. "Your job, Emme—I don't know how you do it."

Emme felt Jaspar's eyes on her as she buried her face in her pint glass. A thousand responses rolled around on Emme's tongue from the innocuous *yeah, it's hard* to the complicated *I don't know how I do it either which is why I put in my notice.* She finished her drink and looked back up at Amy. "You said he was in here last week?"

"Yeah. We chatted for a few minutes, he had a couple of beers and left."

Emme cocked her head. "He was alone?" When Amy nodded, she pressed on. "But you said he told his girlfriend he loved her."

"Oh." Amy brushed a loose lock of hair away from her forehead, tucked it behind her ear. "That was on the phone. She wasn't actually here."

"How do you know it was his girlfriend?"

"I just caught snatches of the conversation, but it was the way he was speaking to her—sort of quiet and intimate, you know? And I mean, I'm assuming it was a her." Amy shrugged. "Pretty sure Max was straight."

"He was," Jaspar cut in.

"Did you see that on your gaydar?" Emme asked.

"Ha." Jaspar rolled his eyes. "No, but I tried to flirt with him once when he came into the bakery and he was completely oblivious. A gay man would've flirted back."

"Unless he wasn't interested," Emme pointed out.

"Who wouldn't be interested in this?" Jaspar framed his face with his hands.

"I would be," Amy said, batting her eyes at him.

"You're married," Jaspar said. "Among other problems."

Amy laughed, a full-throated sound that brought Emme right back to that night in The Narrows, telling dirty jokes about the classmates they liked the least while passing around a joint. "Ain't that the truth. Anyway, when he hung up he said, 'love you too.'"

"It could've been his mom," Emme said. Speculation was part of her job, but it was the messy part that made her feel all jumbled up inside.

"No, it was a romantic 'I love you,'" Amy insisted. "I've been married for eleven years, I know the difference."

"When was this?" Emme asked.

A couple in one of the booths signaled to Amy for her attention. She held up a finger with a friendly smile at them. "About a week ago? I think last Tuesday. I was off after that night until Friday, and I remember the weekend was really busy, I wouldn't have been able to hear a phone conversation like that." She got to her feet. "It's really good to see you, Emme. Let's have a proper visit soon when I'm off work and the kids are in school." She patted Emme's hand and hustled over to the booth calling her away.

"Sounds like he did have a girlfriend," Jaspar said. He held his empty pint glass up for a refill, and Tim nodded to him from down the bar.

"But who was she? And why hadn't he told his family about her?" Emme pushed her plate away, her burger half-eaten. Her stomach was in knots again, trying to untangle the jumbled pieces of information.

"Maybe it was a new relationship," Jaspar said.

"They were already at the 'I love you' stage," Emme pointed out. "What straight man do you know that says 'I love you' that early in a relationship?" Jaspar snorted as Tim set a newly filled pint glass in front of him. "Hey, did that red-haired guy ever come back in?"

Tim scanned the bar, then shook his head. "No. I haven't seen him. Dammit, I think he walked off with one of my glasses."

"Did he open a tab?"

"Yeah, he did." Tim brightened and went to the cash register, dug around for a moment, and returned with an American Express card. "Finn Brackenbury. I don't think he's local."

"Can I have that?"

Tim raised an eyebrow. "What are you going to do with it?"

"Book a flight to Maui and get wasted on the beach." Emme rolled her eyes. "I'm going to return it to him. What time did you see him at The Ugly Mug this morning?"

"Eight-thirty." Tim hesitated a moment, then held the card out to Emme. "I'm only giving you this because you're a federal agent. And I know where you live."

She grinned and snatched the card out of his hand. As Jaspar sipped his beer and looked at her over the rim of his glass, she pulled out her phone. Searching Finn Brackenbury turned up dozens of results: private Instagram and Facebook accounts that had a photo of a Joshua tree as the profile picture, and then several articles with the name Finn Brackenbury as the byline. Emme clicked on a piece from *The Atlantic*.

Next to the title—*Did An Illegal Fracking Operation Cause This Town's Cancer?*—was a thumbnail picture of the author, his coppery hair bright against the black and white text.

"Shit," Emme breathed. She looked up at the door through which the redheaded man had disappeared on his phone call and never returned.

Finn Brackenbury was a journalist.

CHAPTER SEVEN

At eight-thirty in the morning, The Ugly Mug bustled with tourists stocking up on protein and coffee for their day in the park. Emme joined the line that stretched to the door and craned her neck. At the front of the line, a conspicuous head of red hair shone in the sunlight that streamed in through the large picture windows. Emme stepped out of line and sidled her way to the front, just in time for Mr. Finn Brackenbury to pull out his wallet and start frantically rifling through it.

"Looking for this?" Emme held the card between her thumb and her forefinger, dangling it in front of Finn's face. He blinked, looked from her to the card, then plucked it from her hand.

"How did you—"

"You left it at the bar last night," Emme said. "Tim said he'd seen you here yesterday morning, so I took a chance that you're a creature of habit."

"Very astute." Finn nodded to the teenage girl behind the register. "Add whatever she wants to my order."

"Dark roast," Emme told her. Finn paid and made a big show of carefully sliding the card back into its designated slot in his wallet. They stepped aside to wait for their drinks. When the girl handed them over, Emme took a sip and grimaced. Not quite Il Duce, but it was rich and robust and set her veins tingling after the sleepless night she'd had.

"You know, I would've realized that I'd left it at the bar and gone back there tonight," Finn said as they wound through the crowd of people waiting to order. There was an open table tucked away in the corner. Finn dropped into one of the seats and gestured for Emme to join him. After a moment's hesitation, she did. "So why even bother trying to find me?"

Emme leaned back in her chair. "Are you working on a story in town?"

Finn's forehead creased. Then his eyes widened. "Ah. You Googled me."

Emme didn't answer, just shrugged and took another sip of her coffee.

"It doesn't seem quite fair that you know who I am and I have no idea who you are." He rested his elbow on the table, put his chin in his hand, and stared at her. She stared back for a minute, then stretched her hand across the table.

"Emme Helliwell," she said.

Finn took her hand in his, but instead of letting go after a normal handshake, he tightened his grip. "Emmeline Helliwell? From the National Park Service?"

Emme pulled her hand back. "Yes."

"You're actually on my list of people to contact." Finn took his phone out of his pocket and scrolled through it. "You worked on the Hannah DeLeo case, didn't you?"

At the sound of Hannah's name, coming from this stranger, Emme turned cold, as though her blood had turned to an icy slush. "Are you writing a story about her?" It was hard for her to even say the name. It tasted like betrayal on her tongue.

Finn nodded. He seemed not to notice the cold that had shuddered down on Emme. She narrowed her eyes at him. "Why are you in Zion? She was killed in the Grand Canyon."

"Yes, I know. But Max Kerchek contacted me and said he had some information for me." Finn dug into the messenger bag at his side and pulled out a notebook. "He refused to tell me over the phone or even email. I came here to meet with him before heading to the Grand Canyon."

"Max had information about the DeLeo case?" That jumbled-up feeling churned inside her again. "How would he know anything about it?"

"That's what I was coming here to find out. Which is why it was so disturbing to find out he died." Finn shook his head and ran his hand through his hair. Emme noticed that he had a smattering of freckles across his knuckles, matching those that dappled his cheeks. "He was found in The Narrows, right? Do you know how he died?"

"I'm sorry, I can't discuss that." It was comforting to speak the standard line, like falling back onto a soft bed of pillows. "It's an ongoing investigation."

"Okay." Finn uncapped his pen and flipped to a clean page in the notebook. "Can I ask you some questions about the DeLeo case?"

"No." It came out sharper than she intended. Finn snapped his head up and met her gaze. She looked away. She'd come to The Ugly Mug cocky and confident, certain that she'd have the upper hand. And now that had slipped away from her. She grappled herself back into familiar territory. "I am not at liberty to discuss any case with the press until I clear it with my supervisor."

"Oh. Of course." Finn scrunched up the side of his face so that his left eye was barely open while his right one stared straight at her. "Do you think it's worth me taking a trip to Redwater to ask around there about Hannah?"

Emme barked out a half-laugh, half-snort. "For a journalist, you really haven't done your homework, have you?" Finn narrowed his eyes at her. Emme cocked her head. "You know that line in *Lord of the Rings* where Sean Bean says 'one does not simply walk into Mordor?' Replace Mordor with Redwater and you'll have an idea of what that place is like."

"I know about Abraham Murdock and the Warriors for Armageddon—" Finn began, a defensive edge to his voice, but Emme held up her hand and he fell silent.

"Reading about them and experiencing them are two different things," she said. "These are extremely dangerous, heavily-armed people. Do not go anywhere near there."

After a long moment, Finn gave a short nod. "Okay. Thanks for the warning." He rooted around in his bag again and yanked out a business card. "Listen, take my number. When you've cleared it with your higher-ups, I would love to talk about the case."

Now it was Emme's turn to pluck a card from between his fingers. She resisted the urge to crumple it into a ball and slid it into her pocket instead without looking at it. "Max had absolutely nothing to do with the DeLeo case," she said. "I don't know what information he could have possibly had. Maybe you were being played."

Finn shrugged. "Maybe. Was Max the sort to do that?"

No, he wasn't. Emme watched a family of four join the line, a mother and father and their two teenage daughters. They were chattering excitedly about how they'd scored a day-of Angel's Landing permit. She hadn't seen Max in a while, but even that last time he'd still seemed so hopeful for his future, so open to the possibilities that lay ahead. Not the type to lead a random journalist on a wild goose chase. She shook her head in answer to Finn's question.

Finn closed his notebook and dropped it back into his bag, settling back in his seat. "It's a pretty creepy coincidence," he said, "arranging to meet me and then turning up dead."

"I don't believe in coincidences," Emme murmured, like an automatic switch that turned on whenever someone said the word *coincidence*. Finn raised his eyebrows, but before Emme could explain herself, her phone buzzed, making them both jump.

It was an email notification; the medical examiner had finished. Emme grabbed her coffee and stood up. "I have to go." She reached into her bag and pulled out her own business card. "If you find anything else about why Max wanted to meet you, *I* would love to talk to *you*."

Finn smiled as he took the card from her. "Thanks for returning my credit card."

"Thanks for the coffee," she said, squeezing past the family of four to emerge onto the sun-dappled street.

*****

Max's body had been brought to the facility in St. George. Emme followed the winding grey hallways down into the cold, sterile basement and knocked on the door marked MEDICAL EXAMINER. A moment later, the door was opened by a thin, bespectacled woman in a white lab coat, her blonde hair pulled back into a bun so tight that it tugged at her skin. "Agent Helliwell? I'm Rose Young."

"You can call me Emme," she said as she stepped through the door. The smell of formaldehyde assaulted her nostrils, and the frigid temperature inside the room wrapped her in an icy embrace. "Any relation to Brigham?"

Rose peered at her through her glasses, her expression unchanged. "No. Not every Young in Utah is descended from Brigham."

"I know, I—was making a joke." Emme tucked her hands in her pockets. "It was a bad one. Sorry."

"Your victim is over here." Rose Not-Descended-From-Brigham Young led Emme to a curtained area and pulled the curtain aside. The metal rings holding up the curtain screeched against the curtain rod. Emme winced at the harsh sound, but Rose made no notice of it.

Max's body lay beneath a white sheet that draped nearly to the floor. The shape of his nose and his toes protruded under the sheet. Rose reached for the top of the sheet, and Emme squeezed her eyes shut for a moment. She wanted the *before* to last, before his body became a lifeless shell of the person he was.

"Agent Helliwell?"

I told you to call me Emme. She said nothing, swallowed hard into her heart, and opened her eyes. "Yes. Tell me what you found."

"As you can see, there are multiple contusions and bruising around the head." Rose pointed to the dark purple stains that covered the sides of Max's neck. She drew the sheet lower to expose his chest. Welts crisscrossed his torso, nearly black in color. Emme sucked in her breath. She had seen many dead bodies before, but never someone she knew. Even her mom, the nurses had whisked her out of the room so quickly after she'd died. "He also had two broken ribs," Rose continued, "and damage to his internal organs that would be consistent with a fall."

Emme let out a long exhale to steady herself. "Was he still alive when he went into the water?" she asked.

"No. I didn't find any water in his lungs." Rose slid her hands beneath Max's shoulders and lifted him a bit, turning him so that the back of his neck was easier to see. Emme saw how Rose handled his flesh, as though he was an object to be poked and prodded at and not a human being whose life had been so cruelly cut short. She supposed it was how a medical examiner survived in the job, but it made her insides twitch. "Do you see here?"

Emme stepped in beside Rose and followed the line of her thumbs to what she was indicating. Two large, round bruises on either side of the base of his neck, deep red with purpling at their edges, marred his skin. "That's what killed him," Emme breathed.

"Yes." Rose laid him carefully back on the table. "I believe that's what caused the fatality."

"So he fell backwards?" Emme closed her eyes again for a moment, trying to play the scene out in her mind. "He fell backwards, hit his head on—something, probably a rock—then stumbled forward into the river?" She opened her eyes. "But he would have gone into the river alive in that scenario, and there would be water in his lungs."

"Perhaps he hit his head and expired on his way to falling forward into the river," Rose said. "Or he fell from somewhere high and hit his head on the way down."

Emme shook her head. "He wouldn't have been up on the cliffs at that spot. There's no trail."

"Not everyone stays on the trails like they're supposed to in National Parks, Miss Helliwell." Rose's tone was so clipped that Emme balled her hands into fists, dug her fingernails into her palms.

"Of course not," she replied, sharpening her own voice. "But you'd have to bushwhack. I think it's unlikely."

"Unlikely things happen all the time." Rose pulled the sheet back up over Max's head and dropped it with a clean snap. "Whether or not he fell from a height, I do think he fell. Accidentally."

"So, you're ruling his death an accident." Emme's heart pounded, reverberating through her whole body. The formaldehyde smell clogged the back of her throat with a searing ball.

"Yes." Rose moved to the door and held it open for her, a clear invitation for Emme to leave.

"You don't think there's *any* possibility this wasn't an accident?" Emme stayed rooted where she stood.

Rose folded her arms across her chest. "Given where and how he was found, his injuries, and the fact that most deaths in National Parks are accidents, I feel very confident in my ruling."

"Actually, most deaths in National Parks are drownings," Emme said. "Those outweigh falls two to one." Rose didn't respond, but Emme saw her jaw tighten. She was not ready to give Rose the satisfaction of leaving yet, though. "There's not even a shadow of a doubt to rule his death inconclusive?"

"Ruling a death inconclusive opens a can of worms that I don't think is necessary to open in this case." Rose stepped back and nodded to the hallway outside. "If you'll excuse me, I have other bodies to examine. Please let the family know they can pick up the body for burial the day after tomorrow or arrange to have it transported to a funeral home."

Emme didn't move. She met Rose's gaze, whose icy blue eyes didn't blink, didn't waver. A chill slithered down Emme's spine. Something felt wrong here, but arguing with this automaton of a person wasn't going to right it. She broke the gaze and marched through the door into the grey hallway.

"Have a good day, Agent Helliwell," Rose said in that clipped tone, closing the door with a loud click before the words had barely left her tongue.

Emme stared at the steel door. That jumbled-up feeling swirled inside her, but now it was twisted with a red-hot anger. Maybe Rose Young could dismiss Max's death so easily with a wave of her pen, but Emme could not. She turned on her heel and marched down the hall, the concrete walls and mottled floor smearing around her as her mind churned. The hallway dead-ended, and Emme nearly collided with the concrete wall. She stopped and spun in a small circle. A sign pointed to the exit in the opposite direction, back the way she'd come. She leaned back against the wall, pressed herself into its cold solidness and closed her eyes.

That was it, then. Max's death was an accident; the case was over. She would report back to Stace, he would make a record of it, and they would close the file. A tragic accident, that's all it was.

But she could not loosen that knot in her gut. In fact, it pulled even tighter. She took in a long, sharp breath through her nose and parceled out what she knew: *the missing girlfriend, the injuries on the back of his neck, the meeting with a journalist that he never made it to.* Taken separately, each of these things wasn't singular or suspicious. But put together, they felt like pieces of a larger puzzle, one whose picture was still blurry and unfocused. Something was not right, and she knew that knot wouldn't undo itself until she worked out what was wrong.

She launched away from the wall and wound her way back through the maze of hallways until she came to the exit and pushed out into the blinding sun. She drove too fast back to Springdale, taking the exit off 15 onto Route 9 at breakneck speed, almost daring a state trooper to pull her over or her car to go sailing off the road into a ditch. But neither of those things happened, and when she passed the *Springdale: Zion Canyon* sign, she finally slowed down.

She didn't turn onto the road to the house or the bakery; she drove straight through town, straight through the entrance to the park, smashing her Smokey hat onto her head so she could tip it at the ranger in the entry booth, and didn't stop her car until she reached the Weeping Rock shuttle stop. She parked in one of the designated ranger spots, slung her backpack over her shoulders, and crossed the road to the Weeping Rock trailhead.

It was a bright and sunny day with one of those skies where the fluffy white clouds cast defined shadows on the canyon. There were few people on the Weeping Rock Trail; on a clear day like this, everyone flocked to Angel's Landing where the dizzying climb brought views for miles. The trail was short, but it ascended quickly through steep switchbacks. Emme's breath came hard and fast until all she could hear was her own inhale-exhale and the twittering of birds calling to each other across the canyon.

When she hit the fork in the trail, she went right and entered Hidden Canyon. The switchbacks shortened and grew steeper, ending at last at the base of a nearly-vertical stone staircase. She paused for a moment and looked up the length of the stairs. The last time she'd been here was with Addie, right after her sister had graduated from college and they'd both been home for the party that Sunny had thrown to celebrate—two years longer than it should've taken, after Addie had changed her major nearly half a dozen times. They'd taken the first shuttle to get here early, the morning air still chilly and the canyon quiet except for birds just awakening to the day.

Emme started up the stairs, each footfall recalling a memory from that day. It had started so light, both of them laughing about their neighbor who'd gotten sloshed at the party the day before. But then Emme had said something about Sunny finally being done paying college tuition . . . she'd meant it to be off-the-cuff, but Addie had stopped on these very steps, twisting backwards to look down at Emme who was a couple of steps below her, and retorted, "You can't even let me have one day of celebration before you start criticizing me, can you?"

And all the way along the cliff, they'd bickered.

She reached the top of the stairs, threw a glance over her shoulder to see where she'd come from, and continued on the trail. Here, "trail" was a relative term: cut into the side of the cliff, with chains bolted into the rock to help you keep from venturing too close to the edge, the path was sheer rock and so narrow that her feet came within inches of the drop-off. It required total concentration. That was why she'd chosen it today. She didn't want to think about anything except putting one foot in front of the other, keeping the cold chain in her left hand, wiping away the sweat beading on her forehead with her right. She wanted to keep her mind coiled tight, not spiraling outward to all of the things circling inside her.

Past the chains, the trail leveled onto the sandy floor of the canyon, narrowing in and out of slot canyons, under and over fallen trees and scattered boulders. That day with Addie, her sister had gotten so far ahead of her that she couldn't see her around the twisted bends in the trail or even hear her footfalls on the ground. She remembered panicking, the same gripping fear in her belly that she'd felt as a child, tiptoeing around their drunken father, closing the door to Addie's room so she wouldn't hear the sickening sound of his hand smacking Sunny's face. "Addie!" she'd yelled, quickening her pace as fast as she could on the uneven ground. "*Addie!*"

She squeezed through a slot canyon now, the same skinny pathway that had led her that day into an opening where her sister stood glaring at her. "I'm *right here*," Addie had said, rolling her eyes. "Where else would I be?"

The immediate panic had dissipated, like the mist that appeared every morning over the canyon and was gone by noon, but it lingered at her edges. It was always there, that early fear that Addie would be caught by their father's rage, and then later, that she would find out the truth of who he really was. Sunny had created an imaginary world where he was still the hero that Addie thought he was, and Emme had played her part. Her sister had lived her whole life without knowing exactly what had propelled them westward.

The puffy clouds in the sky above the cliffs slid apart, throwing shards of sunshine across the canyon floor. Everything around her crystallized: the leaves, tinged with autumn gold, the red rock walls, the light wind that rustled through the thin trees. A rock squirrel scurried over a tangle of brush and stopped on the trail in front of her. It turned to look at her, assessing whether or not it was safe to cross. Eventually, it deemed her trustworthy, hustled over to a crack in the rock wall, and disappeared. Emme pressed on until she came to the trail's dead end. She dropped onto a flat-topped boulder to rest and pulled her water from her pack.

Shadows lengthened across the canyon floor; if she lingered too long, she'd be traversing those steep switchbacks in the dark. There were few trails in this park that she didn't know well enough to hike in the dark, but she was smart enough not to be foolhardy. One twisted ankle and an overnight exposed to the elements—temperatures that dropped fast, predators that came out at night—could do in even the toughest of rangers.

Emme slid her hands behind her on the rock and leaned back to look up at the sliver of blue sky above her. The quiet wrapped around her. All the things that she'd kept at bay on the trail flooded into her brain. Each individual thought was like a drowning person clinging to a piece of driftwood, and she could not choose which one to save. Was Max's death truly an accident? Something told her there was more to the story than a simple fall. But if she wanted to dig deeper, she'd have to do it outside the boundaries of the ISB, and doing that would acknowledge she still wanted this life, still wanted to get her hands dirty and solve crimes.

And if she was wrong . . . if she made another mistake, the same way she'd messed up with Hannah, she would never be able to trust herself again. Better to close Max's case and walk away for good than take that chance.

Emme squirmed on the rock, unable to settle. Whenever she had a problem, or an intricate case she needed to puzzle out, she would call Sunny. Heat gathered behind Emme's eyes. She shut them tight but couldn't stop the tears from coming. Sunny would end every conversation with the same words: "*Don't ever doubt yourself.*" Emme could hear it now in her head, her mother's voice that she'd never ever hear again. She opened her eyes and let the tears stream out. Here, alone, deep in Hidden Canyon, there was nobody to hear her sobbing or see her being a mess. And for a brief moment, she thought, *I could just stay here. Let the canyon take me, give my body over to the wilderness.*

The thought comforted and chilled her at the same time. Stace would send out SAR when he couldn't get ahold of her. And what if Addie was right at this moment waiting for her at the house, waiting to hug her tight and grieve together? She slapped the tears off her cheeks and drew her knees up to her chest. It was too much to hope. "Where are you, Addie?" she whispered, but only the wind answered her.

And then suddenly, a rage filled her, setting her insides on fire. How dare her sister make her do all of this by herself? How could Addie abandon her like this? Deep down she knew it was irrational, she knew Addie would be there in an instant if she could—but then that thought brought up the terrifying fear that something had happened to her sister, and it was easier to be angry than afraid.

Clouds shifted over the sun and when they slid away, the canyon was no longer filled with light. Emme's stomach jolted as she realized she'd stayed too long. She pulled on the windbreaker shell she always kept in her pack and slid off the rock. In those first few steps back on the trail it was clear in her head—and her heart—that she did not want to be one of those rangers whose bodies they found after days or months or even years of searching. But whether she still wanted to be a ranger was less clear with every footfall.

Daylight disappeared fast in the canyon, dusky shadows lengthening on the trail in front of her. She strapped on a headlamp and followed its soft glow down the side of the cliff, holding tight to the chain in her right hand, placing each foot carefully in the circle of light from her lamp. When she reached the top of the stone staircase, the sky was purple, separated by a thin line of deep pink from the mountains. Her light guided her down the steps and out of the canyon, through the darkness, back to the safety of her car. Once on the main road, she passed the shuttle stops in reverse, her hands turning the steering wheel practically of their own accord. The sweep of her headlights caught a family of deer just off the side of the road, their eyes gleaming at her in the dark. The hike had helped clear her mind, but the further away she got from the trail, the more her brain began to crowd again.

When she got back to the house, it was well past dinnertime and the bakery was dark; Jaspar was long gone. Her phone began to beep and ping with all the notifications and messages that had been silenced in the park, where cell service was nonexistent. As she climbed the steps into the house, one of the emails caught her eye: Max's cell phone records that she'd requested. She stood on the porch with the phone in her hand, staring at the email subject line, her thumb poised above the screen. She could just delete it, she told herself; now that Max's death was officially an accident, she didn't need the records.

Clicking the screen to black, she went inside, shed her clothes, pulled on fleece sweatpants and a warm hoodie. She slid her aching feet into her mother's old sheepskin slippers, the phone tucked inside the pocket of the hoodie, daring her to reveal its secrets. She padded around the house, looking for something to distract her, found the bottle of bourbon and poured herself a glass. Straightened the crooked photo of her and Addie as teenagers that hung on the wall. Wiped the kitchen counter. Knocked over a pile of books, stacked them back up again. All the while, the phone burned in her pocket. She tossed it onto the couch and sat down so that it fell between the cushions. But on the coffee table, her laptop beckoned.

It can't hurt to look. She downed the rest of the bourbon and reached for the computer. The email was a bland form message, the records attached; nothing extraordinary at all, standard practice. Her gaze scanned the pages and pages of pings—near Springdale, which was to be expected, a few random pings in Salt Lake City, but then her eye caught one other place, a place that set every hair on end. A place she was all too familiar with.

Redwater.

CHAPTER EIGHT

*F*ucking *Redwater.*

Home of the Warriors for Armageddon, religious fanatics with multiple wives and too many guns. Where Abraham Murdock reigned supreme, lording over his disciples like a vengeful god on high. Where his son Eli Murdock had been born, married the daughter of his father's closest ally, and then strangled her to death in the Grand Canyon. Where Eli had run to after he'd murdered Hannah and killed himself . . . supposedly.

She stared at the numbers on the page until they blurred and shifted, began to move around in a tantalizing dance. What the hell was Max doing near Redwater? Emme ran her hand through her hair, digging her nails into her scalp along the way. The thing about Redwater was, it wasn't just a town. If his phone had pinged near somewhere like Ogden or St. George, she would've brushed it off. But as she'd told Finn, one did not simply go to Redwater. The entire town was occupied by the Warriors, closed off from the rest of the world by fundamentalism and a perimeter patrolled by an armed militia that called themselves the Horsemen. Lost travelers who took wrong turns into the town were followed until they crossed the border out, and woe betide anyone who dared step out of their car. They were met with an AR-15 and a warning that there wouldn't be a second warning. One ping there could be written off as a mistake, but multiple pings meant he'd been going there with a purpose. The mysterious girlfriend in the purple puffer vest . . . was she the reason Max had been in Redwater so often in the weeks leading up to his death?

She had told Finn that she didn't believe in coincidences, but it wasn't just a quippy thing to say. It was a motto she lived by, deep in her bones. Sure, there were always moments of synchronicity that happened all around her in her job: running into the same hiker in two different parks three states apart or passing a rock climber on the trail to El Capitan just hours before they fell to their death from that famous cliff's face. But a coincidence like this was too big to be chalked up to the slyness of the universe. The Murdock family had dogged her thoughts and nightmares since the day Hannah's body had been discovered, and she could not believe that Max's phone pinging near their hometown was just a simple twist of fate.

Emme glanced at the copper clock on the wall. It was just past nine. Stace always turned in early because he rose at dawn, but she still might be able to catch him. She pulled up FaceTime on her laptop and clicked on his name. The computer jangled through its ringtone once before Stace picked up. "I was about to send out SAR. What did the M.E. say?"

Emme realized that she'd never called Stace after her meeting with Rose Young. She sighed. "Sorry. I went for a hike to clear my head and didn't have any cell service. She ruled it an accident."

"Well, okay. Case closed." He narrowed his eyes, the dim lighting in his cabin throwing shadows across his face. "Or is it?"

"I don't think it is," Emme said. "I just got his cell phone records and—there's a ton of pings near Redwater."

The picture on the screen rustled and shifted, as though Stace had dropped his phone into his lap. "Shee-it." His face appeared again, this time in better light. "Could be a coincidence."

Emme pressed her lips together and tilted her head. Stace rolled his eyes, nodding. "I know, I know. But—"

"But nothing, Stace. I just—it doesn't make sense on its own. And Max had arranged to meet a journalist to give him information about the DeLeo case. It's not a coincidence."

"What do you want to do?"

That question had too many answers, and she didn't know which was the right one. "I think it warrants looking into," she said, rubbing her hand over her face.

"That's not what I asked. What do *you* want to do?"

"Stace—"

"Because if you think it should be looked into, then you need to be the one doing the looking." Stace's face took up the whole screen of her laptop, as though he'd brought his phone closer to him in order to make his point. "Don't you dare ask me to send another agent down there."

Emme dropped her head into her hands to avoid his stare, which felt like one of those Cupid paintings where the eyes followed you everywhere you moved. "What if I screw up again?" she whispered.

"Emme. Look at me."

She lifted her gaze back to the screen. Stace's dark eyes had softened, and he'd shifted further away from the phone so that she could make out the outline of the picture window behind him, with Yosemite Valley, shrouded in darkness, just beyond. She had an intense, sudden wish to be in that room with him, with that view so close she could touch it, a bottle of bourbon between them as they shared their highs and lows of the day. "You're still one of the best investigators I've ever had. You didn't lose that because of one mistake."

"A big mistake."

"Everyone makes mistakes."

"My mistake got someone killed."

Stace blew out a hard breath. "You'd be hard-pressed to find a ranger who hasn't lost someone they should've been able to save. You know what happened on Kahiltna."

Every ranger who had ever worked with Stace knew what had happened on Kahiltna Glacier in Denali National Park. Early in his career, Stace had worked three summers in a row at the camp that sat at 14,200 feet, serving mountaineers gunning for the summit. That last summer, he'd sent six climbers out of camp only to see them disappear in an instant when a crevasse had opened beneath them and swallowed them away from the world. Stace had risked his life rappelling into the dark rip in the earth trying to recover their bodies. Every ranger had a story like that, from death by dehydration in the bowels of the Grand Canyon to an entire family perishing from exposure in Death Valley.

But none of those losses were the direct result of a ranger's mistake. In fact, most rangers had done everything they could to prevent those deaths. Standing at trailheads checking the amount of water each hiker is carrying. Blocking the entrance to The Narrows at the faintest whiff of a flash flood. None of them had failed to recognize a murderer who should've been easy to spot.

Especially by Emme.

"What do you want to do?" Stace asked again. Emme closed her eyes, blocking out his face, and really asked herself that question, this time waiting for an answer instead of shying away.

She wanted to let it go.

She wanted to chalk those pings up to coincidence and accept Max's death as an accident.

But underneath those desires there was another one, pounding away in her gut, telling her not to let it go and that it wasn't a coincidence. "I think I want to look into it further," she murmured.

"Once more with feeling?"

Emme opened her eyes and met Stace's through the computer, through the time and space that separated them. "I want to look into it."

"Good." Stace gave a short, definitive nod. "Keep it off the books for now, until you find some real evidence that it's not accident."

"I will."

Stace yawned, the phone jostling in his hand. "And Emme?"

"Yeah?"

"Don't forget to check in. Okay?"

She smiled. "Good night, Stace."

"'Night."

The house felt so quiet around her after she'd hung up with him, and her body was buzzing, too awake to even contemplate sleep. She slid off the couch and went into her bedroom. Though Sunny had stored more and more of her own stuff in here in the years after Emme had left home, there were still remnants of Emme's time in this room, including the corkboard on the wall where she'd pinned various things over the years. She pulled everything off the board—old flyers for local events, a wild-flower pressed flat between wax paper, a few yellowed photographs, one of which had been taken on that trip into The Narrows after graduation. When the board was blank, she stepped back and stared at its emptiness. It was always this way when she started a case, a clean slate that, little by little, became crowded with theories, trails to follow, and dead ends. She dug out a stack of index cards from her desk drawer and sat on the floor with the board in front of her. One by one, she wrote down each thing she knew for sure: where Max was found, his camping permit was for two people, he was supposed to meet with a journalist the day after he died, his cell phone pinged near Redwater. She pinned the photograph from The Narrows at the top of the board and placed each card below it.

Finn had told her that Max had information about the DeLeo case; whatever that information was, it could explain the pings near Redwater. Perhaps he was digging up whatever secrets the Murdocks were hiding. Emme fished around in her desk and found a spool of red yarn, a staple she always kept in stock for her boards. She stretched a line from the card that read *had a meeting with a journalist re: information about DeLeo* case to *cell phone pings near Redwater*. It was little to go on; she wanted to know what had sent him to Redwater in the first place. Perhaps that was where the mysterious girlfriend came in. But it was a start. She was fully in it now, and there was no going back.

Emme woke up starving, wolves growling in her stomach. She blinked in the grey light and checked her watch. It was early, and her head was pounding from hunger and last night's bourbon, too little food and too much hiking yesterday. She padded into the kitchen, downed a glass of water, and made a three-egg omelet loaded with cheese and onions and red bell peppers. While coffee brewed in the French press, she stood in the doorway between the kitchen and the living room, taking small bites to let the protein absorb into her system. Over her plate, she surveyed the living room, all the piles of crap like a minefield waiting to explode. In some ways, it was a relief to have a case to work on just to be able to avoid tripping a landmine.

After breakfast, she took a mug of coffee back into the bedroom and stared at the board. It was the rule of thumb to start from the inside of an investigation and work your way out, begin at the person closest to the victim and widen your circle with each step. She grabbed her notebook and found Gwen's phone number in the page of notes she'd taken at Max's home.

Gwen picked up after two rings. "Emme?"

"Hi, Gwen. How're you doing?"

There was a sigh, the kind of sigh Emme knew all too well as the only possible answer to her ridiculous question. Of course she was awful. Her brother had just died. Everything was awful. "Listen," Emme went on, releasing Gwen from her obligation of answering, "I wanted to check in with you and see where we are with Max's laptop. Did you have a chance to back it up?"

"Yes," Gwen said. "I can give it to you. But—not at the house. My mom is . . . not doing very well."

"I'm so sorry," Emme murmured, those three little words so insignificant in the depth of their loss. "Why don't you come to the bakery? In an hour?"

"Sure. See you then."

Emme hung up and took a steaming shower, letting the water run in rivulets down her body, scrubbing the bourbon and bad dreams out of her skin. When she was dried and dressed, she made her way over to the bakery to find Jaspar busy at work in the kitchen. "Hey."

"Morning." There were half a dozen quiche shells on the counter in front of him, waiting to be filled.

"Gwen's coming over in a bit to hand off Max's laptop. I hope that's okay."

"It's great, actually." Jaspar held out a large measuring cup to Emme. "Here, help me fill these. They're for Gwen to take home—I was planning on bringing them to her house later anyway."

"That's really nice of you, Jaspar." Emme took the measuring cup. "How much in each shell?"

"About a cup."

They worked in companionable silence for several minutes, her pouring the eggy filling into each blind-baked shell, and him finishing off the tops with a sprinkle of cheese and herbs before putting them into the industrial oven. As they baked, Jaspar fired up Il Duce and set out a plate of carrot-and-walnut muffins for when Gwen arrived.

Gwen appeared at the door a short while later, a canvas bag slung over her shoulder. Jaspar gave her a hug. "I'm so sorry about Max," he told her. "He was a good guy."

"Yeah, he was." Gwen's eyes were shiny and tinged with red, as though she'd only just stopped crying the moment before.

"I have some goodies for you to take home before you leave."

"Thanks, Jaspar. That's very thoughtful." She sat down, holding the bag in her arms as though it was a small child. Emme slid into the chair across from her. Jaspar brought them cappuccinos and disappeared back into the kitchen. Gwen placed the bag on the table and took out an external hard drive. "I just—I couldn't part with the laptop," she whispered. "It was his. He touched it." She slid the little silver box over to Emme. "I brought the back-up instead. I hope that's okay."

"It'll do." She couldn't fault Gwen for not wanting to part with the laptop, but she hoped the back-up had saved Max's passwords. Emme splayed her hand flat on the drive. "Going through all my mom's stuff. . . I understand."

They sat in silence for a moment, grief enveloping them like a thick woolen blanket. Emme cleared her throat. "Listen, Gwen, I spoke to the medical examiner."

Gwen's sad eyes searched Emme's face. "And?"

"She ruled his death an accident. Said his injuries were consistent with a fall."

"But he was found in the river," Gwen said, her brows knitting together. "Where did he fall from?"

"We don't know." Emme reached for the cappuccino Jaspar had left for her and took a sip. *Goddamn*, Il Duce was head-and-shoulders better than The Ugly Mug any day of the week. "Because his death has been classified as an accident, the ISB doesn't have cause to investigate."

Gwen inhaled so sharply the air whistled. "So that's it? We'll never know what happened?"

Emme leaned forward. "No. That's not it. I'm going to get to the bottom of this."

"But—you still think it was an accident, right? What else could have happened?"

There were only a few tiny things that made Emme think it wasn't an accident, and not one of them was something she could hold up in the palm of her hand and show to Gwen. They were all indefinable, a whirring in the back of her mind that she could not turn off, a turning in her gut that she could not lock down. Emme took another sip of coffee, reached for a muffin. "He was with someone," she said finally.

"He was spotted with a blonde woman outside the Visitor Center when he obtained his permit. They were seen kissing."

Gwen stiffened, her back ramrod straight as she blinked at Emme. "What?"

"You really had no idea he was seeing someone?"

"No. He never said anything. I mean—" Gwen swallowed. "I overheard a couple of phone calls that made me think that maybe he was dating someone, but I didn't want to pry. Especially because—he and my mom were very close. He told her everything."

Emme tried not to hear the pain beneath Gwen's words, ancient sibling resentment that probably went back decades. *Oh, how well I know that,* she thought. "But he obviously didn't tell her about this. Why do you think that is?"

"How should I know?" Gwen shook her head. "Sorry. This is just . . . a little overwhelming."

"I know." Emme ate half of a muffin to let Gwen catch her breath. "Do you remember anything about those phone calls you overheard?"

Gwen picked up her coffee, which she hadn't touched yet. Emme kept her face neutral and soft while she watched Gwen drink one sip, then two, then three, clearly delaying answering the question. Finally, she sighed. "I remember catching the end of one conversation where he said he would meet her at some restaurant."

"Which restaurant?"

She shrugged one shoulder up. "I had never heard of it, so it didn't register."

"So it wasn't in Springdale?"

"I don't think so."

"If I said the name, would you remember it?"

"Maybe."

Emme pulled up Google on her phone and searched for restaurants between Springdale and Redwater. "The Red Hen? Sergio's? Mountainside Tavern?" Gwen shook her head as Emme read down the list. "Sloane's Roadside Bar? The Greenlight Grille?"

Gwen jerked her chin. "Yes. I think that was it."

Emme tapped on the map next to the Google entry for The Greenlight Grille. It was thirty miles from Springdale and twenty from Redwater, tucked away in an unincorporated area of farmland. If Max had been dating a Murdock, it was off the beaten path enough to keep the meeting off their radar. She scribbled the name and location down in her notebook. "That's very helpful. Is there anything else you remember from those conversations?"

"I don't get it," Gwen said, setting her coffee cup down on the table with a little thud. "If he was with someone in The Narrows when he got hurt, why didn't she alert the authorities when he fell? Where is she?"

If Max's mysterious girlfriend was a Murdock, Emme knew all too well that the Murdocks were capable of anything. But she did not say that out loud to Gwen. "I don't know," she said slowly. "But I intend to find out."

CHAPTER NINE

The moment Emme ushered Gwen out of the bakery, she turned on her heel and shot through the back door, flew across the patio, and galloped up the stairs into the house. Her mother had an old MacBook Air that she had wiped, intending to sell it on Craigslist, and it was still on the desk in her bedroom in its soft felt sleeve. She booted up the laptop, cycled through the Welcome message and all the steps until she got to the home screen. She plugged in the hard drive, heard it whir to life, and chose the most recent back-up to download. *Approximate time: 2 hours, 17 minutes.*

Emme slumped back and drummed her fingertips on the desktop, willing the thin line to move faster toward 100%. Instead, it jumped backwards. *Approximate time: 2 hours, 43 minutes.* "Ugh," she said out loud and pushed back from the desk. As her mother used to say, *a watched pot never boils.*

She walked down the hall, the floorboards creaking beneath her feet. She'd hinged everything on this laptop, and there was a good chance it would actually yield very little. But this was the nature of the beast.

An investigation never went smoothly. It was never Point A to Point B. There were always a hundred dead ends, leads that went nowhere, obstacles she had to find her way over, under, and through. Emme flopped onto her bed like she was a teenager whose mother had just grounded her. She'd cultivated patience all through her twenties, growing the ability to sift through the painstaking minutiae of a case, and somehow in the weeks since Sunny had died, she'd reverted back to her impetuous, youthful self. Looking up at the tendrils of dust that coated the ceiling fan, she took a deep breath in and rolled onto her stomach. On the floor, the board she'd made the night before rested against the closet door. Emme slid off the bed and grabbed her index cards, wrote *Greenlight Grille* on one and pinned it to the board. She drew a red thread line from that card to *cell phone pings near Redwater* and sat back on her haunches. She was so close to finding the thing that connected it all, she could feel it in her blood, the way it hummed in her veins, setting her teeth on edge.

She crawled back over to her desk, glancing at the laptop (*Approximate time: 1 hour, 57 minutes*) and pulled open the bottom drawer. The folder with all of her notes on the Hannah DeLeo case nestled inside; she'd hidden it there after Eli Murdock had (supposedly) killed himself and the case had been closed. She had never intended to look at the file again, but she couldn't bring herself to destroy it, instead letting it torment her with its continued existence. All of the official evidence was secured in the ISB's storage facility, but this file contained her own personal notes, scribblings, and theories, and a handful of photographs. She shuffled through the documents when a page caught her eye: a little scrap of paper taped to a larger sheet for safekeeping.

Emme drew the paper out of the folder, creaking open the door of her memory that she'd slammed shut after Eli died. A day after Hannah's body had been found, she'd driven into Redwater, followed closely by the four white Ford trucks of Abraham Murdock's Horsemen as soon as she'd crossed the border into town. Abraham himself had greeted her at the foot of the long gravel driveway lined with cacti that led to his yellow farmhouse, an AR-15 slung on one shoulder. When she told him she was there about Hannah's murder, he shifted the weight of the AR-15 into his hands and asked, "Where's my son?"

Emme had raised an eyebrow at this. "Inside your house, I presume," she responded. She was certain that Eli had fled the Grand Canyon back into the safe bosom of Redwater and that his father was shielding him from the authorities.

"I ain't seen Eli in a week," Abraham said. Emme searched his face, sure he was lying. "You can come in and see."

If Eli had come back to Redwater, there was no way that he was simply waiting inside the house for her to arrest him. He would have been alerted to her presence by the Horsemen the moment she'd driven into town and gone somewhere to hide. But she followed Abraham down the long driveway, the gravel crunching beneath their booted feet. The Horsemen fell in behind them and stood in the yard as Emme and Abraham went into the house.

One of his wives served her lemonade, which she accepted with a smile that the wife did not return. She scurried out of sight as soon as the lemonade was in Emme's hand. Abraham guided her around the house while one of his sons trailed closely behind. He opened doors to rooms filled with children sewing, reading the Bible, or older children teaching younger ones to read the Bible. Each room was spare and simple, the only artwork on the walls a cross or a painting of a very white Jesus, save for one room on the third floor. That room's walls were plastered with posters and photographs of the Angel's Landing trail in Zion, so that barely a sliver of wall could be seen beneath. "This here's Josiah's room," Abraham said, jerking his thumb at the son who had tailed them silently throughout the house. "Seeing as he hasn't seen fit to marry yet, he still lives under my roof."

Emme had turned and tried to meet Josiah's eyes, but he kept his head down. "Do you hike Angel's Landing regularly?"

"Any chance I get." He raised his gaze but looked past her, fixating on one poster that showed the view from the summit. "It's the place I feel closest to God," he added, darting a sidelong glance at his father.

"The closest you are to God is right here in Redwater, not some fool land owned by the feds." Abraham slammed the door shut and hustled Emme down the hallway. Without a warrant, she could not look anywhere that Abraham did not show her, but she noted a staircase that led up to the attic, another that went to a basement, and a garden shed in the backyard. "You see, Miss Helliwell," he said as they approached the front door again, "my son is not here."

"I'll be back with a warrant, Mr. Murdock," she said, and handed her glass of lemonade to another wife who stood by the door, so quiet and still that she seemed part of the wallpaper.

"You have no cause for a warrant, Miss Helliwell," Abraham said with a grin that chilled her to the bone, "and we do not recognize any authority but that of God's."

The Horsemen had stood by to let her pass as she made her way back up the long driveway. Only when she had ducked into the safety of her car did she unfurl the small scrap of paper that the silent wife had slipped into her hand when she'd passed her the empty lemonade glass. On it was written *Lara DeLeo* and just below the name, a phone number.

She'd called the number and left a message that was never returned. Two days later, Abraham had reported Eli's supposed suicide, and she'd never needed to follow up.

Now Emme traced the name and number with her fingertip. Whoever Lara DeLeo was, she hadn't been helpful in Hannah's case, but maybe she could be in Max's. She picked up her phone and dialed the number. There was a pause, then three screeching notes followed by a robotic woman's voice telling her, "The number you have dialed is out of service. If you believe you have reached this recording in error . . ." Emme hung up. *Dammit.*

From its spot on the desk, the laptop made its harmonious power-up sound, signaling that the download was finished and it was rebooting. Emme hopped off the bed and tapped her foot as she waited for the screen to load. When it did, the first icon she clicked on was Photos. Surely Max had taken pictures in The Narrows; no one could pass through that beauty without wanting to capture it. Emme held her breath as the images loaded, hoping that the girlfriend had been in at least one of his pictures . . .

But when the images had finished loading onto the page, only a few were dated from the day Max had gone into The Narrows. A picture of his wilderness permit. A panoramic photo of the vast Kolob Canyons viewpoint, which they would have passed on their way to the top-down trailhead to The Narrows. Emme enlarged the last photo. It was taken at the entrance of The Narrows, the reddish-brown walls rising up at the sides of the photo, the muddy Virgin River winding between them. There, in the middle of the shot, a figure stood with her back to the camera, her blonde hair pulled back into a ponytail and her purple puffer vest fitted to her curves. Emme willed her to turn around, but she stayed stubbornly still with her face hidden.

Three photos. Was that really all Max had taken? Had he been killed before he could take any more? But that would place his death early that day he was found, which was unlikely. Emme grabbed her phone again and called Gwen.

"Hi, Emme. Is everything okay with the hard drive?"

"Yes, I was able to load it, thanks. But there are only three photos from the day he had the permit for The Narrows. I'm just wondering—"

"Oh." Gwen sighed. "Max always used his Nikon when he went out on his excursions."

"Ah," Emme said, cursing silently. "Those wouldn't be in the Cloud."

"I'm sorry. I should have mentioned that."

"No, it's okay. You've been very helpful. Sorry to bother you."

"It's all right. Tell Jaspar thank you for the food."

"I will." Emme hung up, tossed her phone onto her bed. Max's Nikon was most likely long gone, gobbled up by the Virgin River. At least the photo confirmed what Ruby had told her, but it was still frustratingly vague. She stared at it for a few long moments, but it only succeeded in pissing her off.

She minimized the photos and searched his desktop for anything useful. Screenshots of receipts and web pages, several versions of his resume, even a few half-written short stories. His calendar had a few mundane appointments leading up to his death—dentist, chiropractor, drinks with a buddy—and nothing after. Emme furrowed her brow. Not one thing scheduled for after his trip to The Narrows? She skimmed through the empty days. It was as though Max knew he wasn't coming back.

Emme pulled up his email, which thankfully loaded without a password prompt, drumming her fingers on the desk as she scrolled past the junk mail that had jammed his inbox since his death, stopping at a name she recognized: Finn Brackenbury. Her heart quickening, she read through the brief exchange, then slumped back in disappointment. After the initial enticement of telling Finn he had information about the Hannah DeLeo case, the communication was sparse, only a brief exchange of where and when to meet up—everything she already knew.

She moved the mouse over the icons at the bottom of the screen and paused on Contacts. It was a reach, but she had nothing to do but stretch right now. She double-clicked, scanned down to the Ds, and caught her breath. There it was: Lara DeLeo, with a different phone number than the one that Abraham's wife had given her on that tiny scrap of paper. With shaking fingers, Emme dialed it.

It rang twice without the screech or the robotic woman breaking in. On the third ring, a soft voice answered. "Hello?"

"Is this Lara DeLeo?"

"Who is this?"

Emme took a deep breath to steady her voice. "My name is Emmeline Helliwell. I'm an agent with the National Park Service. I'm—"

"You left me a message a while back. About Hannah."

"Yes—"

"I don't know if I can help you. Eli's dead."

Emme pushed aside all the thoughts that bubbled up whenever anyone said those words to her. "This isn't about Hannah. This is about Max Kerchek."

"Who?"

"Your name was in his contacts. He died in Zion a few days ago, and I'm looking into his death."

There was an intake of breath. "How did he die?" Lara's voice trembled a little bit, as though she was fighting to keep herself together.

"He—was found in the river."

"Was it an accident?" There was an emphasis on that last word, sharp and pointed like a fine knife.

"That's what I'm trying to find out." No use telling her about the medical examiner's ruling. "Can we meet up to talk? I'd like to ask you some questions."

Lara hesitated for so long that Emme pulled the phone away from her ear twice to make sure they were still connected. At last she said, "Okay. Let me give you the coordinates for where I am. But you'd better come first thing in the morning, because by the afternoon I'll be gone."

*****

The Airstream trailer sat in a small clearing down a dirt road, miles off the highway and halfway between Springdale and the Arizona border. Clouds shifted through the sunroof of Emme's Crosstrek, and a grey chill hung low in the sky, threatening rain. The Narrows would be closed today, with a lot of disappointed tourists turned away at the edge of the Riverside Walk. She guided the steering wheel, veering to the right past a lonely pasture where a single horse grazed. Just beyond the fence sat a mud-splattered pickup truck with an Airstream attached. The car bumped along a pitted and rocky path towards the trailer before Emme stopped it with a jolt. She switched the engine off. As she got out of the car, the door to the Airstream opened.

A thin wire of a woman stepped out, her auburn hair hanging loose down to her waist. She was dressed in jeans and an oversized sweatshirt—a far cry from the long skirts and aprons that most women wore in Redwater, though her long hair still recalled her ties to the Warriors. Emme's boots crunched on the dry ground as she walked toward the trailer. A rainstorm would be welcome; the parched earth needed a good drenching. As Emme got close to the trailer, she saw that there was an awning off the backside that hung over a small table, a couple of chairs, and a small portable fire pit. Lara held her hand out. "Miss Helliwell?"

"Please, call me Emme." Lara's fingers were cold and bony against hers. "Would you like some tea?"

"Sure." Emme took a seat in one of the rust-colored Adirondack chairs beneath the awning while Lara disappeared back into the Airstream. She gazed at the open space beyond the trailer, where the horse was now cantering easily along the fence line. She could do it, too—sell the house and bakery and buy an Airstream, hitch it to her Crosstrek, and go anywhere she felt like. An intense desire for that kind of freedom flamed inside her chest, then burned out. She couldn't do a damn thing until she found Addie—couldn't sell the house or the bakery, not when Addie's name was on half of it, not without Addie's say-so. A bitter anger sniped at her wayward sister, followed by an immediate flush of fear. *Where was she?*

Lara returned, carrying a tray with a porcelain teapot and two mismatched mugs. Emme rose to help her, grateful for the interruption to her thoughts of Addie and the sudden longing to disappear into the wide unknown. When the tray was safely set on the table, they both sat back down. "You've got a cozy set-up here."

"It's easily movable," Lara said. Her voice was soft with a slight waver, as if she was waiting for someone to smack her for speaking out of turn. "I change locations every few days, before my family can find out where

I am." She squinted out to the pasture. "Probably be in Arizona by tomorrow."

Emme took a sip of tea. It left a faint nutty taste on her tongue. "How long have you been out?"

"Eight months, twenty-three days," Lara answered, and Emme knew that instinct, to count your new life of freedom in days or hours or even minutes. It had been that way after they'd run from her father, counting the days since their escape, up until the day he died and she knew they were truly free. "How can I help you, Emme? I don't know why my name was in that man's contacts."

Emme drew out the laptop from her bag. She moved the tea tray a bit so she could set it safely on the spindly table. "I think he may have gotten your name and number from the same person I did," she said. Lara tilted her head. "When I went to visit Abraham Murdock, looking for Eli, one of his wives slipped me a scrap of paper with your information on it."

Lara pressed her hand to her chest. It did not escape Emme's notice how she had shuddered at the mention of Abraham's name. She reminded Emme of a bird perched at the edge of a branch, ready to fly at the first sight of danger. "It must've been Neveah," she murmured. "She always knows where to find me."

Emme opened the laptop and clicked on the Photos icon. "I believe that Max was dating someone in the Warriors." She pulled up the photo in The Narrows, with the blonde figure standing in the muddy Virgin River, the red-rock walls rising up on either side of her. "I was hoping you might be able to identify her."

Lara squinted at the screen. "Can you zoom in at all?"

Emme cropped the photo so that the walls of the canyon disappeared and all you could see was the figure in the river. You still couldn't see her face, and the photo now had that soft, blurred quality that comes from amateur photo editing, but her posture and the curve of her hips were clearer. With her gaze fixated on the picture, Lara slowly slid the laptop closer to her. "I think that might be Sarai," she murmured.

The bottom dropped out of Emme's gut. She gripped the edge of the table, rattling the laptop and the tray, the teapot, and their mugs. "Sarai Murdock?"

"Yes." Lara traced her finger over the figure. "I wasn't that close to her, but of course I knew her." She looked up. "There aren't that many women in the Warriors who are single in their twenties. Most of us—them—are married off in our teens. I was married at eighteen to my second cousin." She folded her arms across her chest. "It wasn't a legal marriage, of course. I was his third wife."

Emme grimaced. "I'm so sorry."

"How do you know Sarai Murdock?"

"I don't know her personally," Emme said. "I'm just very familiar with the family, because of the Hannah DeLeo case. I was stationed at the Grand Canyon when she was murdered and led the investigation into her death." She chewed at her lip; she was here to talk about Max, not Hannah. But now here was the thing connecting the two deaths, and she had to keep her brain from spiraling. "I wonder if Sarai was there," Emme said slowly, "when I went to their house looking for Eli. She's his sister, after all."

"Half-sister," Lara corrected her. "Eli was Abraham Murdock's son with his first wife, and Sarai's mother is his second wife."

"But if Sarai is the daughter of the head of the Warriors," Emme said, puzzling out the family tree aloud, "how would she still be single? Wouldn't she have been married off young, too?"

"She was," Lara said. "I was a bridesmaid at her wedding." Lara's eyes shaded with memory. "Her father was adamant that she be a first wife, so that her marriage would be legal. They got married just a few weeks after her eighteenth birthday."

"But what happened to that marriage? She couldn't have gotten divorced," Emme said.

"He died," Lara said. "Two years ago, he was killed in a farming accident when his foot got stuck in a tractor while it was idling. He accidentally hit the gas and it ran him over." Lara picked up her mug, wrapped her hands tightly around it. "It was horrifying."

It actually seemed a fitting end to any man in the Warriors for Armageddon, but Emme kept that thought to herself. "Okay, so she was widowed. No kids?"

Lara shook her head. "That was a real sticking point. Probably why she wasn't married off again right away after her husband died, because the men thought she was barren. In the Warriors, a woman is only worth the number of children she births."

Emme's lip curled as she took a swallow of tea. It was probably the thing that reviled her the most about the Warriors, how women were nothing more than a baby-making commodity to them. "Was she showing any signs of discontent before you left eight months ago?"

"Discontent isn't really something you show openly in the Warriors," Lara said. "If you do, you get sent to the Garden." Her face darkened, like a cloud passing through her. "It's not actually a garden. It's a concrete building outside of town with a pit for a toilet and where they bring you a bowl of food once a day." Her cheeks were mottled, the edges of her lips white. "I was in charge of cleaning the Garden. That's how I know how bad it is." Lara blew a long breath out. "I wouldn't have known if

Sarai was unhappy. But she must've been, to date someone outside the clan."

Emme set her mug down on the table, a little harder than she intended. She did not remember seeing such a building when she'd gone to Redwater, but it sounded like it was the kind of place Abraham Murdock and his Warriors kept hidden from outside eyes. "And you think that's her?" Emme pointed at the photo, wishing once again that she could make the figure turn around, look right into the camera and show them her face.

"I'd say I'm like ninety-percent certain that's her," Lara said, leaning back in her chair. "So—you think Sarai was dating Max? What does she have to do with his death?"

Emme gazed out over the pasture. The horse was grazing idly by the fence. A single beam of sunlight had broken through the clouds and fallen across the horse's back, setting its chestnut coat ablaze in a fiery glow. "She was with him in The Narrows when he died, and she hasn't come forward, or contacted authorities. I find that odd, to say the least."

Lara stared at her across the little table, and Emme could see her own thoughts reflected back in Lara's eyes. *The Murdocks are capable of anything.* "You think—she played a part in his death?"

"I don't know." Emme felt a drumbeat pulse start up at the base of her throat. "All I know is that I have a dead body and a missing Murdock—and that's the exact same scenario that I had with Hannah."

She was more and more convinced that Max's death was not an accident, and she kept turning everything over and around, backwards and forwards, inside and out, in her brain on the drive back to Springdale. The clouds parted, shedding the rain that had hovered all day, and Emme thought about Lara packing up the Airstream in the mud, getting ready to scuttle away in the night. "You should go east," she'd told Lara as they'd parted; maybe a flight in the opposite direction of the one she'd taken with her mother and Addie all those years ago would offer Lara refuge.

She spent the rest of the day organizing all of her notes, laying out a map of what she knew so far. Rain pounded on the roof and windows, the light outside dismal and grey. As she sketched out a rudimentary Murdock family tree in her notebook, she realized there were too many branches left blank and reached for her phone, hoping Lara could help fill them in.

The phone clicked as someone answered. "Lara? It's Emme. I was—"

"Lara is not available to take your call, Miss Helliwell."

Emme sat straight up as every vein in her body turned to ice. "Who is this? Where's Lara?"

"She is with her family where she belongs." The voice was male, deep and gravelly, a hint of a twang threaded through. "You need not concern yourself with her again."

The call ended. Emme sat very still for a long moment. *They had her.* And the Murdocks, as she knew all too well, *were capable of anything.*

CHAPTER TEN

The back roads between Springdale and Redwater were filled with lonely farmhouses, barns long since abandoned, rusty fences penning in mud-splattered cattle, and gas stations that didn't actually sell gas (but very likely sold meth). Emme gripped her steering wheel with one hand and adjusted the radio with the other. She'd switched between music and podcasts on her phone to country music on FM and religious nuts on AM and back again, unable to settle on one thing for too long.

It was dumb what she was doing, she knew that, but she couldn't not do it, not when Lara was probably locked up in the Garden being fed one bowl of food a day. And if Sarai was involved in Max's death, there was a good chance she was being hidden in Redwater, the same way Eli had been in the days after he'd murdered Hannah. Sarai was the key that would unlock the mystery of Max's death, Emme was sure of that. If she was in Redwater, perhaps Abraham Murdock would see his daughter as a liability, a problem that kept bringing the authorities to their doorstep, and would take Emme's visit as an opportunity to wash his hands of her.

That was wishful thinking, Emme knew deep down, but she needed a wish to keep pushing her forward.

She'd taken precautions. Jaspar was under orders to call the state police if she didn't check in by the afternoon, and she was wearing every item of clothing that identified her as a federal agent, including her gun holstered on her hip. But the Murdocks were capable of anything, and it would take them less than an instant to take her out and deal with the consequences later.

A small green sign by a fork in the road indicated twelve more miles to Redwater. Emme turned right and began the climb to the town, which sat at 5,250 feet above sea level—higher than Utah's lowest point by a few thousand feet, but far below its highest pinnacle at King's Peak. The road twisted and curved around a series of switchbacks. She switched off the radio altogether and navigated the way in silence. The winding twelve miles took nearly forty minutes, but at last she passed a white sign with black lettering:

WELCOME TO REDWATER

"Do not fear what you are about to suffer"

She slowed the car to a stop just level with the sign and reached over to passenger seat where her GoPro sat, strapped it to her forehead, and started filming. The footage would be automatically uploaded to her computer currently sitting on a table in the bakery under Jaspar's watchful eye. "Here we go," she muttered and stepped her foot lightly on the gas.

The outskirts of Redwater were desolate and forlorn: a handful of trailers clustered together on a dirt patch, an empty barn with half its roof missing, a silo that was filled with God-knew-what. Could be grain, could be guns. The heart of the town was a couple of miles ahead, though there wasn't much to that either. But Emme was looking for the grey concrete building at the edge of the town that Lara had described.

As she drove through town, the streets lay dormant and quiet, but Emme knew there were eyes watching her from every direction. She had barely hit the main part of Redwater when the first white pickup truck appeared on the road behind her. Then another, and another, until a line of four trucks followed her into the town. Four trucks, four Horsemen—everything was literal in Redwater.

She kept driving at a steady pace, well below the speed limit—no need to panic until there was a gun in her face. Panic was not in her nature. Still, her heart pounded beneath the barrier of calm she'd learned to build up. It had been a curious part of her training, learning to go against every natural instinct to flee from danger and teach yourself to run towards it.

The town burgeoned like a water stain on dry ground into a cluster of businesses that looked perpetually closed: a feed store, a mechanic, a corner grocery that advertised *Coca-Cola: 50¢* in the window. By now, the four Horsemen were following her at a steady clip, far enough away to be unassuming but close enough to threaten. As the clutch of buildings thinned out, Emme spotted a structure down a side street that looked out of place among the red-roofed adobe houses and old-fashioned Victorians. Square and squat, concrete grey without any windows, she was sure it was the Garden. She made a hard right turn onto the side street, but before she'd made it a hundred yards, one of the Horsemen sped up, passed her, and blocked her path, bringing her to a screeching halt in the middle of the street.

The other three trucks fanned out around her, but before they could block her in she threw the Crosstrek into reverse, backing up until she was wedged between two adobe cottages with a narrow path of escape through the dirt alley that ran along the backside of the houses. She left the car running and stepped out with her badge in hand. "Federal agent," she yelled as she walked out onto the street.

The passenger side door of the truck that had swerved in front of her opened and Abraham Murdock emerged, black Stetson shading his ruddy-cheeked face, cowboy boots kicking up dust at his heels. "Miss Helliwell," he said, his voice low and long, his mouth crowded with chewing tobacco. "Thought we might be seeing you."

"Mr. Murdock." Emme acknowledged him with a tilt of her head while grinding her teeth together. She didn't bother correcting his *Miss Helliwell* to *Agent Helliwell;* every woman in his mind was a Miss until she was a Mrs. "I'm looking for my friend Lara DeLeo."

"Lara doesn't have friends outside of Redwater." Murdock leaned on the hood of the truck. "I don't see what business you could possibly have with her."

"I have reason to believe she's being held against her will." Emme pointed to the angular concrete structure just down the street. "In that building. The place you call the Garden."

Murdock twisted to look where Emme was pointing. "That don't look like a garden to me."

He was toying with her, she knew that, and she would not rise to the occasion, no matter how hot the tight ball of anger in her chest grew. It wasn't that she was afraid of him, not really, but her hatred for him ran bone-deep—it was the intensity of that hatred that scared her. She kept the door to the memory of her father firmly locked, but Abraham's presence somehow creaked that door open.

"You do know that it's illegal to hold someone against their will, right?" Emme said. "It's a little thing we in the federal government like to call kidnapping."

"Well, we here in Redwater answer to a different authority than the federal government." Murdock shifted his weight against the truck. He wasn't armed, but Emme could see the silhouette of the driver inside the cab of the truck, an AR-15 on his lap, leaning against the steering wheel. Without looking, she knew there were probably at least two men in each of the other trucks, and every one of them was armed, too. With so many soldiers to shoot for him, Murdock didn't need a gun of his own. "Thought you were smart enough to recognize that by now."

"I guess I'm just a stupid girl who can't get it through her silly head," Emme said.

Murdock's eyes narrowed. "You know what we do to women who sass around here?"

"I sure do." Emme pointed at the concrete building again. "You hole them up in there and feed them one bowl of food a day."

The Stetson hat shadowed Murdock's face, but Emme knew his eyes were focused on her, so sharp that if they were knives they would've cut her skin. "You make us sound like monsters, Miss Helliwell. We would never harm one of our own, not if they come to us repentant and ready to atone."

"And if they don't?"

Murdock smiled, like he held all the secrets of the universe and had no intention of sharing them. He didn't answer her, just kept that smile pasted on his face as the silence stretched between them, broken only by the rustling of the wind and the sound of a dog barking in the distance. "Josiah?"

The driver's side door opened and Josiah popped up, his AR-15 clenched in his hands. Emme recognized him from the day she'd come looking for Eli, the unmarried son whose room was covered with Angel's Landing photographs. "Yes sir?"

"What do we do with our family members who need a little reminder of their place?"

Josiah glanced from his father to Emme and back again. For a moment, Emme felt a twang of sympathy for him, trapped as he was beneath the heel of his father's punishing boot. But it was so much easier for a man in Murdock's world, not like the women who had no freedom to make their own choices. Josiah leveled his gaze on Emme for a brief instant, his eyes hooded and soft, before he looked back at his father. "We show them the way, sir."

"What way is that?" Emme swept her arm toward the squat little building. "The way into the Garden?"

"You sure are fixated on that garden," Murdock said with a chuckle that may as well have been scripted. "That building ain't nothing but storage. So if you came here looking to find something there, you may as well turn tail now 'cause you ain't gonna find anything but disappointment."

"Lara isn't the only person I came looking for," Emme said. "Where's Sarai?"

Josiah slipped off his perch on the door of the truck and sat back down inside the cab. Murdock cocked his head, that smile playing about his mouth like it was trying to decide whether to stay put or flee. "Now what would you want with my little Sarai?"

"I need to ask her some questions," Emme said. "About a body we found in Zion Park."

"Oh, I don't think Sarai would know anything about that." Murdock spat a wad of tobacco onto the ground. "I don't see how you could possibly think there was a connection from a dead body to our little Sarai."

"Well, that dead body's cell phone pinged all around Redwater," Emme said, "and she was seen with him at the Visitor Center the day before he died."

"Whoever saw her was mistaken." Murdock's voice sharpened into a point. "She ain't left Redwater in weeks."

"Are you certain about that?"

The smile twisted upside down. "Are you questioning whether I know the whereabouts of my own daughter?"

"Clearly you didn't."

A cold silence swept between them as Murdock surveyed Emme. She could see him assessing the situation—the camera on her forehead, her running car, her exit route—and deciding what he could get away with. "Mark David!" he yelled.

The driver in one of the other trucks popped out, standing on the open door of the truck without descending to the ground. "Yes sir?"

"You seen Sarai?"

Mark David's face was an echo of Abraham's—another son, but older than Josiah. His eyes—one brown and one blue, Emme noted—fixated on her face. "I believe she's out in the fields."

"Call her back in, please."

"Cell reception out there is real spotty," Mark David said. He scratched his chin. "Besides, she ain't got a phone."

"Then you won't mind me taking a ride out there to see her in person." Emme moved as though to get back in her car. The doors to the other trucks flung open, and in an instant there was a line of five men training their assault rifles on her.

"That would be trespassing," Abraham said, not a tremor or raise in his voice to indicate he was anything other than calm and collected. "And you know what we do to trespassers around here, Miss Helliwell."

"Well, when a federal agent steps foot on your land, trespassing laws aren't so clear-cut," Emme replied. Her heart thudded in her chest, but her voice's tenor matched Abraham's and she kept her posture easy against the car door. "But by all means, take a shot and see what happens."

Mark David tipped his gun toward her. "No one would even know you were missing," he said.

"Unfortunately for you, that's not quite true." Emme pointed to the GoPro on her head. "See that little red light? I've got some buddies at the FBI who are enjoying the show." She wasn't lying, if by FBI she meant Jaspar.

"Bring it on," Mark David said, and the other men hooted. "We are well-prepared for a siege. Waco forever," he shouted, raising his fist above his head.

"They all died at Waco," Emme said, silently adding *you idiot.*

Abraham held up his hand and all the men quieted. "I don't think you understand, Miss Helliwell," Abraham said, pressing his palms together in a prayer-like gesture that was anything but holy. "But of course, how could you? You are a person of science and law, and we are people of God. The earthly ties that bind you have no hold on us."

A thin shiver ran down Emme's spine. It wasn't that she didn't believe in God; you couldn't set foot in a National Park without feeling the touch of a higher power. But more than any gun, it was zealotry that scared her. She'd talked potential jumpers off the ledge at the South Rim, but there was no reasoning with zealots. They were always going to be right, and no one could convince them otherwise. "The federal government would certainly have something to say about those earthly ties." She jerked her chin. "This doesn't have to get ugly," she said. "Just show me Lara is okay—"

"You ain't getting anywhere near my wife," Mark David snarled. Emme froze, an icy chill unfurling down her spine. Lara had not mentioned that the husband she'd run from was Abraham Murdock's son. No wonder she was so terrified.

"But she's not really your wife, is she?" Emme said. "Not in the eyes of the law, anyway."

"She's my wife in the eyes of God, and that's enough." Mark David traced the trigger of his gun with his finger, glaring at Emme. "And anyone that comes between a man and his wife deserves what comes to them."

"Then let me talk to Sarai," Emme said, "and we can all sleep peacefully in our beds tonight."

"Sarai ain't talking to no one," Mark David said. His voice reminded Emme of a dog barking at a squirrel. "You'll have to run through a whole bunch of us to talk to her."

"Keep your mouth shut, Mark David, and let me handle this," Abraham snapped, his words a whip, and Emme felt the lash of memory as she heard her father's voice in her mind. *Shut your mouth girl*, he'd hiss at her, even if she hadn't said anything. Emme wondered how Abraham spoke to his daughters if his sons earned this much contempt.

Abraham stepped away from the truck and crossed the space between them in three long strides. Emme tightened her grip on the open car door and hated herself for it, knowing they could all see the involuntary reaction of having her personal space invaded. But she kept her feet firmly planted and her face placid as Abraham snarled at her. "You outsiders come in here, thinking you know what's what, and you ain't got the faintest idea what the truth is. The only truth is the Word of God, and He speaks directly into my ear, and if you ain't listening to me, all you hear are lies."

"And is God telling you to keep Sarai from talking to me, Mr. Murdock?" Emme asked. "Does your God approve of murder?"

"When God approves of killing, it ain't murder." Abraham spat another glob of tobacco onto the ground, splattering several drops of it onto Emme's boot.

"And did He approve of Eli killing Hannah?" Emme shot back.

"What happened to Hannah was a tragic accident."

"You're telling me the strangulation marks around her neck were caused by accident?" She could still see it clear as morning, the blackish purple bruises blossomed on Hannah's throat and collarbone in the shape of a man's hand.

Abraham shrugged. "Could be. I ain't a coroner."

"There isn't a coroner on this planet who would rule Hannah's death an accident, Mr. Murdock, and you know it—"

"I only know what God tells me—"

"Did God tell you to kill Hannah DeLeo?"

"I had nothing to do with her death."

"But your son Eli did, and you helped him evade the authorities, didn't you?" *Goddammit.* She'd sworn to herself that she wouldn't bring up Eli and Hannah, that she'd stay focused on Lara and Sarai, and now she'd broken her own promise. But Max's death was inexplicably tangled up with Hannah's murder; she couldn't pull them apart, and that connection breathed fire through her chest. She gritted her teeth as Abraham took another step closer to her, close enough now that she could see the tobacco stains on his teeth.

"Eli is dead." Abraham jabbed a finger at her but didn't touch her, though the veins in his neck told her how badly he wanted to. "How dare you deface his memory."

"Is Sarai in the same place that Eli is?" Emme asked. "Did you spirit her away the same way you spirited him out of the country?"

"You're fucking crazy," Mark David growled.

"Language, boy." Abraham's nostrils flared. "But my son ain't wrong. You're one crazy bitch if you think you can come in here and accuse me of faking my own son's death."

"If you think you can get a rise out of me by calling me a bitch, you are sorely mistaken," Emme said. "I've been called a lot worse."

"You think you're so smart, don't you?" Abraham ran his tongue over his stained teeth. "Some man needs to get in there and teach you a lesson."

"I'd be happy to oblige." Mark David made a crude gesture with his hand in front of his crotch and the rest of the men laughed. He stepped in close to his father, the barrel of his AR-15 within inches of Emme's gut. She couldn't help it; she reached for the gun in her holster.

It was as if a switch had flipped in all of them. They raised their rifles in unison and pointed them at her, like a music cue had just gone off and they were all dancing to the same tune. Emme slid her hand around the grip of her gun and flicked the safety off but kept it holstered. It wouldn't do her any good; they'd shoot her before she even had time to remove the weapon from the holster, but the cool steel against her skin gave her a veneer of control. "Now, now, boys," she said, "you're threatening a federal agent."

"The federal government ain't got no say on this land," Abraham snapped, all pretense of calm gone. "We answer only to God, and God is whispering in my ear." Abraham's voice rose like a cloud over all their heads, showering down his words. His eyes darkened, his lips whitened, and his whole face turned a beet-shade of red. "God gave us this land to survive when the fire and the famine and the plagues come to earth, and after all of humanity has been destroyed, we will still be here," he called out, as though an entire church of people, listening with rapt attention, surrounded him. He raised his arms and tilted his head back and Emme realized with a shiver that he really did think that he was in a church, preaching from the pulpit. "When the rapture comes, there is no man or woman born of this earth that can tear us off this land, and we will be here to birth humanity anew."

"Amen," Mark David murmured, closing his eyes as he listened to his father. The gun in his hands slackened a little. Emme seized the opening. She dropped back into her car just as Abraham's voice notched higher and his followers swayed under the weight of his speech.

"And God is saying to me, anyone who stands in our way must be removed. We will be free from obstacles so that His Way is clear to us, straightforward and unencumbered."

She slammed her car door shut just as Abraham lowered one arm and pointed at her. "And I say unto you, my sons, this woman is an obstacle that shall be removed."

Emme banged the gear shift from park to reverse in one fluid motion. She careened backward between the two houses and cut hard into the alleyway, shot the car into drive, and sped out onto the side street.

The Horsemen had only just been roused from the lull that Abraham's speech had put them under. They jumped back into their white trucks to take off after her, but she was already careening down the dirt road.

Up ahead, a vacant lot filled with patchy grass and a pile of rotting lumber separated her from the main road that led out of town. She aimed for it, pressing her foot as far down on the gas pedal as it would go. Halfway across the lot, one of the Horsemen streaked across her path, the white truck gleaming against the red-dirt ground. She yanked the wheel to the left, her body jolted by the maneuver as the car spun on a dime, narrowly avoiding a collision. The white truck caught up to her, racing alongside the Crosstrek. When Emme glanced over she saw Mark David in the truck bed, aiming his AR-15 at her.

Adrenaline-fueled instinct flooded her insides. She ducked low, steering with one hand, her other hand gripped tight on her gun. If she fired the first shot, they would unleash holy hell on her, and there was no way she could outrun an army of AR-15s. She kept her foot heavy on the gas, pushing the Crosstrek past eighty miles an hour as she squealed onto the main road. The houses that had silently watched her entry into the town were now bursting with noise and color as women and children tumbled out of their doors at the commotion.

The other three Horsemen gained on her until she was flanked on both sides and her rear by the dirt-spattered white trucks. In her driver's side mirror, the slim black barrels of their AR-15s stared her down, held at the ready through their windows. She pressed down harder on the gas pedal, the speedometer swinging upwards of ninety. She just had to make it to Redwater's border. Beyond that, she knew they wouldn't mess with her; outside of their promised land, their bravado turned mute.

Emme slid down in her seat, laying all her weight onto the gas pedal, until finally the *Welcome to Redwater* sign crested into view. She flew past it and kept going, speeding at nearly a hundred out of town. One by one, the trucks disappeared from her rearview, vanishing into a cloud of dirt as if the village of Redwater was some kind of Brigadoon, made of mist and myth and male fragility. Emme's breath began to slow to normal; she eased herself back up in her seat and put her seatbelt on. She twisted the car through the switchbacks down the mountain, going way too fast, and didn't slow until she hit the freeway.

CHAPTER ELEVEN

If anyone had asked Emme about the drive home from Redwater to Springdale, she would not have been able to say a word. The entire trip existed in a blur. All she knew was that when she pulled into the driveway alongside the bakery, her water bottle was empty and her gun was still in her hand.

Jaspar flew out of the back door of the bakery, galloping down the steps from the patio. Emme holstered her gun before he got to the car and opened her door. He reached to help her out of the car, and Emme gripped his hand, realizing that her own was still shaking. He captured her in an all-encompassing bear hug, enveloping her in the scent of coffee and cinnamon and his spicy aftershave. "Are you okay?"

Emme let out a long breath before she answered. "Yeah. I'm okay." She pushed herself out of his embrace and shut the car door. "I'm fine." She wasn't, of course, not really, and for too many reasons to list. But she was standing, unhurt, and she was home. With her legs on firm ground that belonged to her and not some lunatic cult, she felt her balance returning. "I could use a drink."

"I'll take you to Cap's Landing," Jaspar said. "I could do with a cold beer."

"I need to change first," Emme said, suddenly wanting to shed everything off her that had been anywhere near Abraham Murdock.

By the time they left, the sky was dusky purple. Zion Park Boulevard bustled with tourists, lines of people waiting for tables at the most popular restaurants, the art galleries that stayed open late brightly lit and welcoming. The parking lot at Cap's only had a few cars when they pulled in. Amy was working and greeted them as they made a beeline for the bar. "I'll be over in a minute," she called as she made her way from table to table.

They slid onto stools the bar, and Emme nodded to Tim who was pouring a beer from the tap behind the bar. Half the barstools were occupied; she recognized a couple of rangers from the park and the grizzled guy who ran one of the camping supply stores in town. And there, talking to the rangers, his back turned to her but his coppery hair unmistakable, was Finn Brackenbury.

Emme was halfway off her stool to go talk to him when Tim plunked his elbows down onto the bar in front of them. "Hey, you two. What can I get you?"

"Angel's Envy, neat," Emme said.

"Tough day?"

"You don't know the half of it," Emme said.

"Any more news on Max?"

Emme tilted her head with a smile. "Aw, Tim—you know I can't discuss that."

"I see our friend got his credit card back." Tim nodded towards Finn and set a glass filled with a healthy pour of bourbon in front of Emme, then turned away to get Jaspar's beer.

Emme knocked back the bourbon in one swallow and gestured to Tim for another when he set Jaspar's beer in front of him. Jaspar raised his eyebrows. "What? You're driving," she said with a shrug. But when the second glass of bourbon arrived, she sipped it more slowly, let the heat of it fill her belly and her brain. She needed fuzziness right now after the bright sharpness of Redwater.

Jaspar leaned forward. "What made you think you could get Abraham Murdock to give up his daughter? After what happened with Eli?"

There were few people who knew that Emme believed Eli was still alive. It wasn't something she said too openly; they'd found a journal and a personalized knife in the last place he was known to be, and everyone figured his suicide was settled fact. But Jaspar had been there in the aftermath of Hannah's murder and Eli's disappearance, had listened to her rant over the case as she was trying not to cry over her mother, and even through all of her far-fetched theories, he agreed with her. "It was stupid. Stupid, stupid, stupid." She sighed. "But if there's a chance that Lara heard me, that she knows someone is looking for her, I guess it was worth it. I just wish I hadn't brought up Hannah."

Jaspar sipped his beer. "But how could you not?"

Emme closed her eyes as she took another swallow of bourbon. He'd hit the heart of it. She'd never stop bringing up Hannah, not as long as justice for her murder remained elusive, not until she figured out what connection Max had to her. She twisted on her stool to look down the bar at Finn Brackenbury. The journalist held a clue, she was sure of it. "I'm gonna go talk to him," she murmured, hopping off her stool. The bourbon had set her insides alight with a warm glow and she swayed a little as she sauntered over to Finn.

"Don't leave your credit card this time," Emme said, sidling against the bar between Finn's stool and the one beside it. He turned.

"Well, I've got a guardian angel looking out for it if I do." He grinned. "How are you doing, Agent Helliwell?"

"Please call me Emme," she said, waving her hand. "What are you drinking?"

"Glenmorangie on the rocks," he said, rattling the ice cubes in his glass. "But I need a refill."

"Well, let me." She nodded to Tim and he came over, laid down two napkins on the bar. "Two Angel's Flights."

"You got it." Tim winked at Finn, who narrowed his eyes at Emme.

"What's an Angel's Flight?"

"I believe it's more commonly known as an Irish Car Bomb," Emme said, "but seeing as that's offensive to those who suffered through the Troubles, Tim's dad named it in honor of the idiots who've attempted to BASE jump off Angel's Landing."

"Well, as an Irishman, I approve the name change."

Tim set two pints of Guinness and two shots of whiskey in front of them. "You're Irish? I couldn't have guessed," Emme said with a nod at his red hair.

Finn smiled, revealing a dimple on the left side of his face. "I was born there, but my parents moved to the U.S. when I was a baby. So I missed out on the accent, sadly."

Emme picked up the whiskey. "Shall we?" Finn raised his own shot glass and Emme counted out, "One, two, three." They dropped their whiskey shots into the beer and chugged it down. Emme lowered her empty pint glass. She had come over to Finn to talk about Max, to find out what he knew, but suddenly the last thing she wanted to think about was work. The effect of Redwater was starting to leave her, curling away like wisps of smoke from a dying campfire. She deserved one night just to herself, where she didn't have to worry about clues and connections and questions. Finn ordered another round, and Jaspar joined them, counting down loudly as they let their whiskey freefall into the Guinness. The edges of the bar began to soften and blur, the music on the jukebox grew louder. She felt her body sway to the rhythms of one song after another. At some point Amy was next to her, laughing at something Jaspar said. The night smeared around her, a haze of color and music and voices overlapping each other. She let herself become part of it, until the memory of what had happened in Redwater was a distant fog and nothing mattered except the here and now.

*****

Someone was jackhammering inside her bedroom. *I didn't authorize any work,* Emme thought. She rolled over and pulled a pillow over her head. The hammering grew louder, pounding inside her skull. She groaned and pressed a hand to her forehead and slowly, very slowly, sat up. It wasn't her head. Someone was knocking on the front door. She slid out of bed and wobbled her way through the house, knocking into door frames and chairs on her way. *What the hell did I drink last night?* She couldn't remember anything after the first Angel's Flight, except that there'd been at least one more round of them. *That* she remembered.

When she got to the front door, Emme reached for the knob and froze. What if it was one of the Murdocks? They wouldn't knock, she decided. They'd just break the door down. When she opened it, the morning sunlight blinded her. She blinked hard and fast until the figure on the porch came into focus. He was smiling at her, a dimple on his left cheek. Finn Brackenbury.

"Morning!" He was way too awake. She might not have remembered everything from the night before, but she did remember that he'd been drinking right alongside her. "I figured you might need this." He held up a cardboard tray with two large coffees and a couple of blueberry muffins.

Emme didn't move aside to let him in. "How did you know where I live?"

He jerked his chin toward the bakery. "Behind The Sunny Spot. You told me last night."

She definitely didn't remember that. Emme hesitated a moment, then backed up to let him in. He seemed harmless, albeit a little too charming, but she'd taken down men bigger than him. She closed the door behind him. Her gun was hanging just out of sight beneath her flak jacket on the peg next to the door; she could move to it quickly if he turned out to be not as harmless as he looked.

Finn set the coffee and muffins down on the mosaic-topped coffee table in the middle of the living room, took one of the coffees and settled into an armchair. "I didn't know how you take it so it's black," he said.

"I like it black," she said, "but I have cream and sugar if you need it."

"Mine is already light and sweet." He raised his cup to her slightly and took a sip, watching her over the lid of his cup.

Emme picked up a muffin and nibbled at it as she perched on the arm of the couch. "So, uh, no offense, but why are you here? I assume it's not just to bring me coffee."

Finn searched her face with his golden-brown eyes. "You really don't remember our conversation last night, do you?"

"You know, I don't normally drink like that," Emme grumbled. She picked up her coffee and took a long sip.

"Hey, no judgement." Finn held up his hand. "If I'd had the kind of day you did, I'd be downing Angel's Flights too."

Emme lowered her coffee cup. "I told you about that?"

"You think that Max was dating Eli Murdock's sister?"

Dammit. She was never going to drink again. But since her investigation wasn't under ISB's jurisdiction, she wasn't beholden to their rules, was she? She took another sip of coffee while her mind raced. Okay, so she had no idea what she'd said to this guy last night, but the real mystery was what he was going to do with the information. "How's your article coming along?"

Finn set his coffee down on the table. "I'm not writing an article. I'm producing a podcast about deaths in National Parks."

"There's already like three podcasts about deaths in National Parks." She'd tried to listen to one of them, but when they'd started talking about one of her cases, she had to shut it off. It was so easy for them to sit in a recording booth, thousands of miles away, and discuss the dead like they were figuring out what to cook for dinner that night. It wasn't that easy when you were the first one on the scene, watching vultures circle the bodies.

"But none of them are investigative." Finn leaned forward and clasped his hands together, almost as though he was trying to keep his body from vibrating with excitement. "Most of them are outdoor enthusiasts, or true crime fanatics, but I'm coming from an investigative journalist background and that's how I approach everything. And if I can be on the ground while this case is unfolding, that would be huge."

Emme narrowed her eyes at him. "What do you mean, if you can be on the ground?"

Finn straightened. "With you. On the ground with you. Last night, you said we could work together on this."

Emme groaned. Even with less than two weeks left, she might as well hand in her badge right now. How could she be such an idiot? She ran her hand over her face, dug the heel of her palm into her eye sockets. "Listen, I have to be honest. I don't remember agreeing to that last night. And we don't even know if there's a case here," she added, pulling her hand away from her face and blinking at Finn. "The coroner ruled Max's death an accident. The ISB isn't officially investigating it."

"But *you* are," Finn insisted. "That's what you said last night."

"I know, but—"

"And with the Murdock connection, there's bound to be more to the story." Finn stood up. "Look, I know you just woke up and you've probably got a wicked hangover—"

"*Wicked?* You from Boston?"

Finn laughed. "I'm from upstate New York, actually, but I went to school in Boston and some of the colloquialisms stuck, I guess." He started to move towards the door. Emme straightened, swayed, and sank back down. The muffin sat like a rock in her stomach, making her queasy. "Are you okay?"

"Yeah—"

"Let me get you some water." He turned in a small circle, located where the kitchen was, and disappeared. When he reappeared, he handed her a glass of water and laid a card on the table. "I'm gonna get out of your hair. That's my number. I'm kinda assuming you threw out the other card." He winked. "I know things can get sticky between law enforcement and journalists, but I think we could help each other out." Emme cradled the glass of water in her hands. Last night—before the Angel's Flights—she'd been so sure that Finn held a crucial clue to the connection between Hannah and Max's deaths, but now her brain felt like mush. "What did Max tell you to get you to meet with him?"

Finn leaned against the front door frame. "Just enough to get me to Zion," he said, a half-smile playing at the corner of his mouth, "but not enough to be considered concrete evidence."

Emme snorted. She knew the game Finn was playing; she'd played it many times while questioning suspects. "If you know something, you're under obligation to tell the authorities."

"Not if there's no official investigation, right?" His lips curved into a full smile now. Emme stared right into his eyes for a long moment and took a silly amount of satisfaction when he blinked first. "Look, I have to be cagey with information. I'm sure you get that. However, one thing I can tell you is that Max and I were supposed to meet on one of the backcountry trails in the park. I was planning to go there today, but I can hold off until tomorrow if you want to join me." There was a sparkle in his golden-green eyes that the dark bar had hidden last night. "Maybe we can talk more and figure out how we can help each other."

Emme took a sip of water. "I'll let you know."

"Great. Call or text me anytime." A burst of chill morning air blew in when he opened the door, then disappeared as he closed it softly behind him.

Emme stared at the closed door, then went to the table to pick up the card. *Finn Brackenbury, Producer, Twisted Roots Media.* She turned the card over in her hand while she drank the water very slowly, letting each sip settle in her stomach before taking the next one.

In her job, journalists were usually the enemy. They were always digging in places that they shouldn't be, and they had a pesky habit of revealing information to the public that should really be kept private. The days when Stace had to deal with the press were the ones when he cursed the most, and she'd generally taken his line of approach on the matter.

But this was different. She wasn't working for the ISB on Max's case, and they had no say over who she shared information with. And—she ran her finger over the raised lettering—if she did leave the ISB, acting as a consultant for news outlets like this could be a viable source of income.

Emme set the card and the empty glass down on the table. Her mind still felt fuzzy; she needed a steaming hot shower to wash the cobwebs out of her brain. She was still towel-drying her hair when Jaspar knocked on the kitchen door. "I see you're alive," he said with a grin when she let him in. She swatted him with the wet towel and he danced away, laughing.

"Finn Brackenbury stopped by." She rolled her eyes. "I can't believe I told him where I live."

Jaspar filled the kettle with water and set it on the stove. "You don't remember?"

"I basically remember saying 'one, two, three, drink' and the rest is a blur."

Jaspar snorted. "Fair enough."

"How could I be so stupid?" Emme pressed her hand to her forehead. A dull ache still hummed inside her temples. "I am never drinking again."

"Well, I'm sure that's not true." Jaspar turned to face her and leaned back against the counter. "What would be so bad about teaming up with him? He might be a good outside eye." He reached into the cupboard for the bag of coffee. "And, he's cute."

"That has nothing to do with anything." Emme snatched the coffee from him and began to measure out scoops into the French press.

"Yeah, okay. Sure it doesn't." The kettle whistled. Jaspar poured the water into the press.

Emme grabbed a chopstick from the drawer to stir it. She still wasn't sure whether or not to accept Finn's offer to go hiking. On the one hand, she didn't usually trek into the wilderness with men she just met. But on the other, she wanted to squeeze every last drop of information he possibly had out of him. She took down two mugs from the shelf above the sink while Jaspar pressed the plunger down on the coffee. When the hot, bitter liquid hit her tongue, she nearly moaned with pleasure. Now that her stomach was settled and her hangover subsiding, the taste of it was heaven.

Jaspar dumped a splash of half-and-half into his coffee and took a sip, sighed with contentment. "Okay, now that you have some caffeine in you, can I get your help on the patio?"

"Sure." She followed him out the kitchen door. The mid-morning sun was cresting over the mountains, and there was an autumn chill in the air. A whiff of woodsmoke drifted from somewhere down the road.

Jaspar had made more progress than she'd realized. The wooden floor and rails had been sanded and stained a deep redwood color; it looked like a brand-new deck. She trailed behind Jaspar as he pointed out where they were going to run the gas line and how they were going to build the fire pit. As she stood in the center of the deck, she could imagine her mother just inside the bakery, moving between counter and oven, humming to herself as she worked, loving every moment of the life she'd built—the thought was a punch of grief in her gut.

"Emme? Is that okay with you?"

She shielded her eyes against the brightening sun to look at Jaspar. "What? Oh—yes, that's fine."

Jaspar swept his gaze over the patio. "I miss her, too."

Emme bit back a sob, but Jaspar heard it anyway. He pulled her into a hug and Emme cried into his sweatshirt. The only other person on the planet who could understand her at this moment was Addie. Mixed with the grief was a yawning black hole of worry—where was her sister?—and it made her cry harder. After a long moment, she hiccupped and pushed Jaspar away. "I'm sorry to be such a mess."

"Emme, for what you're going through, I'm surprised you're not more of a mess." Jaspar swiped the back of his hand across his eyes. "Listen, I'm meeting the contractor at the store to pick out materials for the fire pit, so I need to run. I promise I'll stay on budget."

"I trust you." She punched his arm. "Thanks, Jaspar."

They exited the deck in opposite directions—him through the bakery and her to the house. When she got inside, she went to the living room and sat on the floor in front of the coffee table. Finn's card lay quiet and unassuming on the table's surface, next to the half-drunk cup of coffee he'd brought her that had long since gone cold. Her skin itched, like it was trying to jump three steps ahead of her. The cure for that feeling was usually to get out into the wild, far away from people and cell service. She picked up her phone and dialed his number. He picked up on the first ring.

"It's Emme," she said. "Let's go for that hike."

Chapter Twelve

Compared to the Zion Canyon Visitors Center, Kolob Canyons was practically a ghost town. Emme parked in one of the many empty spots and hopped out. The sky stretched bright and clear above them, with a few faint streaks of pink morning light threaded through the vast expanse of blue. Finn followed her into the Visitors Center, where a few hikers clustered around the Wilderness Permits Desk and a family of four browsed in the small gift shop. The ranger behind the Information desk looked up from his phone as Emme and Finn approached. "Can I help—oh, hi." He nodded at Emme's Smokey hat and flak jacket. "Are you the ISB agent working on that death in The Narrows?"

"Agent Helliwell," Emme said, sticking out her hand for him to shake. She noted the name on his nametag—Carey—and remembered what Theo had told her at the bar last week. "You were working the East Entrance last Wednesday morning, weren't you? There was some sort of altercation?"

"Aw yeah, that crazy dude!" Carey ran his hand through his dark hair, making it wave to the side. "He was insane, man."

Emme pulled out her little notebook and a pencil from her backpack. "Can you describe him?"

Carey scrunched up his face. "He was medium height, kind of wiry. Had on a baseball cap that sort of hid his face, but at one point he took it off to shake it at me and I noticed—he had one blue eye and one brown. I'd never seen anyone that had that before."

Mark David. Emme inhaled a satisfied breath as she scribbled in her notebook. She'd had an inkling that this incident was connected to Max's death when Theo first mentioned it, and now she had proof she was right. "Okay, that's good, that's really good. What else?"

"He was wearing a dark t-shirt with a long-sleeved, unbuttoned flannel shirt layered on top, jeans, work boots. I think they were Timberlands."

"He came in wanting a permit for The Narrows, right?"

"Yes, ma'am."

Emme made a face at him. "Don't call me ma'am. I'm not ready for that yet."

Carey laughed. "Fair enough. Yes, he wanted a permit. When I told him we were sold out for the day—not to mention you gotta get them at the Visitors Center—he started yelling about how his sister was out there with 'some guy'—he kept calling him 'some guy' and saying his sister was in danger." Carey shook his head. "I told him that she looked fine when they passed through the station, that she certainly didn't look like she was in danger. That actually seemed to make him madder."

Emme looked up. "You saw Max and Sarai that morning?"

"Who?"

Emme flipped to the back of her notebook, where she had tucked a photo of Max and a print-out of the photo he'd taken of Sarai in The Narrows. She held them up to Carey. "These two. You saw them?"

Carey nodded. "Sure. I remember because they came in a little later than everyone else who was hiking top-down that day, and they wanted to switch campsites. I told them if no one else was at the campsite they wanted, they were welcome to use it. They seemed real sweet and in love. So when that guy came in saying she was in trouble I was like, 'dude, you're crazy.'"

Emme's hand flew across the page, trying to capture Carey's story word for word.

"He got so angry he started banging on the window of the ranger booth, and that's when I threw him out."

"Did he put up a fight?"

"He tried." Carey flexed his fingers. "I was bigger than him, so he backed down pretty quick. He ranted at me for a minute, then peeled a U-turn around the booth and left."

"And he was in a white Ford pickup?"

"Yes, ma—sorry. Yes. A white Ford pickup. No plates, though." Carey closed one eye as though he was trying to remember something. "There was a bumper sticker on the truck."

"Let me guess, a Confederate flag?" Finn asked.

"No, although he definitely had that vibe." Carey tapped his fingers on the counter. "It was something about Christ. Ironic, considering how un-Christ-like he was acting."

Bumper sticker with the word Christ, Emme wrote. She snapped her notebook shut with the pencil still inside. "This has been very helpful. Thank you."

"Glad to be of service." The door behind the desk opened, and a young female ranger emerged from the back room. Carey turned to her.

"Hey, Chenoa. This is Agent Helliwell, the one who's investigating that guy who died in The Narrows," he explained.

Chenoa gave Emme a nod. Beneath her Smokey hat, her dark hair was pulled back in a low ponytail, her eyes bright and curious. "You work with Eustace Pompey, don't you?" "I do." Emme leaned against the desk. "Do you know him?"

"No, but he's sort of a hero of mine," Chenoa said with a shy smile. Emme noticed the pin on her lapel, the image of an eagle, its wings outspread and its claws clutching a ceremonial tobacco pipe with black, white, and red feathers spread beneath it: the Ute tribal seal.

"He's a pretty easy person to admire," she said.

"Were you guys planning to head into the park?" Carey asked. A few more people had come into the Visitors Center and were milling around, waiting for them to clear away from the desk.

"Yes," Finn said. He stepped up to the desk and bent over the park map displayed beneath the glass top. "We were going to take the La Verkin trail. We don't need a permit for that, do we?"

"Not if you're just going for the day," Carey said. "You want to take a satellite phone?" he asked Emme.

"Sure."

"That trail has a detour since a mudslide in the spring," Chenoa said. "It can be tricky to follow if you don't know where to go."

"I'm sure we'll be—"

"I'd be happy to go along with you as a guide," she said, glancing between Emme and Finn. "I was planning to hike out that way myself." Emme heard the note in her voice, that eagerness that she'd once had as a young ranger, jumping on every chance she got to tag along with a more experienced ranger.

"Don't you have to work?" Emme asked.

"Nah, I just came in to get my paycheck. And annoy Carey," she said, punching him lightly in the arm. He swatted her away and waved over the people waiting in line. Emme moved to the side and Chenoa shifted along with her, eyes wide and hopeful. Once upon a time, Emme had been just like her, and she owed much of her career to the rangers who had taken the time to teach her what they knew. She looked at Finn.

"You don't mind, do you?"

"Of course not." Finn hoisted his pack onto his back. "I'm going to hit the bathroom before we head out."

"Good idea."

They all met up in the parking lot and piled into Emme's car to drive to the Lee Pass trailhead. "Listen, we need to ask that you keep anything you hear us talk about confidential," Emme told Chenoa as she navigated the twisting road. "But don't be afraid to speak up and share your ideas," she added. "I didn't get to be an ISB agent by staying quiet."

"How did you become an ISB agent?" Finn asked.

"I joined the park service a year or so after college." Emme eased the car around a curve. "My first assignment was part-time in Glacier, at the Granite Park Chalet."

Finn flashed her a grin from the backseat. "*Night of the Grizzlies.*"

"Well, I spent a whole summer there and only saw the backside of one grizzly," Emme said. She could see it in her mind's eye, its lumbering gait, and the swoosh of fear that if it turned around it could be on her in seconds. "Ever been to the Chalet?"

"I have, actually. Not a bad place to spend the summer," Finn said.

"I figured I'd go back the following summer, but then I got offered another part-time job that winter in Yosemite." Emme slowed down as a Jeep came around the bend in the opposite direction, raising her hand to the other driver as they passed. "With the park service, you kind of have to go where the work is. Everyone's chasing that elusive full-time-with-benefits position."

"Tell me about it," Chenoa said.

Emme laughed. "You'll get there. It might be years, but it'll happen eventually."

"Is that why you joined the ISB?" Finn asked.

"Partly. We saw our fair share of deaths in Yosemite—"

"I can imagine."

"—and I just discovered that I was good at the investigating part of it." Emme shrugged one shoulder, trying to ignore the sweep of pride that still filled her chest when she talked about her work. "I caught Stace's attention, and he recruited me."

"You call him Stace?" Chenoa asked, a little breathless.

"*Everyone* calls him Stace." Emme pulled into the small trailhead parking lot. There was only one other car in the lot; they'd have the trail to themselves. "He's a really good guy. Smart, fair, and so, so kind. I'll miss him when I—when I'm out in the field on a case," she said quickly.

"So, you think there's a case here?" Chenoa asked. "It wasn't an accident?"

"That's what I'm going to find out." Emme pointed a finger at her. "And *that* is what you need to keep to yourself."

Emme popped the trunk and they all climbed out of the car. As she organized her backpack and unfurled her hiking poles, she nodded to the pin on Chenoa's shirt. "Did you grow up on the reservation?"

Chenoa nodded. "Most of my family is still there, except my brother who lives in Salt Lake." She shouldered her pack. "I don't get back there as much as I'd like. Or rather, as much as my mother wishes I did."

Emme snorted, covering the grief that swooshed through her at the word *mother*. She tucked a few extra snacks into her backpack. "What about you, Finn? Where did you grow up? You told me upstate New York, but where, exactly?"

"Little town called Rhinebeck in the Hudson Valley, about a hundred miles north of the city," he replied as he adjusted his own poles. Emme noticed how he called it "the city" like all New Yorkers, like the five boroughs were the nexus of the universe. "You've probably never heard of it."

"Actually," Emme closed the trunk and leaned on it, looking at him, "I do know it. I grew up right across the river, in Kingston. Well, until I was eleven."

"Holy shit, really? What are the odds?" Finn stared at her. "That's amazing. What made your family move out here?"

Don't wake your father, Sunny had whispered, tiptoeing across the floor and out the front door, closing the trunk of the car so softly it almost didn't latch. Watching the stars above the sunroof from the backseat, Addie's small sleeping body warm and cozy against her. She'd stayed awake all night even though her mother kept telling her to go asleep, playing sentinel to her mother's wakefulness. Sometime in the early morning they'd gone through a drive-thru for breakfast, and soon after passed a sign welcoming them into Ohio. She knew enough geography to know they were two big states away from her father's rage, and only then did she sleep. She swallowed and forced a smile. "My parents needed a change." It was as close to the truth as she was willing to get. "Do you live in New York now?"

"I have a Manhattan P.O. box, but I travel around so much that I don't really have a permanent place there. I usually Airbnb it when I have to stay for an extended period of time." Finn rested his poles against the car as he slung his backpack onto his shoulders. "I like the nomad life for now, but when I do put down roots, I'm not sure it'll be in the city. I need more space and solitude."

"I certainly get that," Emme said, then nodded to the trail that lay before them. "Some of the best days I've had as a ranger are the days when I don't see another human being. Speaking of which, shall we?"

The hard-packed, rust-colored dirt crunched a bit beneath their feet, tall scrub brush and ponderosa pines reaching up toward the blue sky on either side of the trail. The red-rock cliffs rose alongside them, towering over the land below like a queen on a throne high above her subjects. Their pace was leisurely as Finn stopped every now and then to take a picture of the canyon that encircled them. Emme didn't mind. It had been years since she'd taken this trail; she usually stuck to Zion Canyon since it was so much closer to Springdale.

"What makes you think that man's death was an accident?" Chenoa asked as Finn clicked a few more photos, then walked around recording what he called "ambient sounds" for his podcast.

Emme inhaled deeply, the scent of pine and yucca singeing her nose. "There are a few details that don't add up. And . . ." She trailed off, watched Finn catch the sound of the brush rustling.

"And what?" Chenoa prodded.

Emme squinted up at the brilliant blue sky. "I was going to say gut instinct, but my instinct's been wrong before."

"When?" Finn asked, walking back over to them.

Emme gripped her poles tighter. The day was too beautiful and the canyon too peaceful to think about Hannah. As much as the thought of her was always at the edge of Emme's mind, on the trail it was easy to keep it at bay. "You done? Let's keep going."

A hawk burst out of the top branches of a ponderosa pine and wheeled through the air, high above their heads. Emme tracked it with her gaze until it disappeared behind the jagged crown of a clifftop. They hiked in and out of sun and shade as the trail wound through the canyon. "You were supposed to meet Max on this trail?" Emme asked Finn. "Did he say why?"

"No, but I assumed he would tell me why when I met him." Finn held up his wrist. "Two miles in, that was the spot. I'm tracking it on my watch."

"And he didn't give you any inkling of what he wanted to discuss about Hannah DeLeo?"

Chenoa, who was a few strides ahead of them, stopped and turned around. "Hannah DeLeo? What does she have to do with any of this?"

"The man who died in The Narrows—Max Kerchek—told me he had information about her case," Finn told her. "We were supposed to meet—here, at this trail—the day after he died."

"How would he know anything about that case?" Chenoa's eyes narrowed.

"He was dating Eli Murdock's sister," Emme said. She jerked her chin at Chenoa. "*That's* one of things that makes me think it wasn't an accident. Whenever the Murdocks are involved . . . it's never good news." She shook her head and looked back at Finn. "But what information would he have? That case is closed." She dug her poles into the earth and set off again. Finn fell into step with her, Chenoa just a beat behind.

"That was it, wasn't it?" Finn said. "The case where your gut was wrong. Hannah DeLeo."

Emme didn't answer right away, let the silence stretch between the three of them, filled with the distant cry of the hawk in the mountains and the rustle of the wind through the trees. "My mother was sick," she said finally, keeping her sight fixed on the trail, the little clouds of dirt her footfalls made as she walked. "I was driving back and forth from here to the Grand Canyon. I got called into one of the campgrounds there on a domestic dispute." She could see it all, Hannah and Eli's green tent with a bright blue tarp pulled over it. "It seemed so innocent, just two people getting into a heated argument, like everyone does with their significant other every now and then." Her throat tightened as she heard Eli's voice over and over in her mind, *I know how to handle her when she gets like this.* "I let them go," she said, "and two days later he killed her." The shame made her voice so quiet she wasn't sure Finn could hear her.

Finn exhaled. Had he been holding his breath? "Oh, Emme. That wasn't your fault. How could you know?"

I should've known! Me of all people! she wanted to scream. She'd seen the constant gaslighting her father had used on her mother, on her . . . she should've seen those signs, bright and shining like a flashlight in her face. But she'd been distracted, worried about Sunny, her mind already on the drive back to the hospital and how long it would take with the construction along Highway 89. She blinked several times, the trail in front of her blurring in and out of focus, still not trusting herself to talk. But somehow, with just the three of them and the mountains, it was easier to believe that maybe Finn was right. Maybe it wasn't her fault.

"You know," Finn said, his tone thoughtful as he walked beside her, stride for stride, "I think Eli Murdock is still alive."

Emme stopped in the middle of the trail, breath returning to her body in a big *whoosh*. "*I* think Eli Murdock is alive," she practically yelled, her voice echoing across the canyon. "And everyone thinks I'm crazy."

"I could see it," Chenoa said. "His family never produced his body, did they?"

And as if the bright sun in the cloudless blue sky had shined down to illuminate it, everything clicked inside her. "Oh my god," she breathed, staring at Finn. "That's the information Max had. It was about Eli. Of course he would know something; Sarai would've been there when Eli came back from the Grand Canyon after killing Hannah, and she must have told Max." She dropped her poles and tore open her pack to get her notebook, frantic to capture on paper what was racing through her mind.

Finn scrunched his face up. "And maybe he came to me because he figured he'd get more traction with the press than the authorities . . . or maybe I was a back-up to him going to the authorities. Either way, it tracks—"

"—and it makes sense that it would be Max, because he would've wanted to protect Sarai from the Murdocks," Emme said, tumbling her words over Finn's. "And maybe they did find out that Max was planning to come clean about Eli, and that's why they're keeping Sarai in the Garden."

"What? What garden?"

Emme waved her hand in the air. "It's not a garden; it's a place where they keep dissenters. When I went to Redwater, I saw the building."

"Did you see Sarai?" She shook her head. "No, but I have to assume she was in there. No one has seen her since the morning Max got his permit for The Narrows." She picked up her poles. "Come on, let's keep going. I think the fresh air and the exercise is helping me piece things together."

"The detour is just around this bend," Chenoa said. She'd been quiet during Emme and Finn's revelation, but now she squeezed ahead of them to lead the way. They followed her up the trail, where it curved around a corner and dropped off suddenly in a mess of dried mud, broken branches, and piles of rock. "This trail isn't as popular as the ones in Zion Canyon, or even Cable Mountain, so fixing it has been low on the priority list," Chenoa explained as they veered off onto a crudely-cut path through the brush. It was tall and overgrown, and they had to push branches out of their faces as they hiked. The sun disappeared behind the mountain, leaving them in shadow. A chill swept through Emme.

They pushed through a snarled tangle of prickly bushes and came to a small clearing, encircled by towering ponderosa pines. Finn's watch beeped. "This is it," he said. "This is where I was supposed to meet him."

Emme turned in a tight circle, as though she expected Max to appear and tell them why the hell he'd asked Finn to meet him here. A light wind sighed through the pines, scattering needles and wavering something that hung from one of the trees. "What is that?" Chenoa asked.

They all moved closer to see. A chain of wildflowers hung between two trees, stretched from bough to bough, purple and yellow and white blossoms all twisted together. "That's manmade," Emme breathed, stepping closer. A few blooms had dropped from the chain, littering the ground with petals and drawing Emme's gaze down from the trees to the earth. She jolted to a stop. Chenoa collided into her, knocking her forward. Emme caught herself with her hand on the grass, stained with something wet and dark. When she stood, her hand was covered in blood. She stared at the stain, long and human-shaped . . . Emme walked its length to where it stretched beneath the trees . . . *drag marks*. She followed the trail of blood into the brush, ducking below branches, barely feeling the twigs that snapped against her cheeks.

A stench hit her nostrils, one she'd smelled too many times, putrefying and suffocating. She fished out a mask from the side pocket of her backpack and pulled it on to dull the scent as she crept deeper into the brush. Beneath a twisted juniper, her foot hit something squishy. She jumped back, peering down, her brain trying to make sense of what lay at her feet. She had seen a predator's cache many times before, but always with animal prey—and *this* was decidedly human. Emme squatted down, her heartbeat clogging up her throat. Strips of flesh had been torn away from the body where the animal—probably a mountain lion—had eaten its fill, and a gaping hole in the body's shoulder where the lion had likely dragged it off, to save for later.

But beyond that, the body showed signs of other injuries, wounds that had been inflicted by a human hand. The shock of finding it was beginning to recede as her investigator's brain took over, and Emme let her gaze travel up from the feet, still encased in expensive hiking boots, to the legs, clad in jeans that were dirtied, bloodied, and torn. The body's torso was where most of the damage from the lion was located, but a puffer vest still hung over one shoulder . . . a purple puffer vest, its vibrant color dulled by the stain of viscera. Emme's breath stopped as she slid her gaze up to the body's face, knowing already what she would see there: blonde hair, and the wide, dead eyes of Sarai Murdock, staring unseeing at the bright blue sky above her.

CHAPTER THIRTEEN

A crash in the brush behind her shot Emme to her feet. "Stay back," she yelled, whirling to block Chenoa and Finn from seeing the body. It would haunt them for years to come, and no one needed that kind of trauma. She pushed her way through the tangled branches and met them a few steps from the clearing. "I just found Sarai Murdock," she said, a tremor beneath her voice that she wished she could quell.

"What?" Finn tried to step around her, but she held her hands up to stop him. "I thought you said she was being held in Redwater."

"Yeah, well, clearly I was wrong." Emme ran her hand over her face. Her fingers were cold against her skin. "I—I need to get forensics out here."

"Was she murdered?"

Emme nodded. Finn craned his neck, trying to catch a glimpse through the brush. Emme stepped in front of him. "Listen to me. You do not want to see this. It's clearly been a few days since she died, and an animal has cached her remains. Trust me. You do not need this image in your brain."

Finn searched her face while she kept her gaze calm and focused on his eyes. "Okay," he said finally. "But I want to help."

"Search the immediate area for anything that seems out of the ordinary," she said. "Don't touch anything, just make a note of it to show me and the forensics team when they get here. You can take pictures, but they will be confiscated." She dropped her pack to the ground and dug out the satellite phone. As she was about to dial, Chenoa touched her arm.

"I'd like to assist with the body, if you'll let me," she said.

Emme lowered the phone and looked at Chenoa. She remembered what it felt like to see her first murder victim, all those years ago on the first case she helped Stace out on. No matter how faded the memory became, it had never left her. "It's rough," she told Chenoa. "Very gruesome."

"I can handle it."

"I'm sure you can," Emme said, "but why do this to yourself if you don't have to?"

"Because," Chenoa planted her hands on her hips, "I want to do what you do."

There were so many things Emme wanted to say to her, about how the job would break her down and build her back up, but not quite in the same shape she'd been in before, or about how the work would creep into every facet of her life. But she couldn't say those things; Chenoa had to find them out for herself, if she really wanted to become an ISB agent. "Okay," she said. "Let me call the ranger station, and then we'll examine the body together."

It was going to take over an hour for the forensics ranger, currently at the station in Zion Canyon on the other side of the park, to get to

them. Emme hung up and opened her pack. She handed Chenoa a pair of
rubber gloves—she always kept a few pairs on her—and pulled on a pair
herself. "You probably want to wear a mask because of the stench," she
told Chenoa, who obliged. They ducked below the branches, following
the drag marks, until they reached the place where Sarai's body lay.
Emme turned at the last moment. "You ready?"

Chenoa nodded. Emme pushed the brush aside. As they stepped
closer, she heard a guttural noise escape from Chenoa, as though the
wind had been knocked out of her. But to the young ranger's credit,
she stepped right up beside Emme, and they both crouched down to the
body.

"This is the animal's work." Emme pointed to the flayed torso, rib
bones poking through what was left of the flesh, then moved her hand
to the shoulder wound. "See those punctures? I think that's where it bit
her to drag her off."

"Mountain lion?"

"I would assume. We don't have bears here, and this would be too big
of a job for a coyote or bobcat." She moved her attention to Sarai's neck,
where a deep cut stretched from ear to ear. "But this—this was done by
a knife." She traced the wound with her forefinger hovering just above
the flesh. "An animal would not be so neat."

Chenoa touched Sarai's hand and carefully turned it over so the palm
faced up. A long slice ran from the base of her ring finger up to her
wrist. Gently, Chenoa pushed Sarai's sleeve up to the elbow, then froze.
Emme bit back a gasp. The word Whore had been crudely carved into her
forearm, surrounded by smears of dried blood. Emme crawled around to
the other side of the body and rolled up her other sleeve. This arm bore
the word Slut.

"I think there may have been something else carved on her chest," Chenoa said. They both bent over the body, the tops of their heads touching as they peered at the flesh that remained on her torso. Sure enough, the letters AT and L and HE seemed to have been cut into the space above Sarai's breasts.

Chenoa sat back on her haunches. "Do you think the man who died in The Narrows did this to her?"

Emme jerked her head up. The thought of Max doing this punched her gut; she could still hear his laughter echoing in this very canyon and see the peace sign he'd flashed at the audience when he walked across the stage at their graduation. "No," she whispered. "No, he couldn't have done this."

"How do you know?"

Gut feelings didn't hold up in court; she needed concrete proof that Max was not a murderer. She shifted closer to Sarai's head and smoothed the matted blonde hair away from Sarai's face, which had been virtually untouched by the mountain lion other than scrapes that had probably happened during the dragging. Sarai's skin was tinged a greyish-green, and a reddish-brown foam had escaped from her mouth and nose. Emme pointed to it. "The body is bloated, and leaking fluids, but her skin is still greenish. I'd estimate that she's been dead less than five days." Emme met Chenoa's gaze across the body. "Max likely died eight days ago. Unless his ghost came back for her, there's no way he committed this murder."

"Then who did?"

The Murdocks. Emme had the answer ready in her mind, and the fact that Mark David had been seen at the East Entrance made him a prime suspect. But whether he acted alone, and why, was still unknown and kept her from voicing her deep belief that the family was somehow responsible. "I have some ideas," she said and stood up. "Let's go see if Finn has found anything useful."

They picked their way back through the brush to the clearing, where Finn walked the edge in careful, measured steps. "Find anything?" Emme asked.

"I think so. Come see." He beckoned for them to join him at the other side of the clearing.

Emme skirted around the bloodstain on her way to him. Something brown and twisted lay at Finn's feet in the grass, and Emme bent low to examine it, shining the flashlight on her phone to illuminate it against the dark ground. A long squiggle of twine, broken and frayed . . . she switched to her camera app and took several pictures. When she was done, she shined the phone's light onto the low-hanging branches of the pine trees. Tiny specks of red glinted beneath her phone's harsh white light, standing out unnaturally against the brown bark. "Blood spatter," she muttered. She looked from the spatter, down to the twine, over her shoulder at the large stain on the ground, and back again. A moving picture was forming in her mind, a terrible film of Sarai's last moments . . .

"She tried to get away," Emme said, more to herself than anyone else, but both Finn and Chenoa turned to her. They crowded around her and followed her movements as she played out what might have happened. "I think she was tied up, still alive." She could see it all in colors so vivid and sharp they scraped up against her brain. "She broke free, but before she could run, they caught her." Emme swept her hand from the blood spray on the trees to the stain in the middle of the clearing. "They slashed her throat here, then laid her out over there."

Finn crossed the clearing to where the chain of wildflowers fluttered softly in the breeze. "Do you think she made this before she died?"

"No." Emme began to trace Finn's steps at the clearing's border, looking for anything he'd missed. "I think that was made by her killer."

"How could someone kill her so viciously and then make something so beautiful?" The pain in Finn's voice echoed in Emme's chest, opening a hole there that she desperately wanted to close.

"Whoever killed her cared for her," Chenoa said, echoing exactly what Emme had been about to say. She bit her lip and turned away, swallowing down all her thoughts about the Murdocks. They were certainly capable of being heartless, cold-blooded killers . . . but they were also fiercely protective of their own, the type of family to circle the wagons at the first sign of trouble. Had Sarai stepped so far over the line that they had pushed her out of that circle in the cruelest way possible? Or was something else at play here? Emme paced the clearing, around and around, turning her ideas over and under in her mind. There was something familiar about all of this, but what it was felt just out of reach, no matter how hard she grasped for it. Without saying anything to Finn and Chenoa, she pushed her way back through the brush to where Sarai's remains lay. Moving carefully so as not to disturb the body, she reached inside the pockets of Sarai's vest. Buried deep in the left-side pocket, just below where Sarai's heart once beat, was a little bundle. Emme drew it out and held it up. A small aloe branch, its juices still fragrant where it had broken off from its stem, and a red-flowering plant were bound together by blades of grass, like a miniature bouquet . . . or a talisman. Emme stared at it for a long moment before grabbing a Ziploc bag from her pack and storing it gently inside. Someone had made that for her and put it there, probably the same person who had draped wildflowers above Sarai's final resting place.

She held the bag up. In her short interaction with Mark David, he did not seem the type to weave flowers and leave them for someone he'd just murdered.

She searched around the body for a few more minutes but didn't find anything else. Finally, she kneeled beside Sarai and bowed her head. Without looking up, she felt Chenoa emerge through the brush and lower herself next to Emme. They were quiet for a long time, listening to the rustle of the wind through the pine needles and the chirping of the birds in the trees. *I'm sorry it came to this for you,* Emme thought. Her heart felt unbearably heavy; it wasn't grief like she felt for her mother, but a burdensome sadness that Sarai had been searching for something good, something beyond her life with the Warriors, and that search had been cut so violently short.

"May you always walk in beauty and find the peace you did not find on earth," Chenoa said softly. Emme's throat tightened, and she blinked back the tears that threatened to fall from the corners of her eyes. She put her hand on Chenoa's knee and squeezed.

"Thank you," she whispered, but her words were interrupted by the beeping of the satellite phone. She picked it up and crashed out of the clearing to guide the forensics team on the other line to their exact location.

The "team" was one person, it turned out.

"Hey, I'm Drew," he said, emerging into the clearing. Emme shook his hand, made introductions, and showed him what they had found before leading him to the body. As he began his processing, Emme hung back, watching as he disrupted the peace she and Chenoa had tried to surround Sarai with. There was no helping it, she knew, but the indignity grated at her. "I have to make a phone call," she told him. She walked straight through the clearing and back out onto the main trail to call Stace.

He picked up after one ring. "Hello?"

"Stace, it's me. I'm calling from a satellite phone."

"Ah, that's why I didn't recognize the number. What's going on?"

"I'm in the park. We found another body." Emme paced up and down the trail, her footprints wearing a groove in the dirt. "It's Sarai Murdock. Max's girlfriend. And it wasn't an accident."

"Shit. Do you—" The phone line crackled.

"Stace? You're cutting in and out."

"—if she—"

Emme hiked down the trail a bit and Stace's voice came back full force.

"—was murdered too?"

"Yes," she said, and there was a rush of relief through her veins; she'd been right all along. *This time, anyway.* "I don't believe that he died accidentally and then she was killed. I think there's still a possibility that she was involved with his death, but that seems unlikely now—"

"So back to square one."

"No. More like square three. I have a lot to go on already." She turned as Drew appeared onto the trail and waved her over. She put up a finger, telling him to wait, and pressed the phone to her ear to hear what Stace was saying.

"I'm—in touch with the Salt Lake bureau—send someone—"

He was breaking up again. "Stace? Stace, I need to help the forensics guy. They only sent one person. I'll call you later." She ended the call and followed Drew back to the body.

Sunlight began to disappear into the canyon, and shadows turned the grass beneath them from green to grey. Emme zipped up the hoodie she wore under her flak jacket as she helped Drew take photographs, gather soil samples, scrape wood shavings from the tree trunks where Sarai's blood had splattered. By the time they loaded her remains into a thick, black body bag, twilight tinged the sky a bruised purple above them. The four of them strapped on headlamps and struck out on the trail, taking turns carrying the body bag on the two-mile trek back. In the dark, it looked completely different than it had just a few hours before. Emme's legs moved as though through water. Every step was an effort, and she wanted to cry when she checked the tracker on her watch and saw they'd only gone half a mile.

The sky twinkled with stars by the time she could see the trailhead and the curve of her Crosstrek. She helped load Sarai into the back of Drew's Park Service Jeep and watched as he drove away, followed the glow of the red taillights until they disappeared. Finn and Chenoa piled into Emme's car, and she drove back to the ranger station to drop off Chenoa. "Thanks for your help today. I think you have the makings of a great ISB agent," she said when she'd pulled into the dark, empty parking lot. *Maybe you can take my place,* she wanted to add, but instead she dug into the console between the driver and passenger seats and handed Chenoa her card. "If you need anything—advice, a recommendation, or just a friendly ear—call me."

Chenoa's ponytail had come loose on the hike back, and there were shadows around her eyes that Emme knew all too well. She took the card and held it with her thumb and forefinger. "Can I ask you something?"

"Sure."

"If Sarai Murdock wasn't a blonde, white woman, would you be investigating her case with as much interest as you are?" Her eyes searched Emme's face.

Emme didn't look away, and she swallowed down her instinctual answer of *yes, of course I would be*. She wanted that to be the truth, but she couldn't lie—not to herself, or Chenoa. "I know that I would be just as invested in getting justice for the victim, no matter what color their skin was," she said finally, "but I can't say that I wouldn't be influenced by so many other factors—the media, the public, even my own agency—"

"—and your own biases?"

She nodded. "Yes. And my own biases." She nudged Chenoa's arm with her elbow. "This is why we need someone like you in the ISB. I'll make sure to pass along your name to Stace."

Chenoa smiled. "Thanks. For that, and for your honesty," she said, and she climbed out of the car.

Finn took Chenoa's place in the front seat before they drove off. When they hit the highway, Emme turned to him. "Either you talk to keep me awake or I put on some classic 80s rock. Otherwise I'm gonna fall asleep."

"I'm fine with 80s rock." Finn looked out the window. The mountains made a jagged outline against the night sky on either side of the highway. "I don't know how much a conversationalist I'd be tonight."

Emme switched on the radio and Starship's *We Built This City* blasted through the car. They drove through the night, the music echoing around them. When they were close to Springdale, Emme glanced over at Finn. "Stace is contacting the bureau."

"The bureau—as in the FBI?"

She nodded. "I appreciate the help you've given me so far. But with the FBI on the case now . . . they'll be prickly about a journalist hanging around."

"I can handle prickly." He turned to her, leaning his cheek against the headrest.

She kept her gaze focused on the road in front of her, but she could feel his eyes on her. A tingle crept up the back of her neck. She liked him looking at her, though she knew she must look like a sweat-stained mess.

Springdale was quiet, just a few groups of tourists around the popular restaurants. The bakery and the house were dark; Jaspar must've gone home early, and she'd forgotten to turn on the outside lights when she'd left that morning. Something moved on the porch. Emme slowed the car to an inchworm-crawl and squinted. There was a figure sitting hunched in the wicker chair beside the front door. Emme's breath quickened, and she glanced in the rearview at her holstered gun on the backseat. Did the Murdocks think they could sneak up on her so easily?

But then the headlights swept over the porch, caught the figure full-on in its gleam. Emme's heart stopped and started again with a thump. She slammed the car into park and flung the door open, not even bothering to close it behind her as she ran the rest of the way down the drive. "Addie?"

She pounded up the steps to the porch. Her sister lifted her pale, tear-stained face and looked at her. "I can't believe you buried Mom without me."

CHAPTER FOURTEEN

Emme blinked. Her mind felt like slush. "What? Are you—I—you weren't here, Addie!"

"I know, but you still should've waited!" Addie swiped at her eyes, smearing her tears across her cheeks.

Emme wanted to seize her sister and crush her with the weight of the relief that flooded into her. *Addie was alive, she was here, she was home.* But instead she stood frozen, and the only thing she could think to say was, "Do you know how many fucking messages I left in at least half a dozen places for you?"

"I didn't get them, okay? It's not my fault."

"You didn't—" Emme shook her head, trying to make things come clear, but everything felt fuzzy. "But you must have, if you're here now."

"I did—I mean, I got the messages, I just didn't get them when you left them." In the darkness, Addie's face glowed like a small moon flickering in and out of the clouds. "And there weren't that many. You should've tried me every hour of every day—"

"Emme? Everything okay?"

Emme whirled around. Finn stood next to the car, just an outline bathed in the headlights. She brought her hand up to shield her eyes from the glare and galloped down the steps to him. "Yes. It's my sister. She's—I wasn't expecting her."

"Oh. I'll just go then." He turned away and then looked back at her. "You sure you're okay?"

"Fine—yes. I'll—be in touch tomorrow." Emme watched him get in his own car and execute a complicated multi-point turn to get out of the driveway. She returned to the Crosstrek, switched off the headlights and turned off the ignition, grabbed her bag from the trunk. When she got back to the porch, Addie was still huddled on the chair. Emme noticed the duffel bag at her feet. She picked it up and unlocked the front door. "Come on. It's cold out. You can keep yelling at me inside."

"I'm not yelling—I'm just upset." Addie pushed herself to her feet. "How do you think you'd feel, Emme? I only found out Mom had died like three days ago. I've been on an off-road Jeep, a train, and three planes in the last thirty-six hours—" Addie slammed the door behind her and stood at the edge of the living room. "What the hell did you do in here?" she asked, walking in between the piles of crap Emme had sorted through. "What is all this stuff?"

"It's Mom's, Addie. Who else's would it be?" Emme dropped the duffel bag on the floor with a loud clunk. "I've been cleaning out the house by myself because you weren't here to help, while also working on a case, and it hasn't been easy."

"I would've been here to do all this if you'd tried harder to get a hold of me—"

"Tried harder? Are you fucking kidding me? Do you know how many different people I talked to at the university?" Emme kicked Addie's bag.

It slid across the floor and knocked over one of the stacks of stuff. "I had to do everything by myself. I was all alone with her in that horrible hospital room. I needed you and I couldn't find you. I was so fucking worried that something had happened to you, and now here you are, blaming me for something that's not even my fault—"

Addie sank down to the floor next to one of the stacks. "I would've been here if I'd known, Emme, you have to believe that," she said, and her voice quavered and broke. She bowed her head into her hands on top of a carefully-balanced pile of photo albums and sobbed, her shoulders shaking so hard the albums leaned precariously. Emme let out a long breath. Everything that had happened that day shuddered through her. That morning—so filled with the promise of a gorgeous hike—seemed like a lifetime ago. She ran her hand over her face and lowered herself to the floor beside Addie.

"I'm sorry I had to cremate her before you got here," she said softly, "but I didn't bury her. Look, her ashes are right over there." Addie raised her head and followed the line of where Emme pointed, to the simple grey box on the claw-footed table by the back wall. "I thought we should decide together where to scatter them. I couldn't—I wouldn't do that without you, Addie." Her sister sniffled and lifted her arms around Emme, buried her face in the side of Emme's neck. Emme squeezed her eyes shut, and suddenly they were kids again, scared and quiet in the backseat of the car as Sunny drove them through sunrises and sunsets across the country. She pulled Addie close, and all the makeshift bolsters she'd put into place to keep herself together crumpled. Her sister felt light and fragile in her arms, like a bird whose wings were too tired to fly. She smoothed Addie's long, messy hair and rubbed her back. "She loved you so much," Emme whispered. "Her last words were about how much she loved us."

"What—did she—say?" Addie hiccupped between her words.

Emme closed her eyes and saw that day clear as a movie behind her eyelids. She'd spent the night in the hospital, failing to sleep in the chair beside Sunny's bed, her body cramped and aching when she sat up that morning. Her mother had been in and out of consciousness for the last day or so, but as the sun rose outside, she lifted her hand to the warmth of it streaming in through the window, turning her palm upward as if to catch the golden rays between her fingers. Emme had gone to her bedside and took her other hand. Sunny turned her head slowly toward her and smiled, her eyes clear. "Emmeline. My bright, beautiful girl. Like sunlight."

Emme raised her mother's hand to her cheek. "You're the sunlight, Mom. It's right there in your name."

"You and Addie. You're my sun, moon, and stars." Her voice was stronger than Emme had heard it in days, and a wisp of hope fluttered inside her. "I love you both so much. I'll love you forever even after I'm gone." Her fingers tightened around Emme's. "Tell me you know that."

"I know, Mom." Emme swallowed hard, fighting back the tears that came anyway. "I love you too."

"Good. Tired," she sighed, very softly, and slipped back into sleep. Emme sat watching her chest move up and down. For the next three days, she watched, waiting for her mother to wake up again, speak more words that she could tuck away to listen to later over and over. But Sunny never opened her eyes again.

"She called us her sun, moon, and stars," Emme told Addie now. "She said she'd love us—even after she's gone."

A fresh wave of sobs tore through Addie, and she shook against Emme. "I should've been here," she murmured, over and over and over until Emme's ears hurt. She pulled away and wiped Addie's face with her thumb, the way she used to do when they were kids and Addie had fallen over a rock in the trail and scraped her knee. "You're here now," she said. "We're together again, and that's what Mom would've wanted."

*****

There was barely anything in the fridge—Emme hadn't gone grocery shopping in days—but she scrounged together a couple of plates of eggs and toast for her and Addie. She carried them out to the living room, and they sat on the floor at the coffee table to eat. Emme watched Addie take tiny, deliberate bites of the scrambled eggs. Her eyes had wide, dark circles around them and her cheekbones seemed more prominent. Beneath her baggy hoodie, Emme caught a flash of her collarbone, protruding beneath her pale skin. She cleared her throat. "How was Tanzania?"

"Fine."

"Is the dig still happening?"

"Yes, but I don't know if I'll go back." Addie jerked her chin toward the piles that lined the floor. "I mean, this might take a while, and I want to be here to help."

Emme took a bite of toast. "I'm happy you're here, Addie, but I don't want you to put your career on hold. Mom wouldn't have wanted that, either. We both knew how important your work is to you."

Addie rested her fork against her plate and looked across the low table at Emme. "What about *your* work? I know how important it is to *you.*"

"I—I put in my notice." She didn't think she could take a discussion about her job with Addie right now, but she was too raw and sore to come up with a good deflection. "I just had too much to deal with—with the house and the bakery, and—"

"You quit your job?" Addie narrowed her eyes at Emme. "But you love your job."

"I did love my job, but now—"

"Oh, wait." Addie folded her arms across her chest and leaned back against the couch. "This is about that case Mom told me about, the last time I talked to her. Before she got too sick to—" Addie shook her head as if to shake the memory out of her mind. "This has nothing to do with Mom."

"It does so." Emme flung her arm wide. "What are we going to do with the house? With the bakery? Someone has to deal with it."

"And now I'm here, so I can deal with it and you can work!" Addie picked up her fork and shoved the last of her eggs in her mouth.

"It's not that simple."

"Hang on." Addie swallowed. "You said you were working on a case earlier. If you quit your job, why are you working?"

Emme sighed. "Because I'm still technically working for a few more weeks, and they found a body in The Narrows, and I was the closest agent to the park." She pinched the bridge of her nose. "And today we found a second body in Kolob Canyon, connected to the first, so now the FBI is coming in, and there's a full-blown investigation."

"Well, now that I'm here, I can help so you can focus on your work." Addie turned to the closest pile and began to look through the folders on top.

I don't want to focus on work! Emme wanted to yell, but she bit her lip instead. And, if she was honest with herself, that wasn't entirely true. She wanted to know who murdered Max and Sarai. She wanted to get justice for them. And if the Murdocks had something to do with it, as she suspected they did, she wanted to take them down. "We'll see." She stood up. "You must be exhausted."

"Actually, it's like eight o'clock in the morning Tanzania time, so I'm wide awake." Addie settled herself cross-legged on the floor. "But you can go to bed if you want." She set one folder aside and opened up another. "What are these? Receipts? Do we need these?"

"And that's why I can't go to bed," Emme snapped. "I have a whole system, Addie. Do you want me to explain it to you right now?"

Addie lowered the folder. "I just want to help, Emme. Please let me help."

"Fine." She pointed to the chaotic pile of stuff she'd set aside for Addie to go through. "You want to help? Start here. I had to process a murder scene today, so I'm going attempt to wash that off me and go to bed. Goodnight."

"Emme—"

But if her sister said more, Emme didn't hear it. She'd already left the room, the thoughts inside her head too loud and jumbled up to hear anything. She stood in the shower for a long, long time, letting the scorching water run over every inch of her skin. This was all she'd wanted, for Addie to come home, to be here to help her with all of Mom's stuff so she could focus on the case, and now that she had it all she could feel was anger, bubbling up inside her like a boiling mud pot. She pressed her palms against the tile and pushed hard, as if she could break the walls of this house down and rebuild it all again from scratch.

Sheer, buoyant relief at having Addie home and a heavy crushing weight that there was now one more thing for her to handle warred for space inside her. *Addie is a grown woman*, she told herself, but she'd always looked out for Addie—the big sister forging through the wilderness, cutting a path for the little sister to easily follow. With Sunny gone, she'd have to hold Addie's hand through the grief and all the tiny day-to-day tasks that were piling up.

When she finally emerged from the shower into the steam-filled bathroom, she didn't return to the living room, though she heard Simon & Garfunkel—one of their mom's favorites—playing softly. She turned off her light and climbed into bed, letting the melancholy *Bridge Over Troubled Water* weave its way into her dreams.

*****

Addie was sound asleep when Emme got up in the morning. She tiptoed to her sister's childhood bedroom door and cracked it open. The bed was still made, neat and tidy—and empty. Emme moved to Sunny's room and peeked in. Addie slept on top of the covers, clutching a pillow to her chest while she breathed, deep and even. Emme watched her for a long moment, everything inside her squeezed tight. She'd slept in their mother's bed, too, for several days after her death, breathing in the floral perfume Sunny always wore that still clung to the bedclothes. She closed the door quietly. Tomorrow she'd pester Addie about getting back on Utah time, but for now, she let her sleep.

In the living room, she could actually see patches of floor that had been covered by crap for days, and the big pile of chaos had been separated into two neat stacks. *Huh.* Emme stood in the middle of the room, surveying the completed work and what was yet to be done. Maybe she wouldn't have to hold Addie's hand so much after all. She blew out a hard exhale. Last night's frustration was still there, though it was hard to pinpoint exactly where to direct it.

She made a pot of coffee, poured herself a cup, and wandered out the front door. The sun crested over the mountains, shedding a cold light over Springdale. Across the driveway, the patio of the bakery was in disarray. Jaspar must've been hard at work yesterday while she'd been in the park. A shadow flitted in and out of view through the bakery's windows. *Jaspar and his early worm*, Emme thought. She slid her feet into her Uggs and padded up the driveway to the front door of the bakery. But when she tugged on the handle, it was locked. She knocked. "Jaspar?"

"I'm right here!"

Emme whirled, spilling coffee on her hand. Jaspar stood behind her, the keys to the bakery dangling from his fingers. "What the—did you come from around back?"

"No, I haven't been inside yet." He pushed past her to the door, but she grabbed his arm to hold him back.

"There's someone in there," she whispered.

"What?"

"I saw a shadow in the window. When I walked up the driveway."

"Oh. It's probably the contractor. I told him he could come in through the back if he got here before me." Jaspar gently shook Emme's hand off his arm and unlocked the door.

"Hang on. Let me go first." She poised on the threshold, uncertain of whether to run back to the house and grab her gun. *Stupid, stupid . . .* she should never leave it behind, not when she was working on a murder case that involved the Murdocks.

From deep inside the bakery, she heard the back door bang open. The sound propelled her forward, through the cafe and into the kitchen . . . . there wasn't time for her gun now. When she emerged onto the back patio, she skidded to a stop and swiveled her gaze in a wide arc. A shadow slipped between the house next door and the one beyond, disappearing so fast that when Jaspar caught up to her a few seconds later, it was gone.

"Did you see that?"

"Did I see what?"

"There was someone here. They ran off that way," she said, pointing to where the shadow had vanished.

"It was probably just a deer." Jaspar shrugged and headed back toward the kitchen.

Emme followed him. "Oh, a deer opened the back door?" She opened and closed all the cabinets that ringed the counters. Nothing seemed out of place . . . but there was also nothing of value in the bakery, not since they'd cleared it out to renovate.

As she reached for the refrigerator door, Jaspar grasped her arm. "Emme, it was nothing. Stop freaking out."

Emme tightened her jaw. He was probably right. The sound she heard could have been a deer's hooves on the deck. But every time she closed her eyes, she saw Sarai's ruined body . . . it was no wonder she was seeing shadows where perhaps there were none. She took a shaky sip of her coffee to calm herself. "Addie showed up last night."

"What?!" Jaspar dropped her arm. "No wonder you're on edge." He craned his neck toward the house, as if he could see Addie inside from where he stood.

"She's still asleep. You can see her later." Emme walked to the back door and peered out. The morning lay still, the sun rising slowly on the mountains. "She's pretty jet-lagged."

"Did she know about Sunny?"

"Yes." Emme took another sip of coffee. "Apparently, she got my messages, but not when I left them?" She shook her head. "We—didn't really get into it last night. There were other things to talk about."

"I bet."

Emme thought back to what Addie had said about not getting the messages. There was a story there, she was sure of it, but whether she would get the whole tale out of her sister remained to be seen. "I'm gonna go back over to the house. If you need me here later, just pop your head in."

"Sure. Hey—" Jaspar switched on Il Duce and started pulling stuff out of the fridge: eggs, butter, a tub of cream cheese. "I heard on the radio that another body was found in the park. Any connection to Max?"

"Yes." Through the open back door, the morning brightened, sending golden beams of light slanting across the kitchen floor. "It was Sarai Murdock. Max's girlfriend."

Jaspar froze, hovering an egg in his hand over the bowl he was about to crack it into. "So—his death definitely wasn't an accident, then?"

"Not an accident." Emme leaned on the doorframe and watched the light shift across the floor. "It's an official ISB investigation now. Which means . . ."

"You can't talk to me about it." Jaspar clicked his tongue and cracked the egg on the side of the bowl. "Got it."

"I'll see you later." Emme walked out onto the patio and stood still for a moment, fixing her gaze on the brush that stretched from the back of the house to the base of the mountains. It would be easy for someone to lurk there, watching the house under the cover of the tall grass and tangled bushes. Emme shivered. She needed to double-check the locks in the house; Sunny had always been lax about it, but now with Addie

home, she had more to protect. As she climbed the steps to the front
porch, her feet felt like they were encased in lead. There were too many
things to think about. Her brain was a game of Whack-A-Mole: knock
one thing down only to have another pop right back up. She sat down in
the chair on the porch that she'd found Addie in last night and looked
out at the mountains. They were tipped with red-gold morning light
now, a moment of grace that Emme wished could last forever before she
had to go back inside.

CHAPTER FIFTEEN

E mme didn't need the medical examiner to tell her Sarai's cause of death—knife to the throat—but later that day, she found herself back at Rose Young's door in St. George. She didn't crack a Brigham Young joke this time, but she could not resist digging a little. "You know this is Max Kerchek's girlfriend," she said as Rose led her to the table where Sarai lay. "So his death was likely not an accident."

"I stand by my ruling," Rose said, each word clipped short. "In fact, he could have murdered Sarai himself and then fallen to his death."

"That's unlikely, given everything I've learned in my investigation." Emme folded her arms. "In fact, I believe Max was struck in the back of the head and thrown into the Virgin River—*before* Sarai was murdered."

"Well, that is for you to discern. I am not inclined to change my ruling yet. This body, however," Rose peeled the sheet away, revealing Sarai's head, neck, and shoulders, "was without a doubt a victim of homicide."

No shit, Sherlock, but Emme just pressed her lips together. After all, she was the Sherlock. Rose should be the annoying Watson, but right now she was feeling more like the Moriarty.

A knock on the door echoed in the cold, grey room, but before Rose could answer it, the door pushed open. "Hello? Ms. Young?" A Black woman in a crisp maroon suit stepped into the room, her brown eyes bright behind a pair of tortoise-shell glasses. "I'm from the FBI. Claire Hughes." She stretched her hand out.

Rose held her two blue-gloved hands up. "I'll hold off on shaking your hand at the moment, Agent Hughes."

Emme fought the urge to roll her eyes and stepped forward to grasp the FBI agent's hand. "Emmeline Helliwell, from the National Park Service. I'm the one who found the body."

"Ah, yes. Eustace Pompey spoke very highly of you." Agent Hughes pumped Emme's hand once, firmly, and let go. Emme stood rooted, her gaze fixed on Claire Hughes' face while the FBI agent stared right back. She'd been here before, knee-deep in a case when the FBI walked in, yanked her out, and stomped on all of her hard work. Agent Hughes pushed her glasses up onto her head, where they nestled into her crown of hair, worn natural and pulled back away from her face with a slim maroon headband that matched her suit. "Let's see our victim, Ms. Young."

Emme shadowed the FBI agent as Rose Young walked her around Sarai's body, half listening to the medical examiner while watching Agent Hughes. It was rare that a female FBI agent came in to assist the ISB; usually the agents were brash men who wanted to bluster their way into the wilderness and prove they could start a fire with only two sticks of wood. She tried to go into every partnership with an open mind, but she'd been burned too many times for optimism.

When Rose lowered the sheet to Sarai's waist—or what was left of it—Emme got a small squiggle of satisfaction at Agent Hughes' sharp intake of breath. "What happened here?"

"Mountain lion," Emme answered.

Rose pursed her lips. "Agent Helliwell is correct," she said. Her tone betrayed just how much it cost her to admit that. "The predator most likely tore through her stomach and ate her heart first." She swished her hand over what remained of Sarai's chest. "I believe most of this damage was done by the action of the lion dragging the body. It's also possible that it was a mother feeding her cubs. They'd go for smaller parts of the body."

Agent Hughes peered over Sarai's ruined torso at Emme. "Did you encounter the mountain lion when you found the body?"

Emme shook her head. "If it was still in the vicinity, we probably scared it off. There were three of us, and mountain lions are too smart for those odds."

"I didn't realize mountain lions were that intelligent." Agent Hughes gently rotated Sarai's left arm so that the word Slut flashed out at them, the edges of each letter blackened by necrosis. "Was she alive when these cuts happened?"

"Yes, she was." Rose turned Sarai's other arm, where Whore was carved in deep. "I believe these wounds were self-inflicted."

"Self-inflicted?" Emme raised her eyebrow. "How do you figure that?"

Rose uncurled Sarai's fingers so that her hand lay flat, palm up, and pointed to the slice from the base of her knuckle to her wrist that Emme had noticed when she and Chenoa were examining the body. "This wound appears to be from whatever it was that she was holding to make the cuts. You see there's one on her other hand too, and the cuts on her right arm are cruder, jerkier—as if someone righthanded was writing with their left."

"But she was bound." Agent Hughes traced the raw, red mark on Sarai's wrist.

"I surmise that she was made to inflict the wounds on herself, and then bound," Rose said.

"What about the cuts on her chest?" Emme asked. "Do you think she did that to herself, too?"

"What cuts on her chest?" Agent Hughes bent lower over the body, peering at the place where strips of flesh hung from exposed bone.

"Look." Emme pointed where the faint outline of the random letters could be seen. "Something was spelled out there, too."

"Huh." Agent Hughes looked up at Rose. "Was that self-inflicted as well?"

I just asked her that, Emme thought, pressing her lips tight together to prevent herself from saying it out loud.

"No, I don't think it was. I think that one was done postmortem." Rose moved to the lower half of Sarai's body and pulled the sheet down, exposing her to her knees.

"Was she—" Emme began, but the same question came out of Agent Hughes' mouth, drowning out Emme's voice.

"Was she sexually assaulted?"

"It's hard to tell, given the damage the mountain lion did to her extremities." Rose turned back to the computer sitting on the counter that ran along the back of the cold, grey room. "I did find semen in her cavity, but that could have been from consensual sex with her boyfriend—"

"The other victim," Emme supplied, curling her lip with satisfaction when Rose let out a little exasperated sigh at the interruption.

"Yes, the other victim. I've sent the sample to the lab for DNA testing, but it could be weeks before we get the results back. You'll read this all in my report," Rose added. It was an obvious dismissal, and she did not even turn around to tell them goodbye.

"Great. Agent Helliwell, will you walk out with me?"

The moment the door closed behind them, leaving Rose Young inside her steel box and the two agents out in the hallway, Agent Hughes planted her hands on her hips. "I certainly hope her report is better than her manners."

Emme raised an eyebrow. She felt the same way about Rose Young, but she was not giving this FBI agent an inch before she had the full measure of her. Agent Hughes cleared her throat. "You examined Max Kerchek's body, yes?"

"That's right." Emme leaned against the concrete wall. "But he was already released back to his family, so all I can show you is the report."

"I've seen the report. I had it sent over as soon as I was assigned to the case." She began walking up the long hallway, the heels of her pointed-toe flats clicking on the floor. Emme fell into step beside her. "I have to make a confession."

"I'm not a priest."

Agent Hughes snorted. She glanced sideways at Emme. "I've never set foot in a National Park."

Emme wasn't sure what she'd expected Agent Hughes to confess, but it wasn't that. "Really? I take it you didn't grow up in Utah. You can't spit in this state without hitting a National Park."

"Detroit, and then did my undergrad and training in DC. So not exactly a bastion of wilderness." Her slim black bag, which was stuffed with folders, slipped from her shoulder and she hoisted it back up. "I would not have been able to identify that a mountain lion had cached the remains."

Emme didn't answer. No, she would not have, but she'd danced this waltz before, the one where an FBI agent romances her with compliments only to completely shut her out of a case down the line. They reached the end of the corridor and climbed the stairs to exit out into the parking lot, emerging into the sunshine. It was a bright contrast to the darkened gloom of the morgue. Emme pointed down the line of cars. "I'm down that end."

"And I'm right here." Agent Hughes jerked her chin to a spot close to the door. "I understand you live in Springdale? I'm staying there as well. Let's meet up a bit later to share our notes."

"That's fine. I'd like to see what you've got so far." It couldn't be much, given that she'd only had the case for a day. "Where are you staying?"

Agent Hughes pulled her phone out and scrolled through for a moment. "The Cliffrose? Do you know it?"

"Of course. That's the nicest hotel in Springdale. It's right next to the park entrance."

"Well, what do you know, the FBI didn't cheap out for once." Agent Hughes dug her car keys out of her bag. "Shall we meet at five? In the lobby?"

"Let's meet at Anthera," Emma said. "That's the restaurant in the hotel. They have a nice patio with some secluded tables where we can spread out undisturbed."

"Sounds good. See you later, Agent Helliwell." She clicked her key, and a nearby car unlocked in answer.

Emme bit back her automatic reply of "call me Emme"; it would be easier when the inevitable betrayal happened if things were still formal between them. She watched Agent Hughes get into her car and drive away before starting toward her own car, shaking her head as she walked. She already had one foot out of the door of the ISB. So why did she still feel so territorial?

*****

Agent Hughes was already seated at a table for four in a shady corner of the patio at Anthera when Emme arrived. The maitre d' pointed her out and Emme wove her way around the tables, most of which were unoccupied this early in the evening. The tourists were all still in the park, catching the last rays of sunlight before darkness fell.

"Hello," she said when she got to the table. Agent Hughes, who was bent over a map spread out before her, jerked her head up, nearly knocking over the glass of red wine next to her elbow.

"Agent Helliwell, good to see you." Agent Hughes half-stood and motioned to the three empty chairs around her. "Please, please take a seat. I hope you don't mind, I started without you," she said, picking up the glass of wine and taking a healthy sip. She raised a finger in the air and a waiter materialized at the table.

"Something to drink, miss?" he asked Emme.

"Sparkling water with lime, please." She wanted a perfectly clear head for this meeting. She couldn't risk letting her guard down as she had the other night at Cap's Landing with Finn. After the waiter had brought her water and laid two menus on the table, Emme pointed to the map. "What's that?"

"*These* are all the areas that the Warriors for Armageddon are known to have outposts."

Emme stared at the map. Thin red lines crisscrossed the state of Utah, down into Arizona and Texas, then across into Colorado, Wyoming, and Idaho. Several small bursts of red pen bloomed in rural parts of each state. "I didn't realize they were so far-flung. I thought they were only in Redwater."

"That's their base." Agent Hughes waved her hand in a circle, encompassing the square map. "But their reach goes much farther. We think they might also have a compound in Mexico, but that hasn't been confirmed." She leaned her elbows up onto the table, crinkling the map a little. "When did you first become aware of the Warriors, Agent Helliwell?"

Emme fixed her gaze on the corner of Arizona where the Grand Canyon was located. "When I worked the Hannah DeLeo case," she said.

"Ah. Yes. Director Pompey mentioned you were on that case." Emme could feel the FBI agent's eyes on her, but she did not look up. "You were one of the rangers who answered the domestic disturbance call, weren't you?"

"I was." Emme took a sip of her water, but the cool liquid could not dispel the dryness in the back of her throat.

"Well, that's got to be weighing on you." Agent Hughes settled back in her seat, folding her arms over her chest. Now Emme did look up, expecting to see judgement on the FBI agent's face, but the only expression there was a softly questioning one, and she realized that Claire Hughes was trying to take the measure of her, just the same as Emme was with her. "I'm not going to say that wasn't a screw-up, but if every agent quit the first time they screwed up, we'd have no one left."

So Stace had told her, then. Great. The fact that she had one foot out the door of the ISB was bound to make the FBI more territorial over the case. Emme pressed her palms flat on the table. "I can have Stace assign another agent to the case, if you'd prefer."

"No, I would not prefer. I want you." Agent Hughes took a sip of wine. "I understand you grew up in Springdale. How many times have you been inside Zion National Park?"

Emme shrugged. "I can't even count. We used hike in the park nearly every Sunday when I was a teen."

"And the first time I ever went hiking was when I moved to Salt Lake, two years ago." Agent Hughes shifted forward a bit. "Black people have historically not been very welcome in the wild places of this country."

"Very true, unfortunately." Emme spread her fingers wide on the map, so that Utah's "Mighty Five" National Parks were captured beneath them. "The Park Service has been working hard over the last several years to change that."

"That's good to hear." Agent Hughes nodded once and raised her wine glass to the red cliffs that lay just beyond the patio, their faces jeweled by the dying sunlight. "Regardless, this is your expertise. Crime scenes that have been ruined by wildlife, remote places that most people don't know about—that's your wheelhouse. Mine, however, is *this*." She smoothed the map out. Emme yanked her hands off the table and looked down at the map. Beyond Redwater lay so many other red splotches hidden amongst tiny towns and unincorporated territories. Abraham Murdock was like a spider and the West was his web, his long legs reaching out to ensnare more and more people. "I did my graduate thesis on cults in America. I've been aware of the Warriors for more than five years and seriously investigating them for the last two—long before Hannah DeLeo was murdered."

Emme tilted back in her chair and examined Agent Claire Hughes in this new light. She had readily admitted her shortcoming—something that Emme had in spades—and laid out the knowledge that she possessed and Emme didn't. However . . .

"Have you ever met Abraham Murdock?" Emme asked.

"I have not, although I feel I know him from the interviews I've done with ex-members of the cult."

"Well, I have. He's a lot smarter than most people would give him credit for."

"Oh, I'm aware of how cunning he is." Agent Hughes took another sip of wine and raised her hand to call the waiter over. "It's how he's able to recruit so many people into the Warriors."

Emme raised an eyebrow. "Most of the members are born into it. They don't know anything different."

"You would be surprised by how many people they recruit." Claire tapped her finger on a red splotch in Colorado. "They have a church here that you would think is just like any other church from the outside, and new members join every month. We even think they have a school somewhere, though we haven't been able to locate it."

The waiter arrived at their table and Agent Hughes ordered a burger, Emme the fish tacos. She looked beyond the railing of the patio into the canyon. The sun had dropped behind the cliffs, turning the sky a deep, dusky blue. Day hikers would be hurrying to the park's exit, and overnighters would be cooking their dinner over their campfires.

"So what are your theories?" Agent Hughes asked, bringing her attention back to the table. "About Sarai?"

"And Max," Emme said. "We can't forget him, even though his death looked so different from hers. But they are connected."

"Do you think he was killed first to get him out of the way while she was tortured?"

A woman passing by their table gave them a quizzical look, her eyes wide at the word *tortured*. Agent Hughes didn't seem to notice, but Emme waited until the woman was well out of earshot before she answered. "Yes, I think that's a plausible theory. As for who . . . it has to be someone from the Warriors."

"Well, that still leaves a pretty long suspect list."

Emme balled her hands into fists. "I met with a woman earlier this week—someone who'd gotten out of the Warriors." She dug her nails into her palms as she pictured Lara in the Garden, being fed one bowl of slop every day. "She told me that Sarai had been married when she was eighteen, and that her husband died a couple of years ago. That would mean Sarai was back on the marriage market. If there was someone who wanted to marry her, and found out about Max . . ."

"The murderer could be a jealous rival," Claire said, picking up Emme's train of through. "That would explain the choice of words like 'slut' and 'whore' on her body. I'd like to interview that contact, if you can arrange it."

"That'll be difficult." Emme chewed her lip. "The Warriors found her right after I met with her. Took her back to Redwater and threw her in—"

"—the Garden. Damn." The waiter arrived with their food. Agent Hughes waited for him to leave before she leaned forward, her face hard and determined. "That's why I want to move fast on this case, get enough evidence to get into Redwater with a search warrant. There are people being held there against their will that we need to get out, like your contact."

"If they haven't already killed her." The thought chilled Emme deep beneath her skin. "Abraham Murdock doesn't look kindly on betrayal. If he thought Sarai had betrayed her family, he might have gone so far to order her killing."

"Blood atonement."

"Blood what?"

"Blood atonement." Agent Hughes dipped a fry into the little silver pot of ketchup that had come on the side of her burger and popped it into her mouth. "It's when an apostate—an unbeliever—is made to repent for their sins. The price is—"

"Their life," Emme breathed. "Yes, I could see Murdock buying into that."

Agent Hughes pressed her lips in a straight line while she chewed her fry. "The thing is, I haven't heard of any other blood atonement killings in the Warriors. It doesn't mean there hasn't been, I just have no evidence of one. So for now, we work both theories: jealous rival and blood atonement."

Before Emme could answer, a buzz vibrated her chair. It took her a moment to realize it was her phone in her bag that she'd slung over the back of her seat. "Excuse me."

Finn O'Malley, read the name on her screen. She hit decline, but before she could put the phone away, a text from him popped up.

Hey, just wanted to make sure you were OK after yesterday.

A second later, another text. *Also have some thoughts I'd love to run by you.*

Then a third. *Anyway, call me when you're free. :-)*

"Everything okay?"

Emme looked up from the phone. "Yes—fine. Just—someone."

"Ah, *someone*." Agent Hughes grinned and popped another fry into her mouth.

Emme shook her head. "Not like that." Though there was a little swoop in her chest when she'd seen his name pop up, it was followed by a drop that bottomed out in her gut. She'd have to push Finn off the case now. He wouldn't be happy about that . . . and she wasn't sure how she felt about it herself.

Her phone buzzed again. "I think he likes you," Agent Hughes said, but when Emme pulled her phone out again, it wasn't Finn's name at the top of the text bubble.

There's no food in the house. What have you been eating? I'm going to the store. Any requests?

"No, it's my sister," Emme said, her mind scattering between the two conversations. She had a whole grocery list in her head, but she just hadn't gotten around to shopping or even writing the list down. *Can you wait until I get home? There's a bunch of stuff we need.*

How long will you be?

I don't know—another hour, maybe?

Three dots bounced.

I'm just going to go now & get what I need. You can make a separate trip if I miss anything.

Emme gritted her teeth and couldn't prevent a little growl from escaping her throat. It was just like Addie, charging ahead without thinking about the people around her. She started to type back, then erased it, rewrote it, erased it again and clicked her phone off.

"Sorry."

"No problem. I have a sister too."

"Does yours drive you crazy?"

"Oh yeah." Agent Hughes pushed her nearly empty plate away from her and settled back in her chair to finish her wine. "But she also lives in Boston, and I miss her to death. Where's your sister?"

"Right now? Just up the road at my house. But until yesterday she was in Tanzania."

"Tanzania? Christ. What was she doing there? You must've missed her something fierce."

There weren't words to describe the hole inside her while Addie had been away. But now that she was back, that hole hadn't been filled; so many new worries had appeared in Addie's absence that she felt like a leaky spigot. "She was on an archaeological dig. Yeah, I missed her." Emme slid her plate off to the side. "What else do you have on the Warriors?"

Agent Hughes took a tablet from her bag, tapped it awake, and started scrolling. "These are some of the top dogs in the hierarchy who may have been involved in Sarai's killing." She handed the tablet across the table to Emme.

She clicked through the pictures, taken from high above and far away by the zoom lens of a drone. "Surprised your drone wasn't shot down."

"It was. We've lost three over Redwater."

Emme snorted. She recognized Mark David and a few other Horsemen who had confronted her the other day. "Good luck trying to question them."

"Let me try to figure that out." Claire took the tablet back. "You work on what you know: the lay of the land, where Max might've died in relation to where Sarai was found, their movements in the park."

"I can do that." A twisted feeling wrapped itself around her insides. She was tied to this case now by connections that she couldn't sever easily.

The waiter passed by their table and she flagged him down. "Could I have an Angel's Envy, neat?"

Agent Hughes raised her eyebrow. Emme rolled her eyes. "I guess I'm in it for the long haul now," she said, "even if that means going past my supposed last day with the ISB."

The corner of Agent Hughes' mouth curled up. She stretched her hand across the table. "Welcome aboard, Agent Helliwell."

Emme took her hand and shook it firmly. "Please, call me Emme."

The half-smile on the FBI agent's face turned into a full grin. "And you can call me Claire."

CHAPTER SIXTEEN

The piles in the living room had grown exponentially by the time Emme got back from dinner with Claire. The Foo Fighters were blaring from Addie's phone, and Emme followed the sound of it to the kitchen, where she found her sister putting groceries away. "Hey! How was dinner? I'm so glad Sol Foods is open late now. They used to close at seven, remember?" She slid a carton of almond milk onto the shelf of the refrigerator door. "I didn't get cow's milk. Do you still drink it? I mostly drank goat's milk in Tanzania, but the store didn't have it, so I got almond. I know, almond milk is bad for the environment, but they didn't have the kind of coconut milk I like. I got more eggs, too, for breakfast. I was going to get granola but holy crap, the amount of preservatives in it! I'm going to make some tomorrow."

Emme pinched the bridge of her nose. "Did you, like, drink a gallon of coffee?"

"No." Addie closed the refrigerator door and hung the empty canvas grocery bags on the nail by the door where Sunny had always kept them. "I guess I'm still on Tanzania time. I'm not tired at all."

"Clearly."

Addie leaned against the counter. "So, how was dinner? Did you make progress on the case?"

"Fine. Yes. I can't really talk about it. Can you turn the music down?" Addie made a face. "No, it helps me think. I moved some stuff around in the living room and called Goodwill to schedule a pick up, but they can't come until next week."

"What stuff?"

"Stuff you'd marked donate that I want to keep." Addie moved into the living room.

Emme followed her and stopped in front of a box that she'd written DONATE on in black Sharpie. Addie had crossed it out and scribbled KEEP on the top flap of the box. "You want to keep Mom's bobblehead collection? You always said they creeped you out."

"Some of them are rare. We should at least look into selling them to a collector."

"No." Emme shook her head. "I looked them up on eBay. They're not worth anything."

"How can you say that?" Addie's voice rose into shrill territory. "They were worth something to Mom, and now you just want to throw them out?"

"Addie." Emme caught her arm. "We can't keep everything. Not if we want to sell the house."

"Who says we want to sell?"

"Who's going to live here? You?" Emme shook Addie's arm a little harder than she intended, and Addie yanked out of her grasp.

"Maybe—why not? I could live here."

"What about your work? You're just going to turn down the next dig opportunity that comes along?" Emme followed Addie as she spiraled around the living room, stomping over and around the piles of crap on the floor.

"Well, what about you?" Addie whirled and faced Emme, her hands on her hips. "You just quit your job. Where else do you have to go?"

"I—" Emme pressed her lips tight. The truth was that she didn't have anywhere else to go, but clinging to the house felt like moving backward, not forward. But instead of answering Addie's question, she said, "The bobbleheads go."

"No, they stay." Addie's face settled into a hard expression.

"Addie . . ." Emme trailed off, staring at her sister. Dark circles smudged the skin around Addie's eyes, and shadows shone in the hollows of her cheeks. Emme softened and dropped onto the arm of the couch. "What's really going on?"

Addie's mouth quivered and she bit down hard on her bottom lip. "Nothing," she whispered, a lie so obvious it seemed tangible in the air between them. Emme wanted to hug her so tight it would break all the tension into a million pieces, tell her that she didn't have to keep it together, that her big sister was here to catch her if she needed to fall apart . . . she reached her arms out, but before she could touch Addie, the Foo Fighters cut out and her sister's phone buzzed. Addie crossed into the kitchen to grab it, but when she looked at the screen, she yanked her hand back, recoiling as if she'd been about to pick a flower and realized it was poison ivy. Emme watched her click the phone off, declining the call.

"Who was that?"

"No one. Just spam." She tucked the phone into her pocket and grabbed a bag of trail mix from the counter. "I'm going to read in my room," she tossed over her shoulder as she shuffled down the hallway to her bedroom, leaving Emme in the kitchen to wonder who the hell had called to make Addie react that way.

*****

Her sister was still asleep when Emme rose the next morning and padded to the kitchen to make a pot of coffee. As she stared out the kitchen window, waiting for it to brew, an unfamiliar car rolled to a stop in front of the bakery. Emme tensed and was halfway to reaching for her gun when the driver's side door opened and Finn climbed out. He walked to the front door of the bakery and stopped when he realized it was closed and dark. Emme relaxed and hurried out of the house. The chill morning air wrapped like a cold cloak around her, tingling her nose.

Finn spotted her and jogged to meet her halfway down the driveway. "Morning! Did you get my text?"

"From last night? Yes—I'm sorry I didn't respond—"

"No, from this morning." Finn gestured back to his car. "I'm heading into the park and thought you might want to join me."

"I had my phone silenced. I'm sorry."

"That's okay. I can wait while you change—"

"Yeah, I don't think I'm able to go with you." A gust of wind breathed down the driveway. Emme shivered. "It's freezing out here. Come on in. I just made coffee."

Inside the house, Emme saw Finn's gaze sweep over the chaos in the living room. "Sorry about the mess. It's—"

Finn held his hand up. "No need to explain. I helped my dad clean out my grandfather's house after he passed and trust me, it looked worse."

Emme gave him a grateful smile, which he returned. They stood there for a moment until Emme realized she was still braless in her pajamas. She folded her arms across her chest and turned away to go into the kitchen. Finn followed her, and she could feel his eyes on her as she reached for two mugs and poured the coffee. She handed him a mug and slid the sugar bowl across the counter. "I think the only milk we have is almond. My sister did the grocery shopping yesterday."

"That's fine." Finn opened the fridge and took out the carton of almond milk Addie had placed there the night before. "How's everything with your sister?"

"Okay. I mean, as okay as it can be." Emme took a sip of coffee. "Listen, Finn . . ."

"Uh-oh." Finn poured some almond milk into his coffee and put it back in the fridge. "I don't like the sound of that."

Emme straightened her spine. "I can't discuss the case with you anymore, now that it's an official investigation."

Finn rested his back against the fridge. "Shit. I thought we made a pretty good team."

"Well, that was before I was assigned an FBI partner."

"I know the FBI can be prickly, but—"

Emme held her hand up. "No buts. I'm sorry. I don't want to risk . . ." She trailed off. There was a myriad of things she didn't want to risk, but to reveal them to Finn felt too personal, too soon.

"We could just go hiking," Finn said. "Not discuss the case at all—"

"You know that wouldn't happen," Emme said with a little shake of her head. "I can't step into the park right now without being in investigative mode. Besides, Claire—the FBI agent—wants me to go back to where Max was found and see if anything stands out to me."

"So let me go with you. I'll leave you alone to do your thing—"

"Oh really? You think you're capable of keeping your mouth shut and not asking any questions?" Emme cocked her head and stared at him.

"I—" Finn sighed. "Yeah, I probably wouldn't be able to do that."

"Exactly. You're a journalist. It's in your DNA." Emme took a sip of coffee. "I can't go till tomorrow anyway. I've got a Zoom with Stace this morning and need to organize my notes—" Out of the corner of her eye, Emme saw Addie's bedroom door creak open. Her sister appeared in the hallway, sleep-tousled and groggy, and shuffled toward the kitchen. "Sorry, did we wake you?"

"That's okay. I need to get back on mountain time. Do I smell coffee?"

"There's some left." Emme grabbed a mug. "Finn, this is my sister Addie."

Addie crossed her arms and leaned against the door frame. "You were the guy in the car with my sister the other night," she said, narrowing her eyes at him. "Are you a ranger?"

"No, I'm a journalist." Finn stretched his hand out. Addie waited a beat before she shook it, still appraising him with narrowed eyes. "I'm doing a podcast about the case."

"Ugh, *everyone* has a podcast these days. It's so banal."

"Addie!" Emme thrust the mug of coffee at her, splashing some onto the floor.

"No, it's okay," Finn said, laughing. "She's not exactly wrong."

"I thought you weren't allowed to talk to journalists," Addie said to Emme as she added a glug of almond milk to her coffee.

"She's not." Finn put his empty mug in the sink. "Which is why I'm leaving." He moved toward the front door. Emme pushed past her sister to follow him out. At the door, he turned. "Let me know if you become available to talk. Even just to be your sounding board."

Emme smiled but didn't answer. She waved at him as he walked up the drive, closed the door, and whirled around to find Addie eyeing her from the doorway of the kitchen. "What the hell was that?"

Addie shrugged and walked into the living room. "What was what?"

Emme blocked her path. "You know what I mean. Why were you so rude to him?"

"Why do you care, if you're not allowed to talk to him?" Addie sipped her coffee, looking pointedly at her over the rim of her mug. "Are you into him?"

"No, I am not into him," Emme said, planting her hands on her hips.

"You are such a liar." Addie settled onto the couch and kicked her feet up onto the coffee table. "By the way, I changed my phone number. I'll text you the new number."

Emme dropped her arms along her sides. "Why—"

Addie stood up. "You know, I'm still tired. I think I'll go back to bed for a bit." She grabbed her coffee and turned on her heel, her tousled hair bouncing as she retreated to her bedroom. Emme watched her go. Clearly, the phone call last night had not been spam. But whoever it was, it didn't seem like she was going to get any kind of explanation out of her sister.

*****

The sun was cresting over the mountains when Emme pulled into the Temple of Sinawava parking lot, the iron-grey dawn slowly giving way to a brilliant blue morning sky. The river would still be icy cold this early, without the warming glow of full sun, but she wanted to beat the bulk of the crowds. And indeed, as she hustled along the Riverside Walk, following the twist and bend of the Virgin River as it rushed over itself, she passed only a handful of people. But when she reached the end of the trail, a familiar, copper-haired figure sat on the low stone wall that marked the beginning of The Narrows.

Finn smiled brightly as she approached. "Good morning!"

She stopped and slid her pack to the ground. "What the hell are you doing here?"

Finn shrugged, a gesture so calculatedly casual that Emme balled her hand into a fist to keep from punching him in the shoulder. "Keeping you company. They say to never go hiking alone."

"Who says that? The whole point of hiking is to get away from other people." Emme glared at him. "Also, that does not apply to rangers."

Finn stood up. "Well, I'm here, and I'm heading into The Narrows with or without you. So I can either accompany you, or we can try to ignore each other."

"Let's ignore each other." Emme yanked her hiking poles out of her pack and started to adjust them to the height she preferred. Finn shouldered his bag and climbed over the wall, paused on the rocky shore, and looked back at her. Taking a deep breath, Emme followed him over the wall. "Fine," she said as she marched past him, digging her poles into the gravelly ground. "Hope you can keep up."

Cold morning light filtered into the canyon, slicing the river into stripes of sun and shadow. The sliver of ground that ran along the river was too narrow for the two of them to walk side by side, so Emme forged out in front. She could hear Finn's footsteps close on her heels and the crunch of rocky soil beneath his hiking poles in rhythm with hers. When at last they were forced to step into the water, Emme splashed ahead, but in the wideness of the river, Finn was able to fall into step beside her, matching her stride for stride. A thick, uncomfortable silence stretched between them, one that Emme was not inclined to break. She kept her eyes trained on the river that rushed around her legs, stepping carefully over the slick, treacherous rocks.

But when they reached Mystery Canyon, a mile and a half in, Finn halted so suddenly that Emme jerked to a stop and finally looked at him. She followed his gaze up to the thin ribbon of water that tumbled over the ruddy cliffs into the river below. This early in the morning, the cliffs were empty of canyoneers; it was too early for them to have completed the ten-mile trek to the top of the cliff, where they would rappel down into the river. Emme glanced at Finn; his face was rapturous as he took in the beauty of The Narrows, and for the first time that morning, Emme inhaled deeply. Even her annoyance at his presence couldn't dispel the awe she always felt in this canyon. When they set off again, the silence between them was more companionable, filled with the sounds of water and morning birdsong.

"I knew you had to hike in the river, but I guess I didn't realize how *in the river* you actually get," Finn said as they entered Orderville Canyon. The water sloshed above their calves as zebra-striped canyon walls rose on either side of them, the color variance from the minerals deposited over thousands of years by seeping water.

"I thought you'd hiked The Narrows before." Emme walked a few steps away from him, into a patch of sunlight that slanted in above.

"First time," Finn said. "I've been to Zion before, but the last time I was here The Narrows was closed because of rain." He joined Emme in the beam of light and tilted his face up to the sky. "But you couldn't ask for better weather today."

Weather changes fast in The Narrows, Emme thought, but she kept the thought to herself. She let the sunlight bathe her skin for a moment longer, closing her eyes. But behind her eyelids, she saw Max's corpse, drifting down the river to the spot where he snagged on a rock. Her eyes flew open. She was here for a purpose, not for a leisurely hike. "Stop distracting me," she snapped as she dug her poles into the riverbed. "I have a job to do."

"How can you possibly move through this canyon without being distracted by the scenery?" Finn tried to catch up to her, but Emme kept herself one step ahead.

"If I was alone, I wouldn't be." They crested over a small rise as the canyon walls closed in on them. When they descended, the water level rose to thigh-high.

"Don't you ever work with other people—rangers, agents—in your job?"

"Of course I do." Emme skirted around a large boulder in the middle of the river. "The whole reason you shouldn't be here is because I'm working with someone on this case now."

"Ah yes, the FBI." Finn kicked his foot, splashing water in a wide arc. "A journalist's nemesis. What's the agent they sent down here like?"

Emme hunched one shoulder. "She seems very smart. An expert in cults. She's been investigating the Warriors for Armageddon for years."

"But does she have firsthand experience with them like you?" One of Finn's poles got stuck in between two rocks and he paused to yank it out. Emme didn't wait for him, but he caught up to her a beat later.

"You mean has she been stupid enough to drive into Redwater and confront Abraham Murdock directly? No." The canyon dropped into shadow as the cliffs rose so high above them that they blotted out the blue sky. They'd reached Orderville Junction, where the water level lowered and the walls surrounded them like an embrace. The spot where Max's body had been found was still another mile or so ahead.

"Come on, Emme, you're not stupid. Stubborn, maybe, but definitely not stupid."

Emme didn't answer, just kept her gaze fixed forward to the river's path. She'd been stupid when she believed Eli at the campground, stupid enough that she hadn't recognized she was being gaslit. "I'm sure she'll have her own run-in with the Murdocks' soon." She glanced sidelong at him. "Maybe you should be shadowing her instead of me. She's the one who's going to finish this case."

"Why's that?" They turned a bend and the river deepened again. "Because you quit your job?"

Emme slammed to a halt and twisted to look at him. "Who told you that?"

Finn scratched his nose. Emme knew that tell, when someone didn't want to admit something. Finally, he said, "I spoke to Stace—Director Pompey."

"You talked to—are you kidding me?" Emme's voice bounced off the red-rock walls, echoing through the canyon. Anyone downstream of them would surely hear, but she didn't care. She pinched her forehead. "Why the hell were you talking about me to him, anyway?"

"I called him to discuss the Hannah DeLeo case. Remember how I'm working on a piece about the case? How my entire livelihood depends on it?" Finn stamped one of his poles against a rock in the river. "You're not the only one who cares about these cases, Emme. Who wants justice for the victims just as much as you do? Why do you think I'm out here?"

"He had no right to tell you I'd given my notice," Emme snapped. She stomped away, but the water slowed her down so that it wasn't nearly as dramatic as she would've liked.

"He didn't. It slipped out. He seems to care a lot about you," Finn said, pushing himself to catch up to her. "He sounded pretty broken up that you were leaving the ISB."

"This is none of your business," Emme seethed. She would have words with Stace when she got back into cell service. The canyon narrowed into a slot and she plunged in, glad to have a chance to put distance between herself and Finn. She let the hush of the slot canyon close in around her, dulling everything to a soft hum, trying to dampen her fiery thoughts.

"Holy shit, this is really narrow," came Finn's voice from behind her.

"Hence the name *The Narrows*," Emme tossed back.

"Why are you quitting your job?"

"We are not talking about this." She sidled beneath a jagged rock and around a curve in the rock wall. She couldn't look back; it was too tight to turn around, but she could feel Finn right behind her, hear his labored breath.

"Is it because of what happened to Hannah DeLeo?"

Though she couldn't see his face, the notes in his tone were soft and sympathetic. To her absolute horror, hot tears prickled the corners of her eyes. She dashed them away with shaking fingers, hoping that Finn wouldn't see the gesture.

"How long are you going to martyr yourself for that one mistake?" In the closeness of the slot canyon, Finn's voice felt everywhere, echoing off every surface and surrounding her like a bind. She tried to quicken her pace, but the undulating walls made it impossible. "You have to forgive yourself."

Emme stopped, so suddenly that Finn stepped on her heel. "Tell that to Hannah. She's dead because of my mistake. And maybe if she hadn't died, Sarai would have been able to get out more easily, and she'd still be alive today, too."

"Are you seriously blaming yourself for a sequence of events that probably would've been set into motion with or without you?" Finn was so close that she felt his breath on the back of her neck. She shivered, and she wasn't sure if it was from his question or their nearness. She didn't answer, just pushed ahead and emerged out of the slot into the expanse of the river.

"That's where Max was found," she said, pointing to the opposite shore.

Finn stepped up beside her. "What are you hoping to find?"

To be honest, Emme wasn't entirely sure. Any physical evidence would have been washed away by now, or trampled by hikers. But Claire had told her to *get the lay of the land*, and Emme wanted to prove her usefulness. As she stood staring at the spot where, days ago, she'd crouched beside her friend's body, a droplet hit her nose. She brushed it away and looked up to the sky. Directly above their heads, it was brilliant blue, and the only clouds in view were bright white and fluffy, not a hint of grey to be seen. Chances were, it wasn't even a raindrop. After all, they were in the river; it could've been spray. She crossed the river to the exact cluster of rocks where Max's body had snagged and faced upstream. "He must have been killed further up," she muttered, mostly to herself but aware that Finn had joined her. "And then his body floated down . . ." Emme plunged back into the river. "I need to find the spot where he was killed."

"How is it that the other overnight campers didn't see his body? Or hear the crime in the first place?"

"The sound of the river would have covered it," Emme said. "And not all of the campsites were occupied that night," she added, but it was one of the many questions that stretched between here and wherever he was killed. She twisted around to look at Finn. "By the way, anything I say is off the record." Finn sighed, reached into his pocket, and pulled out his phone. She only had time to see him hit a red button on the screen before he slid it away again. "Are you—were you recording this whole time?"

"I was going to get your permission before I used it—"

"Un-fucking-believable." She jabbed her pole at him. "And you wonder why agents are so prickly about journalists." She whirled around, hiking as fast as she could with the encumbrance of the poles and the water.

"Hey, this is my job. Sometimes I have to be sneaky about how I get my information—"

"Just shut up. Seriously. I don't want to hear anything out of your mouth right now."

"Oh, that's real nice."

"Yeah, well, maybe you can have a nice private chat with Stace about my attitude." She forged ahead to put distance between them and let the river play its soundtrack to drown out the sound of him behind her. Why the hell had she told him she was coming to The Narrows? Her mind was spiraling in too many directions for her to focus. She turned her face to the sky to steady herself, and another water droplet pinged her cheek.

Emme rounded a rock wall and came to a collection of jagged boulders clustered at the mouth where it began to open into a wider path. Growing between the rocks was a familiar red-blooming plant. Emme bent close and plucked one stem free. It was the same plant that she had found in Sarai's pocket. She pulled a Ziploc bag from her pack and stored the plant inside. "What's that?" Finn asked as he reached her.

She didn't answer, just propelled herself forward and away from him. She wanted to press on as much as possible before they began to lose daylight and had to turn back. Somewhere close was the place where Max had taken his final breaths . . . she could feel it . . .

But when she emerged from the narrowed canyon, three more droplets hit her in rapid succession—one on the crown of her head, one on her shoulder, and the other on her nose again. Emme froze and jammed her sunglasses up onto her head. The canyon walls were far apart here, and the sun should be full on them, but there was nothing but shadow. She swept her gaze upriver, up above the cliffs, and *there*—there it was, a dark cloud cresting The Narrows to the north. "Shit."

Finn stopped beside her. "What is it?"

"Rain." She pointed and he followed her finger, his eyes widening as he spotted the cloud. "We need to turn around."

"It still looks far away—"

"Storms move fast in The Narrows. The walls are so close together that the water gets pushed up." She headed downstream a few steps and paused. The stretch they had just come through wasn't quite a slot, but its walls were smooth and slippery, with nowhere to go if the water level rose. As she stood there, trying to decide whether to chance it or not, the sky ripped open, pouring rain down amidst peals of thunder.

"Jesus, you weren't kidding." Finn went to move past her, but she caught his arm.

"There isn't time now," she said, punching down the panic that started to rise in her belly. "We have to get to higher ground." The water around their feet grew angry, rising from the tops of her shoes to her ankles. She looked wildly from shore to shore, seeking an outlet that would give them safety. Finn grabbed her arm and pointed to a spot just downstream. A rock ledge jutted out over the river, about six or seven feet above the ground. "Yes! Come on," she said and dug her poles into the sandy river bottom to balance herself against the rising water. It was nearly up to her shins now.

Rain pelted down and wind howled through the canyon. Emme pressed through the river to the shore, pushing to get to that ledge, but the water was thick and swirling. Thunder rumbled, and kept rumbling. . . the ground beneath them and the canyon walls around them all shook, and Emme realized that wasn't thunder. "Move, move!" she yelled, making sure that Finn was right behind her. They reached the shoreline just as the muddy river swallowed it, scrambling over rocks that were starting to break loose with the force of the water. She pushed Finn ahead of her; ranger training was impossible to shake in an emergency, and her training taught her to rescue civilians first and then herself. "Climb—" Another roar of thunder echoed through the canyon, drowning her voice.

Finn hoisted himself up one jagged rock and then another, twisted down to hold out his hand. "Hurry," he said, and she could hear the raggedy tremor of fear in his voice, his eyes not on her but on the scene beyond. She grasped his hand and let him help her up the rocks, using her poles to leverage her weight as they clambered up. The river below engorged as though it had eaten too much for breakfast, the stones in its middle that they had hiked over just minutes before now invisible beneath the water's swollen belly.

They crawled onto the ledge and pressed themselves as far back as they could. Water poured through the canyon like someone at the mouth of the river had upended a bottomless bucket. The river rose over the banks, swallowing brush and small trees and boulders in its insatiable mouth. Logs twisted in the muddy tide, sludge filled with earth and debris torn away in the river's rampage. It had barely been five minutes since Emme had felt those raindrops pattering on her face, and already the banks of the river were gone, the water level nearly covering the rocks they had climbed over to get to the ledge. "Holy fuck," Finn breathed, wrapping his arms around his knees. "What do we do if it rises above us?"

Emme didn't answer, because the truth was that they would drown. Very few people survived being swept away in a flash flood. Finn's face was white and drawn with fear as a crack of thunder broke over them. She nudged his arm. "Maybe you should turn your recorder back on," she said, keeping her voice calm and light. "This'll make some pretty good ambient sounds for your podcast."

Finn snorted and tilted his head up to the gloomy sky. A fat dark cloud sat over them, refusing to move. The river swelled below their little ledge, carrying dirt and rocks and twigs along in its wake. The water pounded through the canyon, so loud that if she and Finn wanted to talk they wouldn't be able to hear each other. But Emme was not inclined to talk. She watched the water rise, rise, rise, until it was three feet below their ledge, then two feet, then one foot. She forced herself to breathe in and out, steady and deep. Beside her, she felt Finn do the same, until finally they met each other's eyes, breathing in rhythm together. There was nowhere to go, above, below, or sideways. They were either going to get washed away, or they weren't. Suddenly, she heard Sunny's voice in her head, as clear as if she was sitting on the ledge between them. *You're gonna be okay, my love.*

She knew it was her own imagination, but she clung to the sound of her mother's voice as though it were a raft on the raging river below. A moment later, wind whistled through the canyon, blowing away the persistent dark cloud. A strong shot of afternoon sun replaced the dark, so bright and brilliant that it hurt Emme's eyes. She let the sun bathe her face, not caring if Finn saw the tears that crept down her cheeks. "We're going to be okay," she said.

"We still can't go anywhere," he said, and she looked at him fully, saw how his golden-brown eyes glowed luminous against his pale face. "How long before we can move?"

"Probably at least a few hours." She brought her backpack around to her lap and unzipped it to show the provisions she'd hiked in with: energy bars, apples, bags of trail mix, turkey jerky. "Dig in."

Finn reached out to take an apple, but brought his hand to her knee instead. "Thank you. I'm not sure I would've known what to do."

In spite of the cold that seeped to her bones, Emme softened as she met his gaze. "You spotted the ledge before I did. Much as I hate to admit it, you're a smart guy."

The corner of his mouth twisted up as he grabbed an apple. "I *was* shortlisted for a Pulitzer," he said, biting into the apple with a loud crunch.

"Really?" Emme scooted out a little bit on the ledge to look up to the sky. The clouds that had caused all this were now moving back north. She took a stick of turkey jerky and settled back next to Finn. "That's a pretty big deal."

"Eh, it didn't do much for my career." Finn's eyebrows knit together. "But that isn't why I do this. I do this because the people I write about, whether they're dead or alive—I care about them. The same as you."

She looked at him. "I know you do," she whispered.

"And I think what you do is pretty fucking amazing," he said. "Being an investigator—it takes a certain type of brain to do that well. I couldn't do it. That's why I write about other people doing it."

Emme wanted to believe that he wasn't just trying to flatter her. His eyes searched her face, as though he was looking for some resolution to whatever they'd been fighting about only moments ago. "Well, I certainly wouldn't be able to write a Pulitzer Prize-winning piece," she finally said. "It takes a certain type of brain to do *that*."

"*Almost* Pulitzer Prize-winning," Finn said. "Some jackass from *The Washington Post* beat me out."

Emme snorted. She fished around in her pack for the emergency blanket she always had on her and spread it out across their shoulders. As they leaned back against the rock wall, she noticed for the first time that their legs were pressed together in the small space of the ledge. She held herself tense for a moment and then relaxed, tugging the blanket tighter around them. Huddled together as the sun began to shine on the Virgin River once again, they waited for the waters to recede.

CHAPTER SEVENTEEN

Shivering and still drenched, they made it out of The Narrows just as the moon was rising. Once back in Emme's Crosstrek, they turned up the heated seats full blast. "There's a blanket in the back," Emme said, and Finn twisted around to grab it.

"I—I c-can't s-stop sh-shivering," he said, his teeth chattering as he wrapped the blanket around himself. Emme backed out of the Temple of Sinawava parking lot and onto the park road.

"Th-that's a g-good sign," she said, her own shoulders shaking with the cold. "It's when you s-stop shivering that's bad. That m-means you're in hypothermia."

She steered the car down the park road, high beams on to sweep ahead of the curves. The road was quiet, the park emptied out from the rain. She was well over the speed limit, but she wanted civilization, lights, and busy streets. "Where's your car?"

"I t-took the sh-shuttle. C-can you drop me at the B-best Western? On the Boulevard?"

She nodded. Finn rested his head back on the headrest and turned to look at her. She kept her eyes on him for longer than was smart, felt the light of his golden-brown gaze warm parts of her that the heated seats didn't reach. She sped out of the park and up the Boulevard, where a long line of hotels stretched from the park entrance through town. When she eased into a parking spot at the Best Western, Finn put his hands on the dashboard to brace himself. In the wan light of the streetlights in the parking lot, she saw a series of cuts crisscrossing his fingers. "Your hands—"

Finn held them up, flexed his knuckles. "That must've happened when I climbed onto the ledge—"

Emme shut the car off. "I have a first aid kit in my bag. We should clean those up. Can I come up?"

"Sure." There was something hard and glittery in the air between them, and Emme couldn't help but think of his leg pressed against hers on their ledge. She shook her head again to clear it, grabbed her pack, and climbed out of the car after him. She followed him up to the second floor, where the balcony overlooked the pool below. A few intrepid kids played in the water, and Emme shivered just looking at them.

Inside Finn's room, she sat him on the edge of the bed and knelt in front of him, examining the extent of damage to his hands. A deep cut etched itself across his palm, and Emme held his hand in hers, trying to steady herself against the shivering cold that seemed to have taken up permanent residence in her veins. "Can't get warm," Finn muttered, pulling the comforter around him like a shawl. Emme dabbed antiseptic ointment into his cuts and stretched a Band-Aid over the cut on his palm. She began to stand, but Finn caught her wrist. "You've got one too," he murmured, gently turning her forearm. Her jacket had ripped, a red smear of blood shimmering through the tear. She hadn't even noticed it.

Finn stood and guided her by the shoulders to sit where he had just been. "I can do it," she said, but he ignored her, peeled her jacket off, and pushed the sleeve of her shirt up. His fingers were still cold but unbearably gentle. Emme could not remember the last time someone else had tended to one of her wounds. Her breath caught and a tiny gasp escaped her lips. Finn looked up at her. The hard, glittery thing that had been between them in the car crystallized. He reached up and put his hand on the back of her neck, his fingers no longer cold. Her skin seared beneath his touch. She held her breath as she lost herself in his unblinking gaze, barely realizing that she was leaning closer and closer to him until their lips finally met.

She slid into his lap on the floor and his arms wrapped tightly around her, one hand cradling her head as his lips explored hers, tentatively at first, but with a growing urgency that lit a fire within her. Tangling her fingers into his copper hair, she pressed into him. His hands reached up under her shirt; she lifted her arms so he could slide it over her head, then yanked his shirt off an instant later. Skin to skin, they should have been on fire, but the chill of the flood still lingered. Emme shivered. "Shower," she murmured.

"What?"

"Hot shower. It will warm us up."

Finn stood, bringing Emme to her feet, his hand still on the back of her neck, his mouth still so near hers that she could not resist kissing him before he led her to the bathroom. Finn turned the shower on high; they shed the rest of their clothes, and in the harsh glare of the fluorescent light, Emme saw that both their bodies were covered in a mass of scrapes and bruises that were already starting to purple. Finn watched through the mirror as Emme pulled back the shower curtain, stepped inside, and turned back, daring him to follow. Beneath the flow of hot water, she curved against him and felt herself awaken from the heat and his touch. She pressed her lips to the hollow of his throat and felt the pulse of his heartbeat there, fast and so alive.

When they had driven away every last bit of chill from the flood, Finn turned the shower off and lifted Emme up; she wrapped her legs around him and let him carry her to the bed. Whatever lay beyond the door to his hotel room fell away, until all that was left in the world was the two of them, their bodies intertwined long into the night.

*****

When Emme awoke the next morning, it took her a moment to realize where she was. Finn's arm draped casually over her, and he was still sound asleep, a thin beam of morning light etched across his face. It made him look young and innocent. Emme traced his wrist bone lightly with her forefinger, her breasts tingling as she remembered how not innocent he'd been last night.

She slid out of bed and went to the bathroom, found a bottle of mouthwash on the counter, and rinsed the sleep taste out of her mouth. As she met her eyes in the mirror, the unforgiving fluorescent light struck her face, revealing truths that had stayed hidden in the night. What the hell had she just done? She splashed water on her face, trying to clear her thoughts. She'd been so determined to keep Finn at arm's length, and now she'd slept with him. If Claire caught wind of it—if it somehow got back to Stace—well, it was a good thing she'd already given her notice.

Outside of the bathroom, she grabbed her clothes from a pile on the floor—thankfully, they were now mostly dry—and began to dress as fast as her hands would move. When Finn rolled over and blinked his eyes open, she turned so her back was to him.

"Good morning," he said.

"Morning." She glanced over her shoulder at him. "I've got to get going."

He propped up his chin in his hand. "You're sexy as hell, did you know that?"

Emme zipped up her hoodie and picked up her backpack. She took a few steps towards the bed, trying not to notice how perfectly his sleep-tousled hair framed his face or the dip in the middle of his collarbone where she'd pressed her lips last night. "Let's . . . not make this a bigger deal than it is."

Finn sat up. The covers pooled at his waist, revealing the deep V that ran from his abs to his . . . "Emme."

"I really have to—" She moved toward the door.

"Hey." He hopped out of bed, wrapping the comforter around his hips, and blocked her path. "Look, I'm not exactly looking for a relationship either, but can we at least admit that last night was fun? And that maybe there could be a repeat?"

Emme clutched her pack to her chest. "Yes, it was fun. And there absolutely cannot be a repeat. There are lines between personal and professional, and last night," she waved her hand at the bed, with its messy sheets, "blurred those lines way too much."

"Okay, but can I—"

"I've got to go." She stepped around him and pulled open the door. He didn't prevent her from leaving, but on her way out, she caught the expression on his face, somewhere between hurt and longing. She closed the door behind her and stood for a moment in the weak sunlight, still rising over the mountains. She'd fucked up. Literally. She squeezed her eyes shut, as if blocking out the sight of Finn's hotel room door would erase everything that had happened the night before. When she opened them again, the door was still there, and her mistake was still glaring at her.

She couldn't erase what had happened. She just had to shove it in a box and move on. As she made her way down the stairs to the parking lot, she checked her phone. There were multiple missed texts from Addie.

At five p.m.: *Where r u?*

At five p.m., she'd still been stuck on the ledge in The Narrows. There was no cell service in the park, and she hadn't checked her phone when they'd finally left; she'd been too wrapped up—literally—with Finn.

Then at eight: *R u coming home tonight?*

And then, at six minutes past eleven: *WHERE R U?*

Seven minutes past eleven: *I THINK THERE IS SOMEONE IN THE HOUSE*

Eight minutes past eleven: *DONT COME HOME, THERES SOMEONE HERE*

Emme's heart skittered and stopped. She galloped down the rest of the stairs to her car, jumped in, and careened the car backward out of its parking space, almost slamming into a minivan with Ohio plates. The driver, a bespectacled dad with shaggy brown hair, yelled, "Watch where you're going!" at her and rolled by at a snail's pace. She zoomed around him and screeched out onto the Boulevard, speeding way too fast until she came to the bakery. She skidded to a stop in the driveway and jumped out, not even bothering to turn off the car.

The front door was slightly ajar. She flung it open. "Addie? *Addie!*"

Inside, the living room was disastrous, like a cyclone had come through and wreaked havoc. Couch cushions sprawled on the floor, the carefully curated piles of Sunny's stuff had spilled over, and all the drawers in the sideboard and desk along the wall had been removed, dumped out, and tossed aside. A couple of them had splintered. Emme stood frozen in the chaos for a moment, trying to catch her brain up to what she was seeing.

None of it mattered unless Addie was okay.

She ricocheted through the hall, glancing into each room she passed—all torn apart—until she got to Sunny's bedroom. "Addie?" The closet door stood open; it had clearly been searched too, but there was a secret in that closet that only the Helliwell women knew. She shoved aside all the clothes—Sunny's dresses and button-down shirts and pants that her mother called "slacks"—and felt along the back wall. Her finger notched into a tiny groove. She pulled, and the wall opened.

Huddled in the small space behind the false wall was Addie, arms hugged tight around her knees, her phone clutched in one hand and a pocketknife in the other. Emme dropped down and pulled her sister in close. "Jesus, are you okay?" She shook Addie a little, who seemed to have gone mute. "*Are you okay?*"

"Are they gone?"

"Yes—yes, they're gone. There's no one here." Emme pressed her palms against Addie's cheeks. "What happened?"

Addie drew in a ragged breath. "I was in here reading when I heard a noise in the living room. I don't think they knew I was here, because all the lights were off except for the bedside lamp." She swallowed. "I could hear them going through each room. I turned off the lamp, grabbed my phone, and hid in the closet."

"You did the right thing." Emme closed her eyes and remembered the day they'd toured this house, how the real estate agent had shown them the hidden space, and how Sunny lingered in the closet, running her finger over and over along the notch that opened the wall. Even though her father was already dead by then, the fear of him still brought nightmares, and the room was a comfort against that darkness. And now, it had protected Addie against a different evil. "Did you call the police?"

"I was afraid they would hear me," Addie whispered.

Emme cocked her head. "You keep saying 'they.' There was more than one person? Do you know how many?"

"I don't know," Addie said. She chewed at her lip. "I'm pretty sure there were at least two of them. I heard voices—male voices—so there was definitely more than one."

"Could you make out what they were saying?"

Addie shook her head. "I'm sorry, Emme. I should've paid more attention. I was just so scared."

"Oh god, Addie, there's nothing to apologize for." She hugged her sister hard, smoothing her hair away from her tear-stained face. "You're okay. That's all that matters. And besides . . ." she trailed off, not voicing the rest of her thoughts. It was probably better the police hadn't been called, if her suspicions of who had torn their house apart were right. She took Addie's hands and pulled her gently to her feet. "Come on. I'll make you some tea."

While the kettle brewed, Emme went to her room to investigate the damage. The mattress lay skewed on the bed frame, and the covers were strewn over the footboard. Every one of her dresser drawers had been opened and their contents tossed about. Most of the notes she had on Max and Sarai's murders—including her notebook—were in her car or her backpack that she'd had with her yesterday, but the corkboard she'd filled with index cards and red thread connecting the dots of the case was gone. Emme crossed to the small filing cabinet next to the desk and dropped to her knees in front of it. The cabinet held the files of all the closed cases she'd worked on. It had traveled with her from her cabin in the Grand Canyon after Sunny had died, when she knew she'd be here for a while. They didn't belong to the ISB; they were her own notes, her personal writings on each case.

Unlike the rest of the house, the cabinet was not a mess—because the intruder had known exactly what to look for here, where all the files were in neat alphabetical order. Emme thumbed through the files, each name printed in careful letters on each folder tab. Sure enough, when she arrived at the place where *DeLeo, Hannah* should be, it was gone. Emme sat back on her haunches, her suspicions confirmed. The Murdocks—or someone from the Warriors—had broken in, looking for what she had on Sarai's case, and had taken Hannah's file just for good measure. She ran her hand over her face, her fingers shaking as anger snaked through her. They'd breached her home. What if they had found Addie?

From the kitchen, Emme heard the kettle whistle. She stood. They were actually lucky she hadn't been home last night. She would have shot them dead.

Addie was pouring out the boiling water into two mugs of tea. She looked up as Emme entered. The color had returned to her cheeks, and she seemed sturdier now than when Emme had first gotten her out of the closet. "Unless you want coffee?" she asked.

"Tea is fine." Emme took her cup and wrapped her fingers around its warmth. "I'm sorry that all your hard work over the last couple of days has been destroyed."

Addie sighed. "It's not your fault."

"Yeah, it kinda is." Emme leaned against the doorframe. "Pretty sure it has to do with the case I'm working on."

"Still not your fault that people are assholes." Addie pushed past her and stood in the middle of the living room. "I can clean this up. And actually, they ruined some stuff that I was on the fence about keeping, so now I don't have to make that decision." The corner of her lip turned up. "Silver lining?"

"Addie . . ." Emme sat on the arm of the sofa. "Maybe you should go stay in a hotel. Just until I have this case sorted out. I don't know if it's safe for you to stay here."

"I can take care of myself."

"I know you can but—"

"Are *you* going to go stay in a hotel?"

"No, but—"

Addie plunked herself down into the armchair opposite Emme. "I'm not going anywhere without you. I feel much safer being with you."

"But I wasn't here last night!" Emme threw her hand up in the air—the one not holding a hot cup of tea—and dropped it heavily back down to her side.

Addie sat up straight. "Where *were* you last night? Why didn't you come home?"

Oh crap. She'd scrambled home in such a panicked state that she hadn't had time to come up with a good story. "There was a flash flood. I got stuck in The Narrows."

"*All night?* Jesus!" Addie stood up, sloshing a splash of tea onto a pile of papers that had toppled across the floor. The tea stain spread outward in a shape like a humpbacked whale. "Are you okay? That's—wait." She somehow raised her eyebrows and narrowed her eyes at the same time at Emme, looking her down from head to toe and back up again. "You look remarkably clean and rosy for someone who spent the night in the river."

"I wasn't there *all* night." Emme stared down into her mug, hoping that Addie would attribute the flush that crept up into her check to the steam from her tea.

"Oh my god, you were with that guy, weren't you? That podcaster?" Addie stomped her feet until she came within a few inches of Emme. "You were, weren't you?"

"I went back to his hotel room to clean up—"

"I was barricaded in the closet, afraid for my life, and you were out fucking a podcaster?" Addie towered over her; this close, Emme could see how her whole body shook, and shame washed through her.

"I'm so sorry, Addie. You're right, I should've been here."

"You know what I kept thinking, while I was trying to breathe so quietly that they wouldn't hear me?" Addie's voice cracked and her eyes shone with tears. "That I was glad you weren't there, that you were safe and sound somewhere else—"

"And I was!" Emme banged her mug down on the coffee table and stood up.

"Oh really? Screwing some guy you barely know? That's safe?"

Emme jabbed a finger at her sister's face. "That is none of your business." She spun away, took a few steps, and whirled back. "I can either be here twenty-four-seven to protect you, or I can be safe somewhere else, Addie. You can't have it both ways. Just tell me which one you want, and I'll do it."

"I—" Addie bit down on her lip.

"I'm going to clean up." Emme banged her way out of the living room, around the chaos that the Murdocks had just made more chaotic, and into her bedroom. She slammed the door, rattling the hinges, and pressed her back into it. In slow motion, she slid to the floor, curling tight into herself until she could block the rest of the world out.

CHAPTER EIGHTEEN

A tenuous truce settled over the house as the two sisters set about sorting through the mess. At mid-morning, Emme got a phone call from Stace, who sucked his breath in hard when he heard what had happened. "Get out of there, Emme. Go stay in a hotel."

"I'm not running." Emme dumped an armful of papers into the trash bag she'd set up in the middle of the room. "That's what they want."

"What they want is you out of the picture," Stace said. "What would've happened if you'd been there last night?"

"We'd have a couple of dead Murdocks on our hands right now," Emme said.

Stace snorted. "Even so, that wouldn't help our case." There was a pause in which Emme swore she heard his big leather chair squeaking as he shifted in it. "I think I'm gonna come down there."

"Oh, now you're going to come down here? Where were you when I begged to have another agent take over the case?"

There was a pause on his end of the line. "I can't tell whether you're being sarcastic or serious."

"A little bit of both." Emme bent over a pile of books that had been tossed off their shelf and began to replace them one by one. "I can handle this, Stace."

"I'm sure you can." The squeak was more audible. "I just don't like the idea of you dealing with all this on your own."

Addie walked into the living room and sat down on the floor next to a stack of chaos. Emme hunched her shoulders and walked into the kitchen. "So you want to come down here and throw a little weight around? What purpose is that going to serve?"

"It'll show the Murdocks they can't mess with the federal government—"

"No, it'll show the Murdocks that I need more manpower to deal with them." Emme stood in front of the refrigerator and began to rearrange the magnets, one by one forming a pyramid: Abraham at the top, his three sons below him, and then countless other minions spreading out beneath them. She tipped one of the sons over to symbolize Eli, presumably dead. "Just—hold off on coming down here. It would probably be helpful, but flying into town right after the Murdocks break into my house just makes me look weak."

"Fine. But you keep your guard up. And get a goddamn camera or something."

In fact, she'd ordered one online that morning, rush delivery to get there the next day. She called Claire, who answered after one ring without saying hello. "Emme, good. I have some information to share—"

"As do I," Emme said.

"Can you meet later? Back at Anthera?"

Emme shot a look over at Addie, who was carefully placing photos back into one of the albums, her fingers reverent with each picture. "No,

I—I'd rather meet here, at my home . . . why don't you come to our bakery? It's closed so, we won't be disturbed. It's called The Sunny Spot, right on Zion Park Boulevard."

"Sure. Will there be food even if it's closed? I get cranky when I don't eat."

Emme laughed. "No problem. We'll get you fed." She ended the call and tossed her phone on the sofa.

Addie held up a book. "Is this Mom's Bible?" It was the first thing she'd said to her all morning.

Emme walked over and squatted down. "No. To my knowledge Mom never owned a Bible."

"Is it yours?"

"Yeah, right."

"Well, *someone* left it here." Addie tipped it toward Emme, who caught it and turned it over in her hands. The black leather cover was soft and well-worn, the pages falling open easily in Emme's fingers. Someone had read this Bible daily. An alarm began to clang in Emme's head.

"Where did you find it?"

"On the coffee table." Addie cocked her head. "It's odd—it was just lying there as if had been placed, not thrown around like the rest of the stuff."

The clanging alarm got louder. Emme balanced the book on its spine on the flat of her palm and let it fall open where it wanted...right to The Book of Revelation. Pressed into the pages was a little plant bundle, just like she'd found inside Sarai's pocket: a stem of aloe and a red-flowering plant. Emme ran her finger down the text and paused at Revelations 2:10. *Do not fear what you are about to suffer. I tell you, the devil will throw some of you in prison to test you, and you shall suffer tribulation for*

*ten days. Be faithful, even to the point of death, and I will give you life as
your victor's crown.*

Whoever had put the flowers in Sarai's pocket—had been there at the
moment of her death—had been in her house and left this for her to
find. Emme sucked in a deep breath and pinched the book closed with
her thumb and forefinger, carried it by its corner to the kitchen. Before
she dropped it into a Ziploc bag, she removed the plants and put them
in a separate plastic bag. She squeezed the zipper closed and laid the bag
flat on the counter so she could examine the plants. While she knew the
stem was aloe, she couldn't place the name of the red flowering plant,
though she had seen it growing in Zion Canyon. There was a reason
these particular plants had been placed with Sarai; it couldn't be random.
She drummed her fingers on the countertop. Plants had meanings. Was
someone trying to send a message? She drew her phone out and searched
plant symbolism, pulling up the first page in the search results.

Beneath the entry for aloe, the meaning was listed as *grief.* Just a few
lines below that, Emme's eye caught the entry for amaranth. She tapped
on it and a picture of the red-flowering plant flooded the screen. She
clicked back and scrolled over to see its meaning. *Immortality.*

Her heartbeat quickened. It was all connected, from a Bible that was
clearly owned by a Warrior to the scene of Sarai's murder . . . The person
who had pressed the aloe and amaranth—grief and immortality—into
this Bible had left the same message on Sarai's body, and she would bet
good money it was also the same person who had woven the wildflower
chain from the tree above where they'd found Sarai. *Whoever killed her
cared for her,* Chenoa had said, and this was further proof that she'd
been right about that. Emme set her phone down and leaned against the
doorframe, running her fingertip over her lip. Which of the Murdocks

would be cruel enough to murder Sarai but remorseful enough to crown her body with flowers, and then leave a clue for Emme to connect back to it?

If she had to interrogate every Murdock in Redwater, she was going to find out.

*****

The bakery smelled delicious when she ushered Claire inside after meeting her on the front porch. "Oh, this place is lovely," Claire said, and it made Emme's heart shine, knowing how proud it would have made her mother.

"Thanks. We're still fixing it up, but don't worry—the kitchen is in full working order, and we'll have to plenty to eat to keep you from getting hangry."

They sat at the table Emme had laid out with all of her notes—the ones that hadn't been stolen—her notebook, the plant bundle she'd found on Sarai's body, the Ziploc bag with the Bible, and the bundle she'd found inside. Claire pointed to the latter. "What's that?"

"*That* is a little parting gift the Warriors left for me after ransacking my house last night." Emme sat down at the table.

"*What?*" Claire pulled the chair opposite Emme out from the table with a loud screeching scrape along the floor and sat at the edge of it. "What happened?"

"I was at a friend's place last night and came home this morning to find my sister hiding in a closet and the house turned upside down." Claire opened her mouth, but Emme answered her question before she asked it. "My sister is fine. The house is a mess, but nothing valuable was stolen—except for my file on Hannah DeLeo."

"Ah." Claire leaned back in her chair. "So we can assume the culprit was a Warrior."

"Warriors. My sister said she heard voices, so there was more than one of them that broke in."

"What about the materials you have on Sarai Murdock and Max Kerchek? Did they take those too?"

"Fortunately, most of that wasn't in the house for them to take," Emme said. Addie emerged from the kitchen carrying a tray with a pitcher of water and some glasses. "Claire, this is my sister, Addie."

"Nice to meet you." Claire held her hand out. Addie put down the tray and shook it. "I'm glad you're okay."

"Me too." Addie busied herself with pouring out the water. Emme hadn't wanted to leave her in the house alone, even just next door, and when she'd asked her to help out in the bakery, Addie had agreed so quickly that Emme knew she was still shaken from last night. Addie set a filled glass in front of each of them. "Jaspar is making empanadas and a nice tossed salad. Do you want something to drink besides water?"

"Water is fine. Thanks, Addie," Emme said. She brushed her sister's hand with her fingers, but Addie slid her hand away, folded her arms across her chest.

"I'd love some tea," Claire said. "Do you mind?"

"Not at all. Be right back." Addie walked back to the kitchen. Emme noticed how Claire watched her go until she disappeared through the swinging doors, and she cleared her throat.

Claire snapped her attention back to the table and picked up the Ziploc bag. "So, this is their signature?"

"The flowers were pressed into the pages with the Book of Revelation verse that's the Warriors' motto," Emme said. "And they match the flowers found on Sarai's body."

"Okay, so we can assume the same person left the flowers there and the Bible at your house. Or at least pressed them into the Bible after Sarai was killed." Claire withdrew items from the bag she'd brought with her: the map of the Warriors' domain, her file on the Murdocks, her notes. She stood up and surveyed the table for a moment, stroking her lip with her finger. Then she began to walk very slowly around the table. Her focus, as though she had blinders on to everything around her, compelled Emme to her feet. She followed a pace behind Claire, circling the table three times before the FBI agent stopped. "Can I see the print-out of Max's cell phone pings?"

Emme grabbed them from the pile on her side of the table. Claire set the papers beside the Murdock map and picked up a red pen. She began to mark each of the phone pings on the map. Soon the topography of Utah bloomed red with dots like poppies in a field. Most of the dots clustered around Springdale and Redwater, but there was one all the way up in Salt Lake City. Claire ran her finger along the line for that ping on the print-out. "Huh."

"What?"

"This cell phone tower is a block from the Salt Lake FBI office." She met Emme's gaze across the table. "I don't believe in coincidences. Do you?"

"Nope."

Claire picked up her phone and began dictating a text message.

"Natalie, can you pull the visitor logs for Tuesday, October 17th and send them to me right away? Thank you," she said, then sent it off with a little swoosh. "She probably won't get that to us until tomorrow," she said to Emme, "but let's just go with the assumption that he *was* visiting the FBI. Why?"

The gears in Emme's brain began to shift, moving from one theory to another. But before she could voice them, Addie returned with Claire's tea. Jaspar trailed behind her with a tray of food. There were more introductions, and Claire exclaimed enthusiastically over the food. Emme's phone buzzed. She wasn't quick enough to grab it before Addie leaned over to see who was calling and sang out, "It's Finn Brackenbury."

Heat flushed up Emme's neck onto her face. She snatched the phone off the table and caught sight of all three of them looking at her, Claire wide-eyed and Jaspar smirking, and declined the call.

"Is that that hot podcaster from the bar the other night?" Jaspar said, dishing out salad into the bowls he'd brought out.

"Podcaster?" Claire asked. She'd been fixing her tea with milk and sugar, and she looked up at Emme. "Did you tell him about the case?"

"They didn't do much talking," Addie said with a pointed look that Emme recognized all too well. It was the look she got when she had crossed over from anger to revenge.

"Did you sleep with him?" Jaspar asked in a low, whispery voice, like they were in the back booth of Cap's Landing, gossiping about someone the next table over. Addie made a noise, her mouth still full, and nodded.

Oh, she was going to kill her sister. She was going to murder her tonight in her sleep, and when she told the jury why, they were going to acquit her. She shot a death-glare at Addie, who swallowed the bite of salad she was still chewing. "Oops," Addie said as she backed away into the kitchen, flashing Emme with narrowed eyes and a forced shrug. What the hell was she playing at?

"Nice work, Emme. That guy was hot," Jaspar said. Okay, so she was going to be on trial for a double murder now, but hopefully the jury would still see it as a justified homicide. He pointed to the two plates of empanadas. "This one is chicken and rice, and the other is pinto beans and cheese. I'll be in the back hiding the knives so Emme can't stab me and Addie."

Claire snorted, choking on her tea. Emme took a deep breath with her eyes closed, hoping the flush in her face had gone away. It was humiliating. This was the fucking FBI, not happy hour. She was working, for fuck's sake. "I'm so sorry," she said. "That was really unprofessional."

"How much does this podcaster know about the case?" Claire asked, appraising her across the table with an unblinking gaze.

"He was with me when I found Sarai's body. But, to be fair, I never would have been there if it hadn't been for him." Emme flipped to a page in her notebook and spun it so Claire could read it. "Finn had a meeting scheduled with Max on October 20th. We think that he was going to the FBI to give them information about Eli Murdock in connection to Hannah DeLeo's murder, and that he had the meeting with Finn as a backup," Emme said. "That ping near your offices corroborates that theory."

"Yes, it does," Claire murmured.

"So when Finn found out about Max's death, he invited me to go with him to the place where they were supposed to meet. That's where we found Sarai's body."

"In other words, he's been useful." Claire sipped her tea.

"He has been, but I think his usefulness might be at an end. We don't need him on the case anymore." Emme nibbled at one of the empanadas.

Claire raised an eyebrow.

Emme sighed and sat back in her chair. "Look, I know how much the FBI loves the press—"

"Actually, I don't think they're the enemy that many of my colleagues think they are." Claire shrugged. "Sometimes it's better to be in bed with them and get the story you want out there than keep them at arm's length and lose control of the narrative." The corner of her mouth curled up. "Sorry. That was a poor choice of words."

Emme flopped her arms onto the table and banged her head against them. Claire laughed. "Lighten up, Emme. It's practically impossible to keep things strictly professional in our job. When you're working on a case like this, interagency, late nights, too many cups of coffee to count—lines tend to get blurred. Trust me, I know." She dropped her gaze and dug into her salad.

There was a story behind that comment, Emme was sure of it, but she wasn't going to press Claire to confess her past indiscretions. She cleared her throat and pointed to the bag with the plant bundle. "That red flower—amaranth—it grows in The Narrows. I saw it when I was there a couple of days ago."

"You were in The Narrows that recently?"

"I wanted to see if I could find the spot where Max was killed." Emme shook her head. "Unfortunately, I didn't get that far. There was a flood."

"Jesus, you've had quite a couple of days." Claire's forehead creased. "What happens when there's a flood in The Narrows? How do you get out?"

"You get to higher ground, and you have to wait it out." Emme took a healthy bite of her empanada. "I sat on a ledge above the river for hours, watching all our evidence wash away."

"Not necessarily," Claire said slowly. She put her fork down. "Would it be worthwhile to go back, retrace Max and Sarai's steps?"

"Yeah, I think so." Emme stood and shuffled the map of Zion National Park out from underneath the other papers on the table. "But I was going bottom-up yesterday, and Max and Sarai were hiking top-down." She traced the path of The Narrows, showing Claire the two different entrances. "I think in order to truly retrace their steps, we have to take the trail top-down."

"Okay, let's do that."

Emme looked at her. "It's a sixteen-mile trek. In the river. And you have to camp overnight."

Claire inhaled deep. "Well, I brought my hiking boots. I might have to borrow a tent, though. I'm assuming you've done it before?"

"Just once. The summer after high school graduation. With Max." She inhaled deep. "But actually—Addie!" she called, and a moment later her sister appeared. "Addie's hiked it pretty much every year since she was twelve. She could do it blindfolded."

"What now? What am I doing blindfolded?"

"Hiking The Narrows," Emme repeated. "We need to retrace Max and Sarai's steps. Do you want to come with us? Be our guide?"

Addie looked from Emme to Claire and back again. Emme kept her face soft, though she knew there was a pleading look in her eyes. If she had to go into the canyon overnight, with no cell service or an easy way to get out quickly, she didn't want to leave Addie alone at home. And maybe the trip would ease some of the contention between them.

"Yeah, okay." Addie jabbed her finger at Emme. "But you're carrying the tent."

CHAPTER NINETEEN

Emme stood in the middle of the bakery, her hands on her hips. "I could've sworn we had another two-person tent."

"We did," Addie said, shrugging her shoulders in a way that made Emme grit her teeth. "It ripped when I used it in Moab last year."

"Dammit." Emme pinched the bridge of her nose. All of the outfitters in town were crazy overpriced. Jaspar emerged from the kitchen, wiping his hands on a dishtowel.

"Hey, do you have a two-person tent we can borrow?"

He barked out a laugh. "I don't carry my bed on my back if I can help it."

Emme rolled her eyes. She looked at Claire, who held her hands up. "Remember how I said the first hike I ever went on was two years ago? I haven't quite worked my way up to the backcountry."

"Well, if the three of us want to go, we need another tent," she said with a sigh, pointing at the equipment they'd laid out on the floor. "Which means we'll have to wait to go until the day after tomorrow so that I can go buy one."

"It's supposed to rain in two days," Jaspar said. "The Narrows might be closed then."

With a groan, Emme dropped into a chair and pressed her palm against her forehead. With Claire on the case, it felt like they were making progress, and stopping now twisted her up into knots. Addie walked up the row of equipment, assessing each item. Out of the corner of her eye, Emme saw a shadow darken the doorstep of the bakery. She straightened, her mind flashing back to the mysterious figure she swore she'd seen in the bakery the other day, but as she moved to the door, she saw it was Finn peering through the glass, not a Murdock. He lifted a hand to knock, but she opened the door before he could bring his fist down. "Hey."

"Hey." He caught sight of Claire, Addie, and Jaspar. Emme glanced over her shoulder at them, and found they were all smirking at her. She pressed her lips together and raised an eyebrow at him. "I just wanted to make sure you were okay," he said. "After—"

Addie materialized at her elbow. "Do you have a two-person tent?"

Finn blinked. "Um, yes?"

"Do you want to camp in The Narrows with us? Tomorrow?"

"What? Addie! *No*," Emme said, a little harsher than she intended.

Addie shrugged, making her face into an expression of innocence that Emme knew was full-on make-believe. "What? It's better to go with an even number of people anyway."

Claire appeared at her other elbow. "Are you the one who had a meeting set up with Max Kerchek?"

"Yes." Finn nodded. "We were supposed to meet the day after his body was found."

"I'd like to ask you some questions," Claire said. She nudged her way in front of Emme, standing shoulder to shoulder with Addie. Emme stared at the back of their necks, trying to decide the nicest way to smash their heads together. "We could use the hike to discuss that."

"I am itching to get back there, since we were forced out the other day," Finn said. He peered around Claire and Addie and met Emme's narrowed gaze. "If that's okay with you."

Addie and Claire twisted to look at her. From behind, Emme could feel Jaspar's eyes on her as well. If she said no, she'd have to explain why, and she didn't want to revisit how she'd rushed out of his hotel room yesterday morning. A flush seared her throat just thinking about it. With a sigh, she gave a short, sharp nod. "Dress warm," she said. "It can drop close to freezing overnight in the canyon this time of year."

*****

The blue sky sparkled overhead as Emme pulled the car into the Kolob Canyons ranger station and slid into a Staff Parking Only spot. The drive up from Springdale had been smattered with bursts of conversation followed by awkward silences as Finn, Addie and Claire got acquainted with each other, leaving Emme to listen as she concentrated on the road. Finn had told them about some of his travels across the country in a used van with his best friend ("we didn't speak to each other for six months after that," he said, laughing) and Addie told them about her first night in Tanzania when a pack of wildebeests stampeded through the dig site. "Pretty much my first two months there were just cleaning up that mess," she said from the backseat where she and Claire sat, a backpack filled gear in between them. Emme had given her sister another death-glare when she insisted that Finn sit shotgun, but Addie had avoided her gaze and ducked into the backseat with Claire. Halfway through the ride, they fell into a quiet, private conversation, and Emme realized it may have been a calculated act on Addie's part to give Finn the front seat, on a few different levels.

Now, Emme and Claire walked to the station while Addie and Finn waited by the car, stretching their legs in the bright sunshine. The air was warm and still, as though summer had woken up from just having fallen asleep for the year, and the sky was dotted with fluffy white clouds. Not a whiff of rain hung on the horizon; Emme had checked and double-checked the weather forecast for the entire length of the canyon. Even now, as they walked up the sidewalk to the station, she pulled her phone out and re-checked her weather app. *Clear conditions*, it told her.

She put on her Smokey hat as Claire held the door open for her and walked purposefully up to the Information Desk. A tourist cleared out of the way and revealed Theo behind the desk. He leaned on his elbows. "Hey, Emme."

"Hey, Theo. This is Agent Hughes, from the FBI."

Theo and Claire shook hands and he looked from her back at Emme. "Any news on that double murder?"

The tourist who had just vacated the desk whipped around from where she stood at the postcard turntable. "Did you say double murder?"

Emme flashed a grimace at Theo. Like, the first rule you learned on day one of ranger training was *don't alarm the visitors*. She stepped away from the desk and smiled. "It's not what it seems. This was targeted and premeditated. There's absolutely no danger to the public."

"But you haven't caught the guy?" The woman clutched her backpack to her chest, as if it could save her in the face of a killer.

"We're circling him."

"And that's really all we can say." Claire's tone cut clear and firm into the conversation. "I'll reiterate what Agent Helliwell said. There's no danger."

The woman glanced between them, grabbed the postcards she'd been eyeing and beat a hasty retreat to the cash register. Emme turned back to Theo. "And *that's* why we don't ever use the words 'double murder' within earshot of the guests."

Theo scrunched his face up. "Yeah, sorry about that."

"Anyway," Emme said, "we're going to head into The Narrows. I called ahead to make sure there was a campsite available, but wanted to check in here before we headed into the canyon."

"Sure. You want to take one of the station's satellite phones?"

"That would be great. Thanks." She signed the checkout log for the phone and looked up at Theo. "How many permits were handed out today?"

"Only a couple, for campsites nine and twelve," Theo said. "It's getting a bit late in the season."

So they wouldn't have much company on the hike, giving them plenty of space and privacy to investigate. She waved goodbye to Theo and walked back out to the parking lot with Claire.

When they got to the Chamberlain Ranch trailhead, they divided the gear between them and headed out onto the trail, their feet crunching on the dry, red earth beneath them. It was early, and the air still had a morning bite to it, though Emme knew the sunlight would soon feel unrelenting. Addie slid out in front, leading the group, while Claire and Finn hung back. Emme listened as Claire asked Finn about his communications with Max, the meeting they'd set up, what Finn had done when he learned that Max was dead. It was everything Emme had heard before. She tried to listen with a fresh ear, but instead found her attention focused on Addie's back in front of her, a little hunched under the weight of her pack, her swinging ponytail giving nothing away of what was going on in her head. The uneasy truce they'd made after the break-in still seemed to be holding, but they weren't even two miles into this sixteen-mile trek, and Emme knew how easily respect and understanding could break down when your entire body ached, you were starving and drenched in river water, and you still had to set up your tent and cook your dinner.

When they reached Bulloch's Cabin, a lonely, picturesque ruin at the side of the trail, they stopped to take a break and drink some water. Addie slid her pack onto the ground and flopped down next to it. "There's a lunar eclipse tonight," she said, holding up her phone. "And we should be able to see it."

"You're getting cell service?" Finn asked.

"Just barely."

"Hopefully we'll have a good view from the campsite, if the canyon walls don't block the sky," Emme said.

"It starts around eight-thirty." Addie got to her feet. She brushed grass from her bottom and tucked her phone into the pocket of her puffer vest. Emme watched her as she walked out into the meadow beyond the cabin and looked up to the sky. Claire and Finn were preoccupied with their phones, tilting them in every direction in an attempt to find a connection. Emme ducked away from the cabin and jogged into the meadow.

Addie turned slightly as Emme approached, her boots crunching on grass still stiff with dew. "I'm not being a nuisance, am I?" she asked, a sharp edge glittering around her words. "I'm trying to stay out of your way."

"Addie, you don't have to do that." Emme stepped around her sister so that they were face to face.

"I know you only invited me because I've done this trail like a million more times than you." Addie gazed past Emme, not meeting her eyes. "I won't interfere with your work."

Emme lifted her arms and let them drop back down to her sides. "I don't get it. You shame me for spending the night with Finn—"

"*Shame you?*"

"And then you insist that he come with us on this trip. What the hell is going on with you?"

"Nothing is going on with me," Addie said, but her eyes had grown shiny and tears hung at the corners of her eyelashes. "Except for the fact that I walked over here to commune with nature and you're ruining it." She walked past Emme, into a patch of sunlight where the grass rose to her calves.

Emme watched her for a moment, then arched her face to the sky. "You know, I miss her too," she said, softly, but strong enough that she knew Addie heard. "I feel her out here."

"I feel her everywhere," Addie said without turning around. "But especially here. She loved this place so much. It was more her home than New York ever was." She stretched her hand back and Emme took it, weaving her sister's cold fingers into her own. The frustration that had just twisted her up undid itself, scattering away like a cloud blown apart by the wind. They gazed out into the canyon, their mother in every particle of air around them.

"Maybe this is where we should scatter her ashes," Emme murmured.

Addie yanked her hand away. "You want to get rid of her that soon?" In an instant, the cloud of frustration knitted itself back up inside Emme. "I don't want to keep her in that box on the mantle forever. How is that honoring her?"

Thick silence stretched between them for a long moment. Addie hugged herself. "I'm not ready to let her go yet," she whispered. "Can't she just stay in the living room for a little longer?"

Emme swallowed the dense lump that had risen her throat. "Of course she can," she said, reaching for Addie's hand again and squeezing hard. This time, Addie didn't pull away.

"You guys ready to go?" Claire called from the trailside. She'd already hoisted her pack up onto her shoulders. Emme waved to her, and they began to walk slowly back from the meadow, fingers still linked.

"So, you and Claire seemed pretty chummy in the backseat," Emme said before they got back into earshot of the other two.

Addie rolled her eyes. "I told you, I'm not going to interfere with your work."

"I know you wouldn't. I was just saying—"

"I'm not an idiot," Addie snapped, pulling her hand away once again. She turned to face Emme so that she was walking backward toward the cabin. "Do you really think that I don't know how to be professional? For fuck's sake, Emme. Give me some credit."

It was the Hidden Canyon hike all over again, thinking her sister was lost when she was right there all along, making presumptions that only served to raise Addie's ire. "I'm sorry, I just thought I saw a little something between—"

"God, Emme." Addie shook her head. "For your information, I just got out of a relationship and have no intention of getting back into one again any time soon."

"A relationship? With who?"

"Someone in Tanzania." Addie's nostrils flared, her lips pressed thin. "No one you know."

"Is that the person who called the other night?"

Addie's eyes narrowed, squelching something in their depths that Emme didn't have time to decipher before it was gone. Her sister spun and walked swiftly back to the front of the cabin, where Finn and Claire waited with their packs. Emme followed a beat behind, trying to read the tight, tense language in Addie's body that told a story her sister clearly didn't want to speak out loud. Addie settled her pack on her back and walked ahead of them, dust clouds puffing at her feet on the dry ground.

The trail wound its way alongside the river, flowing below them over boulders and fallen logs in its path. "It's definitely not going to rain?" Finn asked, eyeing the water, which at the moment was low, barely ankle-deep.

"I mean, I can't say *definitely*," Emme said, "but everywhere I checked said it would be clear." She glanced at him. "You getting triggered?"

Finn snorted. "No, but getting caught in a flash flood isn't exactly an experience I'd like to repeat."

"You know, I've been managing to keep that fear at bay, and you talking about it isn't helping," Claire said.

"What's the point of living if you're not a little bit on the edge?" Finn said.

"I like my footing firmly on the ground, thank you very much." Claire nudged a loose stone at the edge of the trail and it tumbled down the embankment into the river.

"And you became an FBI agent to stay safe, did you?"

Claire laughed. "Touché." She adjusted the bandanna around her neck. "You would not believe the shit I got from my mama when I told her I was going to Quantico. I thought the roof was going to cave in from all her weeping and wailing."

"What did she say when you told her you were going on a sixteen-mile hike in a river?"

"Are you kidding? I'm not breathing a word of this to her."

Emme listened to their conversation, but her eyes were on her sister, who walked several paces ahead, her back as straight as the poles she carried in each hand. Normally her sister was the one in the thick of a group, the center of the conversation. She wasn't the lone wolf that Emme tended to be; she was the beta, keeping peace, lending support. Emme scrunched up her forehead. Grief reared its head in so many different ways, but the Addie she knew would want to be around others in her sorrow, taking comfort in company. Emme breathed in deep, the crisp air icing her lungs. Whatever the story was behind that relationship she'd had in Tanzania, it had changed her.

As if she could hear Emme's thoughts about her, Addie stopped and turned, her poles resting lightly at her side. Her eyes were hidden behind her sunglasses, but the vein at the base of her throat throbbed as she waited for them to reach her. The trail had tapered to a narrow close; there was no choice now but to descend into the river. "Ready to get wet?" she asked. Without waiting for an answer, she climbed down the embankment.

Emme let Finn and Claire go ahead of her and followed behind, digging her poles in between the rocks to keep her balance. Water splashed over her ankles. The red canyon walls rose up around them. A breeze rustled through the scrubby trees on the banks of the river. Emme looked back at the trail where they'd come from, then plunged ahead after the other three. They were in the river now, and there was no choice but to keep moving forward.

CHAPTER TWENTY

They had only gone a short way downriver when a sense of déjà vu washed over Emme. "Stop," she called to the others. She reached into one of her many pockets and drew out the printed photo that Max had taken of Sarai, in her bright purple puffer vest with her back to him. The other three came to stand next to her as she held up the picture, a miniature, two-dimensional version of the view they were currently standing in. The only thing missing was Sarai's figure, her blonde ponytail swinging as she gazed ahead of her at what should have been a long future.

"So we know they made it this far," Claire said. She snapped a few photos on her phone and jerked her chin at Addie. "Will you go stand how Sarai was standing? I want to see if I can estimate how far away Max was when he took the picture."

"You want me to play the murder victim?" Addie gave a visible shudder, but she sloshed through the water to assume the same position that Max had captured Sarai in, her back to them. Claire moved backwards, careful around the stones and logs in the river. Emme followed alongside, peering at Claire's camera until the angle looked just right.

"That's it," she said, and Claire clicked the button to take a burst of photos.

Though they did not encounter another soul as they hiked on, the canyon was anything but quiet. Birdsong filled the air, and the constant chatter of the river ran underneath it all. They stopped every several yards to examine the places Max and Sarai would have been, though Emme knew it was unlikely they would find any physical evidence. Somewhere between here and the campsites, they had been dragged off the trail to their fates, and though it would be near impossible to pinpoint the exact spot that had happened, they had about nine miles to try.

With each step, the walls of the canyon rose and closed in, illustrating the reason the hike was dubbed The Narrows in the first place. Cliffs of red and grey rock climbed high on either side of the river, worn smooth by thousands of years of erosion, their slippery surface a reminder of the power of water. The group followed the North Fork of the river, picking their way carefully around boulders and ducking under the occasional tree that had uprooted and fallen over to lean on the opposite wall. Emme felt the song of the river and the sigh of the wind deep in her bones; this place was part of what made her who she was. She felt herself sink into the rhythm of the canyon so that the hike became a moving meditation for her, connecting her to the earth and water beneath her feet and the sky above her head. It was odd, she thought as they moved through the canyon, how big and small Zion could make you feel all at once. It was easy to feel tiny beneath the looming rock walls, but beneath their shadows, she was what connected the cliffs to the river running between them. She was everywhere and everything in this place, and that made her feel like a giant. Though she had no ancestral claim to this land, she had sworn to protect and preserve it all the same, and there was never a time she felt the weight of that duty more than when walking through The Narrows, nothing but river and rocks surrounding her.

"Emme."

Claire's voice broke through her reverie. She stopped and turned, waiting for Claire to catch up to her. "What's up?"

"Do you think Max could have been pushed from the cliffs here?" Claire pointed to the top of the canyon walls, lined with scrubby trees and ponderosa pines. "It's certainly high enough to induce the kind of injuries he had."

Emme shook her head. "He had to have been killed further down, and in a couple of miles you'll see why," she said.

"The suspense is killing me. Let's go."

They dug their poles into the water, weaving around and over the rocky, slippery terrain. Addie was still in the lead, but Emme was barely a pace behind her, with Claire and Finn following closely behind. The water rose up to their calves, running in rivulets between stones, a thousand tiny waterfalls in every twist of the river. The canyon widened for a stretch, and the full sun beat down on them. And then, around a bend, the walls closed in like a book, as if a reader were holding their place with their finger, just barely open. "Oh God," Claire breathed, and Emme agreed; who needed a church when you could feel all the secrets of the universe right here in the river?

They entered the slot, the walls undulating like sand dunes on either side of them. Shadows arched over the canyon, turning the air from hot to cool in an instant. Everything hushed in a slot canyon, filtering sound as though through a long tunnel. The canyon narrowed until she could almost stretch out her arms and touch both sides, and they passed through a long corridor where the walls swelled and shrank like they were alive. *But they are*, Emme thought. Even the rocks were living things here, changing every day with the water, the sun, and the air.

The river was calm here, quieter in its babbling, with stagnant pools gathered in between the banks. They climbed over a log that had fallen across the path. Through another corridor, Emme began to hear what she'd been listening for: a rush of water, gathering force until it burst over a steep ledge. "There," she said, her voice too loud against the solitude of the canyon. "He had to have fallen after the waterfall."

Addie had already started down the walkaround that lay to the left of the falls, but Emme, Claire, and Finn stayed at the top, looking down over the flowing water. North Fork Falls had been created by jammed up boulders and fallen logs. The river didn't spill easily over its edge; it hit jagged rocks and shot through crevices between rotting wood. "If Max had fallen from one of the cliffs before the falls," Emme said, "his body would have been caught up here. There's no way it would have traveled all the way to Big Spring, where he was found."

"You don't think the force of the water could have pushed him downriver?" Finn asked.

"It's too calm below." Emme pointed down to where the water flowed gently away from the falls. "And to the side there? How the walls close in and there's a bank to the right?" Finn and Claire craned their necks, followed the line of Emme's outstretched arm to the bend in the river just beyond the falls. "The way the water flows, he would have been pushed up onto that bank. That's where he would have ended up, instead of downriver." Emme dropped her arm. "I think he died between here and the campsites."

"But where would he have fallen?" Claire asked. "It's impossible to get up those cliffs unless you backtrack all the way to where we entered the river."

"I don't think he did fall," Emme said, "in spite of what Ms. Rose Young says. I think all of his injuries, they came from blunt force trauma, from being beaten. And when they were done with him, they threw him in the river."

Below the falls, Addie had wandered back into view from the walka-round and struck out into the river. The water was deeper here at the base of the falls, nearly reaching her waist. She twisted around to look back at them, her hand shielding her eyes from the sun so that her expression was hidden in shadow. When she saw them still gathered at the top of the falls, she turned to face downriver again, her figure still as the current swirled around her.

"Sarai must have been forced to watch as they beat him," Finn said quietly, and Emme shuddered as she imagined the helplessness that Sarai must have felt in those terrible, agonizing moments.

"And then they marched her back up the trail to where you found her, tortured her, and killed her," Claire said, painting the whole nightmarish picture. They stood silent for a minute, gazing at Addie in her bright orange vest, as alive and vibrant as the canyon that surrounded them.

Standing there in the water, with the only sound the rush of the falls, something clicked in Emme's brain. "We keep saying 'they,'" she said. "I think there *were* two of them. Two killers, working as a team."

Claire nodded. "Yes. It makes the most sense. One restrained Sarai while the other killed Max. And while maybe she could have fought off one attacker, it's less likely she would have been able to fight off two."

"Especially if she knew them," Finn said. "Perhaps she thought she could reason with them."

Addie looked back at them again, impatience written in her stance. Emme took her cue and proceeded down the side of the falls, Claire and Finn falling in behind. Just beyond the falls, the river widened into the Deep Creek confluence, the water clear and blue under the afternoon sunlight streaming into the canyon. She and Claire slowed to a snail's pace, examining every rock and crevice for anything that might give them a clue as to where Max took his final breath. High above them, a pair of hawks wheeled in the sky, calling to each other in plaintive cries that echoed off the red rock walls. For a moment, Emme wondered if the hawks were Max and Sarai, haunting the place where they'd been so violently torn apart.

"Emme, which campsite are we at?" Addie asked, breaking through Emme's thoughts.

"Two," Emme called out, sloshing through the water to reach her sister. The river flowed fast and deep here, spraying high into the air as it collided with the large stones scattered across the riverbed. The twelve campsites were spread between Deep Creek and Big Spring, nestled on the riverbank at the base of the cliffs. Each little clearing was marked with rock piles and rough-hewn benches made from logs. When they reached Campsite Two, they all dropped their packs on the ground. Emme stretched her arms high, arching her back. She shimmied out of her hiking pants that were soaked to the thighs, trying not to feel exposed in the skintight bike shorts she had on underneath. The wilderness wasn't a place for modesty. "Let's set our drip line between those trees," she said, pointing to two spindly pine trees, "and catch some sunlight while we still can."

They got down to the business of setting up the campsite. Claire and Finn constructed the tents, their laughter as one of the tents collapsed three times before finally staying upright breaking the somber mood that had settled in the canyon. Emme stretched out the drip line and secured it to the trees, then hung out everyone's wet clothes. Addie took charge of the campfire. Emme watched her wander along the riverbank, looking for rocks to build a fire ring from. Sunlight dappled the shore, crowning Addie's brown hair with gold as she bent and hefted up a collection of sturdy round stones. She carried them back to the campsite and arranged a careful circle in between the tents. Claire emerged from out of the brush near the rock walls, carrying a bundle of sticks and twigs. "Will this work for kindling?" she asked Addie, dumping wood next to the fire ring.

"That's perfect." Addie pulled a homemade fire starter from her pack: half an egg carton, filled with sawdust and melted candle wax, leftover from the stash Sunny had always kept in the house. She tore one cup off the carton, tucked it into the kindling, and lit the very edge of the starter. It didn't take long to catch, the fire crackling and smoke spiraling up above the canyon walls. "We should gather some more wood so we can keep it going." Addie got to her feet and held her hand out to pull Claire up.

Emme breathed in deep, taking the scent of campfire deep into her lungs. Had Max and Sarai made it this far on their fateful trip? Their gear had never been found. Had they even made it to their camp?

Finn climbed out of his tent and settled down by the fire, holding his hands in front of it to warm them. He glanced over at Emme. "It's not even dark, but the fire feels nice. That river is pretty damn cold."

Emme smiled. She stepped carefully around the tents and backpacks still on the ground to join Finn at the fireside. The heat flushed her skin, warming the places chilled by the river. From behind the tents, she heard Addie and Claire rustle around in the brush, looking for firewood.

Finn cleared his throat. "I can, uh, sleep outside tonight if you want the tent to yourself. I don't mind."

"That's very chivalrous of you," Emme said. "But it gets *cold* when the sun goes down. I don't want you to freeze to death."

"I won't. I have a subzero sleeping bag. Really, it's not a problem. Besides," Finn leaned back on his hands and gazed up at the blue sky arcing above them, "I'm not sure how much I'll sleep anyway. This place . . . it feels haunted. By Max and Sarai."

Emme twisted to face him, startled by his echo of her own thoughts. "I was thinking the same thing, when I saw those hawks," she said. "I thought—maybe it was them, looking over us." She pulled her knees up to her chest, hugged her arms around them and rested her chin on her kneecaps. "The last time I was here, in this stretch of The Narrows, was the night I camped here with Max, the summer after graduation. I keep hearing his voice in my head, mansplaining to me how to build a fire, which I already knew how to do perfectly well. I asked him if he wanted to explain to me how to insert a tampon, too."

Finn burst out laughing. "How'd he respond to that?"

"You know, Max was always so good-natured. He pretty much said 'point taken' and let me build the fire." She lifted her chin off her knees. "We were at Campsite Five, I remember. Amy was there too—the waitress from Cap's Landing. She'd smuggled in some weed, and we got so high . . . it was so clear, with no moon, and the stars were so bright. Max pointed out a ton of constellations like The Peeing Boy and Shark Eating Man—"

"Um—"

"—and it wasn't until later we realized that he'd made them all up. We were too baked to know the difference." Emme let the memory wash over her, how they'd dissolved into giggles as he'd rattled off the ridiculous names. It filled her with sweetness, remembering how connected she'd felt that night—to her friends, to the canyon, to herself. But that sweetness was cut by the image of Max lying on that cold steel table in Rose Young's basement autopsy room, his skin blue-grey and his eyes closed forever. She inhaled, her breath hitching.

"You'll always have that memory, you know." Finn sat up straight. "His death—no matter what happened—can't take that from you."

She looked over at him to find his gaze resting softly on her face, and she cleared her throat. "Listen, Finn. About the other—"

Addie and Claire tripped out of the brush, carrying armloads of kindling. Emme stood up, as though she'd been caught in the middle of something she shouldn't be doing, and went to busy herself with the food. The sun began to dip below the mountains, casting shadows across the canyon. Addie kept the fire going while Emme prepared their dinner: salmon fillets, dressed with lemon slices, cooked in foil packets over the fire, with whole potatoes roasted separately that Finn had insisted on making. "It's my campfire specialty," he'd said when he'd shown them the Ziploc bag containing four potatoes and a squeeze bottle of butter.

By the time the meal was ready, dusk had gathered over the riverbank, turning the sky pink, then violet, then an ashy grey. The moon rose slowly, its far-reaching beams visible long before it appeared above the cliffs. By then, they were already roasting marshmallows for dessert. "Addie, yours is on fire," Claire said, pulling her lightly golden marshmallow off its stick.

"Addie likes them burnt," Emme said. She rotated her stick, trying to get just the right ratio of crispy to gooey.

Addie lifted her stick out of the fire and blew on her flaming marshmallow before popping it into her mouth. "Blackened marshmallow . . . *yum.*" She pointed her stick up to the sky. "Oh, look," she said, the words garbled around the marshmallow still in her mouth, "the eclipse is starting."

The moon had settled high above the red rock walls, now washed grey in its light. At the very bottom of its full white orb, a shadow began to creep in, eating away at the light like a caterpillar taking on a very big marshmallow. They let the fire die down so its glow wouldn't compete with the show taking place in the sky above and huddled under the extra blankets Emme and Addie had packed.

"I never thought this would be my job," Claire said, her voice hushed with awe. "Surrounded by wilderness, gazing up at the moon."

"This is all I ever wanted to do," Emme said, and the words punched her in the gut, the truth of them, deep in her heart. But her brain awakened all of her doubts: *why do the job if you are going to fail at it?*

Moonlight limned the canyon in shadow, dissolving color and leaving them in a world of black, white, and grey. "I always like to wonder what ancient people thought when they saw something like an eclipse," Finn said. "How did they explain it? Did they think the world was ending?"

"Maybe," Addie said. "Isn't it, though? Every generation thinks the world is going to end on their watch."

The shadow deepened on the moon, drenching its white face in red like a single perfect drop of pale blood on the black velvet background on the night sky. Some distance away, a fox yelped, followed by a cacophony of several other foxes, yowling at each other in the scarlet moonlight. Finn took several pictures on his fancy digital camera until Addie said firmly, "Put the camera down, you're ruining the moment," and Emme had to hide her grin behind her hand. The canyon was dark all around them but full of so much life and sound that Emme didn't ever want to go to sleep.

"Is that another campsite up there?" Claire asked softly, pointing down river to a small, flickering glow.

Emme leaned forward, peering into the darkness. "The next campsite isn't visible from here."

"There's a cave up there," Addie said.

A prickle went up Emme's spine. "Someone is camping in that cave," she said slowly. "Someone who doesn't have a permit."

She flung off the blanket and scrambled into the tent for her pack, digging into it for her headlamp and her gun. When she emerged, Claire had also strapped her headlamp on and held her own gun at her side. "Stay here with Addie," Emme instructed Finn. He nodded mutely, and the two of them huddled together under one blanket, their backs straight, tense and alert.

Emme and Claire struck out into the river, the water near freezing now without the heat of the sun. Their headlamps made small circles of light on the water, illuminating the stones and rivulets in the river. When they reached the bank just before the cave, they switched off their headlamps. Above the sound of the river, a voice floated back to them from the cave, thin and reedy and male, and singing. Emme froze, held her hand up to Claire. They listened.

"*The errand of angels is given to women,*

To do whatsoever is gentle and human . . ."

Claire looked at Emme and mouthed, "What the fuck?" Emme shook her head. Claire gestured to the two of them, then pointed at the cave and held up three fingers. She gripped her gun and counted down, lowering each finger one by one. When she'd dropped her third finger, they stepped into the mouth of the cave. In the stuttering firelight, their shadows loomed large as phantoms on the rocky walls.

"How vast is our purpose, how broad is our mission,
If we but fulfill it in spirit and deed."

Clouds of smoke filled the cave, obscuring the singing man from view. "Sir," Emme said, "I'm from the Park Service. You need a permit to camp overnight in The Narrows, and this is not a designated campsite."

"Oh, naught but the Spirit's divinest tuition—"

"Sir," Emme said, louder now, talking over his singing, "do you understand what I am telling you?"

"—Can give us the wisdom to truly succeed."

"Federal agent," Claire said, her voice booming in circles around the inside of the cave. She drew her badge out of her pocket with one hand, the other still holding her gun. "Do you understand that you are trespassing on federal land?"

"I don't answer to the federal government," the man said, his voice patchy and hoarse. "I answer only to God."

The words echoed a memory in Emme's brain: Abraham Murdock telling her *"the federal government ain't got no say on this land . . . We answer only to God."* She squinted through the gloomy shadows and shivering firelight, trying to see the man's face in between the wavering of light and dark. "You don't answer only to God. You answer to Abraham Murdock."

In one swift motion, the man jumped to his feet and kicked at the fire. Ash and embers clouded the air, dust thick in Emme's face. Coughing, she stumbled back and hit the rocky wall behind her, pushed herself hard away from its jagged surface, and bolted out of the cave opening. She switched her headlamp back on and lurched into the river, looking wildly in both directions until she spotted the Horseman's outline, moving fast down the river on foot.

"Stop!" she yelled. "It's not safe!" She fumbled forward in the darkness and tripped over a collection of stones, her shin hitting the river bottom hard enough to make her cry out. She hauled herself back up to her feet, but after a few steps, the Horseman had disappeared into the night, not a whiff of him left in the air. "Goddammit," she breathed. Not only had a potential suspect slipped through her fingers, but there was a good chance they'd find his drowned body tomorrow, washed up on the riverbank.

She sloshed back up to the cave, muttering swears under her breath until she stepped back through the opening. "He got away. It's not safe to hike in the river at night, but still—I let him get away. I'm—"

"Emme."

Something in Claire's voice stilled Emme inside and out, and she realized that Claire hadn't followed her out of the cave in pursuit of the Horseman. She stepped deeper into the cave, curiosity pinging in her at what could've kept Claire rooted to this spot. And then she saw it, just above their eye line: the dark splotch staining the wall of the cave, faint lines trailing down from the large spot and tiny dots spraying outward from above it. She moved closer, tilting her headlamp so that the stain was encompassed in its harsh light. A chill swept through her, every nerve ending in her body on edge. She didn't need a lab or a DNA test to tell her what the stain was and who it belonged to.

"This is where he died," Claire said, echoing what Emme already knew deep down. "This is Max's murder scene."

Chapter Twenty-One

A sleepless night brought a restless morning. They packed up the camp in the grey light before dawn, barely taking time to drink the coffee that Finn brewed over the fire. Emme didn't think the chill that had settled into her bones last night would ever leave, no matter how bright the sun shone down on them. When she stepped into the river in her mostly dry clothes, it was cold in a way beyond temperature.

The cave looked completely different in the daylight, shallow and wide, swept clean of shadows. She and Claire took photographs and chipped away a sample of the rock to be tested while Finn walked in circles, looping in and out of the cave with his fancy camera, recording audio on his phone. On their way downriver to Big Spring, they questioned everyone at the other occupied campsites, but no one had seen a man come through. It was like the Horseman was a ghost that she and Claire had imagined, a will-o'-the-wisp that had only appeared in the blood shadow of the lunar eclipse and then vanished when the moon turned white again.

Morning sunlight bathed the red canyon walls, turning them golden. At every step they took, around every bend in The Narrows, Emme expected to see the Horseman's body washed up on the riverbanks, to come upon a scene like how they'd found Max, surrounded by a group of hikers. But they reached the Riverside Walk without finding him. Somehow he had made it out of the canyon alive, in the pitch black of night, through rushing, freezing water, and there was no record of him ever being in The Narrows at all.

But whoever he was, he had now claimed the top spot on Emme's suspect list, and when she finally had his name, she would ride back into Redwater—this time with an arrest warrant.

*****

Paty's diner sat at the edge of town, its façade well-worn and its décor shabby, but its food as delicious as it had been since the day it opened thirty years earlier. The tables were crowded with locals. Emme slid into a booth, facing the door so she could watch for Finn, drumming her hands on the Formica tabletop. When he appeared a few minutes later, he caught sight of her right away and settled across from her. "Hey."

"Hey. Thanks for coming." When she'd texted him, she wasn't sure if he would respond, given the weirdness between them at the campsite, which hadn't been resolved by their hasty retreat from The Narrows. Claire was in Zoom meetings all morning at her hotel, and Addie was still asleep, giving her a bit of a respite. Relief had swooped through her when he'd texted back and accepted her invitation to breakfast.

The waitress, her grey hair piled into a loose bun on the crown of her head, dropped two menus on the table. "Coffee?"

"Yes, please," Emme said, and Finn nodded.

They were silent as the waitress returned a moment later with two mugs and poured the coffee out for them. She looked between them with an arched eyebrow. "I'll give you a minute," she said and sauntered away. Finn reached for his menu, but Emme curled her hands around her coffee cup instead, her eyes on his face.

"Listen," she said, leaning forward a bit, "I'm sorry for my behavior. The other night—morning—leaving your hotel, after . . ." She waved her hand. "I have a lot on my mind, but that's not your fault, and I shouldn't have made you feel like it is."

"Look, Emme . . ." Finn leaned in too, pushing his menu aside. "I appreciate that. I was worried I'd done something wrong."

"You didn't. You definitely didn't," she said, emphasizing the words in a way that made him grin. He sneaked his fingers forward so that they touched hers. She didn't pull away.

"Well, I'm glad to hear that. But, you know, I'm not an idiot or some swoony romantic or whatever. I'm not expecting a big relationship or anything like that," he said, his eyes searching her face.

She pursed her lips and snorted. "I wish I was in a place where I could have a big relationship," she said. "But I'm just not. That said . . ." She met his searching eyes, and his gaze settled on hers, warm and deep. "I wouldn't say no to a repeat, and maybe I wouldn't rush out so fast."

The corner of his mouth turned up. "Oh yeah?"

"You ready?"

They both jumped, their hands breaking apart. The waitress was back, a pencil and pad poised in her hands. Finn grabbed his menu. "I'll have French toast with a side of bacon," Emme said.

"And I'll have the Western omelette." Finn handed the menu back to the waitress. She scribbled down their order and moved to the next table.

Emme took a sip of her coffee. "So, are you recovered from your second excursion into The Narrows?" She hadn't realized how tense she'd been, holding onto that apology. Now that it was out there, her whole body relaxed. The coffee made a rich pool in her stomach, and the din of voices around them was a comforting lull.

"Barely. I'm trying to decide if I never want to go back there, or if I should push my luck on a third time." He dumped a couple of creamers and a sugar packet into his coffee, then stirred as he looked across the table at her. "Why do you think the Horseman returned to the scene of the crime? I know that serial killers often return to the scene of their crimes, but this isn't a serial killer scenario."

"I'll see your question and raise you one," Emme said. "Why was he there alone? I'm fairly certain that more than one person committed this crime."

"Maybe he was ordered to return to the scene and destroy evidence?"

Emme scrunched her face up and shook her head. "If he wanted to destroy evidence, why would he build a fire and sing hymns?" She could still hear the eerie tune in her head, like a plaintive piano. "He would've gone in and gotten back out fast."

The waitress returned with their order, two heavy plates balanced on her forearms. She landed the plates in front of them, refilled their coffee, and left them alone. Emme poured a healthy drizzle of syrup over her plate and dipped her bacon into it before taking a bite.

"Still, it makes the most sense that he was there on some kind of order, and we already know whose orders he would be following." Emme stabbed a forkful of French toast. "But what would Abraham Murdock have told him to do?"

The questions had gone round and round in her brain all night like a Ferris wheel, long after they'd left the park, delivered Finn and Claire to their respective hotels, gotten the car back from the other entrance, and arrived home where Addie had promptly disappeared into her room. Emme had been left alone with her thoughts, trying to separate out all the pieces of the puzzle and make them fit back together again. Sections of the puzzle were taking shape, but others remained unsolved no matter how many different configurations she tried.

A text message popped up on her phone screen from Addie: *Are you coming home soon?* Emme set her fork down and quickly typed back, *No. I left u a note.*

"Lara told me that Sarai should've been remarried to someone else after her first husband died," she said picking up her phone again. "Instead, she took up with Max behind her family's back." Her phone buzzed again—this time a phone call from Addie. Biting back a sigh, she held a finger up to Finn and answered. "Is everything okay?"

"Yes, but I need to know when you're coming home."

"I don't know, Addie. Finn and I are discussing the case. It could be a while."

"But—"

"I'll call you when I'm on my way back." Emme hung up and tucked her phone into her jacket pocket, blowing out a hard exhale.

"Two killers doesn't really track with the jealous rival theory," Finn said, and in an instant Emme's frustration with her sister fell into shadow as she sifted through her thoughts about the crime.

"But a man singing hymns—not to mention leaving flower chains with the body—*does* track with that theory," she said, gathering another French toast-bacon-maple syrup combo on her fork.

"Let's follow that theory for a moment," Finn said, flipping to a clean page in the spiral-bound notebook he'd pulled from his bag. "He does away with Max first, then drags Sarai back up through The Narrows and to the La Verkin trail in an attempt to get her to agree to marry him. There was no sign of a sexual assault though."

"Well, if he wanted to marry her, perhaps he wouldn't have assaulted her in an effort to keep her pure," Emme said, "although that doesn't quite track with the power the Warrior men like to exert over their women. But setting that piece aside . . . yes, it makes sense that the time and distance between Max's murder and Sarai's could have been taken up with the killer trying to get her to acquiesce. When she won't—"

"He kills her. And the condition of her body definitely points to a rage-filled killing. Except for—"

"—the flowers." They were on the same train of thought, the way that she and Stace often discussed investigations, usually over food just like this. "But the flowers could also be a man mourning for the loss of someone he thought would be his wife, and in his warped Warrior mind, he would view the killing as something that God intended or even approved of."

"I think this theory makes the most sense," Finn said. "At the very least, it has the least holes in it."

"But it still has holes, and those need to be filled." Emme used her last piece of bacon to mop up the last drops of maple syrup on her plate. "Like, what information was Max going to give you about Hannah's murder? *Did* he know something about Eli?"

Finn hunched one shoulder. "Both things could be true. He could've had information about Eli *and* been murdered by a jealous rival."

"True. But I have found that either / or situations are much more common than either / and," Emme said. She drained the last of her coffee and held up her hand to catch the waitress's attention for more. The waitress spotted her and nodded before she finished taking the order at the booth on the opposite side of the diner. She left the table to grab the coffee pot, revealing the lone diner who sat pressed into the corner of the booth: a young man in a red baseball cap and white t-shirt with a flannel jacket. Emme stared at the man and realized that, beneath the cap, he was staring right back at her. A memory flashed—the last time she'd seen him staring at her like that, an AR-15 slung over his shoulder . . . "Holy shit," she breathed. What had she just said about coincidences? "That's Josiah Murdock. Don't look," she hissed as Finn immediately did just that.

"Was he the guy in the cave?"

"No. I had never seen that guy before. But Josiah—Abraham's son—he was there the day I went to Redwater." Emme slid to the edge of the booth. "I'm going to talk to him."

She felt Finn's eyes on her back as she made her way across the diner, but she kept her gaze on Josiah, who straightened and removed his cap when she approached his table. "Josiah, right?"

He cleared his throat. "Miss Helliwell."

"May I sit?"

Josiah nodded and wrapped his hands around his coffee cup. "What brings you down the mountain?" Emme asked.

He looked down into his cup. "Sometimes I like to come to town to drink coffee. Father don't allow it at home." He hunched one shoulder. "Everybody slips, sometimes."

"Really. You came here for the coffee." Emme reclined back against the torn cushioning of the booth. "You didn't come here to see me?"

"How would I even know you'd be *here?*"

"I don't know, Josiah, maybe because you have my phone tapped? Or you've got people watching me? Was it you that broke into my house?" Emme pressed her lips together as the waitress returned to the table, placed a cup down in front of her, and filled it to the brim with steaming coffee, all without noticing that she was the same diner from another booth on the other side of the restaurant. When she left the table, Emme leaned forward. "I ran into your buddy in The Narrows the night before last. Any idea what he was doing there?"

"I don't have no buddy." Josiah kept his eyes fixed on the chipped and pitted Formica tabletop. "Sarai was my buddy," he said, so quiet that Emme had to rewind time in her head to make sure he'd actually said it. She stared hard at him and let those words linger in the air between them.

She hated the Warriors and everything they stood for. She remembered the trauma written across Lara's face, plain as a clear blue sky. It was hard to think of any man as a victim of the Warriors, not the way women were in that society where the men held all the power. But Josiah's crumpled posture, his bowed head, how he could barely raise his gaze to look at her . . . he was broken, too. His brother Eli, his sister Sarai . . . perhaps there were only so many times you could get battered before you shattered.

She knew it could be a trap, that he could be playacting to get something from her, but she could not help but soften. She rested her elbow on the table and cupped her chin in her hand. She wasn't going to push, but maybe if she prodded, very gently, she could get something from him instead. The waitress delivered a plate of eggs, sunny-side-up, with toast and jam and a side of sausage and bacon. Josiah removed his cap and held it over his heart for a moment with his head bowed. When he looked up again, he reached for the bacon first. "We don't get bacon up on the mountain," he said. "It's too expensive to fatten up the pigs."

"I try not to eat too much meat," Emme said, "but I've never been able to cut out bacon. It's just too damn delicious." She winked at him. "I like to dip mine into maple syrup."

Josiah's eyes widened like a kid on Christmas morning. "I ain't never tried that."

"No time like the present." She flagged the waitress down and asked for maple syrup. She returned a moment later with a little aluminum pitcher with a flip-top lid. Josiah tilted it over his plate and looked at her. She nodded. He pressed his thumb on the lid and drizzled the syrup over the bacon. "It's good on sausage, too," she added, and soon the entire plate was swimming in maple syrup. Emme sipped her coffee and watched the childlike delight cross Josiah's face as he tasted the sweet-and-savory combination.

"It's got to be hard," Emme said, "losing two siblings so close together."

"I'll see them soon enough," Josiah said, now dipping his toast into the bright yellow egg yolks.

A chill shivered across Emme's neck. "What do you mean?"

"We'll all be reunited when Armageddon comes," he said, his words a little muffled around the food in his mouth. "And after, we'll be together forever. We'll be immortal."

"I guess that's a comfort," Emme said, but the word *immortal* stuck in her mind, spinning in a circle until it stopped on the image of a red flower. Amaranth, the plant that was left with Sarai's body and in the Bible at her house. It meant immortality. She shifted slightly in the booth. "When someone in your family dies, do you have a ceremony? Or some kind of ritual?"

Josiah shrugged. "We bury them in the family plot and Father says some words. Same as any ordinary funeral." He stabbed his fork into the last of his sausage. "Except if they done something bad."

"What happens then?" Emme kept her voice soft, as though she were gentling a frightened animal who could bolt at any moment.

"Then they don't get anything. No funeral, no burial, no words."

"No flowers?"

Josiah snapped his head up, his grip tightening around his fork. "I know how you feel about our beliefs, Miss Helliwell. And I know you're fishing for information."

"And I know that you didn't just come here for the coffee." Emme steepled her fingers under her chin. "I think you came here to tell me something."

Josiah lowered his gaze and picked up his second piece of toast to mop up the last of the egg yolk. He didn't look at her, but the deep grooves in his forehead told Emme that he was thinking, pondering something, maybe weighing whether he wanted to talk or not. She could wait. She turned a little to glance back at Finn, and her elbow slipped off the table.

Addie stood at Finn's table, her gaze following Finn's pointing finger until it landed on Emme. She marched across the diner toward Emme, her eyes like two little bursts of fire on her pale face. "Excuse me," Emme muttered to Josiah and scrambled out of the booth to meet Addie in the middle of the diner. "What are you doing here?"

"Because you wouldn't talk to me!" Several people seated nearby looked over at Addie's exclamation.

Emme grabbed her elbow and guided her outside onto the front porch of the restaurant.

"What the hell? I'm *working!*"

"You had a meeting with the lawyer for Mom's estate," Addie said, her nostrils flaring as she breathed sharply in and out. "He showed up at the house. That's why I was calling you, and you just cut me off."

"Oh, shit." Emme pinched her forehead together as a hot thread of shame twisted through her. She'd set that meeting up so long ago, even set a reminder for herself a week before in her phone . . . and then promptly forgot it in the aftermath of their trip into The Narrows. "I'm sorry, Addie. I—"

Addie held her hand up. "You know, I don't want you to apologize for missing the meeting." She jabbed her finger too close to Emme's face. "What I want you to apologize for is not letting me help. I could have handled that meeting with the lawyer, but instead I was left looking like an idiot because I don't know where you keep any of the documents you have for the house and the bakery. I kept him waiting there while I practically ransacked the house all over again looking for it."

"I moved it after the break-in—"

"And you know what else you can apologize for?" Addie crossed her arms over her chest. "For assuming that I was calling you to bug you or for some stupid reason. It wasn't a stupid reason. It was important."

"I'm sorry, Addie, okay?" Emme pressed the heels of her hands into her eye sockets. "It's not that I don't trust you," she said as bright bursts of light and dark popped behind her eyes, "it's just that I'm the oldest, and it's my responsibility—"

"But it doesn't have to be!" Addie put her hands on Emme's and drew them away from her eyes. Her fingers were calloused against Emme's palms as she gripped them. "I'm not a baby anymore, Emme. It's not like when we were kids, when you always had to watch me while Mom was working. I'm a big girl now. For Chrissake," she said, shaking Emme's arm, "I was just living out of a tent with no running water in Tanzania. I can *handle* things."

Emme sighed and closed her eyes again. She wanted to believe that Addie was right, but her mother's voice was like a playlist on repeat in her head: *you have to take care of your sister, you're the oldest, be the responsible one* . . . Addie had been so little when they'd fled New York, and Emme never wanted her to feel the weight of their escape on her shoulders the way Emme had. She opened her eyes and looked back into the restaurant . . . just in time to see Josiah Murdock jam his cap back on his head and sidle out the back door. "Goddammit," she hissed, snatching her hands out of Addie's. "I just lost my witness because you had to come down here to yell at me."

"That's not—"

"Go home, Addie," Emme said, her voice harsher than she intended, but she couldn't pull it back anymore. There were too many things piled up inside her, and her sister was the only thing within reach that she could knock off the pile. She turned away from Addie's stricken, angry face and slammed back into the diner.

CHAPTER TWENTY-TWO

A frost between the two sisters filled the rooms of the house, so thick it might as well have been snowing. Emme shut herself away in her bedroom, reconstructing her case file board as best she could, while Addie worked on the piles in the living room. The strains of plaintive jazz music wove their way through the halls, bringing a lump to Emme's throat that she tried to swallow down as she stuck her cork board with pushpins. She ran red string from the pin in The Narrows to the pin marking the map at Redwater, then wrote *WHO WAS IN THE CAVE* in Sharpie on a white index card and attached it in the middle of the red string path.

Her phone buzzed on the bed with a reminder. Emme stepped back to assess the board. It was close to where it had been before the break-in, and after the meeting, she was heading out to she expected it to grow even more. She threw everything she needed into her bag, grabbed a down vest from her closet, and stepped tentatively into the living room.

Addie was nearly hidden by the towering piles of stuff, but Emme noticed that there were less piles now. She had them lined up along the floor in front of the couch, and in the corner closest to the kitchen there were bags clustered together either marked *JUNK* or *DONATION*. She didn't look up when Emme entered the room.

"I have a meeting with Claire," Emme said, waiting for her sister to acknowledge her.

"Okay." Addie placed *The White Album* on vinyl on top of a stack of other records.

Emme shifted her bag on her shoulder. "You're not getting rid of those, are you?"

"No, Emmeline, I am not getting rid of Mom's prized record collection." Addie's face pinched, but she still didn't look at Emme. "If you don't trust me to do this I can stop—"

"I trust you," Emme said quickly, but she knew that Addie didn't believe her. She stood there for another long minute, during which Addie added *Yellow Submarine* and *Rumours* to the stack, reached for the wood spray and rag that was on the coffee table, and carefully wiped out the shelf that housed their mother's beloved records. On Addie's phone, the playlist spun from Aretha Franklin to Astrud Gilberto, notes of nostalgia and longing that made Emme's chest pull tight. She knew she should stay, put one of those records on and sit next to Addie to talk through their issues while they worked together. Her phone buzzed with another reminder that she was due to meet Claire at her hotel in fifteen minutes. Emme ran her hand down her face. She could feel them getting close to figuring out who had murdered Max and Sarai, and why; she couldn't stop now.

"I'll see you later," she said finally, earning barely a nod from Addie as she stepped around the mounds of stuff and made her way out the door.

As she reached for the handle, pounding on the other side of the door cracked through Addie's jazzy playlist, wild and frantic. Emme pulled open the door and a slight figure stumbled over the threshold, blonde hair tangled and matted, brown eyes wide and desperate. "Lara!"

"Thank God you're here." Lara DeLeo flung her arms around Emme who, after a stunned moment, hugged her back. Her spine protruded beneath Emme's hands, the sharp bones of her collarbone cutting into Emme's shoulder.

"How did you—"

"I escaped." Lara's voice was raspy, as though it had gone unused for a long stretch of time. "I hiked down the mountain and hitchhiked to Springdale. I didn't know where else to go."

"No, I'm glad you came here." Emme stepped back to assess Lara. Dark circles swallowed up her eyes, and bruises bloomed on her cheek and throat. Her skin was gaunt and grey, and her clothes hung ragged and loose over her skeletal frame; she was clearly malnourished. "I'm taking you to the hospital."

"Can I do anything?" Addie asked. She'd gotten to her feet, and her confused gaze flitted from Emme to Lara and back again.

"I've got it handled," Emme said. She grabbed a spare coat from the rack by the door and draped it around Lara's shoulders before ushering her out onto the porch and into her car. "I can't believe you got out of there," she murmured as she turned the car on and shot off a quick text to Claire, telling her she'd be late. "How *did* you get out of there?"

Lara leaned back in the seat, hugging the coat tight around her. "Neveah. She let me out during one of the shift changes. I hope they don't find out or she'll wind up in there herself."

Emme sped through town, the hotels and restaurants blurring on either side of her. "Who hit you?"

"Mark David," Lara whispered. Her eyes were haunted. "He'll never let me go, not as long as we're both alive."

"Did he kill Sarai?"

"I don't know." Lara blinked, and her eyes filled with tears. "I think he might have. He said that if I talked to you again, I would end up like her." She let out a soft whimper, and Emme stopped asking questions, let her close her eyes and rest until they arrived at the hospital. Emme watched as a nurse wheeled Lara away, then dropped into a chair in the waiting room to call the local sheriff. Not until they had stationed a guard outside her door did she finally leave to make her way to the Cliffrose.

Claire answered the door to her hotel room dressed in sweats with her hair tied up in a scarf. "How's Lara?"

"She's clearly been through hell, but she's getting good care at the hospital." Emme shrugged her vest off and dropped it onto one of the armchairs in the room. "She'll be there a few days, and she'll have an officer on watch round the clock."

"Good." Claire slid into one of the chairs at the table. It was neatly laid out with all of her maps and files, with space cleared for Emme's things.

"She thinks Mark David might have killed Sarai." Emme dropped into the opposite chair and ran her hands through her hair, as though her fingers could ease the swirling in her mind.

"Well, I definitely want to question her. When she's up to it," Claire said.

Emme's phone buzzed with a text from Stace: *Ready?*

"Stace is waiting." She got her laptop out of her bag and launched Zoom. It took a moment, but when Stace's face appeared on the screen, a wave of affection rolled through her. He was in his office that she knew so well, the cracked leather chairs, the big oak desk with the bottom drawer hiding a bottle of single-malt Scotch and two glasses, the view of Yosemite Valley just beyond the window. Even though it wasn't her home, it made her homesick.

"Hello Eustace," Claire said. "It's nice to meet you face to face."

"Good to meet you too. And please, call me Stace. Everyone does." Stace leaned forward a bit so that his face loomed large on the screen. "Emme. You doing okay?"

"I'm okay." The corner of her lip curled up. "I miss doing this in person. We'd be breaking into that bottle in your bottom drawer."

Stace laughed. "I can't promise I won't be reaching for that before this meeting is over."

"I can have room service send up some wine," Claire offered.

"My kind of agent." Stace pointed at the camera, like he could poke through the miles and tap her shoulder. "Glad Bucey saw fit to assign you to this case," he said, naming the FBI supervisor at the Salt Lake City field office. "Let's get into it. Walk me through the crime."

As Emme laid out for Stace how she and Claire had pieced together the murders, she could see it all in her mind's eye, like a movie played on a screen in her brain, filling in details she could imagine were true.

There's a song on the radio in the car that makes them laugh as they drive towards Zion, away from Redwater, maybe for the last time. 'I don't ever want to set foot in that place again,' Sarai tells Max, and he tells her that by the time they hike out of The Narrows, the Warriors will be chasing a different scent down a different trail. They'll hike out of the park and into freedom.

The sun hasn't even risen yet when they drive past the stone entryway, but there's already a line at the Visitors Center for those hoping to score walk-in permits to camp in The Narrows. Max parks the car and gets in line while Sarai waits with their stuff. Behind him are two sleepy young women with enormous cups of coffee that Max is sure they'll pay for later when they'll have to use the sanitary bags the office hands out along with the permits. But Max doesn't say anything, just keeps an eye on Sarai alone in the parking lot. Every car that pulls in sends him on high alert, and he can feel her tension across the lot.

The permits desk opens at last, and Max gets the fourth one of the day. He carries his treasure out to Sarai. Pink sunlight strikes the lot, bathing her in its soft glow, turning her face into a Botticelli painting. His chest pulls as he walks toward her, how much he loves this woman, how this time next week they'll be safely out of the Warriors' reach.

"But he left home on Tuesday. His permit was for Wednesday. So where did he spend Tuesday night?" Stace asked.

"There's a cell phone ping in Salt Lake City—the same block as the FBI office—so we suspect he may have gone there with information about Eli Murdock," Claire explained. "But there's no record of him visiting anyone in the office. I have a request for security camera footage from the reception desk to confirm whether or not he was there."

"As for where he spent that night," Emme said, "there's another ping near Beaver that evening. We suspect they were on their way back to Zion and pulled off somewhere to spend the night, maybe in his car."

"Okay." Stace bent his head, and Emme knew he was making a note in his list of "plot holes" the same way she had done in her notebook.

At the Chamberlain Ranch trailhead they strike out fast, hoping to put some distance between themselves and any other top-down hikers. Max carries the tent and heaviest gear on his back, his trusty Nikon strapped across his chest, the strap loose enough so that he can easily raise it to his eye when the light streams through the canyon just right. When they step into the river, the bright morning sun catches Sarai's figure like a child catches a firefly. 'Hold it, babe,' he calls to her and captures her image with the camera. He looks at it, and she's so beautiful his breath hitches. 'I want to stay in this moment forever,' he thinks, and takes a duplicate picture with his phone so he can set it as his wallpaper.

All morning and into the afternoon, they hike down the canyon. They are unaware of the ruckus back at the Visitors Center at the eastern entrance, of the Warrior who comes looking for them and is forbidden entry to the top-down trail. They do not realize the flaw in their plan: while everyone needs a permit to enter The Narrows from the top, no one needs one to enter it from the bottom.

"So you think whoever that Warrior was, he backtracked down to the main entrance, drove to the Temple of Sinawava, took Riverside Walk on foot, and then hiked into The Narrows from the bottom-up?" Stace arched an eyebrow.

"Yes," Emme said. "The cave where we ran into the Warrior on our trip wasn't that far past the turnaround point for the bottom-up hike. I believe he hiked up the river, found the cave, and laid in wait for them."

How could they know? The sky above them is cloudless and blue, there's a calm breeze through the canyon, and they speak little as they hike down. It's one of the things Max loves most about Sarai, that there is no need for conversation when they are surrounded by such beauty. When they reach the waterfall, Max crouches down and takes a dozen pictures of the way the light hits the water. He'll edit them later on his laptop, maybe even sell them to one of the outfitters in town to use on their website.

They are the only ones in the river now, as the afternoon sun stretches over the cliffs, dappling the rock walls with light and shadow. Campsites one, two, and three are empty when they pass by; Max could not know that they would not be filled, that he and Sarai are the last ones in the canyon that day, that there would be no one between Campsite Four and the trailhead to witness what is about to happen.

Darkness falls early in the canyon, and Sarai ventures out to get firewood. Max is occupied setting up their little tent; one of the poles is missing, and he has to dig around in his pack to find out. It's a while before he notices that Sarai hasn't returned. He stands and looks up the river, listens for her footsteps. But there's only the water burbling over its rocky surface and the distant call of a fox. He calls her name. No response.

Did he know something was wrong when he set foot in the river again, hiking upstream to look for Sarai? He only has to round the slight bend in the river to find out. The cave is awash with firelight, and in its glow he sees Sarai being held by one man while another leans in close to her face, speaking low. Max can't hear what he's saying, but he sees the way his words fills Sarai's eyes with terror. She sees him before they do, and shakes her head hard. He knows she's trying to warn him away, telling him to leave her and go.

But that's not who Max is.

"He went in to protect her," Emme said. She wanted the movie in her mind to end, but she couldn't stop seeing it. "They killed him there, and probably waited until dawn to push his body into the river."

"But Sarai wasn't killed for another couple of days," Stace said. "There's no way they took her directly to the La Verkin trail. Someone would have found her before then."

"We're still working that out," Claire said.

"I think she may have been taken to a remote part of the park, somewhere off-limits to the public," Emme said, "and perhaps held there while the killers tried to convince her to come back to the cult."

"Why not just bring her back to Redwater for that?" Stace asked.

"Again, still working that out," Claire replied.

"I think one of the killers was reluctant," Emme said. She looked out the sliding glass door to the balcony that overlooked the canyon. Late afternoon sun tipped the treetops with golden light. "I think she may have been able to convince them to keep her in the park, hoping that he would change the other one's mind and let her go."

Stace began to list his plot holes: Where were Max and Sarai headed after The Narrows? Where was Sarai taken in the time between when Max was killed and her own death? Who was the jealous rival that was the prime suspect? It was a list of questions that she'd already written in her own notebook. A bird landed on the balcony railing, its feathers brown and speckled white; a canyon wren. Emme watched it hop along the rail, perhaps chasing a tasty insect.

"Okay," Stace said finally, settling back in his chair. Emme heard it creak. "Good work. I know you two will fill those holes and get this solved."

"Thanks, Stace," Claire said.

"Emme, you take care, you hear?"

She half-smiled at him. "I always do, don't I?" she said, and clicked End Meeting for All before he could respond.

"He seems like a good guy," Claire said. She stood up and stretched.

"He's the best."

Claire slid open the door to the balcony, letting in a swish of fresh air. The bird twittered and flew away. "You hungry? How about some room service?"

Emme's stomach growled. She'd been so busy avoiding Addie at home that she hadn't eaten in hours. "That sounds amazing."

They ordered food and wine and Emme wandered out to the balcony while Claire had a call with her assistant in the room. She leaned against the railing and gazed out over the green lawn to the red cliffs of Zion that surrounded the hotel. In the distance, two hawks waltzed in circles above the tree line, and Emme wondered for a brief moment if they were the same hawks she'd seen in The Narrows, the ones she thought were Max and Sarai, watching over them. She squeezed her eyes shut. Of course they weren't the same hawks.

When she opened her eyes again, they were filled with tears.

She swiped at them angrily; this wasn't her, crying at every turn, her emotions riding just below the surface. She was more professional than this—there was an FBI agent in the other room, for god's sake. She could only imagine what Claire would put in her report to her superiors whenever they finally wrapped up this case: *If Emmeline Helliwell is any indication of the sort of agents in the ISB, they are too emotional to withstand the heavy work of investigating federal crimes.* She was an embarrassment—to the ISB, to Stace, to herself.

Claire's footstep on the balcony behind her made her jump. "Sorry," Claire said with a laugh. "Didn't mean to startle you. I'm done with my call. The food should be here soon—hey, are you okay?"

She used to be so good at keeping her thoughts and feelings hidden, shut away in a little box while she puzzled through the intricacies of a case. "God," Emme whispered, "you must think I'm a mess."

Claire furrowed her brow. "I don't think you're a mess, Emme. I think you're human."

Emme choked out a sound that was a snort, a laugh, and a sob rolled into one. But she was supposed to be stronger than the average human, able to climb mountains while packing in rescue gear, rappel from helicopters, and track a killer through dense forest. Surely Claire knew how that felt, she thought. She opened her mouth to ask, but there was a knock on the door.

The room service guy rolled the table right out to the balcony and helped them set up their meal so they could overlook the canyon while they ate. He poured their wine from little carafes into bulbous wineglasses, removed the silver domes from their plates, and even said, "*Bon appetit*," before gliding back out the door.

When they had settled across from each other, Emme sat very still, as though she might shatter if she made any sudden movements. "How do you do it?" she asked. "How do you keep your humanity when you need to be superhuman to do this work?"

Claire considered her for a long moment while sipping her wine. "I think you make a choice," she said finally. "I think you either stay human, or you lose that humanity in your effort to be better than human."

The sentence swirled in Emme's brain like a dangling caterpillar. She knew what Claire meant, but she'd never looked at it like that, so plain and clear. "But staying human makes this job so much harder."

"Isn't that the point?" Claire tipped her glass toward Emme. "Look, we both know the kind of inner strength it takes to do the work that we do. But it also takes an inordinate amount of softness, to empathize with our victims, to put ourselves in their shoes, even to get into the mindset of our killers. You can't solve these crimes if you're too hard."

Emme breathed in deep, put voice to the question that had been silently stalking her for weeks. "What if—you've lost the strength and all you are is soft?"

Claire placed her glass down and leaned her elbows on the table. "Emme. Is that what you're afraid of? That you've become soft?"

She nodded, her throat too tight to speak.

"You just lost your mother. That's going to bring anyone to their knees." Claire tilted her head to one side. "You need to give yourself some grace."

"It's not just my mom." Emme coughed to clear the gravel from her voice. "Hannah DeLeo . . . when I was called to the campground. Eli Murdock, he was so slick . . . he said all the right things, and I let them go. I let them go," she repeated, her words cracking. "Two days later she was dead."

Claire ran her hand over the scarf tying her hair back. "You can't keep beating yourself up about this. We all—"

"Don't say we all make mistakes." She pushed back from the table and paced up and down the balcony. "I should've known. Me, of all people, should've been able to see that he was abusing her and gaslighting me." She stopped right in front of Claire and hugged herself. "My father was the same way. He abused my mother, and he was such a smooth talker; he would beat the living crap out of her and then turn it all around so that by the end she would think it was all her fault and she'd be the one apologizing."

"Oh god, Emme. I'm so sorry." Claire stood. Emme backed away. She didn't want compassion and sympathy, not yet; she needed to live in the cold harsh reality of what she'd done first. "How old were you?" Claire asked.

"When I was eleven, he turned his anger on me." Emme's breath came hard and fast. "That was the push my mother needed to get us out of there. We fled in the middle of the night, came west. We never saw him again. He died a year later in a bar fight. So you see," she barreled on, cutting off Claire before she could speak again, "I know what it looks like. Domestic violence. And I didn't see it. I could've saved Hannah. But I didn't see it," she finished, her voice torn away as sobs broke through.

"Emme." Claire's voice sounded distant, as though they were separated by a long tunnel. "Wasn't your mother sick at the time? Weren't you taking care of her when the DeLeo case happened?"

"I still should have—"

"You're human, and humans make mistakes. God, Emme, you have to forgive yourself." Claire reached out and took her hand. "There is never a balance in what we do. You know? It's life and death, and the scales are always tipped one way or the other. And life is so fragile." Her eyes shined in the gathering dusk, wet with emotion. "The slightest weight can tip the scale towards death. And we try so hard to keep the scale balanced, or tip it back towards life. Sometimes we succeed." She squeezed Emme's hand, so hard her bones creaked. "And sometimes we fail."

"But the price of that failure is someone's life." Emme shook her head. "I don't know if I can live with that anymore."

"Yes, you can. You know why? Because that failure also means that next time you'll do better, and someone else's life will be saved by what you learned." Claire let go of Emme's hand, sat back down at the table, and picked up her wine again. "Now sit and eat. Your food is getting cold."

Emme snorted, but she sat down and stared at the turkey burger on her plate. "You know, I'm supposed leave the ISB. I was on my last two weeks, before this case. I just wanted to fade away and exit gracefully."

Claire paused, a French fry halfway to her mouth. "And now? Have you changed your mind?"

No. Yes. No. Yes. She hitched one shoulder up. "I don't know. I think—I want to continue, but not if I'm going to keep doubting myself like this. And I don't know how to stop doubting myself."

Claire ate the fry, dipped another in the little pot of ketchup, and ate that one, too.

"There are always going to be cases that shake us to our core. And questioning everything is part of our job." She leaned in, her gaze glittery on Emme's face. "But that's where the strength comes in. And you have that, Emme. I've seen it. You're not just softness." She settled back in her chair. "So your core is off its axis right now. That happens to all of us from time to time. You just have to figure out what's going set it right again." Claire took a sip of wine. "I hope you do stay. I think we make a pretty good team." She lifted her glass.

Emme sighed and picked up her own glass. She didn't know what would set her right again, but somehow, Claire had made her feel like she'd eventually figure it out. She touched her glass to Claire's. The sound rang out into the night like a church bell.

She replayed Claire's words over and over in her head as she made her way home. As she pulled into the driveway, her headlights washed over the front porch, and she remembered the night she'd come home with Finn to find Addie huddled on the porch swing. And she knew, without a shred of doubt, that she'd never be set right again if she didn't make peace with her sister.

She cut the engine and galloped up the front steps and through the door. The living room was empty, the piles neat and organized. "Addie?" Her sister didn't answer. She found her in Sunny's bedroom, sitting on the bed, folding clothes into her oversized duffle bag. "What are you doing?"

Addie barely glanced up at her. "What does it look like I'm doing? I'm leaving."

Chapter Twenty-Three

Emme stared, trying to wrap her mind around Addie's words. "You're what?"

"I'm leaving." Addie layered a couple of tank tops, rolled them up into a tight coil, and tucked them into her bag. "The university called. They offered me a Field Director position on a dig in Botswana."

"Oh." Emme twisted her hands together, digging her fingernails into her palms. "But—we still have so much to sort through. What to do with the bakery . . . and Mom's memorial—"

"I'm sure you'll have no trouble handling that on your own," Addie said, and the bite in her voice was unmissable. "You don't need me here for any of that, it seems."

"Addie, that's not fair." Emme stepped into the room, but there was an invisible barrier between her and Addie that held her back. "It's hard for me to relinquish control. You know that about me. You've always known that."

"Well, if there's ever a time to work on that issue, this is it." Addie laid out several pairs of jeans, putting the ones with ripped knees into a pile.

"You want to talk about issues? How about you running away when things get the tiniest bit hard?" Emme planted her hands on her hips and Addie jerked her chin up, anger flashing across her face at the nerve that Emme had just sunk an arrow into. "That's why it took you so long to finish school. You kept changing your major every time you got a B."

"That is not—"

"Grief isn't something you can run away from, Addie." There were so many thoughts tumbling through Emme's brain, and she couldn't put voice to all of them fast enough. "It's going to follow you all the way to Botswana."

Addie balled up a sweatshirt that appeared to have bleach stains on it and threw it in the corner. "You know, this is actually a really great opportunity. It's the first time I'd essentially be leading a dig."

"That's great. I mean it, that really is great," Emme insisted when Addie raised her eyebrows at her. "But you can't delay for a week or two? Until after we decide what to do with the bakery, with Mom? You have to leave right this instant?"

"Flights to Botswana aren't easy."

"Oh for fuck's sake, Addie! This is the twenty-first century. I'm sure I can go into my Expedia app and find a flight to Botswana any day of the week." Emme pulled her phone from her pocket and shook it at her sister. "You are using this as an excuse to run away."

Addie paused her packing, narrowed her gaze right into Emme's eyes. "I'm only taking a page from your book, dear sister," she said, and it was her turn to land an arrow right in Emme's most sensitive nerve.

She inhaled sharply. "What do you mean?" she asked, even though she knew exactly what Addie was getting at. But she wanted it all out in the open, all the words they'd been holding back spoken out loud at last.

"When the going gets tough, the tough leaves the ISB," Addie said.

"That is totally different," Emme said, even though she knew it wasn't. "If we want to keep the bakery, someone is going to have to stay to run it."

"Bullshit." Addie jabbed her finger at Emme. "This has nothing to do with Mom, or the bakery. This has everything to do with Hannah DeLeo's case. You think you fucked up, so instead of sticking around to make up for your mistakes, you're quitting."

"A woman died, Addie! I *did* fuck up." It was easier to say it after the conversation she'd had with Claire. *You're human, and humans make mistakes.* But it still hurt, the pain wedged deeply in her core that was still off its axis.

"Emme, you investigate crimes. Someone *always* dies. That's your job."

"Yes, but I could have prevented—"

"How? How could you have prevented a murder? This isn't *Minority Report*. You're not a mind reader." Addie's face pinched, her lips white. "You can't always recognize abuse. Sometimes you don't even see it when it's happening to you."

Emme fell silent, staring at Addie. Everything in her face, her posture, her tone spoke to a deep personal experience with what she just said, not something she had only read or heard about. "What are you talking about?" she asked gently, the way she talked to skittish witnesses when she needed vital information from them.

Addie chewed at her lip. A drop of bright blood blossomed there. "I was seeing someone in Tanzania," Addie said finally. Her voice was hoarse. "She—wasn't good for me."

"Oh, Addie." Emme broke through the invisible barrier and sat on the edge of the bed. "What happened?"

"She was the Dig Director, so she was in charge of everything, and everyone." Addie looked down and pulled at a loose thread on the bedspread. "It didn't happen overnight. At first she was so supportive and encouraging, complimenting my work, making sure I was assigned to the higher profile spots—"

"Love bombing," Emme murmured.

Addie nodded. "I know now that's what it was. It's very intimate at a dig, like a family—we're all in close quarters, working together, sleeping and eating together . . . it just sort of seemed to happen naturally, going from sleeping near each other to sleeping with each other." She wound the loose thread around her forefinger, so tight that it turned her finger red. "I felt lucky, you know? Like out of all the workers, she'd picked me. And things were really good for a while." She pulled the thread, and it broke with a snap.

"And then?"

"It was little things at first. Like, she'd read my texts over my shoulder and if I was on the phone she was always in the room. And she'd insist on eating every meal with me, even if it meant I had to wait to have dinner at nine o'clock at night after she was finished with all her work. She'd get jealous if I was hanging out with the other workers without her—especially the men," Addie said. "She was fixated on me being bisexual, like I was going to suddenly decide I wanted to be with a guy instead of her."

Emme groaned. "Gross." She wanted to keep Addie talking, spilling out her story, but her gut was twisting into a knot of guilt.

"And it just escalated from there," Addie went on, "until she had complete control without me even realizing it." She looked up at Emme, her eyelashes beaded with tears. "She took my phone, Emme. That's why I didn't respond to your messages. I never got them. She kept my own mother's death from me because she didn't want me to leave," she said, her voice cracking as the tears fell onto her cheeks. "It wasn't until I was alone in the field office one day and took a call from the university. That's when I finally found out."

Emme reached out and put her hand on top of Addie's. The knot inside her was tightening, but she had to know the rest. Addie swallowed. "I went ballistic, screaming at her, and she turned it all around on me, calling me unhinged and crazy in front of everyone. But there were a couple of women who saw what was really happening. They drove me out of the site and got me on a plane back to the States." She sniffled. "I kept telling them that she had never hit me, so she couldn't be abusive. And they said that emotional abuse—control and manipulation like that—is just as dangerous as physical abuse. I couldn't get their words out of my head. The whole trip back, I just stared out the window, replaying them over and over and breaking down everything she'd ever done to me." Addie shook her head, as though she was still hearing those voices. "By the time I landed in Utah, I knew they were right." She crumpled forward, her shoulders shaking. When she spoke, her voice was muffled, pressed against the mattress. "Emme, you have to know I would've been here. If I'd gotten those messages, if I'd known how serious her illness was, I would've been on the next plane—"

"I know," Emme said. She rubbed Addie's back, feeling the knobs of her spine through her thin T-shirt. "I know you would've been."

Addie sat up and wiped her nose with the back of her hand. "I feel so dumb. I should've seen what was happening."

"It's not your fault, Addie." Emme drew in a long, shaking breath. Shame and guilt roiled inside her, like a volcano threatening to erupt. "It's my fault. Mine—and Mom's."

"What?" Addie drew back a little. Her eyes were red and her cheeks splotchy, but she met Emme's gaze in an unflinching way. "What do you mean?"

Emme looked away; it was too much to see herself reflected in Addie's wide, wet eyes. "You were so little," she said, "when we left." *How do you tell a three-year-old that her father is a monster?* But she didn't say that out loud. "Mom already felt so much guilt about what he'd done to me. She didn't want heap trauma on you, too."

"What who had done to you?" Addie had gotten very still. Emme still couldn't look her in the face.

"Dad," Emme whispered. The name shredded her insides; it had been so many years since she'd voiced it or given him any weight in her life. "He used to hit Mom—a lot. You were so young. I would hide you in our room, put music on really loud so you couldn't hear. Then one day . . . he hit me." She finally jerked her gaze back to Addie, who was sitting so frozen it was like time had stopped. "That was the straw that broke Mom. She waited until he was passed out drunk and then we got out, drove all the way across the country to get away from him."

Addie's nostrils flared, the only sign that she was still breathing. "That's why we left?"

Emme nodded. "You were so little. We didn't want—"

Addie held up her hand, cutting Emme off. "So you and Mom just collectively decided to keep this from me? This, like, extremely important piece of our family history?"

"But Mom didn't want it to be a part of our family story," Emme said. Sunny had never told her to come out and lie to Addie, but she was too young to hold onto any real memories of the time before they'd left. "After we got out here, and then he died, he just gradually disappeared from our everyday lives." Emme hunched her shoulders. "There just wasn't any reason to bring it up when you were old enough to understand."

"Well, you should have," Addie said, and now she was an explosion of movement. She tossed the folded clothes aside and jumped off the bed, paced to the wall, slammed her hand on it and spun to face Emme. "You should have been talking to me about it every single fucking day!"

"I wanted to, but Mom—"

"Stop blaming Mom," Addie snarled. "Don't you dare throw her under the bus when she's not here to defend herself. And trust me, if she were I'd be just as furious with her."

"Do you know how long I felt his fists on my face?" Emme slid off the bed, her feet landing on the floor with a loud thud. "Years, Addie. *Years.* I was so angry I got into fights at school. I got sent to the principal's office that first year so many times I lost count."

Addie blinked. "You? Little Miss Perfect got sent to the principal?"

"I'm not fucking perfect!" Emme slapped her hands down on the bed, but it was too soft to be a satisfying gesture. "It wasn't until the assistant principal recommended a therapist for me that I finally started to deal with the trauma. 'Post-traumatic stress disorder,' that's what she told me I had. And Mom was dealing with her own PTSD. She didn't know how to handle mine, too."

"So you dealt with your own trauma, and never figured that I might have some, too?" Addie stalked to the opposite side of the bed so they stood facing each other with their mother's four-poster between them, the space filled with all the ghosts their words had brought back to life. "Because you're fucking wrong, Emme. I do remember when we lived in New York."

Emme inhaled a quick breath, jagged as broken glass. "What?" she whispered.

"Yeah. I remember. Just fragments, but I remember." She clutched at the nearest bedpost. "You used to play the *Mulan* soundtrack over and over because I loved that movie. One time, during one of the quiet parts of 'Reflection,' I heard Dad scream 'you bitch' at Mom." Her knuckles were white against the dark oak wood. Emme couldn't stop looking at her fingers; it was easier than meeting her eyes. "I've never been able to watch that movie since then. In college someone organized a movie night for the live-action remake, and I started shaking five minutes in." She let go of the post and hit her palm flat against her chest. "So you see, I have trauma, too, Emme. I have trauma, too," she repeated, banging her hand against her heart on every syllable. "And unlike you, I was never given the space to deal with it."

"Oh god, Addie." Emme balled the bedspread up in her fists. "I never knew—I thought we'd kept you safe from it—"

"Well, you didn't." Addie breathed in and out so loud and fast it was like a wave crashing to shore. "And maybe if you had explained it all to me, I would have recognized what Kira was doing to me. I would've been able to spot it right off." She smacked at one of the decorative pillows, sending it flying onto the floor. "You thought you were protecting me, but you didn't give me any of the tools I needed to protect myself."

All those years of keeping this hidden from her—everything she and
Sunny had tried to save Addie from—it shredded away from Emme in
that moment. She had never doubted her mother's firm rule that they
never tell Addie the whole truth, but now she saw that it had been
completely wrong. They'd been so stupid to think they'd kept her from
it. Emme sagged against the bed. "I'm so sorry, Addie—"

"No." Addie backed away. "This is beyond apology. You can't make
up for this, Emme." She narrowed her gaze, all the pain in her eyes
compressed into two pinpricks of dark brown light. "Maybe you are to
blame for Hannah DeLeo's murder. You couldn't even be honest with
me about our abusive father. No wonder you missed it with her."

She banged out of the room. Emme sank all the way down to the floor,
pulling the bedspread with her. She pressed her face into its softness, her
body shaking as she tried to keep herself from sobbing. Addie, Hannah,
Sunny; she'd screwed up with all of them, and they were all too good for
her tears. Across the house, she heard the front door open and slam shut.
She knew she should go after Addie, chase her down, talk this out so they
could come to the kind of peace she knew Sunny would want them to
find. But she couldn't move. She was rooted to the floor, in her own little
puddle of guilt. Maybe, if she was lucky, it would just swallow her whole.

CHAPTER TWENTY-FOUR

An insect buzzed in her pocket, biting into her flesh. Emme startled awake, banging her shin on the bed frame. She sat up, trying to remember why she was lying on the floor next to her mother's bed, tangled in the bedspread. In an instant, it all came back to her in multicolored detail, and her insides twisted up in a million knots that would take a long time to unravel.

She grappled for the phone vibrating in her front pocket and answered it without even checking who was calling. "Hello?" she croaked.

There was a rustle, as though whoever was on the other line hadn't expected her to answer. "Agent Helliwell?"

"Who is this?" Her body was creaking awake now, and she became very aware of a crick in her neck from sleeping sideways on the floor.

"It's—Josiah Murdock."

Emme scrambled away from the bed, disentangling herself from the bedspread and nearly dropping her phone in the process. She hauled herself to her feet and swiftly opened the voice app on her phone, hit record. "Yes, Josiah, what can I do for you?"

There was a muffled voice in the background, but Emme couldn't discern what it said. "I—I'd like to talk," Josiah said. "Can you meet me at the Pa'rus trailhead in an hour?"

"What do you want to talk about, Josiah?"

"I ain't telling you over the phone. You're probably recording this."

Emme sighed. "Fine. I can be there."

"Come alone."

"Josiah, I'm not coming alone. But I will promise not to come armed if you show me the same courtesy."

The muffled voice in the background spoke again, followed by something that sounded like a bird screeching. Emme held the phone away from her ear until she heard Josiah's voice again. "Okay. Deal. Pa'rus trail in an hour. See you then." Three consecutive tones beeped in her ear as the call ended.

Emme stared at her phone, wondering if she was still asleep and dreaming. She stopped the recording and replayed the call. It was real. But all of her guesses as to what Josiah was after were too wild to be entertained.

The other pressing matter at hand spun back into her brain. She banged out into the hallway. "Addie? Addie, are you here?" But the living room was empty, as were the other bedrooms and the kitchen. She peered through the window at the bakery—maybe Addie had spent the night there—but it looked dark and empty.

Her phone buzzed in her hand and she jumped, dropping it onto the counter with an echoing thud. When she turned it over—thank goodness for heavy-duty cases—she saw a text from Jaspar. *Addie's with me. She stayed at my place last night.*

Emme exhaled, long and slow, her breath fluttering the kitchen window curtains. *Thanks,* she texted back. *Have to go into the park for work. Try to keep her busy.*

Aye aye, captain, was his reply.

She dialed Claire, who answered sounding chipper and upbeat with her phone on speaker. "What's up?"

"I got a weird phone call from Josiah Murdock, asking me to meet him in the park. Can I stop by and pick you up so we can meet him together?"

"Shit, I'm on my way to St. George to question Lara," Claire said, and now Emme could hear the sound of the highway beneath her voice. "But you shouldn't go alone, Emme. Take Finn with you."

"That's a good idea," Emme said even though she'd already thought of it. "I'll call him now."

"I'll be in touch when I get back."

When she got off the phone with Finn, Emme stood in the middle of her bedroom. Her brain felt sluggish, like it was still asleep on Sunny's bedroom floor. She was still halfway stuck in last night's fight, going round and round the words they'd said like an endless carousel. There were so many things she would have done differently if she could rewind time and make all those decisions over again. She would have entrusted Addie with Sunny's estate the moment she returned home. She wouldn't have made that comment on their Hidden Canyon hike after Addie's graduation. She would've told Addie the truth about their father twenty years ago, even if it had been against Sunny's wishes.

Emme rubbed her hand over her face, scrubbing her cheeks with her palm. Addie needed time to cool off. She'd spend the day with Jaspar, making quiches and muffins, and by tomorrow she'd be ready to talk. Emme couldn't think about that now; she had a job to do today, and whatever was in store for her tomorrow with Addie would have to wait until then. She pulled on hiking pants, zipped up a hoodie over her Parks Project t-shirt, and laced up her hiking boots.

The Pa'rus trailhead lay a short way from the Visitor Center, teeming with tourists getting a late start. Emme got out of the car and scanned the lot for the telltale white truck, but it was all mud-spattered cars big enough to carry camping gear and a couple of kids. She and Finn walked to the trailhead and rested against the low wooden post that marked the start of the trail. Emme checked her watch. "It's been more than an hour since he called."

"Didn't you say Redwater was up in the mountains? Maybe it's just taking him a while to get here."

"Yeah, maybe." Emme watched a mom and dad and two kids, one in a stroller and the other on his dad's shoulders, pass by, the mom pointing out the river that rumbled alongside the trail. Two bikers whizzed around them. Pa'rus was flat and smooth and the only trail in the park open to bikes. It stretched for nearly two miles next to the river and was usually the first trail that families went to after leaving the Visitor Center. She looked up to the sky, morning clouds stretched grey over the canyon. "Let's walk up a little way. Maybe he got here ahead of us."

But they had barely made it a mile when Emme's phone chirped with a message alert. *Too many people on the trail,* read the text, from the same number that Josiah had called her from that morning. *Meet me at the emerald pools, lower pool trail.*

"Goddammit." Emme stopped in her tracks, held up the phone to Finn so that he could read it.

He squinted, pursing his lips as he read, and then looked up and down the trail. "It's not that busy," he said, and he was right; there were people, yes, but not nearly as crowded as high tourist season.

"This feels fishy," Emme said. She blew a hard breath out and jammed her phone back in her pocket. "But let's go." She turned, nearly colliding with a biker who deftly swerved, and marched back to the parking lot. "He needs to trust me," she said as they climbed into her car. "I could tell, the other day in the diner—he was feeling me out, trying to decide whether or not he could confide in me."

She eased onto the main road and sped past the Canyon Junction and Court of the Patriarchs shuttle stops. Exiting the road at Zion Lodge, she skidded into one of the designated ranger spots in the lot. The Lodge was brimming with tourists coming off their morning hikes with ravenous appetites. She and Finn went against the tide of hikers and headed across the road to the Emerald Pools trail. A group of horseback riders forced them to wait at the edge of the bridge over the river. When the last horse had cleared the bridge, Emme crossed it with long strides, barely glancing behind her to make sure Finn was following, the Virgin River rumbling beneath their feet. Although most of the hikers were heading in the opposite direction, the trail was still crowded, making their progress slow. Emme scanned each face as she passed, looking for that telltale red baseball cap. But all the faces along the trail were strangers.

The grey sky cracked open at last and let out a thin drizzle of rain. Emme paused at the side of the packed-earth trail and pulled out the waterproof jacket she always kept balled up in her pack. Finn watched her put it on, zipping up his own jacket all the way to his throat. "This is starting to feel like a wild goose chase," he said in a low voice as a family of five, speaking German, walked by them.

"He's leading us on," Emme agreed, "but I think it will be worth it in the end."

"Can't you have Claire track where his texts are coming from?"

"I could, if I had any cell service here." They continued along the trail as the rain sprinkled down on them, muddying the path into pits and puddles. The rock walls on their left grew slick with water, creating tiny falls that dripped over their heads. It wasn't long before Emme could hear the waterfall that dropped high and far into the Lower Emerald Pool below. Through a thicket of tall trees that lined the trail, the waterfall appeared in its clear, wondrous glory. In spite of the anxiety that was quickening inside her, Emme tilted her head back and felt the spray on her face. Zion was especially beautiful in the rain, when dozens of waterfalls appeared in the park that weren't there in the sunshine.

They followed the path until they were directly under the tumbling water, shielded from its power by the rock ledge it fell from. The sound of the falls was so loud that Emme could hear it inside her head, feel its pulse in her ribcage. Somehow in its din she could hear her own thoughts clearer. *This was a fool's errand.* Josiah had sent her into the park without any intention of meeting up with her. But for what purpose? No matter how she turned it over and around in her head, she could not figure him out.

She turned to Finn. He was standing just beneath the spray, his arm outstretched so he could catch the water in his hand, a soft look of wonder spread on his face. Something warm and sweet wrapped itself up in her chest, but she unraveled it quickly. Now was not the time for that.

"We should go," she said, practically shouting so he could hear her over the falls. He looked at her but didn't move. She went to him. Without speaking, he took her hand and held it in his under the heart of the surging water.

"This place," he said, "it feels like the soul of the world."

That was the magic of Zion at work, and every other National Park she'd ever stepped foot in. They all had their own soul, ancient and timeless, forever in tune with the heartbeat of the universe. She loved that he felt that the same way she did, and she could not help herself from reaching her other hand up to the back of his neck and pulling him down to kiss her. His mouth was so warm against hers that it swept away any chill from the water, spreading through her body so that she forgot, for just a moment, that the Horsemen had screwed her over yet again.

They hiked back and crossed the road over to the Lodge, where Emme's phone lit up with notifications when it reentered cell service. *Too rainy. Meet at end of riverside walk.* Emme seethed and typed back, her fingers shaking, *stop fucking with me. You're not going to be there either.*

There was no response.

She shoved the phone into her pocket. "What a waste of time."

Finn was peering at the Lodge, which had calmed down a bit from the earlier lunch swarm. "How's the food there? I'm starving."

"It's not bad. And I get a discount," Emme said. "Let's go."

With the lunch rush over, only a few tables at the Red Rock Grille in the Lodge were full. They sat by the window that looked out to the canyon and ordered beers. Emme tapped her fingers on the table, unable to dispel the nervous energy that ricocheted inside her. She texted Jaspar to check in; Addie was still with him at the bakery, poring over outdoor furniture options online. She exhaled and tucked her phone away.

"Everything okay?" Finn asked.

"Yeah." She sipped her beer and stared out the window. "Actually, not really." She looked back at him and remembered his hand on hers under the waterfall. "Do you mind if I unload? I know it's not exactly—"

"I don't mind," Finn interrupted. "I'm a good listener. It's why I got into podcasting."

Emme snorted. She stopped tapping her fingers and pressed her palm flat. "Do you remember when you asked me why my family left New York?"

"Yes. You said your parents needed a change." The corner of his mouth twitched. "Not only am I a good listener, I have the memory of an elephant."

Emme didn't smile back. "It wasn't my parents that needed a change. It was my mom. We left because my dad beat my mom, and then he started to beat me. We fled in the middle of the night and just kept driving until we hit the Continental Divide."

Finn said nothing, just put his elbow on the table and leaned his cheek against his hand, his eyes full of the same softness that she'd seen on the Emerald Pools trail. Shadows lengthened across the canyon outside the window as it all tumbled out and Finn, true to his word, listened without saying much. "Everything feels so muddled." Emme ran her hands over her face. "That's never happened to me before. I've always been able to see all the pieces of a puzzle so clearly and figure out how they fit together."

"I think you're being too hard on yourself," Finn said. He grabbed a fry leftover from his burger, pointing it at her before popping it into his mouth. "Emme, you just lost your mother. That in and of itself is its own kind of trauma. Whether you recognize it or not, that trauma is going to cloud everything you do right now."

"You'd make a pretty good therapist if you ever want to switch careers," Emme said, eating one of his fries.

"I did take a few psychology classes in college," Finn said with a laugh, swatting at her hand as she stole another fry.

Afternoon shadows stretched across the sky outside the window, casting a purple glow over the mountains. Emme paid the check, and they headed back to the parking lot. But when she turned the car on, the engine flipped over once, sputtered, and died. She tried it again. This time it groaned like a wheezy old cat and shuddered. "Shit." She turned to Finn. "Are you good with cars?"

"I can change a tire but that's about it."

"Same here." Emme checked her phone; beyond the Lodge, she didn't have any bars. "Come on."

Back inside the Lodge, the lobby was starting to fill up with tourists who were in for the evening, waiting for a table at the restaurant or streaming in and out of the gift shop. Finn went up to the reception desk while Emme called roadside assistance and told them where she was. The very nice lady on the other end put her on hold for several minutes. "I'm so sorry," she said when she came back, "but there's no way we can get someone into the park until the morning. Can you get a ride?"

"Um . . ." She chewed her lip. She didn't want to pull Jaspar away from Addie, and dragging them both into the park to rescue her would probably infuriate her sister more. "Can you hold on a moment?"

"Of course."

She joined Finn at the reception desk. "They can't get here until tomorrow morning," she told him, holding the phone away from her ear.

"We have a cabin available." The clerk at the desk, a young woman with a perky black ponytail whose name tag read Stella, piped up. "The gentleman said you work for the Park Service."

"I was asking if they had a room, just in case," Finn said, his cheeks slightly red beneath his freckles. "But I'm sure if you called the ranger station, someone could come get us."

Emme inhaled deep, aware of Finn's gaze on her face, of Stella glancing between them. Yes, she could get a ride from another ranger. Yes, she could call Jaspar and ask him to come pick them up. But she was suddenly so tired, and the darkness of Zion Canyon wrapped around her like a blanket that smelled of home. She wanted to stay cocooned there for as long as she could, away from the harsh light of day that awaited her at the house. "We'll take the cabin," she told Stella. To the woman on the phone, she said, "I'm okay for the night."

"Good. We should be able to get someone there around eight tomorrow morning, but we'll call about a half hour before to confirm."

"Thanks." Emme hung up the phone. Stella smiled at her.

"Can I see your badge to get you your discount?"

"Oh—sure."

"You're lucky," Stella said as she turned her back to make a copy of Emme's badge. "We're full up, but we just had a cancellation. I hope a queen bed is okay."

Emme looked at Finn, who shrugged, a smile tugging at his lips. "That's fine."

"Cabin 17," Stella said, handing Finn the keys. "Enjoy your stay."

Emme backed away from Finn into the quietest corner of the lobby she could find and called Jaspar. "Hey," she said when he picked up, "my car broke down and I'm stuck in the park—"

"Your trusty Crosstrek? Shit. Do you need me to come get you? Addie and I can—"

"No, no, I got a room at the Lodge," Emme said, glancing at Finn who was rifling through a rack of hoodies in the gift shop.

"Oh, really," Jaspar said, drawling out his vowels in a way that made Emme want to reach through the phone line and pinch him. "You wouldn't happen to be with a certain podcaster, would you?"

"I'm going to ignore that," Emme said. "Listen, can you stay with Addie tonight? I don't want to leave her alone."

"Of course. Absolutely. She's been with me at the bakery all day."

"Thanks, Jaspar." She watched Finn take his chosen hoodie up to the register. "I owe you."

"You can pay me back with details from your night with the hot podcaster," Jaspar said, his laughter still ringing as Emme hung up.

They made their way through the crowded lobby and out into the twilight. Emme used her phone flashlight to guide them across the parking lot; the Lodge practiced minimal light pollution so as not to compete with the night sky. Against a deep blue canvas, the moon was rising, a brief sliver in the sky, waning towards newness.

The cabins were separate from the main lodge, along a path swallowed up by the rising darkness. When they reached #17, Emme illuminated the door handle so Finn could unlock it, but before they went inside, she switched off the flashlight and turned to face the wide-open wilderness beyond the Lodge. "Look," she said, tilting her head back. Stars had begun to emerge above them, scattered like diamonds over the canyon.

The Lodge cabins were simple but cozy, with Western-style furniture and a fireplace in the corner. Finn lit the fire and turned to Emme.

"Listen," he said, "I do not want to be presumptuous. I can totally sleep on the floor—"

"Don't you dare," Emme said, turning up to him and looping her arms around his neck in one swift motion. He pulled her against him and lifted her up, his mouth hot on hers. They toppled onto the bed, and she switched the bedside lamp off. Starlight filtered into the room, dappling Finn's features in pinpricks of light and shadow. He held her close, his breath ruffling her hair as she buried her face in his neck. Everything worrying her felt far away, held at bay by the dripping stars over the dark canyon just beyond the cabin door.

CHAPTER TWENTY-FIVE

Dawn crept through the cabin window, fingers of blue and dusky purple reaching for her. Emme watched the light change outside from night into day, listening to the sound of Finn's even breathing in the bed beside her. Nervous energy fluttered through her as she made lists in her head of all the things she had to do, rearranging them over and over into different sequences. She sat up and rubbed her hands over her face, scrubbing at her skin with her palms to wake herself fully, then reached for her phone on the nightstand. Her finger hovered over Addie's name in her Recent Calls list, then clicked the phone off. It wasn't even six, and waking her sister at this hour wouldn't make her any less mad.

Finn rolled over and settled back into a gentle sleep. Emme slid out of bed, pulled on her underwear and t-shirt, and padded barefoot to the coffeemaker on the table beside the fireplace. There was better coffee in the main lodge, she was sure, but the thought of leaving the safe haven of the cabin filled her with an odd dread. She wanted to stay in this bubble for as long as she could, before she had to step back out into cold reality.

The coffee gurgled as it brewed, filling the room with its rich, bitter scent. Finn breathed in deep and stretched. The bedcovers pooled at his waist as he sat up.

"Good morning," Emme said.

"Morning." He smiled a little lopsidedly at her. "What a treat to wake up to the smell of brewing coffee."

"It probably smells better than it tastes," Emme warned. "But it'll do the trick. Did you sleep okay?"

"Yes, actually. You?"

Emme poured the coffee into the two provided mugs and carried them over to the bed, along with the sugar and powdered creamer. She handed a mug to Finn and took a sip, grimacing at its acidic taste. "Surprisingly well. Considering everything on my mind." She sat cross-legged on the bed facing him. "You seem to have that effect on me. The two nights I've spent with you have been the best night's sleep I've had in weeks."

"I mean, you could chalk it up to being exhausted from waiting out a flash flood and hiking all over the park, but I'll take the compliment." He sipped his coffee. "Oh yeah, not exactly The Ugly Mug."

They drank their coffee in an easy silence for several moments as the sky outside lightened, stretching clear and bright over the mountains. When her phone buzzed on the table, she slid off the bed to grab it, aware of Finn's gaze on her naked legs. "Roadside assistance should be here in a couple of hours," she said when she hung up.

Finn raised an eyebrow. "I have some ideas on how we can pass that time."

Emme grinned and hopped back into bed.

******

The guy from roadside assistance had a farmer's tan even this late in the fall and a handlebar mustache that Emme liked to imagine he had a little comb for in his bathroom. He stayed bent over the engine beneath the hood of her Crosstrek for a long time, and when he finally straightened up his brows were furrowed, the mustache twitching. "You say it just died yesterday while you were inside eating lunch?"

"Yes." Emme leaned against the driver's side door. "It's weird, because I had it serviced not too long ago. It's not the battery, is it?"

"No, it's not the battery." He fingered a coiled wire looped around the car's innards. "I'm going to have to tow it back to my shop in town to really figure it out, but—and I know this sounds crazy—it actually looks like something was done deliberately to it."

Emme straightened away from her car, as though it had just burned her. "What?"

"You see this?" He held up the wire. Emme came around to peer closely at it. "It's been sliced. That doesn't happen on its own."

Her brain rewound, skipping through every call and text from Josiah Murdock yesterday. He'd never had any intention of meeting her. He was trying to get her out of the way, to stall her, to keep her in the park, but why? For what purpose? Her stomach clenched, twisting up her insides, and she wanted nothing more than to get out of Zion, get home, check the doors and locks, and make sure Addie was safe—

"It's going to take a few minutes to get it on the truck," the mechanic said. "You may want to grab anything you need from the car."

"That's fine," she told him. "I have to go check out of the hotel."

"Great. Meet me back here and I'll give you a ride back to town."

She met Finn in the lobby, which was busy with tourists gearing up for their day in the park and guests waiting for a table at the restaurant for breakfast. He handed her a cup of coffee in a to-go cup. "It's from the café, so hopefully it's better than—what's wrong?"

She glanced around, as though the Murdocks had ears in the crowded lobby. And for all she knew, they did. They'd been here last night while she and Finn were eating in the Red Rock Grille, skulking in the parking lot to damage her car. "My car was tampered with. It didn't just die. Someone cut a wire to kill it."

Finn stared at her. "What?"

"It has to be why Josiah sent us on that wild goose chase yesterday. He was keeping us out of the way for something."

"But for what? We know he wasn't after Claire. She was in Salt Lake."

"I don't know." Emme's throat felt paper-dry. Everything was roiled up inside her, and she could not pull it apart to make sense of. "All I know is I have to get home and make sure Addie is okay."

"Of course. I'll grab our stuff from the cabin while you check out and meet you back at the car."

"Thanks, Finn." She squeezed his arm and went to the desk. After she settled the bill, she called Addie, not caring if she woke her up.

It went directly to voicemail.

Emme shoved the panic down. She was probably still asleep and still had her phone off. "Addie, it's me," she said, trying to keep her voice low and even. "I know you're still mad, and you have every right to be, but something is going on with the Murdocks and I need to know that you're okay. Just—please—swallow your pride for one minute and call me back." She hung up and dialed Jaspar. His phone rang and rang until voicemail finally picked up. She ended the call, breathing deep to punch down the fear rising inside her. It was still early; there were a thousand logical explanations why neither of them were picking up their phones.

She kept her phone in her lap as they drove through the park, bouncing her knee up and down and staring at the bars in the corner of the screen to see when she'd have service again. They ticked past each shuttle stop on their way out of the park: Court of the Patriarchs, Canyon Junction, the Human History Museum . . . when they hit the Visitor Center, the bars flared back to life. No messages.

She convinced the mechanic to drop her at her house and that she'd come by later to figure out the car. He'd barely pulled to a stop before she'd flung open the door and ran up the front steps. Inside the house she slid to a halt, colliding with something warm and solid on the floor.

"Jaspar!" Emme dropped to her knees next to Jaspar's prone form, lying crumpled next to the couch. She fumbled to find a pulse. With a whoosh of relief she found it, thrumming beneath her fingertips, his chest moving rhythmically up and down. As Finn banged into the house, she whirled to her feet. "Call 911 and get an ambulance here. He's been knocked out—" Her gaze veered from Jaspar to the remnants of a broken lamp lying a few feet away, then down the hall. "Addie," she whispered.

Emme sprinted through the house to her mother's bedroom and flung open the closet. The false wall gaped wide open, and the hiding space was empty . . . save for Addie's cell phone, which glittered against the dark wood floor.

Emme sank down, her hand trembling as she reached for the phone. Her insides seized up so tight she couldn't make a sound, not even a breath. *They had her.* The Murdocks had her, and they were capable of anything. She pushed herself to her feet and stumbled back into the living room.

Finn had rolled Jaspar onto his side and was holding his hand, fingers resting on his wrist. He looked up at Emme. "His pulse is steady and so is his breathing. It looks like there's a contusion on the back of his head—"

"Addie's missing," Emme croaked. Finn looked wildly down the hall, as if he expected Addie to materialize out of thin air. Before he could say anything, Jaspar groaned. Emme bent over him as he opened and closed his mouth, trying to speak. She fumbled for his hand, and he squeezed her fingers.

"I'm sorry—three of them—" he murmured. His eyelids closed and then opened halfway. "Addie?"

"It's okay. I'll find her." She kept hold of his fingers as the sound of a siren wound its way into her hearing. A few moments later, paramedics clattered through the front door.

Two EMTs hunkered down on either side of Jaspar. "What happened?"

"I came home and found him like this," Emme said, fighting to keep the tremors that wracked through her out of her voice. "He must've been hit with that lamp." She pointed, but as the EMT reached for it, she blocked him. "Don't. It may have fingerprints on it—" The EMT raised an eyebrow at her. "I'm a federal agent."

He put his hands up and backed away from the lamp. Together with the other paramedic they lifted Jaspar onto a stretcher. As they carried him out of the house, Emme jogged along. When they reached the door of the ambulance, Emme grabbed Jaspar's hand, a sob caught in her throat. "Please—take care of him." She kissed his knuckles and let the paramedics load him into the ambulance. As they drove away, Emme pressed the heels of her hands into her eye sockets. She felt an arm come around her shoulders and leaned into Finn for a moment before pulling away. "I have to call Claire."

It took three tries to tap the right buttons on her phone, her hands were shaking so bad. Claire picked up on the first ring, her voice incongruously chipper. "Good morning! Was just about to call you. I got some interesting information from Lara—"

"Addie's missing."

"What do you mean, missing?"

"I mean, Josiah Murdock led me on a wild goose chase through the park yesterday, tampered with my car so that I'd be stuck in the park all night, and when I got home, Jaspar had been knocked out and Addie is gone."

"I'm on my way."

Emme lowered the phone, and Finn guided her back into the house. "Don't you have Josiah's number from yesterday?"

"Yes, of course." She ran her hand down her face, trying to set the clockwork of her brain back into agent-mode. But in her six years as an agent, she'd never had to solve a case involving someone so close to her. She scrolled through the list of recent calls and found the one from Josiah yesterday, tapped it to call. After a pause, a message blared in her ear. *The number you are trying to call has been disconnected. Please check the number and try again . . .* "Dammit."

A moment later, Claire burst through the door. "What do you know?" she asked by way of greeting and Emme laid it out for her: the wild goose chase in the park, the tampered car, Jaspar unconscious in the living room, Addie's phone on the floor of the closet. Claire placed the broken lamp shards into a plastic evidence bag while Emme talked. "Well, we don't need three guesses as to who took her—"

A ringtone jangled, cutting her off. For a second, Emme stared wildly around the room, looking for the source of the sound before realizing it was her own phone, ringing in her hand. She answered with a raspy, "Hello?" without even looking at the number.

There was a pause in which the breath of the person on the other line swept through her ear like wind sweeps through the canyon. "It's Josiah."

Emme jerked her head up, motioning to Claire. "What did you do with my sister?"

"I didn't do anything with her." Josiah's voice was quiet and halting, like he was figuring out what to say only in the instant before he said it. "But my brother—Mark David—he has her."

All the light went out of the room, all the air sucked away, until it was just her and this tiny square pinprick of a phone. "What do you mean, he has her? Why? Is she—"

"Mark David says, an eye for an eye."

"An eye for—" Emme's fingers tightened around her phone. "Because I helped Lara." Josiah's silence was confirmation that she was right. "Where is my sister?"

"I can't tell you where—"

"Can't or won't?"

"Okay, won't." There was a crackle on the line. "I will tell you where she is, but I need assurances from you."

"Assurances for what?" She felt someone beside her, but she could see nothing, hear nothing beyond Josiah's voice.

"I need assurances that I ain't gonna get in trouble for what happened to Sarai."

"Sarai? But—my sister—"

"I will tell you what happened to Sarai and that boy, but I ain't going down for it."

"Ah." Her brain was just catching up through the fog of fear. "You want immunity for whatever role you played in Sarai and Max's murders."

"Yeah. I get that, you get your sister."

"Fine. Done. And I want the whole truth—and nothing but the truth—about the murders—"

"I ain't a liar, Miss Helliwell—"

"—and about Eli."

There was silence on the other end. Emme's heart clenched and un-clenched inside her ribcage. This trade felt dirty, like pollution running though her blood, sacrificing her sister's safety for her job. But she knew, if it came to it, she would break any promise she made if it meant getting Addie back safe and sound. The whole world distilled down into the seconds ticking by as she waited for Josiah's response, and when he finally said, "Deal," she breathed in, and light flooded back into the room.

"Meet me at eight tonight at the top of Angel's Landing."

"Are you nuts? Sunset is at five. I'm not climbing up there in the dark."

"We either meet there, or we don't meet, Miss Helliwell. You named your terms; these are mine."

She squeezed her eyes shut, and behind her closed eyelids she could see the slick rocky path bounded by chains on the way to the place where only angels could land. "I need to know that Addie is okay."

Josiah didn't answer, but a few seconds later, her phone chirped as a text came through. It was a photo: Addie, seated on the floor with her knees drawn up, one wrist handcuffed to the leg of a bed, a handkerchief covering her eyes and another tied around her mouth. Emme's stomach churned—*God, she must be so scared*—but she remembered Addie's own words. *I can take care of myself.*

"If you harm one hair on her head, the deal is off," Emme said. "I mean it. If she has one scratch on her, or one of your fucking 'brothers' looks at her the wrong way, I will rain holy hell down on you and the Warriors so hard you'll think it's the goddamned Flood all over again. Do you understand me?"

"Yeah, I got you."

"And make sure she has enough water."

"Should I invite the Queen over to serve her tea, too?" The phone line crackled again. "Eight tonight, Miss Helliwell. See you there." And he hung up.

Emme lowered the phone away from her ear and held it in her hand, staring at the photo of Addie. She could feel Finn and Claire pushing in on her, questions on their tongues, but for a long moment all she could do was stare into Addie's blindfolded face, turned to the camera as if Josiah had just told her to "Say cheese!" in some bizarre mockery of a tourist photo. Slowly she became aware of Claire's fingers inching towards the phone, finally looking up when Claire removed the phone from her hand.

"I'm sending this to myself," Claire said, tapping away at Emme's phone. "I'm going to try to locate her before you go to meet him."

"I know where she is," Emme said, her voice rough as sandpaper in her throat. "They must be keeping her where they kept Lara—in the Garden. I can show you on the aerial map of Redwater. But—" She grasped Claire's wrist. "I'm going to meet him. He said he would tell me everything about Sarai and Max—about Eli—in exchange for immunity."

Claire hesitated a moment, then nodded. "Okay. But he could be lying, and we need to be prepared for that."

Prepared . . . what did that even mean? Words swirled in Emme's brain, tumbling over one another as she tried to make sense of them. All she knew was she had to get Addie home safely. If she didn't, everything her mother had worked for—had died for—would be in vain, and Emme knew that she couldn't live with herself if that happened. If Addie died, she would too.

Late morning light stretched into the room, the sun meandering across the sky as it inched toward night, but she couldn't stand here watching the minutes tick by. "I need to get ready. He wants me to meet him at the top of Angel's Landing tonight."

"Jesus, are you really going to hike that in the dark?" Finn asked. "That seems really dangerous."

"I have no choice." She pushed past him and headed to her bedroom.

"Emme, it could be a trap," he said, following her down the hall.

"Of course it could be," she tossed back to him over her shoulder. "But I know that place means something to him." She stopped and turned to Finn, who stood in the doorway to her room. "I think he wants to meet there because he believes, in some weird, twisted way, that it will redeem him. For whatever role he played in Sarai's murder." She pinched her forehead together with her fingers, so hard that her skin stung. "I need to prepare for this hike, and I can't think straight."

"On it," Finn said and whirled out of the doorway. In the privacy of her room, she texted Stace a short missive about what was going on. Less than a minute after she sent it, her phone lit up with his picture.

"Don't try to talk me out of it," she said in lieu of a greeting.

"I'm not going to, but may I be the voice of reason to tell you what a bad idea this is?" She could hear the concern in his voice, the undercurrent of fear. She sagged onto the edge of the bed.

"She's my sister, Stace. I have to do what I have to do."

"Then go with Claire to Redwater. Let Josiah rot on top of Angel's Landing."

Emme picked at a pull in the quilt on her bed. He was right, of course. But if there was a chance she could get answers about Sarai and Max, about Eli . . . "I need to hear what Josiah has to say."

"Emme—"

"I have to go—"

"Please, please be safe. You better come back down that mountain."

"You know they're not mountains. They're plateaus."

Stace snorted and, in spite of herself, the corner of Emme's mouth curled up. She clicked off the phone without saying goodbye. The word felt too heavy.

The afternoon blurred into a whirl of color and sound as several of Claire's fellow FBI agents poured into the house, prepping for the mission, dusting every surface in the living room for fingerprints, maps splayed out on the coffee table. At some point, Finn forced her to eat—"you need protein for the hike"—but she barely tasted the food. The hospital called with an update on Jaspar: he was awake and alert, and they were keeping him overnight for observation. She breathed a little easier after that conversation and excused herself to change. When she remerged from her bedroom, dressed in warm layers with her hiking boots tightly laced, she wove through the crowded living room to find Finn in the kitchen, loading her backpack with plenty of water, trail mix, a first aid kit, and flashlights with extra batteries. The gesture flooded her with sweetness that cut through the bitter cold fear in her bones, the way he was there to help lift her up whatever mountain—plateau—she needed to climb. She blinked away the tears that prickled her eyelashes. He and Claire followed her out to the porch.

"You be safe," Claire said. "And don't worry. We'll find her," she added, and Emme knew that if there was anyone in the state of Utah who could rescue Addie, it was Claire Hughes. Finn hugged her tightly until she pushed him away and climbed into the hulking black SUV the FBI had loaned her.

By the time she entered the park, dusk covered the canyon, turning the red cliffs purple. Even in the burgeoning dark, she knew each formation and peak, naming each one as she drove past, until she came to The Grotto. The parking lot was empty—of course it was at this hour—and when she got out of her car, she stood still, looking up to the sky.

Stars dotted the deep blue velvet curtain pulled across the world over her head. Whatever happened on this trail in the next few hours, those stars were her guide, and perhaps the last thing she would ever see.

Chapter Twenty-Six

The first stretch of the trail to Angels Landing is deceptively easy. Emme traversed it quickly, across the Virgin River and along the canyon floor. The light from her headlamp encircled her in a soft white glow, with little help from the thin crescent moon above that drifted in and out of patchy clouds. The sound of her footfalls on the hard, red earth mingled with the sound of her breath, creating a hypnotic rhythm she used to tamp down the rabid thoughts eating away at her brain. She could die on this trail tonight. She could get all the way to the top, and Josiah could play her for a fool again. Addie could already be dead.

She pushed them all away and focused on one step in front of the other; on Angels Landing, one misstep could send you tumbling over a cliff. When she reached the first switchback where the trail really begins to climb, she took a deep breath and looked behind her for a long minute. She was the only human being for miles, but the canyon was alive all around her: wind rustled through trees and grass, foxes yelped in conversation with each other, night birds swooped overhead. As dangerously stupid as it was to attempt this hike in the dark, Emme knew this place the way she knew the layout of her own skeleton. She had to trust herself that she could get to the top in one piece, and that she'd find what she was looking for when she got there.

Heart pounding from the exertion, she reached the top of the switchback and paused to take a drink of water. The trail undulated below her, its pale swath just visible in the darkness. If Josiah was behind her, she would be able to see him, unless he was being a real idiot and not using some kind of flashlight or lamp. No, likely he was ahead of her on the trail or already at the top, watching her progress from on high or laying whatever trap he was setting for her.

The trail narrowed into a thin snake slithering up the cliffs. Overhead, the stars winked at her, mocking her with their steadfastness. In the deep, dark sky, she could pick out constellations, though she was never able to remember their names. *The Peeing Boy,* she thought and inexplicably laughed out loud. *Shark Eating Man.* "Oh, Max," she whispered. With every footfall her mind was on Addie, but there were two other people who were depending on her, too. She thought of the hawks wheeling in circles above The Narrows and hoped that Max and Sarai were watching out for her on this hike, too.

Past the switchbacks, the trail hugged the mountainside under an overhang of cliff: Refrigerator Canyon, the only shady patch on the long trail on a sunny day. Under its shelter, Emme stopped to take another drink of water. The light from her headlamp captured the drop-off at the edge of the path. A low stone barrier bordered the trail, offering measly comfort; if you stumbled hard enough, those rocks wouldn't be enough to break your fall into the canyon below. She swallowed deeply, the cool water a balm to the fiery fear inside her. The worst of the trail was yet to come.

She pushed away from the rock wall and headed into the series of twenty-one switchbacks known as Walter's Wiggles. The name was cute, but the path was not. The switchbacks were tight and narrow, little better than climbing a staircase right up the mountainside. They'd been cut into the rock by the very first superintendent of Zion National Park, Walter Ruesch, and every time Emme had traversed them she cursed him under her breath. If angels were the only ones who could land at the summit, why let humans even try? Her breath came hard and fast, lungs burning in her ribcage. Sweat beaded on her forehead despite the night's chill; she swiped her sleeve across her skin, leaving it cold and clammy. A lizard skittered across the path in front of her, into and out of the circle of her light in a brief second. She felt a kinship to it, like it too was out of its element, on this trail in the dead of night where it didn't belong.

Above Walter's ridiculous Wiggles sat Scout Lookout, where you could gaze for miles across the whole of Zion Canyon. Against the deep blue sky, she could see nothing but the faint outlines of the rock formations and monuments. Even the river, the dominant force of the canyon, was too far below to see from here. Emme tried to calm her heartbeat back to normal. She could just make out the summit from here, but whether Josiah was already up there was impossible to see in the velvety dark.

From here to the top, it was only half a mile, but it was one of the most dangerous stretches inside any National Park, a precipitous ridge known as the Spine. It took two sets of hands to count all the people who had fallen to their deaths along that stretch in the last twenty years, and she did not want to add another finger to the count.

She adjusted her headlamp so that it hit the ground a little ahead of her feet. Rough-hewn rock stairs rose like vertebrae along the Spine, the first of which was called the Step of Faith. She placed her foot on it and closed her eyes, finding stillness for a moment while the night sounds of the canyon washed over her, praying to whichever Great Spirit had ruled this canyon long before white Christians colonized it. *Let my sister come home safe. Let me make it back to meet her.* She opened her eyes, grasped the cold metal chains staked in the ground along the trail, and began the climb.

The chains were the only thing to hold onto on the uneven and rocky path to the summit—if it could even be called a path. It was little more than a fool's hope, really, just a prayer to get there in one piece and have the chance to take a selfie at the place where only angels were able to land. She was no angel, she knew that, but she'd gotten up there many times before and had to believe this time would be the same. But everything was different at night, the absence of light changing everything in a place that was usually bathed in the sun's glow. Shadows shifted over the rocky stairs, giving the illusion of depth where there was none; more than once, Emme placed her foot onto the slippery slope beside the steps, thinking that the step extended farther than it actually did. Her grip on the chains was so white-knuckled, she was afraid to let go even to just replace her hand a few inches further up. With each step she took, her doubt grew. She was very likely hiking to her own death. If she even made it to the top without falling in the darkness, would she be so lucky on the way down?

Even Stace had told her not to do this, and she'd ignored him; she was a terrible agent, a bad employee . . . maybe if she fell to her death, a legend would grow up around her, a cautionary tale of the ISB agent who screwed up a case so badly that she lost her life. She clung to the chains, stubbornly placing one foot in front of the other as her vision blurred.

She blinked hard, letting the tears fall from her eyelashes onto her cheeks, not even sure what she was crying for. There were a million things that could fit the bill. Her breath hitched. She stopped and swatted the tears that dripped down her face. Having your vision go blurry on the most dangerous part of the trail was a surefire way to fall.

Emme stilled. Maybe she *should* fall. Maybe she should just . . . let go.

The night seemed to quiet all around her, as if the birds and animals and even the trees were waiting in hushed silence for her answer. She could almost feel the mountain's glee, its anticipation in claiming another victim, waiting to gobble her up like a witch in an old fairy tale. This is why people hiked this godforsaken trail in the first place—to claim they had conquered death.

She had never felt that way hiking in this canyon. She'd always felt a kinship to this place, like an old friend from a past lifetime. They'd been soulmates, once upon a time, and the canyon had always been generous in its friendship, giving her exactly what she needed at exactly the right time. She'd felt that in so many of the parks all across the country. If she let go now, let the canyon take her, she'd be betraying that kinship. It wouldn't be giving herself to the land. It would be taking something away.

Emme tightened her hand on the chains, the cold metal biting into her palm. She pressed upward, one foot in front of the other, the crosswinds blowing harsh on her cheeks. And then, on those same winds, voices carried down the mountainside to her. "That fucking liar," she said aloud. Josiah hadn't gone to the summit alone as they'd agreed. She leaned forward, listening hard, trying to catch the voices as they blew by her, fragments of words torn instantly away on the wind.

"—but I—"

She could not tell pitch or tenor from here, whether the voices belonged to Josiah or someone else. Could it be Addie? Her heartbeat ricocheted in her chest, threatening to crack open. Had Josiah dragged Addie up the mountain with him? For what purpose?

"—you dare—"

"—No—"

"—God—"

She was taking the rocky, uneven stairs at nearly a run now, but her legs wouldn't move fast enough. The summit still seemed miles away, but she had to be close . . . the darkness seemed to thicken and thin around her, wispy streams of moonlight crisscrossing her path as she heaved herself up and up . . .

"—betrayed the family—"

"No!"

The word cut through the air with a wretched cry that tore at Emme's ears. "Addie!" she yelled.

The clouds shifted, and in the moon's dim glow she saw the outline of a figure at the edge of the cliff just above her. For a brief, wild moment she thought it was an angel, perched on its landing place . . . but then the angel flew into the air with a terrified scream that echoed across the canyon and shattered the night.

Emme froze. "Addie—" It came out as a whisper, the fear so tight inside her that only the tiniest sliver of breath could slip out. *It wasn't her,* she told herself as she forced her feet to move, climb, carry her to the summit . . . *it wasn't her, it wasn't her, it wasn't her . . .*

After a minute, an hour, a lifetime, she reached the top step and stood at the summit, the wide, flat expanse that gazed out over the whole of Zion Canyon from a dizzying distance. But on the cliff where only angels could land, a devil had invaded. Abraham Murdock grinned at her. "Good evening, Miss Helliwell."

"Where's my sister?"

"How should I know?" Abraham's face glowed ruddy in the dark, his breath fast and ragged. "I had nothing to do with that. It was my fool of a son who thought it would be a good idea to use her as a bargaining chip," he said, nodding at the cliff where the body had just fallen.

Emme's stomach bottomed out. "That was Josiah?" Relief flooded her, followed by a gut-punch of horror. "You pushed him."

"There's one thing I cannot tolerate in my family, Miss Helliwell." He raised his arm to point at the cliff, and she saw the gun tucked into his waistband. She shifted slightly so that her back faced the steps. If she reached for her own gun, he would have his out quicker than she could blink. "And that is betrayal," Abraham continued. "'A false witness will not go unpunished, and he who breathes out lies will not escape.' The moment Josiah chose to go against me, he signed his death warrant."

"You—killed your own son," Emme hissed. She wanted to rush at him, push him over the edge herself, rid the world of this monster. It was so deeply unfair that he was allowed to breathe this blessed air while Sunny was not. "Is that why you killed Sarai? Did she betray you, too?"

"I saved Sarai from herself," Abraham said. "She thought she was smarter than all of us, thinking she could outrun the reach of God's hand by sneaking off with an outsider." His eyes shone like the glow of two little campfires in the night. "But God sees all. She should've known that He would chase her all the way into this canyon and that no outsider could protect her."

"But He didn't chase her all the way into the canyon—*you* did."

Abraham shook his head, the corner of his mouth twisting in a mockery of a grin. "When will you learn, Miss Helliwell? God is me. I am God. We are one and the same."

Emme tilted her head to the side. "But it wasn't you who slit her throat, was it? You didn't dirty your own hand with her blood. No, you had Josiah and your other Horsemen kill her for you."

"God speaks, and His followers act," Abraham said. "There wasn't a Warrior alive who didn't feel the weight of her betrayal. I didn't have to command her death; there were plenty who were already sharpening their knives for her blood atonement."

"Oh, really?" Emme kept her hands in front of her, still and empty. Any sudden moves would have Abraham reaching for his gun, she knew, and she wanted to keep him talking as long as she could. "No one in Redwater moves a finger without an order from you. There's no way anyone would kill your daughter without your permission. Who helped Josiah?"

"Josiah acted alone," Abraham said, his tone sharp and his words so fast that Emme knew he was lying. Lara had told her she believed Mark David had helped kill Sarai . . . and there was no way that Josiah overpowered both Sarai and Max, especially considering neither of them had gunshot wounds. Even more so because Emme knew that Josiah had been a reluctant killer. *Sarai was my buddy.* The flowers, the sadness in his face when she'd sat across from him in the diner, the fact that he'd called Emme here to confess . . . No, Abraham was protecting someone, perhaps the other son he considered more valuable than Josiah.

But she let that line of questioning drop for now. "And how did Max betray you? Or was he just collateral damage?" She winced at that term, how it reduced her bright light of a friend to a footnote.

"Max was a nonbeliever, and nonbelievers aren't worth the life God gives them," Abraham said. "He stole Sarai away from her people, filled her head with lies, and convinced her to turn against her own family."

From far away, Emme heard the sound she'd been listening for, the tick-tick-tick of propeller blades whirring in the night. She did not move, keeping her gaze fixed on Abraham. "What sort of lies?"

"Lies," Abraham hissed. "He held such a sway over her that she was going to tell those lies to your people, and betray us all—"

"My people?" And then it all clicked. The cell phone ping in Salt Lake City. "He *was* going to go to the FBI," she said. "He was going to report everything about you and your family to the authorities."

Abraham swept his arm in the air, pointing his finger at her. "You and your meddling is the work of the Devil," he yelled, his voice covering the tick-tick-ticking that was growing louder, notch by notch. "What happens in Redwater ain't none of your business. We are a righteous enclave, and when the Rapture comes, we will rise up on our Holy Land and watch all of you writhing in agony while we are steeped in glory—"

"Unfortunately, what happens in Redwater becomes my business when you bring it onto my land," Emme said, flinging her arms wide to embrace the whole of Zion Canyon. "You could've ordered Josiah to kill Sarai and Max anywhere else and I bet you would've gotten away with it, paid off some redneck sheriff to look the other way." She inhaled through her teeth. "Josiah did that on purpose, didn't he?" she asked, not waiting for an answer as she finally understood. "He committed the crime in the park so the ISB—so I—would have to be involved."

"That was his blunder—"

"No, I think he knew exactly what he was doing." Emme shifted to the side as Abraham stepped toward her. "Betrayal from all sides, Abraham. One by one, all your pawns will fall."

The tick-tick-tick came in louder now, too loud for Abraham not to hear. He lifted the hand that had been pointing at Emme straight up into the air. "But the King will always stand tall, Miss Helliwell," he said, raising his voice to be heard above the whir of the helicopter. "God will always swoop in to save His most loyal followers." He flashed her a full grin, his teeth glistening with spit. "That's my ride, Miss Helliwell. Time to say goodnight."

Abraham dropped his arm to his side and at last reached into his waistband, the move that Emme had been waiting for. She dropped to the ground and rolled toward him before he could shoot, knocking him off his feet. The gun flew out of his hand and hit a jagged rock a few feet away. It went off as it landed, the gunshot cracking the night open with a burst of fiery light. Emme rolled onto her back, slicing her arm through the air as she opened herself up to the sky. The flat of her hand connected with Abraham's throat. He choked, spluttering as he curled onto his side. She clambered to stand, turned him onto his back with her toe, and pressed her foot into his chest as he coughed beneath the sole of her boot. The helicopter swerved toward them from across the canyon. She steeled herself against the wind of its propellers. When the hulking body of the copter hovered above them, the green-and-brown arrowhead logo with the words **NATIONAL PARK SERVICE** in bright white gleamed on its belly. She grinned down at Abraham Murdock. "That's not your ride," she said. "It's mine." Pride swept through her whole body, set her tingling from head to toe. She was a ranger, through and through, and she'd never deny that to herself again.

Abraham struggled beneath her foot, reaching up for her, and she sat down on him, pinning his arms to his side with her legs. The helicopter door opened, and three law enforcement rangers rappelled out with their guns drawn. They landed on the ground like her guardian angels. Only once they'd surrounded her and Abraham did she stand up and step back, gulping in the night air with her face turned up to the stars.

CHAPTER TWENTY-SEVEN

The moment the helicopter flew into air space with cell reception, Emme's phone started pinging with messages, from Stace, from Jaspar and Finn, but her eyes went right to one from Claire, in all caps: I GOT HER. SHE'S OK.

Emme breathed out and leaned as far forward as her seatbelt would allow, a sob of relief shuddering through her. "I didn't think my downfall would make you so emotional," Abraham said from his seat across from her, handcuffed in between two of the law enforcement rangers whose guns were trained on him. Emme straightened.

"My sister has been rescued from your Garden," she said, looking him right in the eyes, "and you better hope she doesn't have a scratch on her ,or I'll make sure you get a well-deserved dose of jailhouse justice."

Abraham smirked, but beneath Emme's lasered gaze he looked away, staring silently out the windows of the helicopter for the rest of the ride to St. George. At the police station there, Abraham was formally charged for Josiah's murder, but before Emme could start on the long list of questions she had for him, his lawyer appeared in the doorway of the interrogation room, like a ghoul materializing on the threshold of a haunted house.

"He's not saying a word," the lawyer said, plunking his briefcase onto the table with a loud clunk. "Now if you'll excuse me, I need to confer with my client."

The prosecutor, bleary-eyed in sweatpants and a down puffer jacket, met her in the long, windowless hallway outside the interrogation room. "I know you must be exhausted, but can I get your statement?"

"Of course." She followed him into a different room and lowered herself into a chair, her muscles stiff and aching from the hike. One of the officers placed paper cups of coffee in front of both of them. Emme wrapped her hands around the cup, taking occasional sips as she laid out the whole story for the prosecutor, from the moment Stace had called her to say, "There's a body in The Narrows," to the confrontation at the top of Angel's Landing.

When she was done, the prosecutor clicked off his voice recorder. "I'm sure we'll get remand," he assured her. "He'll never be free again."

Emme wanted to believe that with every fiber of her being, but oh, how well she knew that sometimes the bad guys win. "Maybe, but the cult is still out there," she said. "Until it's disbanded, they are still a threat." And even after Abraham's cell door was slammed shut behind him for the last time, she knew there would still be loose threads that would never be tied up. The Warriors for Armageddon were a rabbit hole of myth and folklore, filled with smoke and mirrors that would lead even the shrewdest investigator astray.

It was past midnight when, veins coursing with caffeine and adrenaline, she emerged back into the hallway to find Claire striding towards her, a dark blue flak jacket open over a bulletproof vest. Emme broke into a run and collided into her, sweeping her into a bone-crushing hug. "Thank you," she breathed. "Thank you for saving her."

Claire patted her back before gently pulling back. "She's at home, and Finn's there with her. The EMTs assessed her and she's fine. Just a little soreness on her wrists where they had her cuffed. Hang on." She broke away as the prosecutor passed them and blocked his path. "I need a search warrant ASAP for the whole town of Redwater. I only had one for the building where I knew Miss Helliwell was being held, but we need to get into every single structure in that place. God knows what else they're hiding."

"It may take a few hours, seeing as it's the middle of the night," he said.

"I don't care who you have to wake up," Claire said. "They've already had too much of a head start, and I need to get in there before they destroy everything."

"On it." The prosecutor pulled out his cellphone and began tapping at it as he walked up the hallway.

Claire ran her hand over her hair, pulling at the tight bun that crowned her head. "I need to find some coffee," she said. "I don't think I'm going to bed anytime soon."

"Come on." Emme led her down the hall to the main part of the station, where a few officers worked at desks. They eyed the two women as they made their way to a coffee cart in the corner; local law enforcement was always territorial when it came to federal agents, but apparently that didn't extend to coffee. Claire poured herself an oversized cup, and Emme refilled hers, and they wandered back to a vacant interrogation room to wait for the warrant. "Tell me what happened," she said once Claire had taken several sips of her coffee and her breath seemed to even out.

"There's not a lot to tell," Claire said. "We were expecting to meet resistance, but the Horsemen were nowhere to be seen. We saw their trucks parked around town, and saw some of the women on porches, watching us, but we were so focused on getting to the Garden that we didn't stop to question them."

"Maybe they're biding their time, getting ready for a bigger invasion," Emme said, but a squiggle of unease squirmed in her gut. The Warriors were not ones to let the Feds onto their land without a fight. "Who was at the Garden?"

"Addie was the only one there."

The unease spiraled out, made her throat dry. "There wasn't anyone else from the Warriors being held there?"

Claire shook her head. "And guess who was guarding her?"

"Who?"

"Our friend from the cave." Claire took a long sip of coffee as Emme's eyes widened. "We arrested him—he's being held in the room next to Abraham—but I don't think he had anything to do with the murders."

"Oh, come on." Emme tipped back in her chair. "Then why was he in The Narrows that night?"

"Apparently, he was supposed to marry Sarai, before she ran off with Max. He was mourning her. We have him on kidnapping and assault, especially if Jaspar can identify him as one of the men who broke into the house. I'm guessing Josiah and Mark David were the other two. He also spilled a lot on the ride over here." Claire rolled her eyes. "Before he started singing hymns again."

"And Addie—she hadn't been harmed at all?" Emme clutched her cup, her stomach roiling at the thought of what her sister had been through in the past twenty-four hours.

"She was handcuffed and blindfolded when we found her, but she had been fed and given plenty of water. Cave Guy actually seemed relieved when we busted in." Claire's lips twitched. "I guess Addie had been talking for hours about all the archaeological sites she's been at with million-year-old fossils, proving that Creationism is impossible."

Laughter bubbled up inside Emme, and when it burst out, she couldn't stop. Relief and adrenaline coursed through her, shaking loose the fear that had wrapped her tight for days. "Oh god," she gasped, tears rolling down her face, "that must've been worse than waterboarding for him."

"No wonder he wanted to confess everything," Claire said, a few giggles escaping from her. "Listen, I learned something else. My assistant went through that security camera footage. Max *did* come in to talk to the FBI that day. But he was turned away because he didn't have an appointment. He was told to come back in two days. So I think—"

"He went to The Narrows because he wanted to stay off the grid until his appointment," Emme said. She shook her head. Such a small shift in circumstance would've kept Max and Sarai out of The Narrows that fateful night. "And he set the meeting with Finn as a backup."

"I believe so," Claire said. There was sadness in her eyes that Emme was sure was reflected in her own. If someone at the FBI had seen Max that day, would he and Sarai still be alive? It was impossible to know, and Emme knew how futile the *what-if* game could be.

Claire's phone buzzed with a text, breaking their silence. "My backup for the raid is almost here."

"Do we have the warrant yet?"

"No, but I want to be ready to leave as soon as I have that paper in my hand." She pushed back from the table. "You're coming, aren't you?"

"Are you kidding?" Emme stood up. "I wouldn't miss this for the fucking world."

"Then let's get you suited up."

"I'll meet you out there," Emme said. "I have to make a quick phone call."

Stace picked up on the first ring. "Nice of you to call, *finally*," he barked at her.

"I texted—"

"Emme, when you go on some crazy solo mission where there's a high likelihood of not returning, you *call*."

"Okay, sorry. I was just tied up with the prosecutor and Claire—and we're waiting for the warrant so we can go raid Redwater—"

"You're going with the FBI? Stay—"

"—safe. I know, I know." Emme swallowed hard. "Listen, Stace . . ." There was silence on his end of the line, as though he was holding his breath. "Do you think you could . . . tear up my resignation letter?"

He exhaled, so loud she could hear it through the phone, along with the undercurrent of relief and maybe a little smugness. "I already did."

*****

Dawn crested over the mountains as they drove up the switchbacks leading to Redwater, a pink glow that set the red rock cliffs aflame. Emme shifted in her seat, the bulletproof vest that Claire had strapped her into stiff and uncomfortable. Her gun lay on her lap, ready to be drawn the moment they were face-to-face with the Horsemen. Behind her, in the body of the SWAT van, half a dozen officers rocked with the motion of the vehicle as they swerved through curves. Three more vehicles filled with officers followed them. The Horsemen would definitely be outnumbered, but if they'd decided to arm the rest of Redwater's residents, it would be a very different scenario. *Waco forever,* Emme remembered Mark David crowing, and she breathed in deep, hoping that was not what they were driving into.

Beneath her pounding heart, that squiggle of unease refused to flatten. Despite Claire's confidence, and the signed warrant that lay on the console between them that gave them the right to barge into any structure within Redwater's boundaries, Emme could not shake the foreboding feeling that seeped into her bones. She watched the sunrise through the windshield, the sky changing from pink to orange to bright blue, and hoped that by the time it reached its apex she'd be home with Addie.

The white sign—***Do not fear what you are about to suffer***—appeared at the side of the road, provoking guffaws from the officers in the back. "Jesus, that's hardcore," one of them muttered.

You have no idea, Emme thought to herself. Her ribcage throbbed with the quickening of her heart as they edged closer and closer to the main part of town, expecting at any moment for a line of white Ford trucks to appear, the Horsemen in battle formation. But the houses they passed lay quiet and still, and when they reached the center of Redwater, nothing but a windswept emptiness greeted them.

Claire skidded to a stop, dry dirt fanning out beneath the tires as she slammed the van into park. She grabbed the warrant and jumped out.

"Federal agent," she yelled. The only answer was the distant crow of a rooster.

Emme walked around the van, her steps slow and measured. The uneasy feeling had flattened, her fears realized as she swung her gaze up and down the main road through town. "They're gone," she said when she reached Claire's side, her voice hoarse.

Claire didn't respond. She stomped around to the back of the van and yanked open the doors, signaled for the officers in the other vans to come out. "We have the right to search every building in this town, and that's exactly what we're going to do," she announced. She divided the officers into pairs and sent them in different directions, then motioned for Emme to buddy-up with her. Emme could see the wild hope in Claire's eyes, that in one of the lonely houses they would find the Warriors hiding in a concealed basement or, at the very least, a cache of guns that she could add to the charges against Abraham.

But every house was deserted: drawers left open from hasty packing, refrigerators cleaned out, livestock pens yawning open. The officers cut into walls looking for hidden rooms, but the few they found were cold and vacant. The last house they searched was the big yellow farmhouse where Abraham once followed Emme as she went through room after room looking for Eli. Lying on the table in the entryway was a leatherbound Bible, identical to the one Josiah left in Emme's house, open to Revelations, verse 13:7 circled in pencil. *And it was given unto him to make war with the saints, and to overcome them: and the power was given him over all kindreds, and tongues, and nations.*

Emme looked at Claire. "They're not done. Wherever they went, they're going to pick right back up where they left off."

Claire gazed out through the open door of the house, up the long driveway to the abandoned town. "Well, I'm not done, either. Wherever they are, I'll find them."

Chapter Twenty-Eight

The sun streamed through the windows as Claire drove Emme back through Springdale. She gazed out the window at all the places she knew so well: the Mexican restaurant where she drank tequila for the first time, the outfitter that Sunny had worked at before she'd opened the bakery, the local artisan store where she'd bought a present for Addie's last birthday. This was her home, and she loved it, but she couldn't stay here forever. She belonged to the 84 million acres of wild federal land spread across the thousands of miles from Maine to Hawaii, and wherever the ISB took her next would be her home.

Claire pulled into the driveway next to the bakery. "You okay?" she asked.

Emme sighed. "I will be," she said. "You?"

"Frustrated, angry, unsatisfied . . ." Claire gripped the steering wheel tight and twisted in the seat to look at Emme. "But I'm glad Addie is home safe. That's the most important thing."

Emme tilted her head. "I need some time with Addie, but do you want to come by later for dinner?"

"I'd love to." Claire smiled. "Give Addie my best."

Inside the house, Finn was stretched out on the couches in the living room, sound asleep though it was well past noon. She found Addie curled up on the bed in Sunny's room, breathing peacefully in her sleep. Emme removed her hiking boots and socks, flexed her aching toes, and climbed into bed next to her sister. Addie rolled over and blinked her eyes open. "You stink."

"Yeah well, I hiked a mountain and raided a town, so cut me some slack."

"You couldn't take a shower before rubbing your sweat all over my clean sheets?" Addie reached out and punched Emme's shoulder lightly.

Emme caught Addie's wrist. "Addie, I'm so sorry."

"Sorry for what?"

"For all of it. Lying to you for so many years. Not trusting you with Mom's stuff. Most of all, dragging you into my work and, you know, getting you kidnapped." Emme propped herself up on her elbow. "Did they hurt you? I will kill them if—"

"They didn't hurt me." Addie sat up. "I mean, they forced me into a car at gunpoint and blindfolded me, so yeah—that was pretty scary." She pulled her knees into her chest and wrapped her arms around them. "But then they kinda left me alone. They had someone guarding me at gunpoint, but then I started talking about fossils—"

"I heard."

"—and by the time Claire busted in, he surrendered without a fight. I think Claire was actually a little disappointed by that," she added with a snort. "You should've seen her. She came charging in there like Rambo, guns blazing." Addie's lips curled into an embarrassed grin. "It was kinda hot," she confessed in a stage whisper.

Emme snorted and rolled closer to her sister. "Are you okay? Are we?"

"Well, I definitely think I need some therapy, but I'll be okay." Addie slid back down under the covers. "And I'm sorry too, Emme. All those things I said, about you keeping the stuff about Dad from me—I didn't mean it. You were a kid, too. And I don't blame Mom for trying to protect me. She did her best." She curled onto her side, facing Emme. "She was the best mom. And you're my very best sister."

"And you're mine." Emme stretched out on her side, facing Addie. "What are you going to do now?"

Addie scrunched up her face. "I think I'd like to stay here for a while. If you're okay with that."

"Of course I am, but what about work?"

"Well . . ." Addie chewed her lip. "I was poking around the Zion Forever website and I saw that they're sponsoring a dig in the park." She nudged Emme's shoulder. "Do you think you could put in a word for me?"

A slow smile crept across Emme's lips. "Yeah, I think I could do that."

"What about you?" Addie jerked her chin. "Are you still resigning from the ISB?"

Emme let out a long, sweet sigh. "No. I think, deep down, I always knew it was where I belonged."

Addie's eyelids fluttered closed, and Emme felt her own grow heavy. "Mom would be so proud of you," Addie murmured. A moment later, she was asleep again. Emme let her own exhaustion consume her into a deep sleep. She dreamed they were in the backseat of Sunny's car on that long escape from New York, waking up to the red rock mountains of Utah outside their windows. *Look, Addie,* she'd said, shaking her sister awake, gazing in awe at the endless vistas unfurling before them, and she knew they'd found their way home.

*****

The bakery overflowed with people, and Emme had to turn sideways to maneuver herself through the crowd, squeezing past the tables bursting with food. Pictures of Sunny hung on the walls surrounded by pine garlands with red velvet bows, and her favorite music hummed through the air. Tim and his dad poured drinks from a makeshift bar in the corner. As she wove around a group of high school classmates, Amy blocked her path to hug her.

"This is amazing," she said. "I definitely feel your mom's spirit here today."

Emme gave her an extra squeeze. "How's your dad doing?"

"He finished his last treatment a couple of weeks ago, and his scans look really good," Amy said. "Thanks for asking."

Emme sidled away to nudge Addie, who was holding court at the bar with a bunch of regulars from Cap's Landing. "Jaspar's in the kitchen," she said in a low voice. Addie excused herself and they pushed through the swinging doors.

Inside the kitchen, it was warm and smelled of fresh-baked bread and muffins and quiche. The doors muffled the din from outside. Jaspar slid a tray out of the oven and jerked his chin to a Dutch oven filled with bread dough. "Pop that in there, will you?"

Addie put the bread in and closed the oven door. "Jaspar, you should have let us hire someone to help. You deserve to be outside with everyone, not stuck in here." She touched his arm. "Sunny loved you too."

Jaspar mopped sweat off his forehead with the kitchen towel he always kept tucked in his pocket. "I don't do great with grief," he said. "I'd rather show my love through baking."

"The atmosphere out there is definitely not grief-stricken," Emme said. "It's more like a celebration."

Jaspar smiled. "That's what your mom would've wanted."

Emme and Addie exchanged glances. Emme cleared her throat. "Speaking of what Sunny would want—Addie and I discussed it, and we would like to sell you half of the bakery."

"For a very reasonable price, and on whatever payment schedule you can afford," Addie said.

"Are you—" Jaspar looked from Emme to Addie and back again. "Are you serious?"

"This place already has so much of you in it," Emme said. "It's only right that we make that official."

"You're like the brother we never had," Addie said. "So we figured that all three of Sunny's kids should split the business."

"Does that mean you're both staying?" Jaspar asked.

Emme leaned against the counter. "I'm not sure when I'm leaving Springdale, but I'm keeping my job in the ISB. And Addie—"

"—will be hanging out here for a while," Addie interrupted. "I'll be supervising a dig right inside the park. So you're stuck with me for the time being. Just please don't take another knock on the head for me," she said, elbowing Jaspar in the side.

"That's so great. You two!" He exclaimed, crunching them into a tight bear hug that made Addie squeal. Emme tightened her arms, one around Jaspar and the other around her sister. They coaxed Jaspar out of the kitchen just as *Gold Dust Woman* began to play. It was Sunny's favorite song.

Emme poured herself a glass of Angel's Envy and climbed up on a chair. The room quieted. "I just wanted to thank everyone for coming." Emme's gaze swept the bakery. In the corner she spotted Finn, perched on a chair. "My mother and sister and I came to Springdale twenty years ago with little more than the clothes on our backs," she said. "Most people don't know that we left New York because our dad was abusive, and our mother was a domestic violence survivor." The silence in the room thickened, and Emme could feel everyone holding their breath. "When we arrived in Zion Canyon, the red cliffs surrounded us like an embrace. We found a home here, but more than that, we found a community. One that supported us and loved Sunny like she was their own mother." Emme blinked away the tears that had formed at the corners of her eyes. "All of you are a part of the life my mother built for us here, and my sister and I are so grateful." She lifted her glass high. "To Springdale, to Zion, and to Sunny."

"To Sunny," the room echoed back at her. She climbed down off the chair and stepped back as others began to take turns making toasts in Sunny's honor. Behind the counter, Jaspar fired up Il Duce with a grand flourish and a cheer went up. The party lasted well into the evening, a velvety night sky stretching over their heads as the last stragglers left. Emme went to help Addie and Jaspar clean up, but they both shooed her out with a meaningful look at Finn, who had hung behind. Emme splashed the last of the Angel's Envy into two glasses and carried them out to the porch, nodding at Finn to follow her.

The sky was drenched with stars, and Emme tilted her head back to breathe it in, wondering if she would ever look at the constellations again without thinking of Max. She sent up a little prayer that he and Sarai were at peace, wherever they were, and turned to Finn. "Where are you headed next?" Emme asked.

"Back to New York for a bit to edit the podcast," Finn said. "Then I'll just—go wherever the next crime takes me, I guess." He looked at her. In the dim glow of the porch light, his green eyes were as dark as a shaded forest. "You should come visit. To New York. Make sure I'm not cutting out any of your good lines." He leaned over and bumped her gently.

"I hate New York City," Emme said. "It's too loud, too concrete. It assaults my senses. I'm much better in places like this," she said, raising her glass slightly to the canyon that surrounded them.

"Guess I'll have to lace up my hiking boots if I want to see you again, then." Finn smiled. "Hopefully under less morbid circumstances."

Emme lifted one shoulder. "I don't mind morbid." It was the truth, of sorts. She'd come to a restless truce with her job, uncovering the ugly in the country's most beautiful places. It would never bring her joy or peace; she'd have to find those things outside the boundaries of the parks. But with the bakery under Jaspar's wing and Addie ensconced in Springdale, she had a good home base to retreat to when her soul needed respite.

Her phone buzzed in her jacket pocket. "Stace," Emme answered without preamble. "You missed a grand old Irish wake."

"Hope you had a shot of single malt in Sunny's honor for me," Stace said.

"I may have had more than one shot," Emme said. Next to her, Finn snorted and she grinned up at him, hoping that Addie wouldn't mind staying in the house alone for the night.

"Well, sober up. I need you packed and ready to go in the morning."

Her insides flip-flopped. She pushed off the bench and walked a couple of steps away from Finn, her gaze fixed on the faint outline of the ridgeline that ringed Zion Canyon. "Go where?"

"We found a foot in one of the geysers in Yellowstone."

Emme lowered the phone from her ear and breathed in deep. In her mind's eye, she could already see Old Faithful's tall spray instead of the red rock cliffs in front of her. There was never much rest for the weary, not when there was still such wickedness in the world, but her soul was as rested as it would ever be. She glanced back at Finn, who raised an eyebrow at her. At least she'd get a decent send-off.

She brought the phone back to her cheek. "I'll leave at dawn."